D0298029

Against the Tide

By the same author

Daughter of Darkness
Pandora's Girl
Angelina
From This Day Forth

Against the Tide

Janet Woods

ROBERT HALE · LONDON

First published in Great Britain 2003

ISBN 0 7090 7328 3

Robert Hale Limited
Clerkenwell House
Clerkenwell Green
London EC1R 0HT

2 4 6 8 10 9 7 5 3 1

Typeset in 9/12 pt Garamond by
Derek Doyle & Associates in Liverpool.
Printed in Great Britain by
St Edmundsbury Press, Bury St Edmunds, Suffolk.
Bound by Woolnough Bookbinding Limited

With love to my Scorpio son
Andrew,
Life is full of little secrets.

The author is happy to recieve feedback from readers.
She can be contacted via her website.
http://members.iinet.net.au/~woods

CHAPTER ONE

The downpour came suddenly, the rain driving out of the dusk with unrelenting fury.

Eddie Renfrew cursed. Caught halfway along the quayside at Poole Harbour, there was nothing but shadows for shelter between him and Jack Bellamy's boat. Why the hell had he agreed to meet the man responsible for his wife's death?

Because I have a driving need to get my own back.

As suddenly as it had started, the deluge stopped, revealing the low dark shape of Brownsea Island across a stretch of grey wind-whipped water. Shivering, he removed his mackintosh and shook the water from it.

Pale grey eyes narrowed on the boat, trying to calculate its worth. Old, but perfectly maintained, the teak deck was freshly varnished, the brass-work gleamed. The shadow of a head moved across a porthole before a curtain was drawn.

Margaret Jane was painted in brazen gold lettering against the navy blue hull. Eddie's face darkened. His late wife's lover was taunting him by suggesting they meet on a boat named after an adulterer and her bastard.

It was obvious that Bellamy was comfortably off. Perhaps his guilt was such that he intended to offer reparation. Not that it would do him any good.

Three years had passed since Margaret's death. Still rankling in Eddie's memory was the scandal it had created, the knowing eyes of the mourners at the funeral, and the sensationalized newspaper reports.

Bellamy had appeared at the graveside after the mourners had gone. He'd thrown a single red rose on her coffin. Eddie had watched from behind a tree, enjoying his anguish. Nobody took what belonged to Eddie Renfrew and got away with it, even if he had no more use for it.

'Damn the bitch!' he muttered, striding towards the boat. 'She deserves to rot in hell.'

The door was opened before he could knock. There was no greeting and he followed Bellamy into the small cabin.

Bellamy's mouth was a thin, tense line. 'Coffee?'

'Shove it.' Eddie wondered what Margaret had seen in her lover. He was in his early forties, tall and lanky with fair, greying hair. A shiny scar ravaged one side of his face, pulling the corner of his left eye down and puckering up under the hairline.

Margaret had said he'd earned it by saving a pilot from a burning plane. The affair had started shortly after she started work in his boatyard. Some bloody war hero, getting up another man's wife as soon as his back was turned!

Not bothering to hide his hostility, Eddie stared at him. 'What did you want to see me about?'

Bellamy didn't muck about. 'I want to adopt Janey.'

Eddie gave an incredulous bark of laughter. 'Get stuffed.'

'She's my daughter, Renfrew.'

'So you *say*. It's my name on her birth certificate.'

'You *know* she's my daughter.' The man's eyes never wavered. 'Margaret told you Janey was mine when she asked for a divorce. I'll be willing to undergo medical tests to establish the fact.'

Eddie's lip curled. 'My religion doesn't recognize divorce.'

'It doesn't recognize rape either, but that didn't stop you. Margaret married you because she was pregnant and had no one else to turn to, you sanctimonious bastard.'

She hadn't put up much of a struggle and he'd warned her she'd be put in a home if she told anyone. When she'd become pregnant he'd toyed with the thought of walking out, but the lure of the house and her father's bank balance had been too strong. Before the will had gone through probate he'd confessed his sin to a priest, then acting on his advice, had sought permission from the court to marry her.

He frowned as his eyes focused on Jack Bellamy. There was no doubting that Janey was this man's daughter. She'd inherited his fair hair, the deep blue of his eyes and his height.

The girl is unclean, and the sins of the parents must be visited on her. 'I'll never let you adopt her.'

'And if I apply for custody in court?'

'Go ahead,' he said, giving a short, sharp laugh. 'Do you think anyone would award custody to a man who slept with my wife, then caused her death by encouraging her to abort her unborn child?'

Bellamy paled. 'That's a damned lie. I had no idea she was pregnant. If you'd agreed to a divorce she'd never have attempted such a desperate act.'

A nerve twitched in Eddie's jaw as he stood up. 'Are you saying it was my fault? It's debatable who fathered the brat.'

'Does it matter now?' Bellamy said wearily. 'Damn it, Renfrew, Margaret and I loved each other and wanted to get married. No one's to blame. What's important to me now is Janey. She's my daughter, and I love her.'

Eddie choked back a laugh. 'You'll be wanting to buy her next.'

'If that's what it takes.' Bellamy snatched up a cheque book. 'Name your price.'

Temptation gnawed at Eddie's innards. Angrily, he snatched up his raincoat and pushed roughly past him. There were better ways of punishing Bellamy, and keeping Janey from him was one of them. 'Everything you own wouldn't be enough to buy her. My wife died because of you. My eldest daughter watched her mother bleed to death. Pauline has nightmares about it.'

'You can have everything I own. *Everything*!'

Jesus, he meant it! Eddie turned and stared at him. 'You're trash Bellamy. I'm going to make sure Janey doesn't take after you. Take me to court if you like. You'll be laughed out of town.'

'At least let me see her,' Jack shouted after him.

'Go to hell.' He slammed the door behind him before he was tempted to change his mind. He walked fast, anger keeping the cold at bay. When he reached the old customs house he stopped to light a cigarette, sucking the smoke deep into his lungs. After a while, his temper cooled and his mind became analytical.

That Bellamy would contemplate fighting for custody hadn't occurred to him. He wasn't sure what would be involved if he went ahead. There would be blood tests of course, but both Janey and Pauline had the same common blood group as Margaret. Could they conclusively prove paternity from blood tests? He worried that the scandal might blow up in his face again. He didn't relish Margaret's shame being displayed in the pages of the newspapers for a second time.

Then there was Pauline. Hadn't his daughter suffered enough? If he struck a bargain with Bellamy over Janey, he could give Pauline everything she'd ever want.

He drew into the shadows as Bellamy strode past, his head hunched into his turned-up collar. When he reached a sporty-looking Jaguar, Bellamy folded himself into the seat. Seconds later, the engine purred into life.

'Lucky bugger,' Eddie murmured as the tail lights disappeared around the corner. Throwing his cigarette butt into the gutter, he pulled his damp collar up round his ears and set off up the narrow high street towards the railway station. A light drizzle was falling and the shops sent streams of light pouring across the wet pavements. Potential customers were few.

Perhaps he should consult a lawyer as a precautionary measure. He stopped in front of a real estate agency and lit another cigarette whilst he thought about it. Lawyers cost money, and his cash was tied up in investments. Bellamy had probably been bluffing about taking him to court . . . but if he hadn't?

At a pinch he could evict the tenants and sell the house in Bournemouth, the one he'd inherited from Margaret. His glance rested on a glossy photograph of something similar with an astronomical price tag. He shrugged, reluctant to get rid of it. It was worth a small fortune, situated as it was on the cliff top.

'Gotta light?'

Eddie spun round to confront a couple of rough-looking youths with greasy slicked-back hair. Breaking a thinly rolled cigarette in half, the taller of the two gave a portion to his mate.

'Ta,' he said when Eddie flicked his lighter under the end. 'You wouldn't know somewhere cheap we could doss for a few hours.'

'Sorry.'

Eddie thought fast as they began to amble away. 'Wait! How would you like to earn a few quid?'

The larger of the two turned, his pale eyes catching the light. 'Doin' what?'

'There's a boat tied up at the quay. It's called *Margaret Jane*.'

There was an air of expectancy about the two now. 'So?'

'You could stay there tonight.'

'What's the catch?'

Eddie smiled and took his wallet from his hip pocket.

A few minutes after the transaction had taken place, a train whistle blew in the distance. Eddie started to run, making it through the barrier gates just before they closed across the upper end of the high street. He boarded the train with seconds to spare.

Two hours later he joined the crowds on Waterloo station, then took a taxi to the middle of a long curve of regency houses in Regent's Park. He let himself in through the front door with his key, the only one of Sarah Wyman's staff to have this privilege.

'Has Mrs Wyman called?' he asked the butler, helping himself to a finger of scotch.

'Yes, sir. She requested that you ring her. Will you require dinner?'

'A sandwich and a pot of tea will do. Why don't you and your wife take the evening off. Pamela can look after me.'

'Thank you, sir.'

Eddie loved being called sir by the servants. He'd fallen on his feet when he'd applied for the job of personal assistant to Sarah Wyman. She and Eddie had understood each other right from the start. His job involved much more than secretarial work – and for his discretion, she paid well. Eddie despised her, though he didn't show it.

He swallowed his scotch and poured himself another, nursing it whilst he stared at the fire. As far as he was concerned, women should be like his mother; a placid, quiet-natured woman whose mission in life was to make sure her husband and child were well cared for. If she didn't act as expected she got a beating.

'Always rule a women with an iron fist,' his father had advised him. 'They're born with the sin of Eve, and incite lust in the loins of men.'

His mother had died shortly after his father. She'd suffered from depression, and had faded away in the mental ward of the hospital she'd been admitted to. Eddie had never visited her there; he'd been too ashamed of her.

His employer, Sarah Wyman, was a slut, a fact which both excited and repulsed Eddie. He derived pleasure from catering to her appetite for the unusual – as long as he didn't have to be personally involved. Sarah lived apart from her husband, who played the wealthy landowner to perfection, and didn't really care what his wife did, as long as she was discreet.

Eddie was good at his job. Sarah showed her appreciation by introducing him to her stockbroker. Under his expert guidence Eddie's small nest-egg had grown. Eddie had signed over the greater portion of his salary to invest. One day, he'd be as wealthy as Jack Bellamy. He was grinning when he dialled the number of Sarah's Paris flat.

'Good evening, madam.'

'Edward?' she breathed, her voice a low murmur. 'Where have you been all day?'

'I had some business to take care of in Poole.'

'Something naughty, I hope.'

'I'm afraid not, Mrs Wyman. How's Paris?'

'Absolutely divine. I've decided to stay here a day or two longer, so my appointments will have to be rearranged. There's nothing urgent coming up, is there?'

'The usual social engagements. You have a luncheon appointment with Mister Wyman on Thursday.'

'Oh yes. Charles is coming to London to see his solicitor, isn't he? Be an angel and phone him for me, will you, Edward? No doubt he'll be relieved he doesn't have to stay in London longer than necessary, and twice as relieved at missing lunch with me.'

'Certainly.' He glanced up when Pamela came into the room carrying a tray. He waved her away. 'Take it to the dining-room.'

Pamela smiled her shy smile as she backed out through the door, all pink twin-set and imitation pearls. Her grey sunray pleated skirt emphasized her heavy hips and thighs.

'Who was that?'

'Pamela.'

'Tell me, Edward. Are you going to propose to her?'

He shrugged. 'My daughters need someone to look after them. I can't leave them in the charge of your husband's housekeeper for ever.'

'Poor darling,' Sarah cooed. 'Pamela's so drearily domestic.'

'She likes the kids and she won't give me any trouble.'

Sarah gurgled with laughter. 'One of the things I admire about you is your ability to compartmentalize your life. Have fun.'

His eyes narrowed as he replaced the receiver. Striding into his office he removed a slim black diary from a cardboard file taped under a desk drawer, and flipped it open. *Paris flat. Mouluay and Sidi Youssef*, he wrote over several days in January, then returned it to its hiding place. Later in the month, in the private post office box he maintained, Eddie would receive photographs, courtesy of a French gentleman with a zoom lens and leanings towards voyeurism. It was his insurance.

He strolled through to the dining-room, his mouth gritting into a smile when Pamela rushed forward to serve him. 'Shall we go out for a drink after I've eaten?'

'That would be lovely, Eddie.'

He took her to the local tavern, where he proposed marriage and placed on her finger a second-hand engagement ring he'd bought especially for the occasion. 'It was my mother's,' he lied, feeling no guilt when she gazed with doggy-like adoration at him.

They set a wedding date for the following month at the local church. Pamela was no great beauty, but she was sensible. The sooner they were married, the sooner he could bury her in the country with the kids, and get on with his life.

The next morning, two police constables knocked on the door.

'We're investigating an incident that took place in Poole last night, sir,' one of them said.

'Please come in.' Eddie's forehead wrinkled into a puzzled frown as he ushered them into his office. 'How can I be of assistance? I can't remember witnessing anything untoward happening in Poole yesterday.'

One of the constables consulted his notebook. 'I believe you had a meeting with a Mister Jack Bellamy.'

'That's right. We met on his boat.' He managed to keep his perplexed expression in place. 'Nothing's happened to him, I hope.'

'What makes you think something's happened to him?' the other man asked, his glance slowly roving around the panelled room.

'He seemed overwrought.' Eddie bit his lip and lowered his voice a fraction. 'Actually, we had an argument over a private matter. He . . . Jack Bellamy was involved with my late wife, and was making some wild allegations. I'd intended to bring the matter to my lawyer's attention today.'

'What exactly were these allegations, sir?'

'They're of a sensitive nature. To be quite honest, I'd rather not discuss them.'

'It would be helpful if you could verify what Mister Bellamy had already told us. You can be sure of our utmost discretion.'

Eddie closed his eyes for a moment or two, composing his face into a semblance of one remembering past grief. 'This is very difficult for me, constable. There was a lot of publicity surrounding my wife's death.'

'Of course, sir.' The policeman's voice became more sympathetic. 'Would I be right in saying the matter concerned one of your daughters?'

Eddie sighed. 'My daughters have been through enough without adding insult to injury. I can't think why Bellamy is pursuing this matter with the police. If you ask me, the poor chap needs professional help. He actually offered to buy my youngest girl.'

The two policeman exchanged a glance, then one of them said, 'Where were you last night at ten o'clock, sir?'

Eddie stared at him, allowing an edge to creep into his voice. 'Would you mind telling me what this is all about?'

'Someone set fire to Mister Bellamy's boat. It burned to the water line.'

Elation leapt like a tiger into Eddie's chest, and he was hard pushed not to laugh. 'You surely don't think it was me?'

'You haven't answered the question, sir.'

He allowed himself a small smile. 'I caught the five-thirty train from Poole to Waterloo, where I flagged a taxi. I arrived here about eight, then took my fiancée to the Lords Tavern just down the road. We left there about ten. The butler can tell you what time I arrived back from Poole. Shall I ring for him?'

The notebook was snapped shut. 'No need, sir. If the staff at the Lords Tavern can vouch for your whereabouts, we won't need to bother him.'

Seeing them to the door, Eddie pulled on a suitably concerned expression. 'The boat was insured, I trust?'

The two constables exchanged a glance.

'I'm sorry, that would be confidential, I suppose. May I ask if the poor chap was injured?'

'No, sir. He wasn't on board.'

A pity. Eddie closed the door behind them and headed back to his office. Lighting a cigarette, he dialled the number of Sarah's lawyer.

Affably, he said, 'This is Eddie Renfrew. I need the benefit of your professional advice.'

CHAPTER TWO

Janey had been attending school for three weeks when her father married Pamela. She and her sister moved from the big house back into Coombe Cottage.

Janey couldn't stop staring at Pamela. She couldn't wait to tell her best friend Annie the news, except she didn't want to go out in case she missed something.

Pamela smiled as she caught her gaze. 'You must be Janey.'

She nodded. Her glance went to the feather duster. Its reddish-brown iridescent feathers reminded her of the rooster who strutted around the chicken run up at the big house and crowed at the crack of dawn. Ada, the round bodied, red-faced cook who worked there, said she was going to wring its neck one of these days if he didn't watch his manners.

'Please can I dust?'

Her older sister Pauline shoved her aside when the door closed behind their father. She snatched at the duster. '*I'm* going to dust.'

Pamela kept a firm hand on it. 'Let's get things straight. I'm in charge around here. If you want to do the dusting you can ask nicely, like Janey did.'

Pauline threw herself in a chair and her lips drew into a pout. 'I don't have to.'

'Then you can go and clean your own room, because I don't have to help you, either.'

Pauline stormed off and slammed the door behind her.

When their father returned the place smelled of polish and a fire burned in the grate. Pamela blushed when he kissed her. 'Not in front of the children, Eddie.'

There was stew and dumplings for dinner. The meat was chewy, the dumplings not quite cooked in the middle, the sprouts squishy and strong tasting, like the smell of mustard.

'Can't you do better than this,' her father said, a frown appearing above his nose.

Pamela's face turned bright red as she muttered, 'I'm not used to the Aga yet.'

Janey felt sorry for her. Desperately trying not to heave, she swallowed the last of her sprouts without chewing it. 'I liked it.'

The frown was transferred to her. 'Who asked you to stick your nose in?'

When her sister stuck out the tip of her tongue Janey pulled a face at her. A stinging slap across her head knocked her sideways from her seat.

Pamela's voice was a shocked whisper. 'Eddie! She's just a little girl.'

'She's a cheeky little pest who needs to learn some manners.' He scraped his chair back from the table, stood up and glared at her. 'Janey's *my* daughter. I'll thank you not to interfere when I discipline her.'

He strode from the house, slamming the door behind him. Pamela gazed helplessly from one to the other with tears in her eyes. 'He must be tired.'

Janey's face stung and a lump of misery grew in her throat. *I won't cry*, she thought rebelliously. *I won't ever cry again, whatever anyone does to me!*

Pauline smirked. 'Janey always gets into trouble.'

When Eddie returned with the smell of whisky on his breath, Pamela's nerves were twitchy from handling two children determined to be uncooperative. Pauline had ignored her every request, and Janey hadn't spoken one word. The younger girl had cringed away from her when she'd dropped a plate, then scooted into the garden and climbed a tree, her face set and rebellious. It had taken twenty minutes of coaxing to get her down.

Not that she'd have told her off. The poor little scrap had been trembling with fear and her face was a livid red where Eddie had hit her.

She frowned when he threw himself in a chair and scattered ash over the table. 'I've just polished that, Eddie Renfrew.'

He deliberately scattered some more. 'Don't nag, Pam. Come here and give me a kiss.'

This was more like the Eddie she married. 'After the way you talked to me at dinner? Not likely.'

He lunged at her, and after a short wrestling match pinned her to the floor. He laughed when she giggled. 'Do as you're told!'

Her skirt rode up to her thighs and she tried to pull it down when his hand slid between her stocking top and suspenders. He slapped her hand away.

Pamela blushed. There was something shocking about doing it on the floor. 'Put the light out.'

Eddie laughed. 'Why?'

Because I hate you looking at my fat hips and thighs. As soon as the thought entered her mind she tensed up.

Eddie's smile slid from his face when she tried to push him away. 'What's the matter with you?'

'It doesn't seem proper doing it on the floor. I mean, what if one of the children came in?'

His knee jerked up and forced her thighs apart. 'Are you denying me my marital rights?'

'No, Eddie. It's just—'

'Good.' Dragging her knickers down over her legs he threw them in a corner and began to roughly fondle her. 'If a man can't fuck his bloody wife when he feels like it, he might just as well not be married.'

Shock rioted through her. He'd never talked dirty to her before and she didn't like it. She gave a little squeal when he pinched her. 'Stop that, Eddie. I don't like it, and I don't like you talking dirty.'

'Stop that, Eddie,' he mimicked, pinching her again.

He roughly thrust himself into her. Humiliated, she turned her head away from his tobacco and whisky-soaked breath, and saw Pauline. The girl was peering through the crack in the door, her eyes wide.

'Eddie,' she hissed, blushing in shame. 'Stop.'

A hand closed around her throat. 'Shut up you whining bitch else I'll strangle you.'

Pauline smiled and pulled the door shut.

When it was over, Eddie gazed dispassionately at her tear-stained face. 'Try and lose a bit of weight before my next visit. No man wants a lump of lard for a wife.'

Mortified, Pamela dragged her clothes over her legs as Eddie rose to his feet and buttoned up his pants. 'Go and make me a cup of tea before we go to bed.'

Later, in the darkness of the bedroom she felt more relaxed. But he ignored her and fell asleep. She wished Pauline hadn't been watching what was going on earlier, it wasn't right.

Her father was going. Janey watched his car leave, its windows fogged up, its exhaust trailing white vapour. Freedom was an excited little quiver inside her.

Below her, Pamela was huddled in a pink chenille dressing gown. Her hair was dishevelled, her face puffy. Fluffy pink slippers scuffed a mark in the frost as she stamped from one foot to the other, her arms wrapped tightly round her body to ward off the cold.

It was odd having a stranger for a mother, Janey thought as she pulled on the clothing left neatly stacked on a chair. Pamela was better than their last minder, though.

Miss Harding had smelt of mothballs and mints and smacked her hand with a cane when she was naughty. Miss Harding had gone to heaven. Janey had found her lying on her back staring at the sky when she'd come back from visiting her friend Annie's new kittens. She'd been under the washing line with pegs scattered around her.

At first she'd thought it was a game, then the woman's stillness had scared her. Janey had sat on the fence rail and waited. She'd told Griffin Tyler, who'd been the first person to come along the lane. He'd fetched his father, who was a gardener up at the big house. Phil Tyler had gone to the red telephone box outside the village store and called the doctor, who'd sent for the undertaker. Miss Harding had been put in a box and taken away and that was the last they'd seen of her. She and Pauline had gone to the big house to live.

Now they were back in Coombe Cottage with a proper mother to look after them. Pans were rattling in the kitchen, and presently the smell of something frying drifted up to her.

'Breakfast's nearly ready,' Pamela sang out.

Janey was trying to button up her red tartan skirt when Pauline walked in.

'Only babies can't do up buttons,' she scorned.

'I can do them up better'n you can.' Hastily, Janey pushed the last button through the hole.

Pauline gave an odd little grin. 'Dad beat Pamela up last night.'

Janey's eyes widened. 'Liar!'

'I am not! She was on the floor and dad was jumping on her. He called her a bitch and said he'd strangle her.'

'You shouldn't say bitch. It's rude.'

Pauline shrugged. 'How can it be if dad says it?'

'What's strangle mean?'

Her sister's hands came round her neck and squeezed, until Janey fought for breath. She gasped for air when she was let go.

'If I squeezed long enough you'd die. I hope he does strangle her.'

'That's wicked, our Pauline. Our new mum is nicer than Miss Harding was.'

'Well, I don't like her. If you want me to be your friend, neither can you.'

Janey thought about it for a moment. She didn't care whether Pauline was her friend or not. She had lots of friends. Mister Charles Wyman who owned the big house, and Brenda who told all the servants what to do there. Then there was Sam, the head gardener who was really old and had hardly any teeth left, and Phil Tyler, the gyspy gardener who knew where all the wild animals lived, and who had a slow and thoughtful way about him so Janey never felt she was being a nuisance when she asked him questions. She liked him best of all.

At school there was Annie Sutton who'd started class at the same time as her, and Griffin, who was Phil Tyler's son. Sometimes Griffin was her friend, because he stopped the bigger kids teasing her. But sometimes he wasn't, because he teased her himself, though he never hit or pinched her.

Then there was Lord William, who had been born in the big house and had lived there all his days. Lord William sucked mints, and talked and smelt funny. He was so old he'd forgotten when his birthday was, or so he said. He played toy soldiers with her on rainy days and invited her to stay for tea and hot-buttered crumpets. She liked them all better than Pauline.

Her nose twitched as she pushed past her sister and headed for the stairs. 'I don't care if you're not my friend. I'm going to have my breakfast. I don't wanna be late for school.'

Today, school seemed extra special. Pamela had packed them lunch in shiny tins with red lids. There was a crisp bread roll full of grated cheese, a chocolate biscuit wrapped in shiny green paper with a penguin on the front, and an apple.

Pamela smiled as she introduced herself to the teacher. Miss Robbins smiled back.

Miss Robbins took the junior classes, and old Mister James took the bigger kids. The classes were mixed because the school only had twenty pupils. Lessons were held in the village hall, an old stone building with a thatched roof. Its two rooms were heated by a pot-bellied stove surrounded by a mesh guard.

'Janey's a bright little thing,' Miss Robbins said, patting her on the head. 'She's learning her letters faster than any pupil I've had, except Griffin Tyler. She should do well.' The teacher's glance fell on Pauline, who was hovering nearby. 'Run off and play, dear. I want to talk to Mrs Renfrew privately for a moment.'

Pauline flounced off in a huff to join her best friend, Wendy Ryker and her brother, Tim. Janey quite liked Tim, who was a year older than his sister, and was going to be a pirate when he grew up.

She watched Griffin coming down the road, his shoulders hunched into a brown and cream checked lumber jacket. He was the oldest in the school and had no friends because he had gypsy blood. Everyone said gypsies couldn't be trusted, but only behind his back. Janey trusted him. Griffin had saved the life of a mouse she'd almost killed.

She hadn't meant to make the mouse sick when she'd caught it and put it in a jam jar. She'd forgotten it, and had discovered it lying on its side three days later. It was stiff, its little feet curled under it. She cried when it wouldn't wake, and took it back to where she'd caught it from in the hedge.

Griffin had come across her there. He stopped and stared at her. 'What's up with you then, cry baby?'

She held out the jar. 'It won't wake up.'

Taking it from her cupped hands he tipped the mouse into his palm and gently ran his finger down its side. His dark, gypsy eyes gazed at her. 'Blubbering won't help it. Come to the garden shed when I whistle for you, and I'll have made it better.'

'How you gonna do that?' she asked him.

'I'm learning to be a doctor, so I'll operate on it.' He was humming softly to himself as he walked away.

A long while later, Griffin placed the warm, living mouse in her hand. Gruffly, he said, 'Here, go and put it back in the hedge. Don't you ever shut a living creature in a jar again. How would you like someone to do that to you?'

Janey knew she wouldn't. As the mouse scampered away she felt so happy she could have burst. Griffen had become her hero and she lived for a smile from him.

She smiled at him when he came into the schoolyard, but he barely flicked her a glance.

'Your mother is quite nice, really,' Annie remarked as they hung over the five-barred gate to watched Pamela set off on the walk back to the cottage.

'Yes, she is,' she said, feeling proud when Pamela turned to smile and wave at her.

Although school absorbed her, Janey missed being outside. She couldn't wait for Saturdays to come so she could visit the big house, and the ginger cat and the owl who lived in the barn. Lord William's old horse, Wellington, had lived in the barn too, once, but just before Christmas he'd grown angel wings and flown away to heaven.

Wellington's empty stall always made her feel sad. There were reminders of him everywhere: his hair stuck on the wooden rails, his bridle hanging on a nail, now green with mould. For a long while she could smell his musty hay smell, then it seemed to fade, until one day she couldn't remember what his smell had been like.

Pamela kept Coombe Cottage spotless, and made friends with Brenda. Sometimes the housekeeper came over for tea and a chat when Janey was home.

'Mister Wyman said to tell you that his dog is going to have some puppies in the spring,' Brenda said one day. 'When they're old enough you can come over and see them.'

Janey couldn't wait.

When their father came on his monthly visits, Pauline's sullen manner improved. Janey tried to keep out of his way, but never quite managed to get through the weekend unscathed.

Pamela was different when their father was around. She cooked special dishes to please him, and wore make-up. She didn't laugh quite so loudly though.

On the Sundays when he was home, they all went to the big church in Dorchester. Her father prayed long and hard on his knees and the service went on forever. The incense made her throat tickle.

Janey began to dread his visits. After church they'd have to sit at the table and read passages from the Bible. When she couldn't, he'd smack her legs and mutter, 'Child of the devil. What are they teaching you at that school?'

Tears came into Pamela's eyes.

'Enough of that,' her father would say, and send them outside to play.

When they were called back in, Pamela would be jolly and smiling, though her eyes would be puffy and red. Once she had a bruised eye. She told them she'd walked into the door.

'I expect dad punished her,' Pauline said when they were alone. 'He hates her as much as he hates you. He only married her so we could have a mother.'

Pamela was offered a job at the big house. Her wages bought some curtains for the cottage. Pauline got a pink bedspread with a ballerina on it, and a pair of shiny patent leather shoes. Pauline surprised them both when she said politely, 'Thank you, mother.'

Pamela smiled. 'I'm glad you're getting used to me, Pauline. I want us to be friends.

The following week Janey was given a blue bedspread with a rabbit on, and a red duffel coat with brown wooden toggles. There was a hood she could pull over her head.

Pauline stared enviously at it. 'Dad said Janey had to make do with my cast-offs.'

'She needs something new of her own.'

There was a row when their father came down. For once, Pamela shouted back. 'I bought them with the money I earned, and I'll spend it how I like.'

Janey stared in shock when her father back-handed Pamela in the same way as he did her. She fell on to the sofa and blood seeped from the corner of her mouth.

Face contorted with rage, her father stared down at her. 'You'll do as I say.'

Pauline's face turned as pale as putty. Janey took her sister's hand. 'Come outside, quick.'

Her father turned and stared at her. 'You're going nowhere. Go and get the coat.'

Silently, Janey did as she was told, her hate for her father a hot, clutching fist in her chest.

'Give the coat to Pauline.'

'But Pauline's gonna be si—'

'Shut up. Do as you're told!' he barked.

As she handed Pauline the red duffel coat her sister threw up over it.

Her father gazed at her in disgust. 'Isn't it about time you grew out of this stupidity.'

Shocked at being the object of his scorn for once, Pauline gave a great, gulping sob. 'It isn't my fault. I can't help it.'

'See what you've done,' he snarled at Pamela, then turning, headed for the door. 'I might as well stay in London for all the respect I get.'

A few seconds after the door slammed shut they heard the car drive away.

Pauline threw herself face down in a cushion and screamed, 'Nobody loves me, and I hate you all. I hate you!'

Pamela was trembling as she rose to her feet. 'Look after her, Janey love. As soon as I've tidied myself up I'll come and see to her.'

It took a while to calm Pauline down. Pamela's lip was swollen on one side, and she looked pale and sad.

There were some snowdrops under the hedge. Janey picked some to cheer her up. Pamela placed them in a tumbler on the window sill, gave a tremulous little smile and kissed her. 'Your father must have been working too hard.'

With a cat and canary smile on her face, Pauline wore the red duffel coat, still smelling faintly of sick, to school on Monday.

The onset of spring was an unexpected delight, even though Janey had been watching for it.

Every day for a month she'd watched the brown buds on the trees swell, touching the sticky casings gently with her fingers. One morning a feather of green emerged, and within a week the casings fell to the ground, revealing boughs covered with bright green leaves.

Bluebells appeared, spreading through the woods in a brilliant fragrant carpet. Creamy lilies meandered along the brook. Birds chased each other through the air and a pair of house martins took up residence in the thatch above her window.

Her wobbly front teeth fell out in April, when the wind played chase-me with showers of rain and sent grey rags of clouds streaming across the sky. May brought her two new ones. It coincided with the white hawthorn blossom, when the air was drugged with perfume and hummed with the sound of bees. All manner of flowers opened in the fields and hedges, and white daisies spread across the land.

The puppies arrived, glorious, fat, squirming creatures with squealing voices. Proud of her litter, their mother watched anxiously when Pauline and Janey cuddled them in their laps.

Janey wished she could have one but knew her father wouldn't let her, so why bother asking. Besides, hadn't Mister Wyman already said they all had good homes to go to?

'How do you like school, Janey?' he asked her.

She smiled. 'I can nearly read, and Miss Robbins said I'm good at drawing so I'm going to be an artist when I grow up.' Remembering her manners she asked. 'How is Lord William?'

Mister Wyman's face became grave. 'He's not well, Janey. I'll tell him you asked after him. He'll be pleased you remembered him.'

Her fingers went to the lead soldier safe in the pocket of her skirt. It was her favourite, and she hadn't been able to resist taking him home. Later that day she took a posy of wildflowers to Brenda to give to Lord William.

Her elderly friend died the following month.

'Snuffed out like a candle in a puff of wind,' Ada, the big house cook said to her, and wiped her eyes on the corner of her apron. 'Eh, that will be some grand funeral on Saturday. Who knows, Queen Elizabeth might even come.'

The Queen didn't come, and the funeral wasn't as grand as Ada had said it would be. Hidden behind a gravestone with Annie, Janey watched a black hearse pull up at the church. It was followed by Mister Wyman and Brenda, and some of the staff from the big house. Curious locals looked on from the boundary of the church wall.

Ada, the cook, wore a black coat and a hat with a feather in it, despite the warmth of the day. Phil Tyler stood at the back with Sam, the head gardener, their caps doffed as a coffin with shining brass handles was lowered into the grave. Mister Wyman threw a shovel of earth into the hole.

Prayers were said by a clergyman in a long black robe and a purple scarf with a gold fringe on the ends. Then everyone sang, 'In England's Green and Pleasant Land.' Cook's determined voice rang loud and clear above the rest, and she kept dabbing at her eyes with a lace-edged handkerchief.

Afterwards, when the mourners trooped off to the big house for tea and biscuits, Janey and Annie crept over to the grave and gazed down at the coffin.

'It's a long way down,' Annie said in awe.

Janey's hand closed round the lead soldier. 'Lord William's gone to heaven to see his horse, Wellington.'

'How can he be in heaven when he's in a box in a hole?' said the more practical Annie.

Cocking her head to one side like a bright-eyed bird Janey gazed at Annie, wishing she hadn't asked. 'I suppose he's growing angel wings, then he'll open the lid and fly away.'

'What if he comes out now?'

The coffin made a thumping sound as a pebble fell on it. Janey's heart began to race and she scrambled to her feet. Annie gave a high pitched yelp and began to run.

'Scat, you kids,' a voice rasped.

Janey took off after Annie, catching her up at the gate. 'Quick,' she yelled, 'The Lord's after us.' Jumping on their bikes, their legs pumped furiously at the peddles as they sped away.

Sam pushed his cap back on his head. He was laughing as he straightened up from his hiding place behind Betty Potter's tombstone. Shovel against hip, he watched them go, then transferred his gaze to the coffin.

'I have a favour to ask, My Lord,' he whispered, looking about him to make sure Phil Tyler wasn't watching. 'I'd be much obliged if you'd keep watch over that young-un you liked so much. If you asks me, something's not quite right inside her father's head.'

'You know what they say about people who talk to themselves.' Phil screwed a finger at the side of his head as he sauntered towards him, shovel over his shoulder. 'We better get this filled in, pronto. Mister Wyman wants us up at the house when the will's read. I reckon the viscount has left us a little something.'

'He was a grand old man.' Sam stared at Phil as the younger man bent his back to the pile of earth. 'He thought the world of that young Renfrew lass.'

'He ain't the only one from what I just heard.' Phil's smile was sly as he gazed at Sam. 'They'll be putting you in the funny farm if they catch you talking to dead folk too often.'

'You can talk. Everyone knows you're soft in the head when it comes to that lass.' Giving a sheepish grin, Sam punched him on the shoulder, then took up a shovel of earth and hurled it into the hole.

Jack Bellamy stretched his legs towards the fire, and reread the letter from Eddie Renfrew's lawyer.

'Damn him!' he said, his scowl making the scar on his face pucker. 'He can't deny a man the right to see his own daughter, Mary.'

His sister glanced up from her darning for a moment. 'The lawyer said it's only your word against his. Leave it alone, Jack, or he'll take out a restraining order against you.'

'Leave it alone, be damned!' Jack lumbered to his feet. 'I'm going out for a while to think things through.'

'Put on your coat. It's chilly out.'

He stooped to kiss her cheek. 'Go home to your husband, and stop darning my socks. I can buy new ones.'

Mary sighed as she watched him stride from the room. She'd disapproved of his relationship with Margaret Renfrew. Not that she'd disliked her, but the girl had been married, and a good fifteen years younger than Jack. But to give Margaret her due, she'd seemed to be genuinely fond of Jack.

Staring at the sock, Mary tried to picture Janey. She'd only seen her once, a fair-haired baby in a pushchair who'd looked like thousands of other babies. Had Mary known then that the child was Jack's daughter, she'd have taken more notice of her.

He'd been devastated when Margaret died. Her lips tightened a fraction. Jack had blamed himself, and his only thought now was to see his daughter. She hoped he wouldn't do anything stupid.

Jack had no intention of doing anything stupid. He also had no intention of letting Eddie Renfrew have things all his own way.

A plan was forming in his head. Nothing radical, just an easy way of solving the problem. He intended to buy a cottage in the village near where Janey lived. At least he'd be able to watch her grow up whilst he worked on his paintings.

He'd started painting during the war, when he'd been recuperating in hospital after crash-landing his Hurricane. He'd been in a fever of impatience whilst he'd mended. Painting had become his therapy whilst the battle of Britain had continued in the skies above him.

It had become an absorbing hobby, one he continued to practise under his given names of John Gregory. His skill earned him a modest income that was infinitely more satisfying than the business profits.

Without knowing it he'd walked along the quay to where his boat had once been moored. Scowling, he stared at the charred length of rope still attached to the bollard. The boat had been his father's, and had crossed to Dunkirk for the evacuation of troops. She'd been called *The Maggie* then, after his mother. The boat had been strafed by a German fighter plane at Dunkirk in May 1940, and his father had lost his life.

Jack had toyed with the idea of building another boat just like her, but she hadn't been insured and the materials were too costly to justify it. Besides, he'd never be able to reproduce her brave history, nor the bullet holes in the teak decking he'd so carefully caulked.

The fire had been deliberately lit. He still thought Eddie Renfrew had something to do with the fire, though the police had told him Eddie's alibi had checked out.

He tossed up whether to tell Mary about his decision to move nearer to Janey, then decided against it. She'd only worry.

It was nearly dusk when he returned home. He cut through Poole Park. Mist breathed on the surface of the boating lake. Lovers were entwined on seats, and a pair of swans, their necks arched and graceful, flapped their wings and hissed at him.

A group of youths were larking about on the cricket oval, watched by three girls sitting on the steps of the cricket pavilion. All wore the latest fashion – circular skirts in a colourful paisley design, tight ribbed sweaters and elastic belts to nip in their slender waists.

They were well-dressed, well-fed, and carefree, enjoying their youth.

Jack grinned. He'd been apprenticed to his father at that age, and had been just as carefree, not knowing war was just seven short years away.

He fingered the scar on his face. He'd got off lightly, he'd survived and become successful with his business. But for what? Money. He had nothing else of value. The only woman he'd ever loved was dead, and his daughter was denied him.

But not for long. He could watch Janey grow up, and when she was old enough to know the truth he'd tell her. His mood suddenly lightened, and he quoted softly as he inserted his key in the lock. *'There is a tide in the affairs of men, which taken at their flood, leads on to fortune. Omitted, all the voyage of their life is bound in shallows and misery.'*

The tide had brought him both fortune and misery. For once in his life he intended to swim against it.

He gave a wryly astonished smile. Everything changed. Even him.

Three months later Jack met his daughter face to face.

In that time, Canford Cottage, which he'd bought cheaply, because it had been in such a dilapidated state, had been rewired and the plumbing fixed. He'd made a start on the internal repairs.

Feeling happier than he'd been for some time, he hummed to himself as he spread plaster over a hole in the wall. No need to be too careful, the uneven walls were part of the cottage's charm. It would look nice painted a soft buttery yellow to tone in with the new carpet he'd chosen. Next, he'd have to tackle the garden. He bent his head to look at it through the tiny, square-paned window upstairs on the landing.

Flowers of every description and colour grew amongst the lush green nettles. A tangle of pink and white dog roses rambled over the fence, yellow and pink hollyhocks climbed the outhouse wall, and a patch of sunflowers stretched their faces towards the sky.

There was a small orchard of mossy-trunked apple trees, pears and plums at the bottom. A stone wall, set without mortar and mellowed with lichen, separated his garden from a meadow. It looked as though it had been there forever.

A flash of red caught his eye. A child – two children, their heads bobbing up and down as they walked behind the wall. One was a dark curly-haired imp, the other had flaxen braids tied in red ribbons. One ribbon trailed like a flaming red banner.

'Go on, Janey. I dare you to look through the window and see if he's as ugly as everyone says.'

Goose-bumps prickled along Jack's forearms. Breath held, his eyes were riveted on the fair-haired child as she scrambled over the wall and, with the caution of a fox, crept towards the house.

She was halfway across when the other child spotted him. 'He's upstairs at the window.'

Janey came to an abrupt halt and gazed up at him. The hem of her blue checked dress was a darker colour where it had been lengthened. Her white socks had slid into the heels of a pair of shabby brown sandals.

Janey, my daughter! Jack's heart turned slowly in his chest. She'd inherited his colouring, but her mouth was petal soft, just like her mother's had been. Her head was cocked to one side in a little gesture of defiance. Bright blue eyes stared in wary contemplation of him.

Dry-mouthed, he managed to say, 'Hello, Janey.'

'Run!' the other one yelled.

Janey's mouth turned up in a grin and she giggled. Then she turned and sped away, scrambling over the wall like a monkey. The pair of them went dashing across the meadow, jumping from tuft to tuft and laughing.

He watched until distance swallowed them, his smile fixed in place. When his sight blurred he realized he was crying.

He closed his eyes, allowing his body to absorb his sense of loss. The grief he'd lived with over the past few years seemed to wash away with his tears, leaving him vulnerable, and somehow renewed.

'Thank you for this gift, Margaret,' he whispered. 'She's the most beautiful child I've ever seen.'

CHAPTER THREE

To Janey, winters were Christmas cards glittering with frost – spring was warm, delicate pastels. She loved summer with its freedom and blossoming, but autumn was her favourite, a season of ripeness, its flamboyant colours giving her a sense of achievement.

There had been many seasons since Pamela's arrival, but the coming of autumn had something special to look forward to.

Arms outstretched, she moulded her body against the warm earth, her sketching pad forgotten beside her. The baby would be born in a few short weeks when the earth was wearing red and gold. She hoped the baby was a boy, because Pamela had said she wanted a baby boy.

'Now you're eleven you'll be able to help me look after him,' Pamela said just that morning. Her eyes had been soft as she'd taken her hand and placed it against the swell of her stomach. It had been strange and exciting to feel the baby moving under her hand, and to know Pamela would give birth to a new life.

She closed her eyes, a smile drifting across her face. Once the grass beneath her cheek had been new. Now it had an old smell, and had coarsened to the touch like old people's skin, as if the juice had been sucked up by the sun.

Spring, summer, autumn, winter, seasons turning over and over. The earth rested in autumn, the disturbances of spring and summer quiet and calm. It was a good time to bring a baby into the world.

She pressed her ear against the earth's skin. Phil had told her the earth was a wise old woman who spoke to those who took the time to listen. She listened now, feeling it slowly revolve as she clung to its surface, as small as a speck of dust. Being small made her feel secure, as if she and the earth shared a secret.

'Miss Robbins said I have a good chance of going to grammar school next year,' she whispered. 'And John Gregory wants to enter a painting of mine in the council competition. If I win it I'll be able to buy a present for the baby.'

She liked John Gregory, though the others laughed at his scarred face behind his back. Janey didn't mind it. It was shiny and smooth where he'd been burnt, and had felt like silk under her fingers when she'd touched it. He had kind eyes, and a kind face if you imagined it without the scar.

Every Tuesday afternoon she went to art class in his cottage. Mister James had arranged the classes for the senior students.

'Janey.'

Ignoring Pauline's voice she rolled over on her back to look at the sky. The blue was so intense it shimmered and glimmered into minute flashes of different coloured particles that went on forever. It was a dizzying sensation, as if the world had speeded up.

'Janey?'

She sat up and gazed at the cottage. Pauline stood at the gate, her eyes shaded by her hand against the sun.

'Dad wants you.'

The smile slid from Janey's face. Why was her father at the cottage mid-week? Her feet dragged as she made her way down the hill. The day had lost its joy.

Her father's eyes blazed with annoyance. 'Look at the state of this kitchen. You're supposed to help with the housework when your mother goes for her check-up.'

Janey shot her sister a frown. 'It's Pauline's turn to do the kitchen. I cleaned the bathroom and made the beds before I went out.'

'Liar,' he snarled. 'Pauline had just finished making the beds when I came in.'

Pauline smiled her smug smile. 'She probably forgot. All she thinks about is her stupid drawing and painting.'

Janey stiffened when her father grabbed the sketch book from under her arm. The anguished cry she gave didn't prevent him from stuffing the book into the fire-box of the Aga. The pages blackened and curled, then little blue flames licked around the edges. It flared up briefly, becoming red and grey flakes that were sucked up the chimney pipe.

It isn't fair! It isn't fair! Janey carefully hid her rage, but her fingers curled into tight little fists against her skirt.

Her father turned to give her a hard stare. 'Let that be a lesson to you. From now on you don't go out until you've finished your chores. Is that understood?'

Janey's teeth worried her bottom lip. It was easier to say nothing. He wouldn't believe her word against Pauline's. Her sister was lazy, and would do anything to get out of the housework. She would have been reading comics all morning.

'*Do you understand!*'

She jumped, trying not to wince when he gripped her arms and dug his fingers into her flesh. Her chin lifted a fraction, though she kept her eyes lowered and her voice quiet.

'Yes, father.'

'Good.' He thrust her against the table. 'Pauline and I are going to pick Pamela up from the clinic. Make sure the kitchen is clean by the time we return.'

The kitchen was spotless when they returned. Her father grunted as he ran a finger over the surfaces for dust. 'Better than nothing, I suppose. See that it's kept like this.'

Pamela looked pale and tired as she lowered herself into a chair.

'Shall I make you a cup of tea,' Janey offered.

'Thanks, love. I don't know what's wrong with me lately.'

'Nothing,' Eddie was saying as Janey went into the kitchen. 'You're having a perfectly normal pregnancy. I don't know why you wanted me here. Mrs Wyman was furious.'

'I'm sorry, Eddie.' Pamela had tears in her eyes. 'I feel so tired all the time.'

'You ought to make Janey do more instead of letting her moon about all over the place.'

'She does her best,' Pamela protested. 'Besides, she has her exam to study for. Mister James thinks she's got a good chance of going on to grammar school.'

'Waste of an education if you ask me. She'll never amount to much with her head always in the clouds.'

'I hope I won't have to put up with her at *my* school,' Pauline said in the toffee-nosed voice she'd adopted since she'd boarded at the Catholic girls' college. 'It would be *too* embarrassing. Wendy Ryker thinks she's stupid.'

'I don't see what that little madam has got to be so proud of?' Pamela sounded unusually snappy. 'She can't add two and two together – and neither can you.'

Janey grinned as she took the tea caddy from the shelf. All Pauline and Wendy talked about was film stars, boys and make-up. Pauline was always looking at herself in the mirror when she was home, inspecting her face for pimples, her armpits for hairs or sticking out her chest and measuring it with a tape.

'Janey won't be going to your school, love,' her father said. 'If she doesn't pass the exam she can go to secondary school in Poole.'

'And how's she going to get there with me stuck in the country with no car?'

Janey held her breath. She'd heard this argument before from Pamela, and it usually ended in a fight.

But not this time. Her father gave a funny sort of laugh. 'I've decided to let you have the Morris. I cashed in one of my investments and bought a Ford Zephyr. I'm picking it up in an hour.'

An unbelieving smile inched across Pamela's face. 'That's wonderful, Eddie.'

He crossed to where she sat and playfully patted her stomach. 'Let's hope you and my son can fit behind the wheel.'

'Now don't you get your hopes up, Eddie Renfrew. The baby might just be a girl.'

He scowled as he headed for the door. 'It had better not be.'

'You're not going back tonight, are you?'

'Of course. Mrs Wyman is going to Paris tomorrow. Hurry up and finish your tea, then you can drive me into town. I'll wait in the car.'

'Oh, Eddie. I'm that tired I could weep.'

Eddie fixed her with a stare. 'Don't be so bloody selfish. You don't expect me to walk, do you?'

'Of course not, Eddie. Couldn't you get a taxi? I've got to get dinner prepared, and there's the washing to bring in.'

'I haven't got money to burn,' he snarled. 'You get off your fat backside and drive me into town, otherwise I might change my mind about the Morris.'

Pamela placed her tea cup back on the saucer and struggled to her feet.

'If Pauline gets the washing off the line I'll start on dinner,' Janey offered.

Pauline pouted. Moving to their father's side she laid her head against his arm. 'Can I come with you?'

He slid his arm around her and kissed the top of her head. 'Of course you can. You're my favourite girl, aren't you.'

Janey fought to control the wave of hurt that engulfed her. Her lip curled, but not until she'd turned away from her father's flat, grey stare.

She sighed with relief when the car chugged away. The tension had evaporated, and the cottage seemed silent. Her fingers uncurled from her palms, leaving tiny red marks where her nails had dug in. There was a pain in her chest – like a wound that never quite healed.

She closed her eyes for a moment. Silence surrounded her, hugged her close and comforted her. After a while she didn't hurt any more.

By the time Pamela returned she'd peeled some potatoes and put peas and carrots in the steamer over the top of the pan. The table was set, fat sausages sizzled in the frying pan. Neatly folded into the wicker basket was the washing, waiting to be ironed.

Pamela looked exhausted. 'I met Mrs Ryker in the village. She invited Pauline to stay the night with Wendy.'

The two of them exchanged a glance, then mutual smiles.

'Then it's only us for tea.'

Pamela kissed her on the cheek. 'We can have an extra sausage each. You can get on with your painting for the competition after, and I'll do the ironing.'

'Dad threw my sketch book in the fire.'

'I know, love. He didn't mean it. I expect he was tired after the drive down.' She placed a paper bag on the table. 'I bought you another one while I was in town, and a new box of paints. Those squirrels you drew were lovely, just like real ones. I bet you'll win the first prize in the competition.'

Janey wished Pamela would stop making excuses for her father's behaviour. She gave her a hug. 'You sit down and rest. The painting can wait. I'll finish dinner *and* do the ironing. It won't take me long.'

'You're a good girl, Janey. I don't know how I'd manage without you.'

She wanted to tell Pamela she loved her, but didn't know how. She could only show it. She was going to paint the best picture she could, and when she won the prize she'd buy Pamela a present as well.

Eddie didn't go back to London straight away. He drove his new Zephyr slowly round Poole Park, then parked to watch a couple of teenage girls feed the ducks on the pond. It was dusk when they split up, one heading towards the main entrance. The other took the path in the opposite direction that led to the back of the park. His eyes narrowed in on her, and he turned the key in the ignition.

When he arrived back in London, he was met by Sarah's latest maid. She gave him an angry glance.

'Mrs Wyman is in a right mood. Fetch this, fetch that! She's had me at her beck and call half the night. If she keeps this up I'll hand in my notice, just see if I don't. I wasn't hired to be her bloody slave.'

'Anita?' Sarah called out. 'Fetch me a fresh pot of tea, at once. This is lukewarm.'

'I'll do it. You go on about your business.'

'Thank God you're back,' Sarah snapped when he carried in the fresh tea. 'Where the hell did you hide my plane ticket?'

'It's with your passport.'

Sarah was propped against the pillows, her dark hair hanging around her shoulders, her face pale. Her breasts thrust against her white negligee. She looked like hell.

'You look tired,' he said.

Sarah stared viciously at him. 'I spent all of yesterday afternoon chairing the functions committee.' Her yawn exposed teeth as perfect as cosmetic dentistry could make them. 'They're boring old farts. I had to pop a couple of uppers to stay awake during the meeting, then some downers to get to sleep. Now I feel like shit.'

He dropped a small cellophane packet on the bed. 'Try this as a pick-you-up.'

Her face dimpled into a smile. 'You're an angel, Edward. What have you got lined up for me in Paris?'

'Wait and see.'

'How was dearest Pamela?' she cooed.

'Perfectly healthy.'

'And the *enfant-terrible*?'

'Try your claws out on someone else, Sarah,' Eddie ground out.

'Is that an order?'

It was about time Sarah Wyman was put straight. 'I know too much about you for your own good.'

'I see.' Slipping from the bed she drifted towards him, gazing through flint-hard eyes. 'Be careful, Edward. That works two ways.'

Despite his unease he managed a faint smile. She was bluffing. 'If you're talking about the circumstances of my former wife's death, it's on public record.'

Sarah patted him on the cheek. 'Poor Edward.'

He jerked his head away from her touch. 'Is there anything else you want?'

She gave him a wicked grin. 'I doubt if you're man enough to take advantage of it.'

He was tempted to slap her. One day she'd go too far, and when she did, he'd show her whether he was man or not.

Turning away, he strolled from the room, pulling the door quietly behind him.

He leaned against the wall for a couple of minutes, taking several deep breaths until he got a grip on himself.

Sarah was trash. She wouldn't get anyone else to pamper for her needs like he did, and it was about time she realized that.

His eyes narrowed as he turned back towards the door. In a few minutes her mood would have improved and he'd persuade her to show her appreciation. A nice little bonus wouldn't go amiss.

Pamela was restless. Two weeks to go. The midwife had told her everything was proceeding as normal.

She felt lethargic and swollen. The day was overcast and humid, as it had been for days. Her back ached. She placed her hands against it, trying to ease it with a cautious stretch as she gazed critically at the shabby lounge suite. She'd patched the covers on the chairs so many times there was hardly any of the original material left. Eddie kept her too short of money and now she didn't even have her job to fall back on.

Going upstairs, she opened the drawer containing the baby's clothing and eyed the contents. Ada had knit a complete layette in a pretty shell design. As she fingered the delicate edging on the shawl she gave a watery smile. Ada had a good heart.

Her hand tenderly caressed her stomach. Her very own baby, at last. It had been an accident. Eddie rarely touched her any more. Her smiled faded. Her child should have been conceived in love, not anger. But that didn't make any difference to her. She already loved her baby and nothing would alter that.

At the sound of the gate squeaking open she lifted her head. Janey already?

She was surprised to find Phil Tyler standing on the doorstep, his wiry arms clasping a basket of fruit and vegetables.

'These are for you, missus. Mister Wyman asked me to bring them over.'

'That's very nice of him. Thank you, Phil.' She stood aside to let him through and watched him deposit them on the kitchen table.

Removing his cap, Phil gazed at her. 'Ada's put in a blackberry and apple pie, and some iced fairy cakes for young Janey.'

Tears pricked Pamela's eyes. Everyone was being so kind. 'Would you like a cup of tea?'

'You sit down, missus. I'll make it. If you don't mind me saying, you look done in.'

'I'm just tired.' To Pamela's horror tears slid down her cheeks. 'I'm so sorry,' she said, trying to dash them away. 'I don't know what's come over me. It must be the weather making me depressed.'

'Don't you pay no mind to me.' Phil put his arm around her shoulders. 'You have a good cry if that's what you want. It'll do you a power of good.'

So she sobbed like a baby against his chest. When she finished she blew her nose and washed her face on the flannel he handed her.

She managed a wry smile. 'I suppose you think I'm stupid.'

He set a mug of tea in front of her. 'If crying hadn't a purpose, nature wouldn't have given us the ability to produce tears, I reckon.'

'I've never thought of it quite like that.'

'People never do. They think they've got to be brave all the time.'

She jumped as lightning lit the room, and struggled to her feet. 'I'd better go and fetch Janey from school.'

'Don't you fret about young Janey,' Phil said comfortably. 'She'll be coming through the door any minute.'

Just as he finished speaking the door flew open and Janey bounded through. She stopped when she saw Phil, and gave him a big smile. 'Mister Gregory said he saw some badgers in his garden last night.'

Phil nodded. 'They've got a set in the thicket, the run probably goes through his garden.'

'Will you show me where it is?'

A smile inched across Phil's face. 'We'll have to go at dusk and wait until they come out of hiding.'

'Not tonight surely, not with this storm brewing,' exclaimed Pamela.

'No missus. Some other time.' Phil finished his tea and stood up, cap in hand. 'I'd best be off, then. You look as though your time be near, missus. Don't you go overdoing things, now.'

'Thank you, Phil. I'm sure I'll be all right. Eddie got the phone put on for me, and when the time comes all I have to do is ring the midwife. Eddie said he'll come straight down from London when I call.'

'I'll be off, then.'

For some reason she couldn't fathom, Pamela was reluctant to see him go. 'How's that boy of yours doing at grammar school?'

'Griff's doing right nicely, I reckon. It's university for him next year. He's set his heart on being a doctor.'

'You must be very proud of him.'

'Aye, I am that. Thank goodness the old viscount left me a little something to put by, otherwise I don't know how we'd manage all the books he'll need.'

'Tell him I wish him good luck, and thank Ada and Mister Wyman for me. I appreciate how kind they've been.'

'Some people are worth bothering with, some ain't,' Phil said sagely as he set his cap on his head and made his departure.

Pamela stared after him for a few seconds. 'I always thought Phil was a bit strange, but he's a nice man for all that. He told me you were home just before you came through the door.'

Janey laughed. 'It's his Romany blood. He senses things other people don't.'

'You're a queer one yourself sometimes, Janey Renfrew,' Pamela chuckled. 'Go and put the kettle on. I could do with another cup. We'll sample a couple of the fairy cakes Ada sent over.'

Janey gave her a closer look. 'You've been crying.'

'You don't miss much, do you? The weather's getting me down a bit, that's all.' She smoothed her hands over her stomach. 'And I feel fat.'

'You *are* fat.' Janey grinned. 'I'm surprised you haven't noticed it before. It's the talk of the village.'

Both of them burst into laughter.

'Mister Gregory has asked me to stay to lunch when I take my painting to him tomorrow,' Janey said as she moved into the kitchen. 'He said his sister and her husband will come to pick me up in her car so you can meet them. Will that be all right? Mister Gregory has a telephone, so you can call if you need me.'

'I don't see why not. Pauline will be home.'

As if that made any difference, Janey thought as she made the tea. Pauline was useless, just making work for them both.

The storm didn't eventuate that night, apart from a few warning grumbles of thunder and flickers of lightning. Pamela spent a restless night. Her back ached incessantly, and she couldn't get comfortable.

Pauline sulked when her request to go to Wendy Ryker's house was denied.

'You can go tomorrow,' Pamela told her. 'I need you to help me today.'

'Why couldn't Janey have stayed home?'

'Because she's been invited out to lunch. Besides, Janey helps me all week when you're at school.'

Pauline had turned into a selfish little madam, she thought with a sudden flicker of dislike for her. She was pretty to look at, and dainty when set against Janey's coltish frame. Janey would have a graceful elegance once she became a woman, and her gamine features would mature into classic beauty. If she had a daughter, she hoped she'd take after Janey rather than Pauline.

She shivered. Eddie wanted a son, and when he didn't get his own way it didn't bear thinking about. Sometimes she questioned her wisdom in marrying him. She was beginning to dread his visits, mostly because Janey usually bore the brunt of his anger.

Leaning on the window sill she returned Janey's wave as the car pulled away. Mary and Douglas Yates were a nice couple. They treated her stepdaughter like one of the family.

A spatter of wind-driven rain hit the window. As she leaned forward to pull it shut, pain lanced though her back. Carefully, she straightened up and took a deep breath. She grimaced as the pain faded to a dull ache. She'd be glad when it was all over.

CHAPTER FOUR

Two red squirrels filled the picture. They were perched on a branch, the one in the foreground nibbling a pine cone, the other standing alert and watchful.

'What do you think of it, Mary?'

'It's good for someone of Janey's age.'

'It's more than good. The animals have life. Look how she's captured the lustre of the coat and eyes. Not many kids would observe that.'

Mary gave a light laugh. 'You sound exactly like a proud father.'

Jack grinned as he took her hands in his. 'I *am* a proud father, I just wish I could shout about it. It's been hell having to hide when Eddie Renfrew's in the district.'

Mary slid a troubled glance towards the window. Janey was racing around the garden with Goldie, Jack's Labrador in tow. Her hair was free of its usual braids and fell about her shoulders like pale silk. Her dress was faded and patched, a piece of contrasting material sewn round the hem to lengthen it.

She could understand Jack's point of view. She'd grown to love Janey and it was frustrating not to be able to adopt the role of aunt. She'd love to fit the child out with some new clothes.

'I'm going to tell her,' Jack said. 'As soon as she's old enough to understand. Renfrew can't keep us apart for ever.'

'Be careful, she's sensitive. The shock could drive her in the opposite direction.'

Jack's brow furrowed. 'Then perhaps I could approach her stepmother. Janey thinks the world of her.'

'Pamela Renfrew is a sensible woman, but don't forget she's married to Janey's father. It's possible she might not be aware of the situation.'

Jack hunched his head into his shoulders and scowled like a scalded bear. '*I'm* Janey's father.'

'Stop being so grouchy. You know exactly what I mean. If you take my advice you'll wait until she's a grown woman. You're already skating on thin ice.'

'OK, I get the message.' Slanting her a glance, he grinned. 'It's odd how she never mentions Renfrew.'

Driven by a gust of wind, rain splattered against the window. Janey and Goldie headed for the shelter of the house. Janey took the seat opposite Mary's husband. She liked Douglas a lot. He was round-faced and jolly, and had doggy brown eyes like Goldie. 'It's started to rain.'

'There's going to be a storm later. Fancy a game of snakes and ladders?'

'No time I'm afraid,' Mary said. 'I think we'd better drop Janey off and head for home. I don't like the look of this weather.'

'I'll drive her home,' Jack offered, loath to relinquish his daughter so soon. 'She wants to see her picture being framed.'

'Be careful, Jack,' Mary said softly.

He nodded. 'I'll ring Mrs Renfrew and ask if she can stay another hour. It's not as if Janey has school tomorrow.'

The phone was engaged.

Unease prickled down Janey's back. Her father said no one was to use the telephone unless it was an emergency. The unease stayed with her for a short while, then fled as she watched her picture being framed. The frame was almost the same colour as the squirrels. Inside, bordering the painting, was a cardboard square of a soft oatmeal shade.

'It makes it look like a real picture.'

'I'm proud of you, Janey. It's a lovely painting. I'm sure you'll do well in the competition.'

'You can have it as a present afterwards, if you like,' she offered.

'Why, thank you, Janey. I'll treasure it.' He gave into the urge to kiss her cheek, and watched her blush. Tears in his eyes, he turned to blink them away. 'We'd better get you home before this storm hits. I'm going on into town afterwards so I'll drop you at the end of the lane.'

By mid-afternoon the sky was a cauldron of dark ominous clouds. Perspiration beaded Pamela's body and she shifted uncomfortably on the bed.

There was a rock and roll special on. Pauline's transistor radio blared out one song after another. She beat time to it, taping something against the adjoining wall with annoying persistence. She turned on to her side and pulled the corner of the pillow over her ear. Almost asleep, she was jerked awake by a deafening crash of thunder. The radio went dead.

Pauline sidled into the room. 'The electricity's gone off.'

'Yes, I know.' Her head spun for a second or two as she hauled herself upright. 'We'll have to find some candles.'

Together, they went downstairs and searched through the cupboards. Pauline set the candles in saucers, then threw herself into an armchair.

The atmosphere was oppressive in the cottage. The windows were small, allowing in more gloom than light. Pamela tried to concentrate on finishing the tiny blue matinée jacket she was knitting. The idea was stuck in her head that if she made something blue, her baby would be a boy. Not that she really minded if it was a girl – but Eddie would.

Pauline sat opposite, her face sulky, her legs drawn up under her skirt. 'Some weekend this turned out to be.'

'Why don't you go and make us some tea. There's some of those nice fairy cakes Ada made left.'

'I'm not going into the kitchen. A big spider ran across the floor when we were looking for candles.'

'The storm must have driven it indoors.' Setting aside her knitting, Pamela slowly rose to her feet. Her back was killing her, and her pelvis had begun to ache. 'I'll make it.'

She was halfway across the room when Pauline gasped. She turned, gazing at her ashen face.

'What is it?'

'Blood, on your dress and legs.'

Pamela's fingers found the sticky patch. She gazed at the blood almost uncomprehendingly, then her heart lurched against her ribs. Suddenly, water gushed in a torrent from her, cramp clutched at her pelvis. Bent almost double by the pain, she groaned. 'Quick, the baby's coming. Phone the midwife.'

Pauline stared at her like a cornered rabbit, then her eyes rolled up in her head and she slid to the floor.

Cramps came one after the other. Pamela cursed as she staggered towards the phone. She should have known Pauline would be useless in an emergency.

The midwife's line was engaged. She remembered that John Gregory lived almost opposite the midwife – but she'd forgotten to ask Mary Yates for the number.

Sobbing under her breath, she rifled feverishly through the phone book. Of all the Gregory's listed, not one lived in Winterbrook. As she tried to ring the nurse again, there was a blinding flash of lightning. The line went dead.

Pain walloped her again, squeezing relentlessly at her innards. She doubled up, falling to her hands and knees. When the pain subsided, she crawled to Pauline and gently slapped her pale face.

The girl's eyes fluttered open, then awareness came into them. She scrambled in panic to the corner of the chair.

'Don't touch me. You're going to die, just like my mother.'

Prickles crept up Pamela's spine when she remembered that the girl had found her mother dead in a pool of blood.

'It's all right, Pauline. I'm not going to die.'

'I want you to die,' she spat out, her face contorted with loathing. 'You're not my mother. I hate you and I hate the baby! I hope you both die!' Leaping to her feet she made a rush for the door. 'I'm going to Wendy's house.'

When the door slammed behind her fear salted Pamela's tongue. 'Someone please help me!' she managed to cry out before the pain consumed her again.

Buffeted by the wind, Janey didn't see Phil and Griffin in the lane until she almost ran into them. Griffin had outgrown his father now. As tall and as straight as a sapling, his dark hair was a mass of curls. He looked nice now he was nearly grown up.

'You Renfrews are in an almighty hurry today,' Griffin said, his deepened voice coming as a surprise after not seeing him for a while.

It was a nice voice, she decided, her head aslant as she gazed shyly up at him – sort of soft and growling.

'Your sister was running towards the Rykers' place as if her tail was on fire.'

Fear touched her heart. 'Mum,' she whispered.

'What about her? We were just going to drop in on her to see if she needed anything.'

'She hasn't been well lately, and she's all by herself.'

Phil didn't stop to ask questions. Grabbing her by the hand he hurried towards the cottage, dragging her after him.

The sky opened when they reached the porch. For one fleeting moment, before the sight of Pamela drove everything else from her mind, Janey prayed Pauline would drown in it.

Pamela's face was contorted with pain. 'Thank God! I think the baby's about to arrive.'

Griffin promptly headed towards the phone.

'Now don't you go panicking, missus,' Phil soothed. 'Childbirth is a natural thing. I'll help you to your bed so you can relax.'

Pamela felt calmer now she had someone with her.

'The phone's dead,' Griffin called out a few seconds later. 'I'll run to the village and fetch the nurse.'

Janey took her hand. 'Griff won't be long. As soon as the nurse gets here, everything will be OK.'

Pamela arched her back and groaned.

Phil took her aside. 'The baby's not going to wait that long. I want you to get some towels whilst I wash my hands.'

Janey scurried to do Phil's bidding. When she returned, Pamela was on her back under a sheet, her knees making a tent. Phil folded the bottom of the sheet back and placed the towels under Pamela's bottom.

Janey averted her eyes.

'This is no time to be squeamish, Janey. You've watched that old barn cat give birth to her kittens. This is exactly the same. That there is the baby's head, I reckon.'

Fascinated, Janey watched the baby's head emerge as Pamela gave long, straining groans. Then the head slowly turned. A few seconds later the baby emerged in a slithering rush. Immediately, it started to howl. Pamela lifted her head, her eyes frantic.

'What's wrong with him?'

'Nothing, missus, but it ain't a him.' Wrapping a towel round the infant, Phil lifted the baby to show Pamela. 'She's a bonny little lass, but I'm going to have to leave her down here while we wait for the nurse. There's still the afterbirth to come, and you're bleeding a bit.'

He placed a towel between her legs and pulled the sheet down over her knees.

'Janey, you get acquainted with your new sister. I'll wait downstairs for Griff to come back.'

Pamela lifted her head to glimpse the baby. Janey fetched a mirror from the dressing table and propped it against the foot of the bed.

When her eyes lit on her squalling daughter Pamela forgot her discomfort. 'She's so sweet. Look at her hair, Janey love, and her little fingers and toes. Isn't she beautiful?'

Janey thought so too. Full of awe, she stared at her baby sister and her heart filled up with love. After a while the baby stopped crying and opened her eyes. They were dark, like Pamela's. It was odd that she wanted to cry when she felt so happy. She swallowed hard to stop herself. 'Shall I make you a cup of tea whilst we wait for the nurse?'

Pamela didn't take her eyes from the baby. Like her smile, they were soft. She looked exhausted, but the strain of the past few weeks had gone from her face. 'That would be nice, Janey love. I'm parched.' Her gaze left the baby for a moment. 'I don't know how I would have managed without you. I'm going to make sure your dad knows how helpful you've been. Would you like to choose a name for your little sister?'

'Susan,' Janey said.

'What about Joy for a second name? Susan Joy Renfrew.' Pamela's hand curled around hers and gently squeezed. 'It's a lovely name.'

Eddie was furious. Another girl, and he'd have to stay at the cottage until Pamela got out of hospital.

Bloody useless woman! he fumed. *She's ruined my whole weekend.* He felt embarrassed by the whole affair. There was something distasteful about having a gypsy deliver the baby. Didn't Pamela have any shame, exposing herself to a stranger like that? She must have known she was in labour.

His eyes narrowed. And where was Janey at the time? Shirking her responsibilities by visiting one of her teachers. She knew Pauline had a weak stomach.

He watched her bring in the ashtray he'd sent her for. She was taller than Pauline now, and her long fair hair was untidily braided. Her eyes flicked up to his as she set it on the arm of his chair. They were bluer than Pauline's, bluer than her mother's. Every day, she grew to look more like Bellamy.

Aggrieved at the reminder of his first wife's lover, he stared with loathing at her. She had a double serving of bad blood in her, and needed strict discipline to curb it. He watched her move away to straighten up a candle on the sideboard before returning to the kitchen.

There were lamb chops, vegetables and mashed potatoes for dinner.

'The gravy was lumpy,' he said.

He detected a spark of insolence in her eyes when she murmured. 'I'll try and do better next time.'

He was sure she said one thing and thought another. 'Make sure you do.'

Taking a cigarette from his pocket he put a match to it, then sucked too savagely at the smoke and started to cough. Janey watched him with a steady, unblinking gaze.

'What the hell are you staring at?' he snarled, stubbing the cigarette out on his plate as he stood up. 'Get the table cleared and the kitchen tidied before I get back.'

Pauline kissed his cheek. 'Will you drop me off at Wendy's? Mister Ryker said I can sleep there tonight, and he'll drop me off at school tomorrow.'

Janey stared at her, thinking: *Liar, you just want to get out of the washing-up*. Relieved when they both left, Janey tidied the kitchen, then stared out of the window at the clouds building up in the sky. They were a dark shade of purple, threaded through with silver. Now and again, lightning sheeted against the undersides. Beneath their awesome magnificence, the landscape looked drab and black.

A rumble of distant thunder rolled across the hills and Lord William's old grey horse suddenly popped into her mind.

What had Phil said all those years ago? *When you hear thunder, that will be old Wellington kicking up a fuss.*

As she set a match to one of the candles the wary expression left her eyes. Then she shrugged, and gave a gently ironic smile. She no longer believed in fairy tales.

The second storm hit as Eddie drove up the lane.

He'd spent an unproductive evening in a public house in Poole. The available women had been blowsy old hags, the whisky suspect. He'd been thrown out after accusing the landlord of watering it.

His mood was foul, his stomach sour. He switched off the engine and stared at the cottage through a torrent of rain running down the windshield. What a dump!

The only light burning was a candle flickering on the bathroom window sill. Janey should have left one lit downstairs, so he could find his way in.

Eddie scowled. Bellamy's by-blow had probably forgotten on purpose. It was about time he taught her another lesson. His mouth set in a sneer as he dashed through the wind and rain towards the house. Was *she* in for a fright.

The front door was unlocked. Fighting the urge to laugh, he groped his way across the pitch-black room, then tiptoed upstairs. Through the crack under the bathroom door a thin yellow light flickered. Water gurgled as it was sucked down the plug hole. Easing the door open, he peered through the crack.

Janey's back was towards him. Slightly bent, she was drying her legs with a towel. His throat dried up. *Christ!* She was as long and slender as a Madonna, with pale, gently rounded buttocks. As she straightened, candlelight played over her body and silvered her hair. There was something innocently sensual about her.

Eve must have looked like this when she tempted Adam with the apple. Something tore at his guts as rage built up in him. Her mother had been a temptress, too. Janey had to be punished. Only by descending to the depths of baseness would he be able to cleanse her of sin.

First he'd weaken her, like the biblical harlot Delilah had weakened Samson.

The towel came defensively up against her body when he slammed the door open. Backing against the sink, she gave a tiny, scared gasp.

'Sinner,' he growled, pushing her on to the pedestal. Snatching up a pair of scissors, he took a hank of her hair in his fist and hacked it off.

Janey didn't utter a sound as her father slashed at her hair, just bowed her head so she didn't have to look at his terrible eyes.

'The Lord wants me to punish you, Delilah.' Long strands of hair gathered around her feet. Suddenly, he threw the scissors in the bath and stared at her. 'Your mother was a sinner. She gave herself to another.'

Tremors of fear jagged through her. Her father had never looked at her in this terrible, frightening way before.

'God took her life as punishment.'

She shrank back when his hand brushed her shoulder. Was he going to kill her?

'A daughter who loves her father, shows respect. Do you respect me, Janey?

She stared at him. How could she respect a man she hated so much?

'Tell me you love me, Janey?' he whispered against her ear.

She closed her eyes for a few seconds, shutting him from her sight. Lightning danced across her lids and thunder crashed above the thatched roof.

His hand closed around her throat, jerking her to her feet. 'Answer me?'

She whimpered, then something escaped from the pent-up hurt inside her, a spark of defiance she couldn't control. Her hand lashed across his cheek. 'I hate you.'

Breaking free of his grasp she ran, dry-mouthed and fearful, across to her room. He came after her, crashing his shoulder against the door before she could turn the key in the lock. She retreated to the bed, huddling in the corner as his shadow advanced towards her. As the lightning flickered, fear forced a jittery scream from her.

'I'm going to punish you, Janey. I'm going to teach you to respect me.'

She closed her eyes and silently started to pray. When the first stroke landed, she stopped. What was the use? The pain went on and on, each stroke of the belt raising fiery welts on her buttocks. She gripped the bed-sheets with her hands and bit down on her lip. She wouldn't give him the satisfaction of crying. *She wouldn't!*

Despite her resolve, she screamed out just once – but it was after the beating had stopped. Her plea for mercy was lost in the roar of thunder overhead. The lightning sent brilliant flashes against the wall, setting into relief a moving, menacing shadow. It became ingrained in her memory, the shadowy evil ogre hunched over her – and the storm of its voice muttering curses against her ear.

When he finally left, she curled herself around her pain and stared blankly into the darkness. Racked by trembling, she wanted to cry but couldn't find any tears. Like the old grass, she was brittle and used up. Later, she experienced an overwhelming shame, as if she'd been soiled by her father's vileness.

For a long time she stayed awake. Sleep came in reluctant little snatches, jerking her awake to remember the heaving evil shadow on the wall. She fought it, filling her mind with the roar of the wind, absorbing the thunder to destroy her thoughts. Rain lashed against the window, crying the tears she couldn't find. Gradually, the storm abated to a sigh. Through the window Janey saw a sprinkling of stars amongst the chasing clouds. Heaven didn't exist. God didn't exist.

Her body gave up its tension slowly. Her pain was absorbed, becoming smaller and smaller until it fit into a tiny room with a stout wooden door. She turned the key in the lock, then made the room as small as a dot and threw the key in the ocean. But the tide was strong. The key grew larger as it floated back towards her.

She knew she could be stronger than the tide. Relentless, she churned the dark water into a terrifying whirlpool. The key circled the edge, then was drawn inexorably into its flow. Round and round it went, faster and faster. Finally, it was sucked into the yawning hole at the centre, down ... down ... down into the darkness. The water closed over it in unruffled serenity. Her eyes drifted shut. Peace came, and with it sleep.

When she woke she remembered nothing. Rising from her bed she went into the bathroom and stared at herself in the mirror. Her hair was all different lengths and stuck up all over the place. She frowned, unable to remember cutting it off. She'd go to the big house and ask Ada to trim it properly for her before she went to school.

She felt dirty. Filling the bath with cold water she immersed herself in it, scrubbing at her skin with a nail brush and soap until she was numb.

She dressed for school, made her breakfast and packed her lunch. The Aga had gone out, but she didn't bother to relight it. She had to hurry.

Her father came down just as she was ready to leave. He had dark circles under his eyes. He began to cough when he lit a cigarette, and inhaled on the smoke.

'Where's my breakfast?'

She ignored him. She experienced nothing but a strange sense of detachment as she left the cottage – as if she belonged only to herself, and he didn't exist.

Two weeks later Janey's squirrel painting won the art competition. Pamela was enormously proud of her, especially when her photograph was printed in the local newspaper shaking hands with the mayor.

She showed it to Eddie when he came down for the weekend. He stared at it for a few seconds, then screwed it up and threw it on the table. 'Where's the prize money?'

'I've opened a post office account for her.'

'Then you can damn well close it again. Any money coming into this house goes towards the family.' He glowered towards the pram. 'We've got an extra mouth to feed.'

'Since I'm feeding Susie myself, she doesn't cost anything. Besides, Janey bought her a teddy bear with some of it, and a box of chocolates for me. She's thoughtful like that.'

His eyes raked critically over her and his lip curled. 'No wonder you're getting fat, if all you do is sit around eating chocolate.'

Pamela flushed.

Eddie picked up the cutting again, smoothing it between his fingers.

Something about it bothered him. He examined it. Janey was shaking hands with the mayor, and behind him, just visible, was part of a man's head. He seemed vaguely familiar. 'Who's that?'

'Janey's art teacher, John Gregory. He's a nice man. It's a pity about the scar on his face.'

Forgetting about the prize money, Eddie crumpled the cutting into a ball and hurled it at the wall. A roaring sound filled his ears. He frowned ominously as Pamela scrambled to pick it up.

'Mister Gregory said he'd be willing to give her an extra art lesson every week,' Pamela said, her voice determinedly bright. 'He works during the day, but could manage it on Friday evenings.'

Jack bloody Bellamy! Concealing his rage, Eddie stood up and stretched. 'Where does this John Gregory live?'

'He moved into Canford Cottage about six years ago.'

Six years. Bellamy had lived in the village for all that time without him knowing? The sneaky bastard had been seeing Janey behind his back! Eddie's mind began to work overtime. What he needed was a plan to get rid of him permanently – short of murder, of course. If anything happened to Bellamy, it wouldn't take the police long to come looking for him.

'Is that all right then, Eddie?'

'Is what all right?'

'The art lessons.'

An idea began to ferment in Eddie's brain. It was possible that Jack Bellamy had played right into his hands.

He smiled and said slowly, 'As long it doesn't cost me anything.'

Winter arrived with a vengeance. It snowed before Christmas, slushy stuff which froze into ridges overnight.

The bitter wind found its way though the windows of Coombe Cottage and sent icy streams of air whistling under the doors. Drafts pushed down the chimney, puffs of smoke and particles of soot flew into the rooms.

Susie had a runny nose, and was being fractious at night. She seemed all right during the day, due no doubt to the warmth of the kitchen up at the big house.

'Teething,' Ada had announced that morning. 'You can see the teeth in her gums. They must giving her gyp.'

Pamela was pleased she'd been able to get some work up at the big house. It was only a few hours in the morning, but at least it brought in some extra money.

Her brow furrowed as she polished the dark wooden banister that curved down into the main hallway of the big house. The grammar school was strict about uniform, and the list they'd sent her was a mile long. Everything seemed so expensive these days, and she wondered if she could get hold of a second-hand uniform. But Annie Sutton had also passed the exam and was kitted out with new uniform. She didn't want Janey to be at a disadvantage.

She glanced up as she heard footsteps coming down the stairs and stood respectfully to one side.

'Good morning, Pamela. How's the baby coming along?'

Pamela smiled at the thought of Susie. 'She's fine, thank you, Mister Wyman.'

'And Janey? I haven't seen her for quite a while.'

Pamela's smile faded. 'She's been a bit on the quiet side lately. I think she might be worrying about going to grammar school.'

'I don't think she needs to worry. The girl's as bright as a button.'

'It wouldn't be that.' Pamela shrugged. 'Perhaps she's worried that she'll be out of place.'

Charles Wyman's astute blue eyes took in Pamela's shabby clothes. Edward Renfrew earned a decent salary, and the cottage was let at a nominal rent. So why were Pamela and Janey always so badly dressed when the older girl lacked for nothing and attended a private school.

He suddenly remembered his wife telling him there had been doubt over who had fathered Janey and Renfrew had married Pamela for convenience. Poor Pamela. She seemed a nice enough woman to him, and hard-working – even though Sarah had belittled her.

His lips tightened a fraction as he carried on downstairs. Sarah had been quite malicious about it. He'd dismissed it as gossip. Now he wondered if it was true.

Charles frowned as he thought of his wife. He'd known right from the start that she'd married him for his money. As for him, he'd been temporarily smitten and had wanted a beautiful young wife to show off. Unfortunately, her beauty had been only skin deep. He'd been unable to satisfy her, either sexually or emotionally.

They'd agreed to live separate lives – he in the country where he was at his happiest, and she in London. All he'd asked was she maintain the façade of their marriage, and be discreet.

Now he wondered if he'd done the right thing. Sarah had become a wealthy woman in her own right. Although he applauded her for that, she'd not kept her part of the bargain. Her visits were becoming rarer, and on the occasions he visited London she was always in Paris.

It was always Renfrew who answered the phone, perfectly polite and apologetic as he passed on her messages, or took her calls.

'Mrs Wyman had to go out of town. Would you like to leave a message? Perhaps there's something I can help you with.'

Charles had an instinctive dislike for Edward Renfrew. Pamela was right. The way Janey was dressed she *would* be the odd one out when she started at the grammar school. Strolling into his study he did something totally out of character. He rang his lawyer, and asked him, 'Rob, how would I go about getting some information on someone?'

'Are you thinking of getting a divorce then, Charles?'

He chuckled, though his eyes lingered on Brenda as she came into the room with a bowl of flowers. He gave her a smile when she whispered an apology, and waited until she left. 'Have you heard anything to suggest I should?'

'Not a thing, old boy. Sarah smells like a rose around town. Her frequent trips to Paris are arousing speculation in certain quarters though. Who do you want investigating, Charles?'

'A man called Edward Renfrew.'

'Any particular reason?'

'Curiosity more than anything. He works for Sarah.'

'I see. I might know someone who can help you. He's very discreet.'

'How discreet?'

'Take my word for it, Charles. Shall I ask him to ring you?'

'I'd rather meet him face to face. Why don't you bring him down with you at the weekend?'

'I can't promise anything on such short notice, but I'll put it to him.'

Later, Charles called Brenda into his study. 'What's the best way of setting young Janey up for grammar school without causing embarrassment to Pamela?'

'You could tell her about the bequest.'

'No. William didn't want anyone to know. I promised him it would remain in trust until she comes of age.' Charles leaned back in his chair, his eyes alight with amusement. 'I'd never have predicted the old man would have taken such a liking to a girl of that age.'

'Why not? You did?'

Charles grinned. 'OK, I admit it. She's an engaging little minx. I hope she does well at school.'

'My niece used to attend that school.' Brenda looked thoughtful. 'I could put some new uniforms through the dry cleaners and tell Pamela they're second hand. If I throw in a couple of worn garments as well, we might get away with it. My sister's bound to have something left over. She never throws anything away.'

'I'll leave it to you then.' Taking Brenda's hand in his he gently squeezed it. 'What would I do without you?'

'You're an old softy, Charles. Who else would have allowed Lord William to remain here after they bought the place.'

'He didn't take up much space. Besides, it was his home.'

Brenda kissed the top of his head. 'Now you know why I love you so much.'

'I'm a fool,' he said gruffly. 'I should have divorced Sarah long ago and married you.'

Her eyes met his in complete understanding. 'I'm content to leave things as they are, as long as you're happy.'

But am I happy? Charles asked himself after she'd gone. *Or am I just being selfish because divorce is a messy business, and Brenda demands nothing of me?*

He rang Rob again, catching him just before he left for lunch. 'Tell your friend there will be two people to investigate.'

'Now you're talking,' Rob said softly.

CHAPTER FIVE

Head bent against the March Wind, Eddie strolled back to the house in Regent's Park. Confession had sanitized his soul.

A voice from the past intruded on his state of grace. *'Little sewers need disinfecting.'* He scowled. Confession didn't burn as much as a penis dipped in vinegar.

Pouring himself a brandy, he lit a cigarette and subsided into a chair. The house was empty of staff today, so he could relax. Then he noticed Sarah Wyman's bag on the table. *Shit!* She was supposed to stay in Paris for another week.

Downing his drink, he stood up, then moved into the hallway. His ears strained to catch a sound. A soft gurgling laugh floated down to him. 'I know you're down there, Edward.'

She sounded as high as a kite. Eddie sighed as he mounted the stairs, hoping she wasn't going to be difficult. She was clad in a short navy blue tunic, and a Breton hat of the type French schoolgirls wear. Her hair was tied in two braids with ribbon bows. Her face, unblemished by make-up, looked incredibly young.

Blood rushed to his face. *Bloody hell! Had she found out?* He wouldn't let it rattle him. 'Why aren't you in Paris?'

She pouted, one finger hooked over her lip. 'Don't be cross with me.'

Despite his unease, Eddie was fascinated. Sarah was playing the part to perfection, just as long as it wasn't aimed at him. He swallowed, taking a grip on himself. 'Are you expecting someone?'

She nodded, childlike, her eyes shyly provocative as she walked towards him. Her pupils were black dots in a sea of innocent blue. 'I'm expecting you, sir.'

'You're being stupid.'

'Is teacher going to punish Sarah for being naughty?'

His glance followed hers to a cane lying on the end of the bed. His reaction made a mockery of his recent confession. Bending the cane across his knee he snapped it in half 'You're trash, Sarah.'

'And you're fired,' she snarled.

He grinned, enjoying his moment of domination. He'd amassed enough information on her to keep the tabloids busy for years. Now was the time to cash in on it.

'Let's get one thing straight. I know too much about you, and have evidence to back it up. You might decide to give me a substantial raise after you've seen it.'

Turning his back on her outraged face, he left her to think about it. From now on, Sarah Wyman would dance to his tune.

Charles Wyman smiled. There was nothing about John Smith to suggest he had once worked for Scotland Yard. He was of medium build, had greying brown hair going thin on top, and a face so ordinary it was instantly forgettable. The only extraordinary thing about the man was his name – the standard for anonymity.

'Edward Renfrew,' the investigator said in a dry voice. 'Born 1923 in Kent. Only child of Joseph and Agnes Renfrew. Oddly enough, the father studied for the priesthood before his marriage. Both deceased. Catholic school education. Conscripted into the army in 1941. Spent the duration of the war in the paymaster's office in Aldershot. Honourable discharge. After demob he took a position in a bank in Bournemouth.'

He sent an inquiring look over his sheaf of papers. 'There's more of the same, but absolutely nothing out of the ordinary, unless you consider the age of his first wife and her subsequent death. You already have information on the circumstances surrounding it. Renfrew has no convictions, prior to, or since taking the position as your wife's secretary. One item of interest you should note: four months ago he received a substantial raise in salary.'

Charles nodded. 'Thank you, Mister Smith. You needn't read it all out.'

The investigator put the papers in a manila folder, placed them on the table and opened his briefcase again. 'Sarah Wyman is more interesting.' Astute brown eyes quizzed Charles.

Charles nodded for him to continue.

'Because of the frequent trips, I've concentrated my investigation of her in Paris. I've included a comprehensive list of her business and social interests as well. I really think you should study my report in private. Most of it is based on hearsay, and is of a sensitive nature. If you wish to proceed with the investigation I could provide you with evidence. It will just take a bit longer and cost a bit more.'

'How sordid is it?'

'I'd prefer not to offer an opinion.' John placed the folder on top of the other and stood up. 'Let me know your decision after you've studied it. You have my number.'

An extraordinary man, after all, Charles thought, and one he could grow to like. After he'd gone, he picked up his wife's folder and flipped it open. Half an hour later he opened the safe and distastefully shoved it inside.

He felt sick, inside and out. Shrugging into his jacket he whistled for his dog. He needed fresh air, and lots of it – and he needed to think.

Janey had turned thirteen in the winter of 1962.

Now it was summer, and the holidays had arrived. Pauline was in France with the Ryker family. Lazy days in the woods or on the beach beckoned – and time to draw, and to play with her baby sister.

'Sit still for five minutes,' she grumbled, quickly sketching in Susie's dark, mischievous eyes and springy curls. 'If you behave, I'll take you to see the kittens in the barn when I'm finished.'

Pamela laughed. 'You'll be lucky. She's on the go all day, and into everything now. She broke an ornament this morning. I don't know what your dad will say when he finds out. It was a wedding present from Mrs Wyman.'

Janey's smile faded. 'He isn't coming down this weekend, is he?'

Pamela shrugged. 'He might. He hasn't been down for some time now.'

Eight whole blissful weeks to be exact. Janey's arms circled Susie as she scrambled on to her lap and she kissed her sticky, upturned face. 'You're a pest, Susie Renfrew.'

'Kitties,' Susie demanded.

'OK.' Janey stood up and marched her sister through to the kitchen. 'But first we wash your face, otherwise the wasps will gobble you up.'

Pamela smiled indulgently as Susie had a short-lived fight with a flannel-wielding Janey. Susie was strapped into her pushchair, then the pair of them headed out through the door.

Pamela hummed to herself as she watched them go, her eyes shining with love.

There had been a subtle change in Janey of late. Her face had fined, revealing a delicate bone structure, and her hips had a softer, rounder shape. Her hair had grown long again. Drawn into a pony-tail on the crown of her head, it cascaded down her back. She'd never understood why Janey had cut if off.

'She must have been jealous of the baby,' Ada had said, nodding her head wisely. 'It was hacked off without rhyme or reason.'

Yet Janey had never displayed any sign of jealousy. Susie adored her. It was only Pauline, Susie hadn't taken too. Not that Pauline cared. She didn't care for anyone but herself. Just turned sixteen, she was too aware of herself, aware of the heads that turned her way. She was like Eddie – diffcult to live with, especially when she had the curse.

'Anyone would think she was the only female who had to put up with it,' she grumbled as she surveyed the mess in the girl's room. 'All that fainting and complaining gets on my nerves.'

She gathered up the scattered clothes, sorted out the clean from the dirty and hung the rest in the wardrobe. It was stuffed full, some of it hardly worn.

Eddie catered to Pauline's every whim, whereas poor Janey walked around in rags most of the time. It was as if Janey didn't belong to him. She stared in shocked astonishment at the wall. Could that account for the way Eddie treated her? What if Janey wasn't his child?

She remembered the small leather case Eddie had brought down from London the last time he'd visited. Personal papers, he'd said, and had put it in the roof space. She'd thought it a strange place to keep personal papers, but hadn't dared question him.

She fetched the stepladder. An hour later she was none the wiser about Janey – but she was a lot wiser about her husband. All those photographs! They were so disgusting they made her skin crawl. She slumped into a chair, not knowing quite what to do about them as she stared at the case.

After a while she fetched a spade from the shed. Wrapping the case in a plastic shopping bag she buried it in a hole at the bottom of the garden. She doubted if Eddie would cause trouble if he discovered they were missing – he wouldn't want to admit to them.

Jack decided he'd tell Janey when she was sixteen.

I'm your father, he would say. Your mother and I loved each other.

Jack watched her mix a subtle shade of blue on her palette. She was working on a seascape – a present for Charles Wyman. She'd known exactly what she'd wanted to paint, and had borrowed his camera to take a photograph of yachts racing out of Bridport and rounding the buoy. They were strung out across the sea, spinnakers billowing to the breeze.

She had a good eye for a scene and colour, but not much patience for the finer details. Tonal colours merged one into the other, shadows and shapes making suggestions as she experimented with style.

She put the finishing touch to a sail, a shadowy sweep of blue, then stood back, her eyes intent and serious. 'It's finished.'

'You're sure?'

She slanted him a glance, her eyes still absorbed. 'This is exactly how I want it to be.'

No hesitation or doubt, yet her eyes questioned his, inviting comment. He smiled. 'You've forgotten to sign it.'

Her laugh was a tiny, breathless morsel as she picked up a brush. 'Does it always feel like this when something comes to an end?'

'Like what?'

She finished her signature and turned. 'I feel like a boat without a sail.'

'Cast adrift?' He thought of the years following Margaret's death. 'It's a sort of bereavement, like when someone you love dies. You have to start planning another project to take your mind off it.'

'Has someone you loved ever died?'

Jack's throat constricted. 'Someone I loved very much.'

'And you found another project to take your mind off her?'

'Eventually.'

Her hand touched his and she gave a sad little smile. 'I'm glad you did. Thank you for the lesson, Mister Gregory. I enjoyed it.'

She never lingered after her lesson, unconsciously aware of the proper relationship between student and teacher. Jack could imagine Pamela Renfrew reminding her of it every time she came to him.

Don't overstay your welcome, and don't forget to say thank you.

For once, Jack felt like breaking the mould. 'Would you mind if I gave you a hug before you leave?'

She nodded, allowing him to clasp her in a brief embrace. She pushed him away almost immediately, then hurried down the path into the lane-way beyond, her pony-tail swinging. 'Good night, Mister Gregory,' she called out. 'I'll see you next Friday.'

Goldie pressed against his leg and made a small whining sound. He fondled the dog's ear. 'Go on then, fetch your leash. I'll get the car out and take you to the beach before it gets dark.'

The district nurse was watering her garden when Jack backed out of the driveway. He nodded pleasantly to her. 'Good evening, Mrs Adams.'

'Mister Gregory.' Her smile faded as soon as he'd gone. She'd observed the hug, and wondered at it. Janey Renfrew was a strange child in her estimation. She was too quiet, a dreamer, and usually shied away from intimacy – but she was growing to be a beautiful girl.

John Gregory was a loner, and in her experience, people of his ilk usually had something to hide.

Janey lingered on her way home. The dusk was mauve velvet and breathed a dewy soft moisture against her skin.

It was nearly time for the night creatures, tiny voles, and moles that burrowed under lawns, leaving little mounds of earth where they popped their heads up for air. Owls glided on silent wings to hunt the unwary, and hedgehogs snuffled in the undergrowth.

Moths were white ghost shapes that fluttered up from the grass at her feet as she walked, to be snatched from the air by bats swooping in from nowhere. Only the bats weren't really silent, and they didn't come from nowhere. Griffin had told her they gave high-pitched squeaks to help them locate their prey, and to stop them bumping into things in the dark.

The bats inhabited a cave hidden from sight inside the hill. Griffin had taken her there once. They'd watched the bats emerge at dusk, exploding through a tiny fissure like a handful of black rags thrown into the air.

The quiet dusk was broken by the purr of a car engine, but there was no gleam of light and it didn't come down the lane.

She stopped to watch the moon slip up from behind the hill, throwing the pines into stark relief and sending long shafts of light through the trunks. The soft yellow light turned to a silvery blue as it swiftly climbed upwards, bathing her face and arms in its glow.

When a twig snapped nearby she quickened her pace. Pamela didn't like her being out in the dark. About to pass Suttons' old cow-shed, something clinked against a stone. Probably Tim Ryker trying to scare her, she thought, then remembered he was in France. She gave a squeak of alarm as a shadow moved in the doorway.

'Phil?' she quavered, but the shadow was too tall. 'Griff?'

As she turned to take flight, something dusty came down over her head. A hand cut off her scream, her flailing arms were pinioned to her sides.

Helpless, she was dragged into the building and thrown to the floor. As she tried to scramble to her feet something smacked against her head and everything went dark. Consciousness came, and with it a claustrophobic suffocation. Rough against her face was a hessian sack. Sucking in a deep breath, she inhaled dust and began to cough.

There was the taste of blood, and pain – unbearable pain. When she tried to resist, blows – against her stomach, her ribs, her face. Then her arm was twisted in throbbing agony up behind her back. She screamed when something gave.

The torment continued long after, just under the surface of her consciousness. Shadows came to haunt her. She cast herself adrift, riding the dark maelstrom until it became a drift of calm water.

Janey woke to a different kind of pain, struggling up from sleep into an astringent smelling brightness.

'You're awake then.'

She stared at the nurse, bewildered. *A hospital, was she sick?*

'Thirsty?'

She nodded, then groaned when the movement lanced pain into her neck.

'Your shoulder was dislocated. Try not to move too much, dear.' A glass of pale liquid was held against her lips and trickled sweetly into her parched throat.

A doctor came to see her. A light shone in her eyes, questions were asked that she couldn't answer. The nurse held her hand when she cried out during the examination. Humiliated and sore, she wished he'd go away.

Doctor and nurse exchanged a glance. 'Her memory might come back when she gets over the shock, but perhaps it's better if it doesn't. Arrange for the district nurse to look in on her.'

The nurse patted her hand. 'Cheer up, love. You'll soon be home.'

Pamela was awkwardly cheerful as she tucked her up in bed the next afternoon. 'Your father was very upset about your accident. Thank God Griffin and Phil found you.'

The last thing she could remember was leaving John Gregory's house after her painting lesson. 'Was I hit by a car?'

Pamela's eyes slid away. 'More than likely, dear.'

Shortly after, her father arrived. He gave her some chocolate and an Enid Blyton book she'd read two years earlier. He sat on the end of her bed.

Made uncomfortable by his proximity she traced round the pattern on the bed cover with her finger.

'They've caught the man who did this to you. It was John Gregory.'

'John Gregory ran me over?' Shocked, Janey stared at him.

'That's right. There's a policeman downstairs. He needs to ask you some questions. Make sure you tell the truth about John Gregory, else you'll be in serious trouble.'

The policeman's uniform and gruff voice intimidated her.

'How long have you been having art lessons?'

Janey couldn't remember exactly. She gazed mutely at Pamela.

'Several years, but she's been having private lessons for just over two.'

The policeman wrote it in his notebook.

'Mrs Adams said John Gregory hugged you that night. Did he often hug or kiss you?'

Her father's grey eyes were intent on her face.

'Sometimes,' she said reluctantly.

'Did he ever touch you?'

Her head began to throb. 'I don't know.'

'Did he ever tell you he was your father?'

She closed her eyes and wished the policeman would go away. 'Why would he say something stupid like that?'

'I'm asking the questions, miss. Can you tell me what happened last night?'

Tears trickled down her cheeks when she remembered what her father had told her. 'John Gregory did it. I can't believe—'

Pamela's hand closed around hers. 'Leave her alone,' she snapped. 'The doctor said she's got to rest. Hasn't she been through enough?'

Later, Janey heard her parents arguing.

'This is your fault for allowing her to roam all over the countryside at night.'

'And where were *you* when this was going on. In London. You only married me to have a mother for your children. You're a rotten father, and I wish I'd never—'

Pamela cried out as the sound of a slap rang out.

'You're my wife, you'll do what I tell you,' Eddie snarled. 'If you don't, I'll take Susan and leave you.'

'You wouldn't.' Pamela sounded close to panic. 'You wouldn't take Susie from me.'

Susie started to cry, long drawn out sobs.

'Just try me.' Footsteps thudded across the floor and the door slammed shut. Seconds later the car roared into life.

Janey waited until the sound of the engine died away, then rose from her bed and went downstairs. Sitting on the threadbare sofa Pamela cuddled Susie fearfully against her chest.

Janey experienced a desperate rage when she saw the red welt on her face. She crossed to where she sat and gently touched it. 'I want you to know I love you – and I love Susie.'

'I know, Janey. I know.' Pamela drew her again her shoulder. 'I've loved you from the first moment I saw you.'

Janey gave her a tremulous smile. 'I didn't know how to tell you before.'

Pamela wondered where the girl found her strength. Her face was swollen, her arm was in a sling. Bruises covered her body, and she'd been violated in the worst way possible.

'You should be in bed,' she said gently.

'What will happen to John Gregory?'

'I expect he'll go to prison if he's convicted. You might have to give evidence.'

'I can't remember anything.' *John Gregory in prison?* The short, sharp sense of loss she experienced was overtaken by a deep hurt.

'I wonder if Mister and Mrs Yates have been told,' was all she could think of to say.

The evidence against Jack Bellamy was circumstantial, but it was enough to convict him. On the doctor's advice, Janey was spared the ordeal of court and the case was heard in camera.

Witnesses for the prosecution included the lawyer Eddie had sought advice from – who verified the warning letter he'd sent to Jack. Mrs Adams said her piece with breathless relish, pointing out that she'd seen the man mauling Janey earlier that evening and the girl pushing him away. The policeman damned Jack straight away when he flipped open his notebook and read the record of his interview with Janey.

'John Gregory did it,' the girl said. His accusing eyes gazed straight at Jack as he re-emphasized. 'John Gregory did it.'

The fact that Jack had moved to the village to be near Janey, and had concealed his real name, did nothing to help his case. Two people gave him a character reference: Phil Tyler and Mister James. After the schoolteacher said Jack was a war hero who'd served his country well, and was a bloody fine bloke and an expert painter, the judge commented caustically, 'So was Adolph Hitler in the eyes of the misguided.'

Jack received a long jail sentence.

A week later, Mary and Douglas put the boatyard up for sale, then travelled to Winterbrook to close up Canford Cottage.

'Jack wants me to take him the squirrel painting,' Mary said bitterly. 'Even though it was Janey's statement that convicted him.'

Douglas took Mary in his arms and held her close. 'Don't blame young Janey. Think instead, of what *she* went through. Someone attacked that poor little lass and it was so traumatic she lost her memory of the event. When she made that statement she'd have been in shock, and wouldn't have known what she was saying.'

'If you ask me, that Eddie Renfrew put words in her mouth.'

'Be that as it may, you'll never be able to prove it. Let it be, Mary. Jack's accepted the fact that he'll never be able to prove his innocence, and so must you.'

'Never,' Mary said fiercely. 'Janey knows the truth, and one day she'll remember. When she does she'll want to clear his name.'

'Of course she will,' Douglas said soothingly. 'So we'll just have to find some way of keeping in touch, and wait, and hope.'

The only person Mary could think of to keep in touch with was Pamela Renfrew. Though loath to do so, she was determined to see her before she left.

Leaving Douglas to board up the windows, she took Janey's seascape to Coombe Cottage and knocked on the door. Pamela's Morris was parked in the drive, but no one answered the door.

She left the picture in the porch, then thrust one of Douglas's cards through the letter box.

Arms folded over her chest, from the upstairs window Pamela watched her drive away.

Six weeks after the trial, Eddie Renfrew's diary went missing from its hiding place.

Sarah's lawyer called on him later in the day. He didn't pull any punches. 'I believe you have some incriminating photographs, Renfrew. If you hand them over without any fuss Mrs Wyman will allow you to resign with a reference, and a handsome pay-off.'

'And if I don't?'

'Amongst other things, you'll be charged with blackmail.'

'What other things?'

'Theft. A large amount of cash has gone missing from your employer's safe.' His hand went to the phone and hovered over the receiver. 'If the police are asked to investigate, they'll probably find it in your bank account.'

Eddie took the key to his safety deposit box from his pocket and jiggled it on his finger. 'You won't mind if I check the amount in my account first.'

'Of course not.' The lawyer gave a bland smile and stood up. 'I suggest we visit your bank together before it closes.'

The amount in his bank account was generous, but not generous enough.

'The negatives will cost a little extra, of course,' Eddie murmured.

'I thought they might.' The lawyer slid an envelope from his pocket. 'One thousand in cash. The negotiation is now over. Go and get my client's package, there's a good chap. I'll wait for you in the park.'

They exchanged envelope for envelope, the lawyer comparing the photographs with the negatives before shoving them in an inside pocket. He relieved Eddie of his house keys. 'You'll find your suitcases in your car, and your car parked in Grosvenor Street. By the way, you have a week in which to vacate the cottage.'

'Toffee-nosed git!' Eddie snarled as the man walked rapidly away.

Ripping open the envelope he feverishly started to count the money. He didn't see the two men closing in until it was too late. Something hit him in the stomach. As he doubled over he received a blow to the chin. He fell sideways to the ground. A boot caught him in the ribs. Still conscious, he was dragged behind some bushes and his assailants systematically set about him.

When he came to he'd been robbed. He staggered upright, then bent double again as he began to retch. At least they hadn't broken any bones.

Staggering to a water fountain he splashed water over his face and in his mouth, spitting it into the grass. 'Bitch!' he snarled. 'Don't think you'll get away with this. I've got copies of those photographs.'

Half an hour earlier Pamela had returned from shopping to find the cottage in a shambles. There was nothing missing, so she didn't call the police.

She had a good idea what the intruders been looking for, so when Eddie arrived home in a foul temper and told her to start packing, she wasn't surprised.

What *did* surprise her was the pleasure she experienced at seeing him so bruised and battered. A pity they hadn't killed him, she thought, hiding a smile as she added insult to injury by telling him about the cottage being ransacked.

His face fell and his eyes became frantic.

She could have told him not to bother checking the roof space, but she didn't. She enjoyed listening to him cursing, and scrambling around in the dust.

Later, when he found some excuse to hit her, it didn't seem to hurt quite so much.

The news they were leaving Winterbrook affected them in different ways.

Pauline was excited because the Ryker family had recently sold their property to a development company, who intended to build retirement bungalows in the area.

'They've bought a place in Branksome Chine,' Pauline said to her father. 'It's got six bedrooms and two bathrooms. It's only a short walk from the sea. Wendy said it's miles better than the one they're in now. She's bragging madly about it.'

'The one we're going to is just as big, but it's right on the cliff top in Bournemouth and overlooks the sea. We used to live there when you were little. Can you remember it?'

'Not really.' Pauline's eyes began to gleam. 'Wendy's going to change schools. Can I go to the same one as her?'

When Eddie appeared dubious, she said prettily. 'You won't have to pay boarding fees if I do, and I'll be able to see you more often. Besides, the nuns are a bore and the uniform's such a drag.'

'Janey won't have to change schools. She can hop on a bus,' Pamela said brightly, but neither of them were listening. She felt sad to be leaving the village and her friends, and the thought of seeing Eddie every day made her sorrier still. Still, she had to resign herself to the fact that she had no money of her own and had Susie to look after, so she really had no choice.

Janey didn't know whether to be sad or happy. Since her accident, people had changed in a subtle, but unsettling manner. They seemed to stare at her when they thought she wasn't looking, then when she smiled at them they avoided her eyes. Sometimes, in the village shop, the customers would fall silent when she went in.

Annie Sutton had made a new best friend at school. Janey thought it might be because she'd won both the English and art awards at prize-giving, when Annie didn't win anything. Mr Wyman hadn't changed. He'd looked sad when she'd gone to the big house to say goodbye. He'd made her promise to write, and to visit him when she was grown up. He'd had her seascape framed, and hung it on one of the dining-room walls. Brenda handed her a box of handkerchiefs with her initial in the corner embroidered in blue, then gave her a big hug. 'We'll miss you.'

Phil was in his shed, his back towards her. He was sharpening the curved blade of a scythe with a flat stone held in his palm. It keened along the blade with a thin metallic zinging sound that made her teeth clench. She watched him work in a smooth fluid motion, waiting until he'd finished, because she didn't want to startle him into cutting himself. Spitting on the ball of his thumb, Phil ran it along the edge then gave a satisfied whistle. He hung the scythe on a hook and without turning round, said, 'You're leaving, then?'

'Yes. I've come to say goodbye.'

He poured tea from a flask into two cups, then turned and handed her one. 'You won't forget old Phil?'

She suddenly felt miserable. Tears pricked her eyes as she sipped at the tea. 'Why do things have to change?'

'You know why, Janey. Life is a journey.'

'But what if you don't want to go on a journey? What if you want things to stay exactly as they are?'

'Is that what you want for yourself? Never to learn, never to experience life? Sometimes we have to leave, so we can find ourselves.' His eyes were on hers, dark and intent and full of the mystery of the woods and the earth 'We all have our journeys to take.'

'I'm scared,' she admitted, because she could always talk over her fears to Phil. 'Sometimes I think I belong to this place, but then I'm not sure.'

He gave a glimmer of a smile. 'This place will still be here when you *are* sure. Griff says you won't be going for good, so saying goodbye is a waste of words.' His thumb jerked towards the bench. 'He's made you a little something to remember us by.'

Janey picked up a small wooden disk attached to a leather thong and ran her fingers over the carved relief. It looked like a lion with the wings and head of an eagle. She'd never seen anything like it before.

'What is it?'

'A mythological creature called a Griffin.' Phil took it from her hands and tied it around her neck. 'It will give you strength and courage in the years to come. Griffs mother named him after it, because she knew she wouldn't be around to bring him up.'

'Did she die?'

'Aye. She had a heart problem, though we didn't know it until she was carrying our child. She went quick and easy just after he was born.'

'I'm glad you had Griffin to love.'

'Aye. It was a rare gift she gave me.' His calloused hand reached out and ruffled her hair. 'Off you go now, Janey. I'll be seeing you.'

She knew she should get back home but the woods beckoned her. Autumn had come in a hurry and was now in its dying stage. The glorious colours had faded to brown, and the trees were nearly bare. Leaves piled on leaves, decomposing, pressed into the earth by rain. The brook choked on them. The air of decay depressed her.

She walked through it, making her way to the top of the hill and staring out over the sea. Here, the air was tangy with salt, alive with the pull of the tide. She laid on the ground and spread her arms, hugging the earth to her body.

'I'm leaving.'

The ground was as cold as the wind on her face.

Feeling stupid and angry she scrambled to her feet. *What did I expect, that the earth would talk to me, make everything as it was? That's kid's stuff.*

Yet, as she made her way back home a certainty grew in her. She *did* belong here, she'd always belonged.

Suddenly, she couldn't wait to leave. She had a journey to take, and the sooner she started the sooner she'd return.

The wind changed direction as she passed the big house, pressing eagerly against her back. It sent the cockerel on the weather vane quivering towards the west.

She looked at it, and smiled.

CHAPTER SIX

The cloth formed soapy circles on the green and white checked linoleum. Janey knew every inch of the floor, from the worn patch near the door to each tiny pock mark left by the steel tips of Pauline's stiletto heels. The house her mother had grown up in was large, but after two years she'd grown used to it.

It had taken her a long time to get used to Bournemouth, to the crowds of people who thronged through the town centre. Everyone seemed so busy and well dressed, the cafes full of happy-looking people.

The summer holidaymakers brought with them an unexpected bonus. She'd discovered that if she went to the beach very early and dragged a forked stick through the sand, there was money to be found. Each precious coin she unearthed was carefully hoarded into her post office savings book. One day, when she had time to paint, she'd use it to buy materials.

Sometimes she visited a small art gallery on the other side of town. Entrance was free, and it was filled with the most marvellous paintings. Her favourite was a battle scene with a central figure on a horse brandishing a sword. He looked like her lead soldier Lord William, the grey mount he rode evoking a vague childhood memory of a horse called Wellington.

Sometimes, she woke with the smell of the countryside sharp in her nostrils, and wondered if her friends there ever thought of her. But Coombe Cottage seemed far in her past now, and although she wrote letters, neither Phil nor Mister Wyman answered them. She'd tucked the lead soldier away in a drawer, and didn't often look at him now.

Her sister Pauline was marrying Tim Ryker tomorrow. Settling back on her haunches, she wrung out the cloth. It was to be a white wedding, despite the circumstances.

Her mouth slid into a rare grin. Her father had been incensed. 'You cheap little tramp, you're only seventeen years old,' he shrieked, slapping Pauline across the face.

He'd stormed off, returning a little while later in a calmer mood, and with the smell of alcohol on his breath. 'It's all arranged. You and the Ryker boy will be married next month. The pair of you will live here until Tim's old enough to earn a decent wage.'

Releasing the twisted cloth, she mopped up the remains of the suds and stood up. It seemed a stupid exercise to clean the kitchen when it would be filled with caterers making a mess in the morning. Habit died hard. She always tidied the kitchen before she went to bed, so it would be clean for Pamela to cook the boarders' breakfasts.

The wedding reception was being held in a marquee in case it rained. She drew the curtains aside and gazed through the window at the clear, star-speckled sky. August wouldn't dare rain on Pauline's wedding – it just wouldn't dare.

On her way upstairs, she heard Wendy and Pauline giggling together.

Pauline sneered. 'Pamela told the salesgirl in the bridal shop that Tim was a good catch. How absolutely lower class.'

'I hope she's not going to wear that ghastly blue suit. I'll die laughing.'

'The old man gave her some money to buy a new dress. It's pink crimplene, with short sleeves and a pleated sun-ray skirt. She looks hideous in it.'

'I suppose your sister will look as if she's just walked out of a jumble sale again. Honestly, Pauline, she's got no idea of style. No wonder you didn't want her as a bridesmaid.'

Janey's cheeks burned as she headed to the room she shared with Susie. It wasn't her fault she had nothing to wear. She hadn't been paid a penny for the work she did in the boarding house since she'd been forced to leave school.

Her request for pocket money had been denied. 'You have a roof over your head and food in your stomach. What do you need money for?' he'd said.

What do I need money for? she'd thought resentfully. *Lots of things. I'd like to be able to buy some paints. I need a new pair of shoes and a dress for the wedding I'd also like to buy a brassiere.*

She gazed at the small breasts that had sprouted on her chest. Her periods had started a few months ago. She wished she could buy the sanitary napkins Pauline used instead of having to wear linen squares fashioned from old sheets. They rubbed the inside of her thighs raw.

But she couldn't tell her father about her intimate bodily functions. She kissed Susie and slid into bed. It would be too embarrassing.

Pamela was in a flap the next morning. The caterers arrived just as she'd finished preparing the breakfast trays. Janey took them up to the three boarders, listening to the complaints of one of them about the noise of the caterer's van waking her up.

Later, Mrs Ryker arrived to help the bride and bridesmaids get ready. Eager to oust Pamela from a role she'd never been asked to fill, that of mother to the bride, her overbearing manner soon had Susie in tears.

'I told you it was a mistake having Susan as a bridesmaid. Sit still, child. If you get dirty you'll spoil the look of the wedding party.'

Janey's temper began to burn when Susie gave a heart-rending sob. Her eyes were fiery as she pushed open the door. 'If you stop shouting at her she'll be fine.'

Giving Mrs Ryker an exasperated look she took the weeping Susie by the hand and led her away. 'Leave her to me.'

'Well, I never?' Mrs Ryker spluttered. 'Who does she think she is?'

'Cinderella,' Janey muttered, 'and you're the ugly stepmother.'

'I don't like being a bridesmaid,' Susie whined.

Squatting to her haunches, Janey smiled at her. 'You look beautiful, like a fairy princess. Did I ever tell you the story of Sleeping Beauty?' Susie was soon smiling again. When it was time to leave for the church, she handed her over to Wendy with the instruction. 'Make sure she has a wee before you leave.'

Wendy gave Janey's faded green gingham dress a critical glance. 'Is that what you're going to wear?'

'It's all I have.'

Pity filled Wendy's eyes. 'Your father's a mean sod where you're concerned, isn't he? There's a dress in my bag that should fit you, and I could arrange your hair better for you.'

Tempted, Janey remembered Wendy's hurtful remark from the night before and determined she wouldn't be patronized. 'Thanks, but I'm quite happy as I am.'

'Please yourself.' Wendy stalked away on her high heels with a pink-frilled Susie in tow.

The wedding went off without a hitch. Pauline looked self-conscious, and beautiful in her white, empire line dress. Her short veil was attached to a garland of daisies.

Tim Ryker had an embarrassed look on his face as he mumbled his responses. He was sweating. A lock of his slicked-back hair kept falling on to his forehead like Elvis Presley's. Janey felt sorry for him, but then she'd feel sorry for anyone who married Pauline.

Afterwards, they went back to the marquee, where people stood in little clumps talking and being polite. The women looked like bunches of flowers in their pastel chiffons and silks, their lips pursed to sip champagne and orange from shallow glasses.

Her father made a speech. Pauline and Tim turned red when he told an awful joke about the patter of tiny feet, and everyone laughed. The pink crimplene dress Pamela wore collected a brown stain on the bodice. Nobody noticed until Mrs Ryker thought to point it out. During the course of the afternoon the hats wilted, the men became glassy-eyed and loud, and the women began to neigh like horses. Dragged on to the dance floor by the best man, Janey was whirled around until she was dizzy and almost tripped over a chair. Embarrassed, she muttered an excuse and retreated.

Pauline changed into a powder blue dress with matching coat. A pill-box hat adorned her head.

'So chic. She looks just like Jackie Kennedy,' someone gushed.

'Poor dear,' another said, and they all fell silent, remembering the shocking assassination of the American President two years previously.

A shout went up. 'Where's the groom?'

Amid much laughter, Tim was hauled out from under the table by a couple of his friends. White-faced and staggering, he was sick in the flower bed. When the taxi came to take the bridal couple to the railway station for the start of their honeymoon in Cornwall, Pauline was tight lipped. They were arguing as the cab sped away.

Soon the marquee was empty of people, but full of dirty glasses and plates.

Janey lifted the arm from the middle of the record to set it back on its rest, then carried the remains of the wedding cake into the kitchen whilst Pamela put Susie to bed.

Together, they began to tidy up.

Her father came out of the house just as they'd finished lining the full garbage bags up against the wall. He got in his car and drove away without looking at either of them.

They exchanged a glance, smiled, then went into the kitchen and put the kettle on.

Janey had taken Susie to the beach, and Pamela was alone in the house when the doorbell rang.

The last person Pamela had expected to see on the doorstep was Mary Yates.

'I'm sorry I didn't ring first. I thought you wouldn't see me if I did.'

She was probably right. Pamela stood aside, allowing her entry. 'You can't stay long. Eddie will be home from work soon.'

'I've come about Janey,' the woman said. 'Douglas and I have had a talk. We'd like to see her now and again if you'll let us.'

'After what your brother did to her?'

'Jack didn't do anything. He'd die rather than harm a hair on her head. Why didn't your husband allow her to give evidence?'

'Because she couldn't remember anything, and Eddie didn't want to put her through it. She thinks she was hit by a car. It's best to let sleeping dogs lie, if you ask me.'

'Did anyone ask you?'

Pamela lowered her eyes from Mary's shrewd glance and gave a sigh. 'She's Eddie's daughter, not mine. I haven't got much say in what goes on.'

'Janey is *Jack's* daughter, and I'm her *aunt*.' Sounding determined, Mary took a photograph from her pocket and thrust it into her hand. 'That's Jack at eighteen. Deny it if you like, but she looks just like him.'

Janey was the spitting image of the man in the photograph. He'd been nice-looking before he'd been scarred. Sadly, Pamela handed it back. 'I believe you, Mrs Yates, but I can't help you. I daren't. Somebody attacked Janey, and everything pointed to your brother.'

'I think it was more of a chance for revenge. Jack was in love with Margaret

Renfrew.' Mary shrugged. 'I didn't really approve of the relationship. Margaret seemed too young to be married, let alone have children. I didn't know the circumstances then.'

Curious now, Pamela gazed at her. 'What circumstances?'

Mary hesitated. 'I'm sorry, it's not really my business. I keep forgetting you're Eddie Renfrew's wife.'

Pamela took a deep breath. 'Don't let that stop you. To be quite honest, I sometimes wish I wasn't.' She glanced nervously at the clock. 'Look, could we meet somewhere and talk. Janey could walk in at any moment.'

'I thought she'd be at school. Is she sick?'

'Eddie insisted she leave as soon as she turned fifteen. She helps me in the boarding house.'

Mary looked shocked.

Pamela's voice thickened with tears. 'Eddie never did treat that girl right. I wish I'd had the guts to leave him. Then I think of Janey here all alone with him, working in the boarding house for no pay, and I think of my daughter, Susie.' Fishing around in her pocket she brought out a handkerchief and blew her nose. 'He threatened to take Susie from me if I left him. Besides, where could I go without money?'

Mary placed an arm around her shoulder in a sympathetic hug. 'Look, I didn't come here to cause you trouble. Why don't you visit me. I don't live far from here.' She slid a card from her bag and placed it in Pamela's pocket. 'This is my address. Come tomorrow if you can get away. We can chat then.'

'I will.' Pamela managed a tremulous smile. 'Janey will be coming up the cliff path from the beach soon. Please don't mention what happened in Winterbrook. She has enough problems to cope with.'

A kiss landed on her cheek. 'Thank you, Pamela. I promise I won't even speak to her unless she sees me.'

Mary found a seat under a tree a little way from where the path emerged. Ten minutes later she was rewarded when a tall, slender girl appeared with a dark-haired child clinging to her hand. She looked shabby in a faded pink blouse and a pair of patched pedal-pushers. An elastic band secured one long pale braid.

Janey's face had matured into fragile beauty, but her eyes had a haunted look. The child with her was just as poorly dressed, but was gazing up at Janey with undisguised adoration in her dark eyes.

Mary's breath caught in her throat when Janey walked past her without a glance. She'd never seen anyone look so vulnerable. Yet when she turned to smile at something the child said, her face was illuminated by love.

Dear God, Mary thought, shaken to the marrow by the flood of feeling that ripped through her. *She smiles just like Jack*.

At least she could tell Jack she'd seen her when next she visited him. It might cheer him up to get some news. And if she could get Pamela on side, Janey might be able to visit them.

She felt a niggle of guilt at encouraging Pamela to deceive her husband. The woman seemed to be on the brink of a nervous breakdown as it was. But she had to put Jack first. His mental and physical health was slowly deteriorating in that place. She knew he was innocent, and was determined to clear his name.

There had been a spate of attacks on young girls in the district round about the time Janey had been attacked. A man had lured girls into his car on some pretence, then drugged them before raping them. But the police hadn't bothered to take that into account.

If she could win Janey over she might be able to encourage her to remember what happened, and clear Jack's name.

She sniffed disapprovingly at the thought of her niece being used as a maid of all work by Eddie Renfrew. If Janey lived with *her* she'd still be at school, not working in a boarding house.

Pamela was soon informed of her predecessor's story.

'There was little sympathy for Margaret from the public.' Mary showed Pamela newspaper cuttings describing Margaret as a loose woman, and depicting Eddie as a martyred saint.

'Pauline looks like her mother,' Pamela said, 'though Margaret had a softer look to her.'

'She certainly wasn't what they made her out to be. She was a nice girl who'd been treated badly. Half the time she was frightened of her own shadow, that's why she took to Jack. He's gentle, dependable and kind. Not the type to hurt anyone, let alone his own daughter.'

Pamela remembered the photographs she'd buried in the garden of Coombe Cottage. *If only they knew*, she thought, feeling a strange sense of rapport with the dead Margaret Renfrew.

Between them, she and Mary came to an arrangement. They'd wait until Janey's eighteenth birthday before telling her the truth. In the meantime, an accidental meeting was arranged in the public gardens.

Janey was delighted to see Mary again. They chatted whilst Pamela took Susie to the café for an ice-cream. It was only natural that Mary should ask her to visit, and whilst she was there, encourage her to use Jack's painting equipment.

Janey couldn't resist the lure. Every Wednesday she joined the Yates's for lunch, then spent a couple of hours painting. She was working on a still life – blue hyacinths growing in a bowl on Mary's window sill.

They were careful not to mention the man Janey had known as John Gregory. When Jack's old Labrador greeted Janey with unashamed delight, tears pricked her eyes. Mary couldn't help wondering what the girl was thinking of as she knelt and hugged the dog.

Aware of her father's temper, Janey didn't need reminding to keep the visits a secret. For a few short months, her life took on a new meaning. Until Tim Ryker inadvertently gave the game away.

*

Janey's sixteenth birthday coincided with her Wednesday visit to Mary.

A cold wind was blowing when she left the house. She shivered as she dodged across the traffic in the square, and pulled up the collar of her thin raincoat.

Mary and Douglas lived in Westbourne. Resisting the urge to take a bus, she walked through the gardens. It was pretty along the stream, the grass crunchy under her feet where it was layered with frost. Bare willow canes dipped gracefully towards the stream, the dormant brown nubs along their length waiting for spring to wake them. The banks were lined with them all the way along. In the summer they were a pretty fresh green.

This would be her last visit for a while. Douglas had recently retired, and he and Mary were leaving for a four week holiday in Australia, where Douglas had a brother he hadn't seen for many years.

Goldie was going to a boarding kennel in the country. Janey wished she could look after her, but knew she'd never be allowed to have a dog in the house, even if she dared to ask.

Finishing off her painting, she made her way through to the kitchen, where the table was laid for lunch. There was an iced cake with sixteen candles on it. Next to it was a small present wrapped in tissue.

'This is for you,' Douglas said with a smile. 'I hope you like it.'

They watched her open it, smiles on their faces. Inside, was a gold chain with a heart hanging from it. There was an inscription on the back. *'To Janey with love.'* She'd never seen anything quite so lovely.

She gazed at them, almost overwhelmed by their generosity. 'It's so beautiful. Thank you.'

'Let's see what it looks like on, then.' About to clasp it around Janey's neck Mary fumbled with the thong she found there. 'We'd better take this old thing off first.'

'No.' Janey's hand closed over it. 'It was a present from Griffin Tyler.'

'Isn't that the gypsy lad who found. . . .' Mary's voice trailed off as she lifted the wooden disk to examine it. 'Didn't he live in the village?'

'Griff's only part gypsy.'

'He's good at carving. I suppose he sells these from door to door. Does he make wooden pegs as well?'

'He's at university,' Janey said quietly. 'He's going to be a doctor.'

Feeling as if she'd patronized Janey and come off second best, Mary grimaced at her husband.

Douglas winked at her. 'I'm sure there's room for two necklaces.'

Impulsively Janey gave Mary a hug when it was hung around her neck. She felt choked up, as if her mind couldn't decide whether to cry or laugh.

Mary didn't know whether to laugh or cry either at the totally unexpected gesture of affection. She wished she could tell her the necklace was a gift from her father, but Jack had expressly forbidden it.

'Let sleeping dogs lie,' he'd said. 'She's suffered enough.'

Afterwards, Janey blew out the candles and ate some of the cake. Mary and Douglas sang happy birthday, then Mary put some cake in a bag for her to take home for Susie.

'There's something else,' Douglas said as she was preparing to go. 'We've bought you a warm coat.'

Janey vaguely remembered a new coat she'd had as a child. Her father had given it to Pauline. The smile left her face.

'It's all right, love. Your mum will pretend she bought it in a jumble sale if anyone asks. We've put the spare house key in the pocket in case you want to come up and paint now and again whilst we're away. You know where everything is.'

The three-quarter length duffel coat in warm blue wool had a checked lining and a fur-edged hood. Janey had never owned anything so nice in her life. She was wearing it as she left, her old raincoat stuffed in a bag.

Tim Ryker had just finished valuing the house for a prospective client in the street when he glanced up and saw her walk by.

He felt sorry for her. She and Pamela were little more than slaves in the Renfrew house. He hated living there, hated the tension that was always present in the household.

His dislike of Eddie Renfrew had turned to loathing. The man was a hypocrite. Smooth and urbane to outsiders, he attended church on Sundays without fail. Yet he treated his wife and two younger daughters like rubbish.

He'd been an idiot to have allowed himself to be trapped into marriage. Pauline was a lazy, selfish bitch, who constantly complained about the coming baby. She'd once been fun, but Tim knew he'd never have married her if she hadn't become pregnant.

At nineteen, control of his life had been taken over by others. Knowing it was his own fault didn't help matters. He'd only just left school, and already he'd been obliged to abandon his plans to make the navy his career. The pregnancy had forced him to do what his father had always wanted – join him in the real estate business.

Briefly, Tim wondered what Janey was doing in this part of town before he turned his attention back to his client. It was a few days before Tim had a chance to ask her. Sunday lunch was over and Janey was clearing away the dishes.

He gave her a smile as she picked up his dirty plate. 'What were you doing in Westbourne Crescent on Wednesday?'

The plate slipped from her hand as she gazed at him, eyes horrified.

Realizing he'd made a blunder, he tried to cover it up as she picked the broken pieces of the plate from the floor. 'Come to think of it, it couldn't have been you. The girl I saw was wearing a new blue duffel coat.'

Audible in the sudden, tense silence, was Pamela's swift intake of breath.

Eddie saw deception in his wife's eyes when he flicked her a glance. She'd lied when she'd told him she'd bought the coat at a jumble sale. Placing his napkin on the table, he fixed Janey with a stare.

She gazed back at him, seemingly indifferent.

Pauline gave a nervous titter. 'I'm going upstairs.'

'Stay there,' Eddie snarled, his scowl daring Tim to intervene.

Tim nervously shuffled in his chair, and Pauline rolled her eyes and gave an exaggerated sigh.

'Well, Janey,' Eddie said silkily. 'Answer Tim. What were you doing in Westbourne Crescent on Wednesday?'

'Running an errand for me,' Pamela said defiantly.

Eddie's hand thumped on the table, making everyone jump. 'Answer me, Janey.'

'Visiting friends.'

'Friends? What friends?'

Janey didn't answer. Her father could beat her black and blue if he wanted. *Nothing* would make her tell him. She experienced a certain inevitability, as if something momentous was about to happen. The only happiness she had was when she was with Mary and Douglas. She wouldn't let him spoil it. *She wouldn't!*

'Am I to take it you're refusing to tell me?'

'That's right.' She was sick of being the object of her father's anger, and sick of being a slave in the boarding house. The Yates's had shown her a different way of life. They treated her with respect, made her feel special.

Eddie's neck turned a mottled shade of purple. 'You'll do as I tell you.'

Something strange happened to Janey. Her mind seemed to detach from her body. She took a long, hard look at herself. She observed someone who was brow beaten, and frightened of her own shadow – someone she didn't much admire. Her fingers touched the Griffin hidden under her shirt. It would give her strength, Phil had said.

Her chin lifted. 'All my life you've treated me like dirt. I'm not taking it any more.'

Dishes and cutlery scattered as Eddie shot to his feet. His mean little eyes swept round the table and came to rest on Pamela. 'See what you've done by taking her side.'

Pamela gazed down at her hands. Susie began to whimper.

'Shut up,' Eddie shouted.

Susie scrambled from her chair and buried her head in Pamela's lap.

'Leave her alone. It's me you're in a temper with, father.'

Eddie glared at her. How dare she speak to him like that in his own home? Her Bellamy eyes were full of contempt. He felt his control slip. He needed to hurt her, to bring her back into line.

'I'm not your bloody father,' he snarled.

Pamela gasped, and Pauline gave a tiny whimpering cry as he moved towards Janey and gazed into her defiant face. 'Your mother was an adulterous whore, who aborted her baby in this very house. She was a sinner, who right at this very moment is burning in hell. Oh no. I'm not *your* father!'

'Thank God!' Janey spat back, her shock tempered by a strange sense of relief. 'Because I hate you, I've always hated you.'

Eddie's face blazed. He back-handed her across the mouth and she staggered backwards and fell. Mouth dripping blood, she cried out when he grabbed the carving knife with one hand and her hair in the other. 'Didn't you learn your lesson the last time I cut off your hair. This time I'll scar your face so no man will ever look at you.'

'No you won't!' White-faced, Tim shot to his feet and pinioned Eddie's arms to his sides before he could slash at her. He twisted the knife from his hand, managing to nick himself at the same time. Blood sprayed as he threw the knife on the table, staining the white cloth with startling, bright red drops. 'That's enough. If you don't calm down I'll ring the police.' He pushed him into a chair and stood threateningly over him.

Pauline sidled to her feet and backed towards the wall. 'That's right. Stick up for her, but not for me.'

'Why don't you belt up for five minutes,' Tim shot back at her.

'Get out of my house, you ungrateful bitch,' Eddie shouted. 'Go and join your mother in hell, for all I care.'

Head held high, Janey left the room. She could hear her father coughing as she stuffed her clothes into two plastic bags. *No he wasn't her father*, she reminded herself. *Someone else was*. At last, something to explain his treatment of her.

There was a sense of unreality about the situation. *She was free – free from his tyranny at last!* Hysterical laughter bubbled up in her. She felt deliriously, euphorically happy as she took Lord William from the drawer and placed it in her pocket.

Life was a journey, Phil had told her, and hers was about to start.

The house shook as a door slammed shut. Her laughter stilled in her throat. How would Pamela manage without her?

They were waiting for her in the hall. Pamela's face was strained as she whispered in her ear. 'Get word to me through Mary if you can.'

Pauline looked terrified. Ashen-faced, she was swaying on her feet as Janey gave a tearful Susie a hug. 'You made him do that, Janey. I hate you.'

'Take Pauline upstairs. She's going to be sick,' she said to Tim.

Tim ignored her words. Following her to the door he said apologetically. 'It was my fault. I'm so sorry, Janey.' He pressed a wad of money into her hand. 'It's not much. If you need any help contact Wendy at work. I'll tell her what happened.'

There was more to Tim than she'd first thought, though he'd shown appalling taste in marrying Pauline. 'I thought you were going to grow a beard and be a pirate when you grew up,' she said, making him smile when she took his handkerchief from his pocket and wrapped it round his cut hand.

He brushed a gentle kiss against her bruised mouth. 'And you had dreams of being a famous artist.'

'I still have.' She experienced a dangerous sense of freedom, as if this was a turning point in her life of some significance. 'Now, perhaps I *can* be. I'll invite you to my first exhibition.'

She heard Pauline throw up and grinned. For once in her life, she wouldn't have to clean up anyone's mess but her own.

With no set plan to follow Janey spent the night at the Yates's house. One thing she knew, she wasn't go to stay in Bournemouth where she might bump into her father. She'd take a train, something she'd never done before. It would be an adventure.

Before she left for the railway station she wrote Mary and Douglas a note, explaining she'd left home, and thanking them for their kindness. She promised to write when she was settled. Still with no set destination in mind, she closed her eyes and stabbed her finger at the map on the station wall.

'How much is the fare to London?' she asked the man in the office.

Her heart was beating overtime as she handed over the money. The thought of going to the capital city was frightening, but it was as good a place as any to start her new life.

CHAPTER SEVEN

To Pauline's relief she miscarried in the fourth month of her pregnancy.

Two weeks later, Tim told her with awkward candour. 'I'm sorry, Pauline, our marriage was a mistake. Now you've recovered, I'm leaving. I suggest you seek an annulment.'

The copious amount of tears she shed left Tim unmoved, as did Eddie Renfrew's ranting threats. He'd been accepted at Dartmouth naval college, and nothing was going to stop him from following his chosen career.

The Ryker family dropped Pauline. Wendy made friends with a girl at the hairdressing salon where she was apprenticed, and studiously ignored her when they crossed paths.

Stuck up bitch! Pauline thought angrily. *I'll show her.*

Within a month, Pauline persuaded her father to pay for a course at secretarial college. For once, she diligently applied herself whilst Eddie arranged an annulment of her marriage.

Conveniently forgetting the failed pregnancy, Eddie told himself that Pauline was the injured party. He managed to convince both himself and the powers-that-be that the marriage had never been consummated.

Six months later Pauline was free, and she'd learned enough to land a job as a receptionist in an accountant's office.

Andrew and Robert Pitt, Accountants, was a small, but exclusive partnership of two brothers. Their suite of offices was the epitome of good taste with leather chairs, wood panelled walls and the company name discreetly advertised on a small brass plaque outside.

Pauline shared reception with Miss Frobisher, a spinster secretary of straight-laced disposition who'd been there since the stone age. Under her eagle eye, she answered the phone, made appointments, did the filing and kept the staff and clients supplied with tea and biscuits.

The job suited her. Before too long, she managed to charm herself into the good graces of the Pitt brothers, as well as Miss Frobisher.

Then she set eyes on Martin, the son of Robert Pitt. Martin was in his final year at university. He was ordinary looking, with straight, sandy-coloured hair and eyes a muddy mixture of green and brown. His hooded eyelids and long lashes gave him a sexy look.

More importantly, Martin Pitt was a good prospect. He drove a nice car, spoke with a cultured accent and always had money. When he asked her out to dinner she didn't hesitate.

She *did* hesitate when he tried to kiss her goodnight. She'd learned that a girl had to hold back if she wanted to catch her man. There would be no sex without a ring on her finger. Fluttering her eyelashes a little, she said in a breathless voice, 'I'm not that sort of girl, Martin.'

Martin knew exactly what sort of girl she was, one who had her eye on the main chance.

He was heir to both partners. His father and uncle were establishment, and expected him to marry. Pauline's virtues had been pointed out to him. Had they known his time at Cambridge had revealed to him a side of his character he kept hidden, they'd have been deeply ashamed.

Martin was confident of his ability to live a double life with Pauline. All he need do was produce a child. He could manage that, if he had to.

He didn't press the point with Pauline. Let her play her stupid female games. If she believed he loved her in the end, so much the better.

Sarah Wyman was furious.

'Damn Charles,' she said to her lawyer. 'If he thinks he's getting half of my investments he can think again. He can take me to court.'

'Up to you of course, old girl,' Noel Chatterton said affably. 'It will be more money in my pocket. But, take my advice and accept. He has enough on you to keep the gutter press in copy for the next century.'

'And where did he get it? Edward bloody Renfrew, that's who.'

'Don't be tiresome, Sarah. Nothing in the diary or photographs has surfaced. All Charles has got he's picked up over the past three years. My guess is, he's had a private detective on your tail. You should have agreed to a divorce when he asked two years ago. He said he'd provide you with grounds.'

'What, some trumped up assignation with a prostitute? How stupid would that have made me look?' Sarah chewed on her fingernails. 'Isn't there something you can do?'

'Like what?' Noel downed his drink and stood up. 'Charles is being more than fair under the circumstances. Same grounds. Everything split down the middle. In addition, you get this house and the Paris flat, and he keeps his estate. Nice and clean if you ask me. No scandal.'

'No scandal!' Sarah shrieked. 'What's to say Renfrew didn't tip off Charles? He might have copies of those photographs.'

'Stop being a bore. Charles wouldn't pass the time of day with a piece of pus like Renfrew. If you will play the whore?' Distaste clouded his eyes as she took out a rectangle of cellophane and laid a row of white powder along the table. 'You should knock that stuff off.'

'Mind your own bloody business,' she snapped. 'What would a poofter like you know about it?' Renfrew had grown rich at her expense. What's more, he'd rejected every approach she'd made. She'd made a fool of herself on the last occasion, though at one stage she'd thought she'd discovered his vice. Her eyes narrowed. She knew men, and could have sworn her schoolgirl outfit had turned him on.

Eyes half-closed she recalled the session in the French brothel. How had Charles found out about that? He wouldn't have discovered it by himself. Renfrew *must* have tipped him off. She wondered if Edward was still a client of her stockbroker. Perhaps William Reith could be persuaded to throw a spanner in his financial works. Her eyes began to gleam. He'd made several approaches to her in the past.

Feeling good now, she dialled his number. 'William,' she cooed in a little girl voice. 'Can you come. I've got a bit of a problem.'

'I can come any time.' William's voice was smooth and yellow, like camembert cheese. 'But I've got a meeting with a client scheduled after lunch, sweetie.'

'Cancel it,' she said huskily. 'I have this *personal* problem I thought you might like to help me with.'

He chuckled, his voice dropping to an intimate whisper. 'I think I might be able to help you with that, Sarah, darling. Perhaps we should meet in private. I have a nice little flat in Chelsea.

Five minutes later Sarah left her house and swept past the casual chauffeur, who relieved her regular driver on Wednesdays.

Tipping his cap, he respectfully held open the door of the Daimler for her. A nondescript little man, he didn't rate a second glance. As she seated herself she adjusted her coat over her thick black stockings.

'Chelsea please, Smith.'

'Certainly, Madam, The address?'

The following week Sarah had to take a taxi, as the chauffeur didn't turn up for work. Having discovered William Reith preferred other diversions to schoolgirls, she was dressed for the occasion as she let herself in.

William was sitting on the couch in the other room, a rather plump Roman gladiator in imitation leather. She laughed as she shrugged out of her coat. He'd turned out to be fun. But William wasn't laughing, and hers became a dismayed gurgle as she stalked into the room to discover Charles and his lawyer occupying the two chairs opposite him.

Charles looked as though he wanted to puke as he surveyed her slave girl get-up.

She gazed steadily back at him. He'd lost none of the quiet elegance that had once turned her on. A pity he'd turned out to be such a square. 'Charles,' she drawled. 'How lovely of you to join the party. Would you like a grape?'

'For God's sake,' William whispered piteously. 'If this gets out it will ruin me.'

She gazed at Charles. 'Will it get out?'

'My client has instructed me to tell you he intends to sue for divorce on the grounds of adultery with William Reith, and several unnamed men who visited an establishment in France in July 1964. The owner of the establishment has agreed to give evidence in court.'

Her eyes became hard blue chips as she gazed at her husband. 'How did you find out, from Edward Renfrew?'

'Who's Edward Renfrew?' the lawyer said to Charles.

His lip curled. 'Someone we should consider using if Sarah doesn't agree to the terms.'

So it wasn't him. Head to one side, Sarah considered for a moment. It must have been the relief chauffeur, Smith! He was the only one who knew about this place. For the life of her she couldn't remember his first name or his face.

'She gazed at William, who looked green around the gills. 'For God's sake, Willie, go and puke if you've got to.'

The doorbell rang. Charles smiled. 'That should be Chatterton now.'

'What the hell's going on,' Noel said as he swept into the flat. He stopped dead and surveyed the scene. William looked ludicrous, Sarah absolutely divine. Charles and his lawyer were po-faced. It was a classic. He grinned, he couldn't help himself. 'Right, I get the picture. I suggest we adjourn to my office and talk business, gentlemen.'

'Don't let Charles bluff you,' Sarah called out as they left.

'Be quiet, or get yourself another lawyer,' Noel said pleasantly as he shut the door behind him.

Janey washed the counter top and ran her eye over the tables and chairs. Everything was clean and ready for the morning. The chrome on the espresso machine shone and the juke box had been turned off at the wall socket. She took off her frilly red apron and hung it on the peg.

'I'm off home now, Mister Levy.'

'Samuel Levy will walk you home. Hammersmith is no place for a nice young lady to be alone in at night. Wait until I fetch Winston. He can water the lamp-posts.'

Janey dutifully laughed at the joke, but didn't argue. In the two years she'd worked at the café, her boss had always insisted on seeing her safely home when she worked late.

She bade him goodnight outside the bedsitter she shared with Sandy Carter, and let herself in. She'd met Sandy on the train and they'd swapped similar stories before deciding to team up. She had flaming red hair, worked in a Soho club as a hat-check girl, and was going to be an actress.

The bedsit was situated above a tobacconist shop. The place consisted of one large, shabbily furnished room, divided in half by bamboo screens. The bedroom was behind the screen.

The bathroom was situated halfway down the stairs, and shared with the tenant of the downstairs flat. They'd never set eyes on the occupant, but sometimes they heard the toilet flush, and a door opening and shutting.

'It's probably a pro,' Sandy said knowledgeably.

'What's a pro?'

Sandy laughed. 'Haven't you learned anything since you've been in London? You know, one of those tarts who sell sex to men.'

Janey's blush made Sandy laugh again.

They pooled their tips to buy food, and sometimes had enough to pay the rent as well. Janey saved as much of her wage as she could, and the small amount in her post office savings account had nearly tripled in the first six months. It felt good to be earning money, but her frugal upbringing had taught her thrift.

Urged on by Sandy, she'd enrolled herself in a part-time arts course at a nearby college.

Sandy had joined the drama class, and dashed around London in her spare time attending auditions.

One day Janey met the mysterious tenant. She returned from art class one evening and picked up the letters lying on the mat. Gas bills. The one for the downstairs tenant was addressed to J. Smith, Esquire.

There was a crack of light under his door and she listened for a moment. There was a violin concerto playing. It was lovely. When she shoved the bill under the door the music suddenly stopped and she heard footsteps.

Switching on the dim hall light she'd headed for the stairs and was halfway up when the door to the downstairs flat opened. Silhouetted against the light was the figure of a middle-aged man.

He gazed up at her for a second, smiled and said, 'Thank you, miss. Goodnight.'

Sandy was disappointed when Janey told her she'd finally seen their elusive neighbour, who wasn't what she'd imagined. She suddenly brightened. 'Perhaps he's a spy.'

'Living in a Hammersmith bedsitter?' Janey laughed. 'I might invite him to dinner on Sunday. He looks lonely.'

When Sunday came there was no sign of J. Smith, Esquire. The next day a card advertising the flat to let appeared in the window of the tobacconist. The flat was taken by a couple of effeminate young men who painted the bathroom pale lilac and hung a perfumed atomizer in the toilet.

Both hairdressers, their names were Stephen and Dion. They borrowed sugar, milk and tea, and sprayed the hall with air freshener.

'Nine bob notes,' Sandy declared. 'And before you ask what that is, it means they're queer.'

Janey thought they were fun.

'Hello, daaahling,' Dion called out when she let herself into the hall one evening. 'There was a handsome spunk looking for you earlier. He said his name was Griffin.' He handed her a note, adding slyly. 'I didn't know you had a boyfriend.'

'I haven't. Griff's a friend from school. Hand going to her pendant, she raced upstairs, experiencing a deep disappointment at having missed him. Feverishly, she tore open his note.

'Dear Janey, I'll be starting work at Hackney hospital in the New Year and will contact you again. Perhaps we could meet for coffee and a chat? Regards, Griffin Tyler MD.'

She puzzled over the MD for a few seconds, then her face spilt into a huge grin. Griff had finally become a doctor!

That winter, Sandy got her first job as an actress, abandoning the nightclub job on the strength of it. 'It's nothing much,' she said, her casual tone at odds with the excitement in her eyes. 'I'm a village maiden in a pantomime, and an understudy for the wicked witch.'

For weeks, Sandy learned her understudy lines, and rehearsed the songs and dance steps, dragging Janey along to the rehearsals and grumbling afterwards.

'Did you see how that Barbara keeps trying to upstage me all the time. I'm going to kick her bum if she gets in front of me again.'

Finding it all bewildering, Janey sat near the back of the stalls, trying to be as unobtrusive as possible in case she got thrown out by one of the two men who directed the show, and sometimes tore at their hair, ranting and raving and swearing at all the actors. But they hardly gave her a second glance.

Come opening night the witch took sick. Sandy was almost tearing her hair out with stage-fright.

'You'll be fantastic. Everyone says you've got miles more talent than her, anyway,' Janey told her.

Sandy's nerves fled as soon as she hit the spotlight. She proved to be marvelously nasty. Everyone booed when she raised hooked hands and flung her arms about, cackling and snarling and casting spells over both players and audience alike. Her huge false nose, wild matted grey wig, and blacked-out front teeth made her look terrifying. When she got her just deserts everyone cheered.

Susie would have enjoyed this, Janey suddenly thought, a surge of homesickness hitting her.

Pamela had written the day before. She'd said Pauline was engaged to her boss's son, Martin, and that Eddie had been in bed with bronchitis for the last week. Susie was doing well at school. She'd sent her a drawing of a bright green stick man with a purple dog on a lead. It was pinned up over her bed.

Janey intended to send Pamela some money for Christmas like she had the year before, and ask her to buy Susie something new to wear. Her father treated Susie only marginally better than he'd treated her all her life if she read between the lines of Pamela's letter correctly.

Only Edward Renrew wasn't her father, was he? With a sudden shock she realized Pauline was only her half sister, and Susie – her dear, darling Susie – wasn't related at all. An arrow of grief shot through her, followed by curiosity.

Who was her father? She decided to go to Bournemouth on her day off and ask Pamela if she knew. She could catch the train at Waterloo Station and be there in two hours. A great choking lump settled in her throat. She was dying to see Pamela and Susie again.

Sandy's success inspired her to paint her portrait as a memento of her first theatre job. She was painting in every spare moment she had, putting into practice everything she learned at art class, like perspective and form. The bedsit was littered with canvasses.

'You should try and sell some,' Sandy said. 'It'll put some extra cash in your pocket. Think of what you can do with it?'

Janey toyed with the idea, but when the mail arrived she put it from her mind, telling herself she wasn't good enough to sell – yet.

The mail came. There were Christmas cards from Phil Tyler, Charles Wyman and Brenda. Brenda included a note saying she and Charles were marrying in the village church in April, and she was invited to the wedding.

There was also a letter from Tim. He'd run into Pamela in Bournemouth, and had badgered her into giving him her address, he wrote. He said he was being posted to Malta in the New Year, and would try and visit her before he left.

It would be nice to see everybody again.

To her disappointment, Pamela was alone when she met her in Fortes café.

'Where's Susie?'

'I left her with the mother of a friend she made at school.' Pamela glanced nervously over her shoulder. 'I daren't let her see you, love. If she let anything slip to your father there would be hell to pay.'

'He's not my father, remember?' she said bitterly – then as casually as possible, because Pamela had given her the perfect opening, 'do you know who is?'

Mouth open, Pamela stared at her. She'd worried herself sick after Janey had been thrown out. Now she realized the girl was more resourceful than she'd imagined.

She'd filled out a bit, and although she was still slender, her figure was that of a young woman. Her face was free of make-up and her hair was caught back into a slide at the back of her neck. She was wearing the blue duffel coat over a pair of drainpipe trousers, and carried a tartan drawstring bag over one shoulder. Her cheeks were flushed from the cold.

Pamela didn't quite know what to say. She and Mary had agreed not to tell Janey until she turned eighteen. Still, that wasn't too far off. What did a couple of months matter? Yet somehow, she couldn't bring herself to tell Janey that the man she'd known as John Gregory – the man who'd been convicted of attacking her – was her father. Hadn't she been through enough?

'Eddie didn't tell me,' she hedged, wishing Mary was on hand to advise her. She swiftly finished her coffee and stood up. 'Have you got time to visit the Yates's? They'd love to see you.'

'I intend visiting them before I catch the train back.' Janey placed a hand on her arm. 'Must you go so soon? I've got heaps to tell you.'

Pamela heaved a sigh of relief as she sank back onto her seat. 'I've only got half an hour. Eddie creates hell if I'm out for too long, and I've got to pick Susie up.'

'Things haven't changed, then?'

'If anything, it's worse. Eddie can't get rid of his cough and is bad-tempered all the time now.' Unconsciously, her fingers strayed to the yellowing bruise on her cheek. 'I keep Susie out of his way as much as possible.'

Janey's blood began to boil at the thought of him hitting Susie. 'Why don't you leave him? You could come to London and we could get a place together. Both of us could work.'

'If only I could,' Pamela said sadly. 'But I daren't. He threatened to take Susie away from me if I left him. Eddie never makes idle threats.'

'What's Pauline doing these days?'

'Working in an accountant's office.' Pamela sniffed. 'She's become all hoity-toity since she got engaged to the boss's son.'

'What's he like?'

'Oh all right, but you get the feeling he's looking down his nose at you all the time. Eddie's thinking of consulting Martin about his investments. Something went wrong, and he lost a bit of money. He wasn't very happy about it.'

'Serves him right for being such a scrooge.'

'The trouble is, he takes it out on me.'

Janey noticed the threads of grey in Pamela's hair and the dark circles under her eyes. She looked older than the last time she'd seen her, sadder.

She cheered her up by telling her about her job and her art classes. When it was time to go she slipped some money into her hand. 'This is to get Susie something for Christmas. I wish it was more.'

Pamela hugged her tight for a moment, then watched her go. Her long slender form carried her gracefully in the direction of the bus station. When Janey disappeared from view, she wiped the tears from her eyes and hurried to the nearest telephone box.

Mary waited until Janey had nearly reached the end of her visit before she told her that Pamela had called her.

'I believe you want to know who your real father is?'

Puzzled, Janey stared at her. What had Mary Yates got to do with this?

Mary placed a photograph in her lap. 'That's your father.'

Uncomprehendingly, Janey stared at it, then spluttered in astonishment. 'That's John Gregory, your brother.'

'His name's John Gregory Bellamy,' Mary said quietly, relieved the girl wasn't taking it as badly as she'd feared. 'Most people call him Jack.'

Janey gazed from the photograph back to her. 'Then you're my aunt?'

'Yes.'

'I'm glad.' A wary look came into her eyes. 'He's in prison, isn't he?'

'Yes, but—'

'I see.' The photograph fell from her lap as she stood up, her face suddenly strained. 'I'd better go now. I don't want to miss my train.'

'He's innocent, Janey. He didn't do it.'

Janey's head began to ache and she closed her eyes for a few seconds. 'Didn't do what?'

'Attack you.'

'No, he didn't attack me. He ran me over.' She experienced a strong urge for fresh air, and pressed her fingers against the knot of pain on her forehead. 'I'm afraid I can't remember much about it.'

'Try, Janey,' Mary urged.

Douglas came to stand between them. 'Get your coat, love. I'll drive you to the station.'

The station smelled of soot and grease, and rain dripped steadily from the curved ironwork that arched above their heads. The smell made Janey's headache worse.

The three of them stood in an awkward knot until the train came thundering into the station. As they exchanged brief hugs, Mary noticed a stiffness in the girl that hadn't been there before. 'You'll still write?' she said, terrified she'd never see her again.

Janey gazed at her, her blue eyes clouded. 'Of course I'll write.' She hesitated for a moment, then smiled slightly. 'Thank you for the present . . . Aunt Mary.'

Mary experienced a rush of love for the girl, but it was tempered by relief. She'd accepted it! 'He'll be out soon . . . your father. In twelve months.'

'Leave it alone, Mary,' Douglas said.

'He'll want to see you.'

'That's impossible.' Her head was beginning to pound now. She wished Mary would go away. 'I've got a dreadful headache.'

'Get on the train, Janey love,' Douglas urged. 'Don't you worry about anything.'

The carriage was almost deserted. Douglas and Mary's' faces were pale opaque ovals through the steamed-up glass. They waved as the train pulled out, but she didn't wave back. When she could see them no longer she put her throbbing head in her hands.

John Gregory was her father. *Her father!* She wished she hadn't asked. How could he have left her to die after running her over. How could he? And did Mary really expect her to see him? Why should she? She owed him nothing.

'Excuse me,' a soft drawling voice said after ten minutes had passed. 'Are you feeling all right?'

Glancing up, Janey saw a young man in a brown-checked lumber jacket leaning over her. He was big, his light brown hair was shoulder-length and tangled. His eyes were a clear, liquid green. She'd never seen eyes of such a glorious colour before.

'It's just a headache, that's all.'

'I have some aspirin and a flask of coffee in my pack. Would it help?'

'That's very kind of you, Mr. . . ?'

'Darius Taunt, late of New York in the United States of America.' He chuckled as he hefted his pack from his seat, and took the one opposite her. 'But don't stand on ceremony. My friends call me Drifter.'

'Jane Renfrew.' Her glance went to the guitar strapped to his pack. 'Are you a musician?'

'No ma'am. I just like to strum now and again.' He shook two aspirin into her hand and poured some coffee into a cup. His smile sent a trickle of pleasure down her spine and made her feel shy and breathless.

Janey felt a bit of a fraud as she swallowed the aspirin. Her pain had disappeared as suddenly as it had begun.

CHAPTER EIGHT

'I was named Darius Rhodes after my Greek grandfather, and Ingram Fairfax Taunt after my English grandfather. Hence, the name, Drifter – from the initials, and my pressing need to drop out of the rat race for a while.' He gave a lazy chuckle. 'I was sent down from Oxford last year.'

'Groovy!' Impressed, Stephen flicked ash from his best purple shirt. 'My grandfathers were called Sam Higgins and Ian Tully.'

'Shiiit!' Sandy said, and they all fell about laughing. When they finally stopped, she gazed owlishly around the bed sitter. 'I know this sounds stupid, but I'm going to miss living in this hole.'

'The cockroaches will miss you too, daaahling.' Dion sloshed cheap red into their empty glasses and proposed a toast. 'To Sandy. May we see her name up in lights.'

Solemnly, they all drank.

'Now I'd like to propose a toast to Janey.' Stephen raised his glass to a fantasy painting of a witch stacked against the wall. 'I hope her paintings sell so she can stop working for Samuel Levy.'

Fat chance, she thought. I'll have double the rent to pay now Sandy's moving on.

'They won't sell if nobody ever sees them.' Dion jumped excitedly to his feet. 'Let's turn the hallway into an art gallery and hang them.'

Drifter smiled as his eyes took in the witch. 'I'll buy that one.'

'Like hell, you will!' Sandy crawled across the floor and sat defensively in front of it, her arms spread out. 'Janey painted it for me. It was my first role in theatre.'

A church bell started to ring, and they smiled at each other.

'To 1967.' Sandy's face was softly glowing. 'May the New Year bring us all success and happiness.'

They hugged and kissed, and wished each other a teary Happy New Year.

'I'm going to whitewash the hall,' Dion shouted, suddenly springing to his feet. 'Who's going to help?'

'We haven't got any whitewash,' Stephen pointed out.

'I know where I can get some. A painter and decorator lives around the corner. He has plenty in his van.'

Janey's eyes sprang open in shocked surprise. 'You're not going to steal it?'

'Of course not, my innocent little duckling,' Dion cooed, his dark eyes glittering. 'Would I do something naughty like that? I'll push some money through his letter box.'

By dawn, the hall was a pristine white background for her paintings. Stephen cocked his head to one side. 'They look absolutely fabulous.'

'Like an ancestral home.' Dion gave a tired sigh. 'We'll invite all our clients and friends to a viewing. How much shall we charge for them.'

Janey left them arguing about how much her work would sell for, and made her way upstairs. The amounts being bandied back and forth were preposterous. Despite her tiredness, she glowed with warmth at having such good friends.

Drifter was sprawled on his back on the couch, his long legs dangling over the arm. Gazing at his sleeping face, tenderness stirred and she gently kissed his cheek.

A chance meeting on a train and I'm in love. How very odd.

She wondered what Drifter would say if he knew. Probably smile his slow beautiful smile, kiss her on her cheek and say in his relaxed way, 'Hey, that's nice, babe. Real nice.' The place smelled of stale smoke and cheap wine. Out of habit, she emptied the ashtrays and tidied up before she went to bed.

Sandy was curled up in bed fully dressed. Her battered suitcase stood in a corner, jealously guarding her painting. It was wrapped in brown paper and tied with string, *Property of Sandy Carter. Keep your thieving hands off!* was written across it in thick black letters. She'd miss Sandy, she thought as she crawled under the blankets, but it would be nice to have the place to herself for a while.

By the time she woke, both Sandy and Drifter had gone. There was an envelope on the table containing a fifty pound note. *For number 11*, was written on the outside.

Pulling on her robe she rushed to the top of the stairs.

Halfway down was a blank space on the wall where Tower Bridge had hung. Drifter had paid fifty pounds for it? She'd have given it to him if he'd asked.

Sinking on to the top of the stairs she gazed down at the makeshift art gallery and began to laugh. She'd sold her first painting and was now a bona fide artist. Was everybody but herself mad, or was it the other way around?

It was Sunday. Sub Lieutenant Timothy Ryker stopped in front of the tobacconists shop and checked his bearings.

To the right of the tobacconist and set back a bit, was a black painted door set into a pebble-dash wall. Number 179 was painted in yellow over a brass letter box.

There seemed to be a party going on inside. Dusty Springfield was belting out *You Don't Have to Say You Love Me*. That and the sound of laughter beat against his ears.

His thump on the door was answered by a pink-skirted man with quiffed hair. Tim took a step backwards when a pair of Latin eyes carefully looked him up and down. The man gave him a thin smile. 'I'm Dion. Can I help you, ducky?'

'I was looking for Janey Renfrew. I must have the wrong address.'

'Are you a friend of hers?'

'I'm her brother-in-law,' Tim said, stretching the truth a little.

The door opened wider, revealing a seething mass of people with glasses in their hands. The man jerked a thumb. 'Janey's skulking upstairs. Be a dear and see if you can persuade her to come out and meet her public.'

'Shut the jolly old door,' a dark-skinned gentleman in a turban shouted. 'It's cold enough to freeze a fart.'

'Not yours,' Dion muttered. 'You eat so much curry they'd melt the bloody South Pole.' Tim's chuckle brought a friendly expression to Dion's face. 'Just elbow your way through the crush, dear. Pinch Cynthia's arse on the way up, would you. She's partial to sailors.'

'Which one's Cynthia?'

'The one with the frightful moustache. Wouldn't you think she'd get it waxed?'

Dusty Springfield became Englebert Humperdink, the song throbbing with passion as Tim made his way through the heaving mass of humanity. The smell of sweat mingled with perfume and cigarette smoke tickled his throat. The whiff of marijuana lingered round a lilac painted door labelled *Powder Room*.

A brunette in a short, white crocheted dress, flapped a pair of heavily mascaraed eyelashes at him. 'Hello sailor.' Her nipples poked through the holes in the bodice like a couple of cherries. Tim pinched her arse, and she gave a little squeal.

At the top of the stairs, a middle-aged woman in tweeds was talking to a younger man. Her voice had balls. 'I can't make up my mind between *The Serpentine*, or *Thames By Night*. What was the artist was called?'

'Jane Renfrew,' Tim said pleasantly. 'Actually, I rather fancied those two myself.'

'Piss off,' she said frostily, then turning to her companion said as decisively as an Alsatian about to attack, 'both, I think, Bobby. See to it, would you.'

'Hey, Dion,' Bobby shouted down the stairs. 'Cynthia wants numbers 2 and 7.'

'Sorry, luvvy. Devlin wants *Thames by Night*.'

Tim grinned, unable to believe what his eyes were telling him as he knocked at the door. What had happened to mousy Janey Renfrew?

She was still there, tucked behind a stout door flaking green paint. An anxious whisper came to his ears. 'Who is it?'

'Black-beard, the Pirate.'

The door opened a chink and one blue eye peered out at him. The smile she gave was almost incandescent. 'Tim?' Then he was inside, and they stood grinning awkwardly at each other.

'You look great,' he said.

Her fingers fluttered nervously to her hair in an unconsciously feminine gesture. She laughed as she indicated her paint-spattered jeans and a faded black T-shirt sporting a CND sign. 'Don't lie. I look a mess.'

Not so, Tim thought. Here was a girl of unusual beauty. That she seemed unaware of it was endearing. There was nothing artificial about her. Fine high cheekbones cradled huge blue eyes that were fringed with pale brown lashes. Her mouth was a wide, soft curve, her hair caught into tie-dyed scarf at the nape of her neck.

Tim stared at her, entranced. She was taller than he remembered. Slim hips tapered down to long legs, her feet residing in a pair of scruffy flat black pumps. Firmly rounded breasts jutted against the fabric of her shirt. Janey had grown up with a vengeance.

When a blush of colour tinted the creamy skin of her cheeks he realized the girl he'd always known was still inside. 'I can't believe it,' he said softly. 'You're stunning.'

She turned away, embarrassed. 'Would you like some tea?'

'I was hoping to take you out to dinner.'

'That would be nice.' Her face was one big smile as she turned back again. 'There's an Italian restaurant up the road that opens on Sundays. They do a good meal for next to nothing. I'll get changed.'

She disappeared behind a bamboo screen draped in a flowered curtain. Whilst drawers opened and shut, he studied the painting on the easel by the window.

It was nothing like those on the wall outside. There was a swirl of different shades of colour merging from black to dark green. In the middle, and taking up most of the canvas was one creamy lily. It unfurled from the background with stark simplicity, and had immediate impact.

She came up behind him. 'It's not finished yet. What do you think?'

'It's sensational. I can almost smell the perfume.'

'It's the best I've done so far.'

She'd changed into a pair of clean jeans and a blue, ribbed sweater. Over her arm she carried the blue duffel coat, the cause of her leaving home.

He tugged the scarf from her hair when he helped her into the coat and watched it drift around her shoulders. 'What about your guests?'

Her spontaneous giggle made him smile. 'They're not really my guests. Dion and Stephen had this stupid idea to show my paintings. Nothing will sell and I shall feel an utter fool.'

'I wouldn't bank on it. There was some brisk trading going on when I came up.'

Anxiety came into her eyes. 'If Dion wants me to say anything on the way down, I'll die.'

He tucked a hand under her elbow and steered her towards the door. 'No you won't. Just drift down the stairs, smiling graciously at everyone.'

Stephen's squeal when Tim pushed her through the door brought an instant hush. 'Here she is. Stand back everyone. Let her pass.'

Janey died a thousand deaths when a sea of faces gazed up at her, then they melted against the wall at either side as if Moses had appeared to part the waters of the Red Sea.

Dion minced up the stairs to take her hand, and kissed it in a flamboyant gesture. 'The artist, Jane Renfrew, everyone. Smile,' he hissed from the corner of his mouth.

She pasted a smile on her face. The staircase seemed twice as long as she regally descended it. When she turned to see where Tim was, everyone clapped.

'For pity's sake, say something, daaahling,' Dion implored.

'Thank you,' she said, her face beginning to resemble a neon sign. She hoped the staircase didn't collapse under their weight. 'So nice of you all to come.'

'I could kill you,' Stephen said sulkily to Dion. 'Her grand entrance was *my* idea.'

'Honestly. You're such a prima donna at times, Stephen. . . .'

Then Tim was by her side, laughing. They escaped through the front door into the cold, fresh air. Feeling ridiculously exhilarated, she began to run along the pavement, then leapt into the air.

Tim grabbed her up, swung her round, then set her on her feet, his eyes reflecting his amusement.

'They applauded,' she said unbelievingly. 'They applauded Miss Jane Nobody from nowhere.'

'You're selling yourself short. The applause was for a very talented artist.' He kissed her cheek and tucked her hand in his. 'And a girl I happen to be very fond of. Tell me, Janey, is there a man in your life.'

'No . . . yes. . . .' Drifter came into her mind; Drifter who came round to visit and talk, but never asked her out, or indicated if he felt anything other than friendship for her.

'Does that mean you're gone on someone.'

'Yes, I guess so.'

So yearning, that yes, as if she was in the first throes of puppy love. Tim experienced an ache in the region of his heart. He hoped she wouldn't be hurt. 'Anyone I know?'

She gazed shyly up at him. 'He's an American.'

Worse! Tim had met American sailors. Loaded with charm and money, they could worm their way into any woman's heart – or bed come to that.

He wondered if Janey was still innocent. He shook his head when he recalled what had happened to her as a child. It had kept village tongues wagging for ages. He recalled Mrs Sutton saying to his mother in the shop once, 'It's likely she'll grow up promiscuous. I'm keeping my Annie away from her, just in case.' His jaw tightened. The crime against Janey had set her apart and he wondered if she'd ever regained her memory of the crime.

'Is something wrong, Tim?'

His arms came round her in a brief hug. 'Any sailor worth his salt has a girl in every port. I don't want to let the navy down, so promise you'll write.'

'Try and stop me,' she said, and gave him a sisterly kiss on the cheek.

It had been nice seeing Tim, Janey thought a little later as she sat in the armchair in front of the spluttering gas fire. He'd looked handsome in his uniform, though he'd argued when she'd tried to pay him back the money she owed him.

'Send it to Pauline,' he said offhandedly. 'She gave me hell over that, so tell her I hope it chokes her.'

She'd arrived back home to find the hall had been almost emptied of her paintings, but littered with dirty glasses and fag ends. An envelope containing cash and cheques had been shoved under her door. *Gone out. See you tomorrow, luvvy* was written on the front.

She counted it after she'd cleaned up the mess. It was more money than she'd ever seen in her life. On impulse, she extracted one hundred pounds from the pile, then wrote Pamela a letter explaining where it had come from. She scribbled a short note to Pauline, enclosing the money owed to Tim.

The rest of the money was deposited in a proper bank account the next day. She couldn't believe the total! At long last, she was an artist!

Drifter gazed at the girl from under hooded lids as she padded naked across the floor. Nice tits, he thought as she slid on to the bed beside him.

She did what she was paid to do with an efficient ease, grinding against him with a few practised grunts and moans, whilst he – brains suddenly concentrated on one spot – was helpless to stop his involuntary thrusting.

Afterwards, she used the bathroom, then left, smelling of vinegar douche.

Relaxed now, he picked up the paper and read the latest news on Vietnam. 'What a stupid bloody waste of life,' he muttered.

Disgusted, he threw the paper to the floor, got out of bed and strode to the window. The flat he was living in belonged to a titled gentleman, a friend he'd made at Oxford. Fully serviced, not only was it a place of elegant beauty, he didn't have to lift a finger to help himself.

He ate out, and didn't bother to answer the phone in case one of his grandfathers called him. By now, they'd know he'd been sent down from Oxford, and would have a private detective on his track. Once they found him, he'd be hauled back home and made to learn the publishing business from the ground up. He wasn't ready for it. He wanted to live a little.

He grinned. He wouldn't mind having a go at something like the new *Oz* magazine that had hit the streets the previous day. Man, *that* was really something. The sharp, witty satire would have his grandfathers wetting their pants.

The publisher had hit on a novel way of advertising. The name of the magazine was daubed all over town, on bridges, buildings and the steps of the underground. They were out to shake up the establishment. Yeah, he really dug that!

He should move on again. Join a commune, perhaps. There was safety in numbers. Better still, he could start one of his own. Perhaps Janey would move in with him. Now, that was a chick he couldn't figure out. She didn't fuss about her appearance, or discriminate against people. He wondered how she'd respond if he made a move on her. He'd buy her some flowers, treat her to some good grass, then when she was nice and relaxed, move in. He suddenly remembered she disliked grass. Champagne would have to do. It would loosen her up fast. 'Yeah,' he said softly, imagining her long shapely legs wrapped around him.

Devlin Cox gazed at the painting of the lily. It was a gem. By comparison, the paintings in the hall had been ordinary. They'd showed promise, nonetheless. She had a good eye for form and colour, but this went beyond that. It had soul.

'Have you any more I can look at?'

She shook her head.

'How long have you been studying art, Janey?'

Her voice was hesitant. 'I've been going to evening classes once a week for two years.'

He raised an eyebrow. 'Is that all?'

She shrugged. 'When I was young, I was taught by a man who lived in the village where I grew up.' She pressed a couple of fingers against her forehead. 'His name was . . . John Gregory.'

'Ah yes, I know of him. War paintings, mostly planes. Gregory's work is competent, but confined. He seems to have dropped out of sight over the past few years.' Draughtsman stuff wasn't to Devlin's taste. 'I'm glad to see his perfectionism didn't influence you.'

She steered the subject away from John Gregory. 'Would you like a cup of tea or something, Mr Cox?' Scrabbling around in a cupboard she came out with a tin. 'I think I've got some biscuits left.'

'No thanks. I'd like to hang the lily painting in my gallery. If it sells, I'll take a commission and show more of your work.'

'I couldn't allow you to do that?'

'Couldn't *allow* me to do it? Devlin spluttered in astonishment. 'Why the hell not? Most artists would sell their grandmother for the chance I'm offering you.'

'It's a wedding present for someone.' Her eyes became dreamy as she gazed at the painting. 'Those lilies grow along the banks of the stream where I grew up. They perfume the air in early summer.'

'Spare me the rustic scenery,' he growled, then felt guilty when the rebuke made her flush.

'Look. I'll buy the painting outright.'

She shook her head.

'Please yourself' He ambled towards the door, giving her a chance to change her mind.

'Thank you for showing an interest in me, Mr Cox.'

He turned, knowing he was being stupid. 'Let's do a deal. You allow me to hang the lily painting and I'll offer you space for five more in a showing of emerging artists in June. If the painting attracts interest it will bring people into the gallery to see the rest of your work.'

That made sense to Janey. 'You won't sell it?'

Devlin sighed. 'I won't sell it. I promise.'

'And you'll bring it back in April?'

I should walk out of here right now! 'Professionally framed.'

The brilliance of her smile made him blink. 'Thank you, Mr Cox.'

'Call me Devlin.' He sank on to the ancient couch and wondered what the hell had happened to him to allow this young woman to dictate her own terms. 'I'll have that cup of tea now, Janey, whilst I give you some free advice. When an agent approaches you he'll expect you to kiss his arse, not the other way round.'

She laughed, like he'd made a joke or something.

When Devlin left, he passed a tall, hairy young man with a bottle of champagne under one arm and a bunch of flowers in his hand.

Green eyes met grey, assessing and unfriendly. Neither spoke.

'Who was the fancy-looking dude,' Drifter said, experiencing a small, annoying thrust of jealousy when she admitted him.

'Devlin Cox. He's going to be my agent.' Her eyes lit on the flowers. Immediately, she became an endearing mixture of shyness and excitement. 'Are those for me?'

'Who else.' He placed the champagne on the table and drew her into his arms.

'That's nice,' she sighed after he gently kissed her. He kissed her again, longer and more lingering. 'I think I love you,' she blurted out afterwards.

Shaken, Drifter opened the champagne. He needed it. He gazed at her over the glass, at her soft eyes and vulnerable, trembling mouth. She was some chick.

'Hey, that's nice babe,' he said, and wondered why she giggled.

Later, when the champagne was finished, the petting over, he took her to bed and made love to her. She was inexperienced, and stiffened in his arms, but she didn't make a sound. When it was all over he gazed down at her face. Tears glistened in her eyes.

He felt like a heel. 'I'm sorry, babe. I didn't mean to hurt you.'

'It's all right, Drifter. It's just, I've never made love before. I didn't know exactly what was expected of me.'

Good God! She'd been a virgin. There was something touching about the thought. He grinned as he ran his fingers through the pale hair spread across the pillow. Its perfume triggered a memory of a holiday in France, of a cool breeze that had whipped a woman's long hair into strands about her face. He'd stood in the mistral wind with his nanny, waiting for his parents' yacht to return. It hadn't.

Janey's hair reminded him of his mother's. Moonbeams on water. Mistral hair. He breathed its perfume. He could fall for this chick. 'Mistral,' he whispered in her ear. 'My own darling, Mistral. Next time I'll make it better for you, I promise.'

Janey hoped so. She'd felt nothing but an all-pervading tenseness, as if her body belonged to someone else.

A month later Drifter found the perfect place for his commune: a large empty residence in Finsbury Park.

He took a year's lease on the place, paying in advance by cash, and using another name. The estate agent didn't question it when he saw the colour of his money.

At Drifter's urging, Janey resigned from her job to paint full time. They moved into the self-contained flat on the top floor, where she was ecstatic to discover a large airy studio to paint in. Drifter had furnished it with enough paints, brushes and equipment to last her an age.

Stephen and Dion took the basement flat, and another couple moved into the ground floor. Felicity was an upper-middle-class type. She talked with a nasal whine, and was slumming it with her unattractive, poet boyfriend, Connor – who managed a passable imitation of Donovan.

As the five paintings she was working on took shape, Janey had never been happier. She'd used a flower theme, as Devlin had suggested. She put the finishing touch to some poppies and stood back to inspect them, a smile playing around her mouth. Blood red, they scattered over a polished table dusted with grains of pollen.

The beauty of it made her ache inside.

Lined up against the wall were various canvases. She'd experimented, using fast-drying acrylics and long swift strokes to paint a series of work that was dark and different. All were fantasies based on Connor's poetry. She didn't like his verse, but it reflected a part of his personality, and that was what she'd attempted to capture. She signed them Mistral, Drifter's pet name for her.

Every day she fell in love with Drifter a little bit more. He was gentle and kind, and made her laugh. Beneath his casual poise she'd discovered a quick and intelligent mind. She found pleasure in his gentle touch, but she never experienced fulfilment in the heights of passion as he did.

She wondered if there was something wrong with her. Always, a sense of detachment stole over her, as if she were watching him make love to another woman, someone with no feeling. Though it pained her to deceive him, she learned to act, convincing herself she did it for him.

By April, her flower series was finished.

Devlin arrived, bringing with him the lily painting, framed in gold.

'I've had several offers for it.'

Smiling, she shook her head and led him to her studio. 'You want lilies. There they are.' Devlin tried not to let his surprise show. There was a whole bank of them, their serene elegance reflected in a stream. Bluebells stood in a jam jar on a windowsill, a snail climbing up the side. Yellow dandelions grew from a crack in a path with forget-me-nots in the background. White daisies bathed in sunlight, and spilled over a bank. Dark purple irises, gold throats resembling richly embroidered satin, speared from a pool covered in lily-pads. Poppies. He couldn't tear his eyes away. *What poppies!* Glorious red, on a table so glossy Devlin reached out, tempted to run a finger over its surface to wipe away the pollen. He decided to buy it himself.

'It's still wet,' she said, reading his mind as he reached out to it.

Smiling, he took her face between his hands kissed her mouth in celebration of her talent.

'That happens to be *my* girl,' Drifter said quietly from the doorway.

Devlin's grey eyes flicked him a dismissive look. 'Lucky you.'

His attention was caught by the series of fantasy scenes. He walked along the line of paintings, absorbing the impact of them. 'These could prove to be commercial.'

He collected them the same afternoon, sliding them carefully into the racks in the back of his van.

'I don't trust him,' Drifter said to her, watching the van drive off. 'I think he's got the hots for you.'

'It won't do him any good.' She slid her arms round his neck and gazed into his eyes. 'I think I'm pregnant.'

Drifter's eyes hooded slightly. 'You're sure?'

'Almost.' Her smile faded. 'Are you upset?'

He forced a smile to his face and summoned up some enthusiasm. 'Are you?'

Her eyes became all misty and soft. 'Just imagine. Our own baby to love, someone who's part of both of us.'

At least she hadn't mentioned marriage. His smile became as soft as hers. 'I love you,' he said, and meant it. 'Let's go and tell the others. We'll have a party to celebrate.'

Removing her arms from his neck she turned away. 'Must we tell them? I haven't even been to a doctor yet.'

'Hey, Mistral.' His arms slid round her waist from behind, and he nuzzled into her neck. 'If you want to keep it a secret that's OK by me. We'll celebrate by ourselves. I'll take you to see the *Sound of Music* and we'll sit in the back row and hold hands. If you're good, we'll feast on fish and chips on the way home.'

'Last week you said the film was romantic crap.'

'For you, babe, I'll force myself to suffer romantic crap by the shovel-load.'

Laughing, she twisted in his arms and put her lips up to his to be kissed. 'You're on, Dad.'

'Pops,' he reminded her. 'I'm an American, remember?'

CHAPTER NINE

Janey had forgotten how soft April was in the country, forgotten the way the wind shredded the clouds into streamers and chased them across the sky.

She exchanged a glance with Griffin, her grin reflecting her exhilaration at finally returning to Winterbrook. The fatigue had fled from his face now and his dark eyes were alive with amusement.

'Shall we make a run for it?' she said. Laughing, they sprinted to the spreading branches of an oak tree, then shook the glistening raindrops from their hair.

'At this pace, the wedding will be over before we get there.'

'It was your idea to walk from the station,' she reminded him.

'I needed the fresh air.' Disregarding the damp, he placed her parcel on the ground and leaned against the trunk of the tree. 'Thanks for letting me sleep on the train.'

'I didn't have any choice. One minute you were gazing at me all goggle-eyed, the next minute . . . comatose.'

'I haven't seen you since you were a kid. Believe me, you're worth a goggle.'

'Borrowed plumage.' She gazed down at the belted culottes and matching calf-length boots. The dress was made from fine wine-coloured wool, and boasted a designer label. 'These rags belong to Felicity.'

'This suit belongs to a fellow internee.' He chuckled. 'Felicity has great taste.'

'She can afford to. Daddy's a banker.' Hefting her bag from one shoulder to the other she slanted her head to one side, gazing at Griff in curiosity. 'You make the hospital sound like a prison.'

'It is, more or less. If I'm not working flat out, or attending lectures, I try and snatch a bit of sleep.'

'Is it worth it, Griff?'

His mouth stretched in a wryly mocking smile. 'I've had my doubts these last few months – but yes, I guess so. In the end it will be worth all the sacrifice and hard work. Besides, I owe a debt to Charles Wyman. He had enough faith in me to advance the money to help me through my initial training. I can't let him down.'

The shower stopped as suddenly as it started, and he lifted the parcel to his shoulder. 'What is this?'

'One of my paintings.'

'Is it good?'

'When it's opened you can judge for yourself.'

His eyes caught hers, dark and intense. In his young man's face she saw a trace of the boy she'd idolized. Warmth touched her heart as she experienced the depth of her affection for him.

'How do *you* feel about it, Janey?'

'It's perfect.' She reached out and touched his hand. 'You *will* come and visit me when you get time, won't you Griff?'

His hand closed around hers. 'Try and stop me. Come on. Let's go before it rains again.'

They made the church with a few minutes to spare, and paused in the doorway to scan the pews. Miss Robbins was playing an asthmatic Bach fugue on the organ, her head nodding in time to the music.

Ada was halfway down the aisle. She'd gained weight. Wisps of grey hair escaped from her blue hat. Next to her sat Phil, exactly as she remembered him. A lump lodged in her throat.

Phil's head lifted slightly as if he was listening to something. Then he turned, his face creased into a smile. 'I knew you'd make it,' he said, his voice echoing out in triumph. 'Damned if I didn't say so to Ada.'

'You watch your language in the Lord's house, Phil Tyler,' Ada admonished. Her eyes widened in shock as she turned towards the door. 'Well I never! If it isn't Janey Renfrew, and as pretty as a picture. I never thought the day would come when I'd see you again.'

Charles Wyman, a red rose in his buttonhole, blew her a kiss and smiled at Griff as they walked down the aisle. Miss Robbins began the bridal march, and all heads turned towards them.

'Anyone would think we were the bridal pair,' Griff whispered as they settled themselves between Ada and Phil.

'And a nice pair you'd make, if you ask me,' Ada said loudly.

Janey coloured when Griff gave a low chuckle.

The organ suddenly wheezed to a stop, then started the wedding march all over again. Heads turned again, the whispers and rustles faded to a hush.

Brenda looked elegant in a cream suit and a veiled hat. Her eyes glowed as they met those of Charles. The neatly dressed man who escorted her in was of medium height, with thinning brown hair. He delivered Brenda to Charles, then sat in the nearest pew.

Janey thought he looked familiar, but she dismissed him from her mind when the service began.

She'd never forget this wedding, never forget the fragrance of the flower-filled church. Huge vases of lilies and roses almost obscured the altar, candles sputtered. Light shone through the stained glass window, and dust motes danced in the air.

It was more than the ambience she'd remember. There was an atmosphere of love, almost sacred in its emotional intensity as the vows were exchanged and the songs of celebration sung. Charles and Brenda were amongst friends who wished them only happiness, and she experienced it in every fibre. Tears pricked her eyes and she felt like bawling.

Griff offered her his handkerchief. Careful not to smudge the eyeshadow Felicity had applied, she dabbed the tears away and managed a smile as she handed it back. He took her hand and led her outside – out into an April day that sparkled with sunshine, diamond bright showers, and birdsong.

'I wish I could stay longer.'

'You can.' Griff's voice was a low enticing murmur. 'Stay the night. We'll walk through the woods, then watch the bats fly out of the hill.'

'I thought you needed to rest.'

'It *will* be a rest.'

'A renewal, you mean.'

Their eyes met in complete understanding.

Dear, dear Griffin, she thought, his face quiet and serious, his smile enigmatic. How well they knew each other. He sensed the need for solace in her, a hunger that matched his own. 'Will we always feel like this?' she said.

'Always.' His dark eyes held the secrets of the universe in their depths. 'Wherever we go, whatever we do, this place will always call to us.'

They posed for photographs, two people pulled together by an invisible thread and close in spirit. Yet they were apart. She with her art, her lover and the tiny spring bud of her child curled close to her heart – he with his need to heal.

Brenda and Charles approached them at the reception, claiming astonishment at the change in her, as if they'd expected her never to grow up. 'Such a wonderful painting. Everyone has admired it.'

Charles took her aside to inform her that Lord William had left her a small bequest when he died. It's invested until you're twenty-one, so don't forget to come and claim it.'

Vaguely, Janey remembered an old man she used to play soldiers with, and a horse called Wellington. It all seemed so long ago now. Her hand closed around the lead soldier, hidden deep in her pocket. *Thank you, Lord William.*

Later, when the reception was over, she borrowed some jeans and a sweater from Griff and they walked in the woods. Nostalgia gave everything a sharp piquancy. The damp mushroom aroma of leaf litter, the green moss clinging to root knuckles and the pungent smell of the bog called to her. *Childhood smells. Childhood fancies.*

'I thought Goblins lived in the bog. I used to hide behind a tree and try to catch a glimpse of them.'

Griff gently squeezed her hand.

On the hill they watched the bats tossed skywards into the purple dusk. Sprawled on the ground she felt at peace. The world was turning in the damp grass beneath her cheek, and she was cradled against its heart, turning with it.

'Are you pregnant?' Griff said abruptly.

She scrambled upright, staring at him. 'How did you know?'

He took her in his arms, and holding her against his chest whispered 'Do you love him – the father of your child?'

She felt Griff's hurt, like a tiny ache inside herself. 'Yes, I love him.'

'Call me if you ever need me.' He kissed the top of her head, then pulled her to her feet. 'Let's get home. Dad will be annoyed if he doesn't get to spend some time with you. He loves getting your letters.'

'Why doesn't he ever answer them?'

'He can't read and write, except for his name.'

'Then how does he—'

'Ada reads them to him.'

So later, whilst Phil and Griffin talked before the fire, she quickly sketched father and son together. When she gave it to Phil as a parting gift he gazed at it for a long time, then said with a trace of moisture in his eyes, 'That's the best gift I've ever received.'

He was talking about Griff, not her sketch. Her hand slid unconsciously to cradle her child, and she exchanged a smile with Griff over his head.

On the train the next day, when Griff slept, she saw the man who'd brought Brenda into the church sitting further down the carriage. He was reading a newspaper, his eyes intent on its pages. Recognition came to her suddenly. With a quick intake of breath she rose and made her way towards him. 'Mr Smith?'

A pair of eyes peered at her over the newspaper.

'I was at the wedding yesterday.'

'Ah, yes. I remember. I don't think we were introduced. How did you know my name?'

'We met once before. You used to live in the bedsit below me in Hammersmith. I slid your gas bill under the door, and you opened it and wished me goodnight.'

The paper was lowered. 'You have remarkable powers of observation. You only saw me for a second, Miss. . . ?'

'Janey Renfrew.' He gave a small start. 'My flatmate thought you were a spy, because we sometimes heard you – but never saw you.'

He chuckled. 'Nothing so exciting, I'm afraid. I'm quite a boring chap. When I'm not working I like to play a little music, then go to bed.'

'What work do you do, Mr Smith?'

Janey thought she'd been too nosy when he hesitated. She was about to apologize when he said, 'This and that. I was a chauffeur when I lived there. I hope you're not too disappointed.'

'On the contrary. I must tell Sandy if I see her again. She'll be crushed to discover you're not James Bond.'

'And what keeps you occupied, Miss Renfrew?'

'Please call me Janey.'

'Only if you call me John.'

She smiled as she told him she was an artist, because sometimes she didn't believe it herself. Encouraged by his polite questioning, she chatted non-stop all the way to London. She invited him to her first professional art exhibition as they pulled into Waterloo.

'I'd be delighted to come.'

'Goodness.' She grinned as she scrambled to her feet. 'I've been talking your head off. I'd better wake Griff.'

John watched her walk away, a thoughtful look on his face. He didn't usually believe in coincidence, but had to admit it was odd seeing the girl he'd once shared a building with at the wedding – and odder still to discover she was the daughter of a man he'd once investigated.

He'd kept out of her way at the wedding, and had been surprised that she'd recognized him. She was a nice girl. He took a quick look at the address she'd scribbled on his paper, committing it to memory – Finsbury Park.

'Come to dinner one day,' she'd said. 'You can meet Drifter.'

He doubted if he would, but he'd certainly go to the art exhibition. The painting she'd given Charles and Brenda had been surprisingly good for one so young.

Throwing the paper on the seat, he joined the other passengers on the platform and disappeared into the crowd.

Four more tenants moved in with Felicity and Connor over the next two months. The two females said they were feminists, though Drifter called them dykes. They discarded their bras, walked around on dirty, bare feet, and grew long sweaty hair in their armpits.

The other two were men. One was tall and wore round glasses. The other was smaller and cur-like. 'Fuckin' right on, man,' he answered to anything said by Connor.

The house began to smell of hash and incense – dirt gathered in the corners. Stephen and Dion rarely visited, and Janey knew it was because they had to run the gauntlet of the latest tenants.

The crude language and sneering comments upset them, and annoyed Janey. Drifter found it amusing. 'Forget it, babe,' he drawled when she commented on it. 'They're making a statement.'

'They're creeps.'

The mixed exhibition was a success, her oils selling quickly. Devlin followed up with a showing of the Mistral series, and sold those as well.

'They brought better prices than I expected,' he said, 'so you've got to go with the flow while it lasts. Think big and acrylic for the Mistral signature. In twelve months time I'll be arranging a major oils exhibition for you, so start work.'

'Mistral's pregnant.'

The flat statement from Drifter sent Devlin's head swivelling round. He gave him an unfriendly stare. 'So what! She can still use her arms, can't she?'

Drifter lumbered threateningly to his feet. 'Listen, man. I don't want her tiring herself. She'll have a baby to look after soon.'

'I don't recall asking for your opinion. Janey's *my* client. She can decide for herself whether she's prepared to work.'

'Well?' Drifter said to her.

Both men wore the same disgruntled expressions as they gazed at her. She grinned. They looked like kids spoiling for a fight.

'Of course I can do the work. I *want* to. The baby's not due until early January.' Crossing to Drifter, she linked her arm through his and laid her head against his arm. 'I'll have to rely on you to keep the others out of my hair.'

'Anything you say, babe.' He was annoyed, though. After Devlin had strutted off like a victorious turkey cock he gazed at her with wounded eyes. 'I was only thinking of you.'

'I know, and I love you for it.'

His arms came round her. 'That guy's a Svengali. He'll work you until you drop if you let him.'

Irritation niggled at her. Drifter had grown up taking money for granted. She needed to work, to get ahead with her painting and grasp every opportunity. Drifter didn't understand that her work was more than just a job to her. She needed it like she needed to breathe.

By Christmas, their relationship was coming apart at the seams. Drifter needed people around him and he filled the house with them. Stephen and Dion moved out, their place taken by several students, who didn't seem to study, but played loud music and smoked pot incessantly. One of them had a set of bongo drums that throbbed half the night.

There were parties. People walked around half naked and drunk. She nearly tripped over a couple making love on the stairs outside their door one night. Drifter laughed when she complained. 'Cool it, babe. There's nothing like a little loving to make a man mellow.'

Her blood pressure rose after Christmas. Because the baby was overdue, they admitted her to hospital and induced the birth. The labour was short, the infant slipping from her like a calf from a cow. When Drifter was allowed to visit, she had the baby tucked protectively against her chest.

He pulled back the shawl and smiled. 'She's a cutie with that bald head. Why is she that funny colour?'

'Jaundice. They said she'll be all right in a day or two.'

He chuckled as he put his arms around them both. 'Saffron, that's what we'll call her.'

Griff came to see her after she returned home. He brought a teddy bear for the baby and was pleasant to Drifter. He was taken aback by the nature of the people living in the house. 'This isn't a good environment to bring a baby up in,' he said when Drifter went to make some coffee. 'I hope you're not messing about with drugs.'

'Do I look that stupid, Griff?'

A grin slid across his mouth. 'You look disgustingly healthy, and totally smug.'

'Saffy's beautiful, isn't she?'

'The best baby I've ever laid eyes on. I hope you're going to ask me to be her godfather.'

Drifter set three mugs of coffee on the table. 'We're not having her christened. All that conventional crap is old-fashioned.'

When disappointment touched Griff's eyes, anger trickled down her spine. If Drifter thought he'd make decisions like this all by himself, he could think again. 'Who the hell decided Saffy wasn't going to be christened?' she exploded, after Griff had gone.

'Hell, I'm her pop, aren't I?'

'Then why did you insist your name be left off her birth certificate?'

'Aw, hell.' He slumped into a chair. 'Don't get mad, Mistral. If you want Doc Tyler to be her godfather, it's all right by me. You know why I'm not taking any chances. If my grandfathers catch up with me they'll shove me in a suit and glue my arse to a chair behind a desk.'

'And you think they're going to check every new birth certificate. For God's sake, Drifter, get real.'

His eyes shifted to the door. 'I think I'll go downstairs for a bit. I expect you want to paint.'

'I've got to feed Saffy first.'

'There's a few people coming up on Saturday to celebrate her arrival. That all right with you, babe?'

Her heart sank, but he looked so pleased with the idea she had no other choice but to summon up a smile.

Saffy took over her life. Nappies, washing, feeding, bathing. After a month she'd organized her life sufficiently to fit in her painting. She was so tired that when she fell into bed, she hardly had the energy to wish Drifter goodnight.

Devlin was pleased with her Mistral paintings. It wasn't what she wanted to express on canvas, but they were quick to paint and brought in money. Not that she needed any, because Drifter insisted on paying for everything. Her bank account got fatter and fatter.

'You're my girl,' he said, but never once suggested they make it legal. Not that she wanted to get married, she told herself, but it would have been nice to be asked.

She sent money to Pamela with her next letter.

By return post she learned that Pauline had married. There was a photo of Susie, taken at school. She was smiling, but her eyes were unhappy. She'd be eleven in autumn.

Drifter threw a surprise party for her twentieth birthday, to which even Devlin was invited. Janey's heart sank when she returned from putting Saffy to bed, and found the residents gathered in their lounge room. She forced a smile to her face as they shouted, 'Happy birthday!'

Drifter drew her into his arms and kissed her, then pulled a small box from his pocket. 'Hush everyone. I'm about to propose to my girl.'

Horrified when he dropped to one knee, Janey didn't know quite what to say. 'I . . . I suppose so,' she stammered. There was a cold glitter of diamonds as a ring was slid on her finger, then everyone cheered. Drifter was borne away, and a glass was placed in her hand. 'I can't drink that. I'm breast-feeding.'

'It's fruit punch. Connor made it especially for you.'

Felicity looked stunning in a sleek black dress, but her eyes were shadowed underneath, and her smile fixed. Her hand trembled as she bore a glass to her lips.

'Are you all right, Felicity?'

'Perfectly, darling.' She gazed to where Connor sat, spouting his poetry to a dirty-looking group of students. 'Connor's being a frightful bore, that's all. He's begun to believe he's some sort of genius.' Felicity sounded as stunned as Janey felt as her eyes flickered to Drifter. 'Congratulations, I didn't think he wanted to tie himself down.'

Devlin wasn't quite so generous when he drew her aside. 'You little idiot,' he snarled. 'When he decides to grow up that whoremonger will break your heart.'

Something was stuck to the side of the glass. Fishing it out with her finger she murmured, 'What's this?'

Devlin swore as he took the tiny speck of paper from her. 'It's a blotter. If I'm not mistaken your drink's been spiked with acid.'

'Acid?'

'LSD, ducks. Where does that doctor friend of yours work?'

Fear sent goose pimples rioting along her spine. 'Hackney hospital.'

'Good. Fetch the baby and get in my car. Be quick, we haven't got much time.'

'What about Drifter?'

'I'll see to him.'

As she left with Saffy bundled under a shawl she saw Drifter on the floor with a crowd of people round him. Blood gushed from his nose.

'What have you done?' she whispered when he came back.

'Nothing he didn't deserve.'

Fear was rippling along her body like little waves, one after the other. 'What's going to happen to me, Devlin?'

'I guess you're going on a trip.' The eyes he turned her way were glacial. 'For your sake, I hope it's a good one.'

'And if it's not?'

His hand covered hers for a second and he sighed. 'Don't worry, I'll look after you.'

Colours, brilliant colours, singing like a choir of different winds coming from the centre of the universe. Reaching out, she caught one. It changed into a key that seared into the flesh of her palm.

The pain was so intense that she cried out, and plunged her arm into the ocean.

The waves boiled up around it, steam filled her mouth, her eyes, her nostrils! She was choking on it.

Saffy was locked in a room, calling her with a thin reedy cry from far away. The shadow was taking her child.

'Saffy!' she screamed.

'She's fine.'

Griff's voice, calming her. But Griff didn't understand. Her hand closed around his wrist.

'The shadow will hurt her.'

She took Griff's hand with hers as she plunged into the whirlpool and swam to the door. It was locked. Desperate, she pounded on it. 'Let me in.'

You have the key, a voice in her head said.

'I've lost it.'

It's in your hand.

'That's a scar.'

It doesn't have to be a scar.

She tried to peel the scar from her hand but it wouldn't let her. Saffy gave a silent, wrenching cry.

She struggled with her hand, prising each stubborn finger from around the key.

'Leave me alone,' it said. 'I'm the keeper of the shadow.'

'The shadow is mine,' she argued. Seizing the key she thrust it in the lock and entered the room. The shadow was hunched on the wall, moving, threatening. She experienced Saffy's pain, absorbing it, making it her own so her child wouldn't have to suffer.

The shadow was unaware of her creeping up on it. The choking dust muffled her footfalls. It had its back to her, and she couldn't see its face.

She inched her way on to the pillow, melting into a shaft of moonlight coming through the window.

It was him! He was punishing her child!

Giving an anguished scream, she picked up a candle from the dressing-table and thrust hot wax into his eyes. His vision soaked up the light and she stared into the face of evil.

'I'm your daughter,' she cried out, 'Why are you doing this to me?'

'She's not making much sense.'

'She is to me.'

Devlin glanced at the clock. 'How much longer?'

'Could be another six or seven hours.' Griffin smoothed the tangled hair back from Janey's forehead. 'Why don't you catch some sleep.'

'What's the point. Saffy will be yelling for another feed or a nappy change soon.' Devlin grinned. 'I hadn't realized babies peed so much.'

'In one end and out the other. She hasn't had any trouble taking to the bottle, then?'

'Soaks it up like a wino on the slops, then belches half of it down my shirt. I stink to high heaven.'

'If you burped her halfway through, it might help.'

'*You* try taking the bottle out of her mouth. She's got a suck on her like a vacuum cleaner.' Griff chuckled, then turned towards the bed as Janey gave a drawn-out moan.

'What is it Janey? What's happening?'

'He's waiting for her, in the cow-shed.'

His eyes sharpened. 'Who's waiting, Janey?'

'The shadow. She doesn't know yet, but she senses something.'

'*Phil? Griffin? Is that you?*'

Her frightened, little-girl voice made the hairs prickle on Griff's neck.

Saffy gave a short, sudden cry from the other room.

'*Don't hurt me, daddy . . . please don't hurt me . . . I can't breathe. . . ?*'

Devlin rose to his feet, his face pale. 'Is this what I think it is?'

'I'm afraid so.'

'I'm out of here. Is there anything I can get you?'

'I could do with some coffee and a sandwich.'

'*I'm suffocating.*' Janey's eyes suddenly snapped open and focused on him. Her pupils were pinpricks. 'Don't leave me alone with him, Griff,' she begged. 'Last time you came too late.'

'I'm here now, Janey.' He took her hand in his. 'Hold on to me. I'll help you through it.'

Tears flooded Devlin's eyes. Leaving the room he poured himself a stiff brandy, and raising it towards the bedroom door, muttered, 'Here's to you, Griff Tyler. You're quite a guy.'

Saffy gave a furious, demanding yell from the other room.

'Shit! I hate babies.' he said. Placing his untasted drink on the table he hurried through to the spare bedroom. Saffy was a bundle of furious rage, her arms punching the air like a heavyweight champion in a title fight. 'What are you all steamed up about?'

She stopped crying and turned her head towards his voice. Eyes a clear shade of green gazed up at him.

His nose wrinkled. 'Did anyone ever tell you that you stink?'

When she gave him a gummy smile, he melted. 'How would you like me for a godfather,' he said.

There came a time when Janey saw a dark whirlpool amongst the brightness. She fell towards it with a silent scream, but jerked awake before it could suck her in.

She'd had a nightmare. She tried to move, but her limbs felt as if they were coated in treacle. Then she saw Griff asleep in the chair, and remembered.

Her fist beat against the cover. '*No! No! No!*'

In an instant, Griff was at her side. His fingers peeled open her unresisting eyelids and he shone a light into her eyes. 'Good,' he grunted.

'Not good. The light feels like ice.'

A stethoscope was placed against her chest.

'Boom biddy boom!' she said, then laughed hysterically at her own joke.

Griff managed a tiny, humouring grin. 'You're feeling pretty rotten now, but you'll soon improve.'

She pushed aside the blood pressure cuff he was trying to wrap around her arm. 'Stop playing doctors for five minutes. Why didn't you tell me, Griff?'

His eyes came to rest gently on hers. 'Tell you what?'

'You know damned well what! That it wasn't a car accident. That I was . . . you know?'

'I wasn't there. You tell me, Janey.'

She felt close to tears. He was being deliberately obtuse and making her angry. Rage rose in her like a white-hot column. She lashed out at him, her fists beating furiously against his chest with a hollow thumping sound. *'You do know, Griff. You do know!'*

'Say it, Janey. Spit it out and get rid of it!'

'I was raped! Edward Renfrew raped me, and somebody else went to prison for it. *Damn him! Damn him to hell!'*

Griff's arms came round her and he hugged her close. 'It's a mistake to disassociate yourself. Are you telling me that your father raped you?'

She pushed herself from his arms, her face horrified as she sank back against the pillows.

'I wish it was that easy.' Her head began to throb. 'No, my father didn't rape me, Griff . . . it was Edward Renfrew.' Her hands came up to her face and she began to sob. 'Oh God, what an awful mess. My father . . . my *real* father is Jack Bellamy.'

CHAPTER TEN

Drifter stuck his elbow on Devlin's doorbell and kept it there. If the man so much as looked at him the wrong way he'd rip him into little pieces, and to hell with the consequences!

The door opened so suddenly he fell through it. Sprawled face-down, he found himself staring at Devlin's expensive Italian shoes. He sprang to his feet, fists at the ready. 'I want to see Mistral, and nothing's going to stop me.'

Devlin's voice dripped acid as he turned and walked away. 'Wait here. I'll enquire if Janey will see you. If not, you'll find yourself arse-up on the pavement.'

Just like the goddamned superior British butler they had at home. Drifter inspected the hallway whilst he waited. The limey sure knew the value of understated elegance. Marble floors, wood-panelled walls supporting a painting or two. A half-table displayed a statuette of a woman. She leaned slightly backward from her hips, her perfect figure outlined under a filmy gown. 'I bet you were some chick before your head and arms were cut off,' he muttered.

In an alcove stood a *chaise longue* covered in red velvet. Above it, discreetly spotlighted, was a painting of poppies spilling across a table. He gazed at it for a long time, then moved on to the other paintings. Andrew Wyeth, an André Derain landscape, one of his later works and certainly far from his best . . . a Picasso drawing. Mistral was in hallowed company.

He moved back to the statue, picked it up and examined it.

'Tang dynasty, sixth to seventh century,' Devlin said drily, then taking it from his hands, placed it back on the table. 'It's a pity it's only a copy. The original is priceless.'

'Cut out the small talk, Devlin. Will she see me or not?'

Devlin gave him a long, level stare. 'God only knows why. Top floor, first door on the left.' A hand closed around his wrist before he could move. 'Upset her and I'll remodel your entire body.'

'Let go, or I'll shove your fake Tang dynasty up your arse-hole.'

Devlin's grip relaxed and he gave a tight grin. 'Grow up, pussy-cat. My arse-hole could bite your arm off at the elbow.'

They eyeballed each other for a second, then by common consent both men turned away. Drifter moved towards the stairs, and Devlin towards his study.

'*Mistral, baby!*'

Janey rose from her chair at the window and placed the sleeping Saffy on the bed. 'How are you, Drifter?'

His heart took a dive when he saw the set look on her pale face. 'Hey, babe,' he said softly. 'What's eating at you? I didn't feed you that crap. You know I never touch the stuff.'

'Why, Drifter, why did Felicity do it? Are you involved with her?'

Taking note of the suspicious nuance in her voice, he shifted his eyes to Saffy for a few moments, smiling as he lied. 'You've got it all wrong, babe. It was Connor.'

'Connor?' Her eyes widened in complete bewilderment. 'Why would he do such an awful thing?'

'He was jealous of the success of your exhibition.'

'My exhibition?' She crossed to where he stood, placing her hand on his arm. 'Why should he be?'

'Because you based the paintings on his poetry. He approached Devlin and asked if he could do some readings. Devlin told him to get lost.'

'Oh. He should have asked me.'

'He was given the impression it came from you.' His fingers smoothed her pale mistral hair back from her face. 'Believe me, he's a sorry son of a bitch now.' His finger lodged under her chin and he tilted her face up. 'When are you coming home?'

'I don't know. Griff said I might get side effects from the drug, flashbacks and things. I might need him.'

Janey was worried about what she might say if she did, though Griff had assured her they'd only last a few minutes, at most. She couldn't tell Drifter about her childhood trauma – she just couldn't!

'Hey, we can handle it.' He pressed a small tender kiss against her mouth. 'Besides, there's nothing to stop Doc Tyler dropping in any time he wants. I like the guy. I love you, babe. You, me and Saffy . . . we're a family.'

She sighed as she laid her head against his chest and listened to the slow steady beat of his heart. It would be so much easier if she didn't love him. And there was Saffy to think of. Drifter was her father, and he loved her.

Twenty minutes later Devlin seethed as he watched them drive off in Drifter's battered old van.

Thanks! she'd said, kissing his cheek. *Thanks, for Christ's sake!* Couldn't she see Drifter was acting a part, that eventually he'd break her bloody heart?

He slammed the door shut with some force. The Tang dynasty replica statue rocked back and forth, then toppled over and slid to the floor.

'*Shit!*' he said, staring at the pieces. '*Look what that bastard made me do!*'

Janey accepted Connor's muttered apology with as much grace as she could muster, but she'd never forgive him for depriving her of the pleasure of feeding her child, for her milk had dried up.

Everything remained as it was. The Finsbury Park house was full of strangers she didn't much care for. Drifter was totally at ease with them, but she couldn't bring herself to mix with them. As often as possible, she locked herself in her studio and immersed herself in preparing for the forthcoming exhibition.

Spring brought blossoms to the street trees but she hardly had time to enjoy them between looking after Saffy and painting. The physical relationship between herself and Drifter continued to be unsatisfying. She didn't deny his needs, and if he noticed her lack of enthusiasm, he didn't mention it. As a precaution she went on the pill.

She tried to put the drug episode behind her. Sometimes, and without conscious thought she experienced a gnawing sense of guilt because Jack Bellamy was paying for a crime he didn't do. She told herself there was nothing she could do about it.

When she wrote to Mary and Douglas she was tempted to tell them what had happened. Then she remembered her father was due out of prison soon, so what was the point of making waves? It was in the past. Dragging it out into the open would do more harm than good.

Out of the blue she received a letter from Pauline. She said she was pregnant. *I'll be in London in June. Let's meet for afternoon tea somewhere.*

Somewhere proved to be a smart hotel in the Strand, where Pauline and her husband were staying for the weekend. Smartly dressed in a blue linen suit, her sister was perfectly groomed. Her mouth puckered into lines of discontent as she explained that Martin had an appointment with an old university colleague.

'You know what men are like when they get together,' she said with a falsely indulgent titter. 'And you can't stay more than an hour. We're going out to dinner tonight, and guess who's invited us? Father's old employer, Sarah Wyman.'

'I expect she wants you to toady to her, like he did,' Janey said, giving a soft laugh.

'She's got nothing to be uppity about. She grew up in a slum.'

'*There but for the grace of God, go I,*' Janey quoted.

'You've changed since you left home. You're more self-assured.'

'It's the company I keep. I doubt if you'd approve of them.'

Pauline gave Saffy a cursory glance, saying maliciously, 'When Dad heard you'd produced a bastard, he was furious.'

'I'd prefer it if you didn't call Saffy a bastard, Pauline.'

Pauline flushed. 'I was only repeating what dad called her.'

'Since he's not my father, I'm not really interested in his opinion.' She gave Saffy a kiss, in case she'd understood the slur on her character, and was hurt. 'How are Pamela and Susie?'

'Pamela's her usual frumpy self. Susie has turned into a sullen, obstinate little wretch. I don't know how dad puts up with them.'

'Haven't you noticed yet? He's unstable. He's the type of man who needs a punching bag around the house.'

'You *would* say that!' Pauline glared at her across the table. 'You never got on with him, and no wonder! How would *you* feel if you had someone else's daughter foisted on you?'

'Considering that the child wouldn't have been given any choice, I'd probably welcome her. I certainly wouldn't *abuse* her.'

Abuse, a word with several nuances, like tonal shades of one colour. You were never really sure which was the true shade, but the mind selected one that pleased it most. A smug little word really – just right for Pauline.

Pauline gave a light, brittle laugh and tapped a long pearly fingernail on the table. 'Oh, don't let's quarrel. We haven't seen each other for years. Where's that damned waitress with the tea trolley?'

Almost as soon as she said it there was a knock on the door.

When Pauline frowned at Saffy when she cried for her bottle, Janey felt uncomfortable and out of place. She wished she hadn't come. 'You can feed her if you like,' she offered, feeling a moment of perverse pleasure at the alarm on her sister's face. 'It will give you the feel of things.'

'I'll probably have a nanny to do that. Besides, Martin doesn't want me to lift anything.'

Janey gave her sister a long, steady look.

'I didn't want a child, but Martin insisted, to keep his father and uncle happy.' Pauline's smile was wry. 'Neither of us really likes kids, so we won't be having any more unless this one dies.' Her voice became a self-pitying whine. 'I don't want to go through all this again.'

Janey wondered how she could be so unfeeling. If anything happened to Saffy she wouldn't want to live herself. When it was time to leave she smiled, and hiding the pity in her eyes, said gently, 'Won't you kiss me goodbye?'

'I really don't think we're that close, do you?'

'We could have been if the circumstances had been different.' Janey kissed her gently on the cheek, anyway.

When she arrived back home, it was to find the hallway crowded with people. They stared at her as she came in, their faces avidly speculative.

The sound of long drawn-out sobs came from upstairs.

'What is it? What's happening.'

'Robert Kennedy's been shot,' Connor said. 'Drifter had a couple of reefers and went off his rocker.'

Drifter smoking marijuana? She hurried up the stairs, expecting to comfort him. Felicity was already there, straddling Drifter's lap on a kitchen chair. Both of them were as high as a kite – and completely naked.

'Ride me again, babe,' he was saying, tears running down his cheeks. 'I want to know I'm still alive.' Drifter's eyes were half closed and full of sorrow. He gave a miserable sob when he saw her. 'Hi, Mom. I thought you'd died and gone to heaven.'

An aching sadness filled her. They didn't really know each other. They'd never scratched below each other's surface. Now she saw something she'd never wanted to admit to. He'd bought her, and all the awful people living in the house. They were misfits, puppets to his master. He was manipulating them, observing them – laughing at them, probably. *And he'd called Devlin a Svengali!*

When she walked past the two people copulating on the chair she felt sick. But she knew she'd stay – just so she'd learn to despise him.

Later, when he tried to put things right between them, she asked. 'How long has it been going on?'

He picked up a lock of her hair and twisted it around his finger. His eyes were green and guileless as they gazed into hers. 'I can't even remember it. I must have been off my brain.'

He was lying. When he tried to make love to her later that night, she was stiff and unresponsive in his arms. 'Haven't you had enough for one day?'

He gazed down at her, his eyes suddenly charged with anger. 'Why are you always so goddamned frigid?'

A week later, John Smith lunched with a distinguished-looking American at a small, but exclusive restaurant not far from the Houses of Parliament.

If Ingram Fairfax Taunt was impressed by his surroundings, he didn't show it. He was too wealthy, too well bred, and too used to dining in style. He *was* impressed, however, when a couple of people stopped at their table to shake John Smith's hand and exchange the time of day. Both were politicians of some status, and one was a Lord.

His estimation of the man sitting opposite him, who unconcernedly continued to enjoy his roast beef and Yorkshire pudding, suddenly rose. Perhaps he'd do after all. He'd come highly recommended, and he figured that a man didn't attract powerful friends unless he was very rich or very able. In Smith's case, it must be the latter.

He waited until coffee was brought, then lit a cigar and slid a photograph across the table. 'My grandson. Darius Rhodes Ingram Fairfax Taunt.'

Some handle? John examined the photograph of a young, unshaven man with a pleasant look to him. Typical American face, wide smile, nice straight teeth, clear green eyes and mid-brown hair.

'He was expelled from Oxford university about two years ago for drug-related offences.' Ingram Taunt gave a small, embarrassed cough. 'It wasn't the first time something of that nature had occurred.'

Something niggled at the back of John's mind as he gazed at the photograph, but he'd never seen the young man before – he'd have recognized him if he had.

'I want him found, and I want him found fast.'

Didn't they all?

'I'll pay you a flat fee plus expenses, and a generous bonus if you find him within the next month. You know where I'm staying.' A gold-embossed card was slid across the table with some figures scribbled on the back. 'Is that satisfactory?'

John managed to stop his eyes popping out of his sockets, but only just. His dream of a retirement bungalow in Winterbrook had suddenly become a reality.

'Tell me about him,' he murmured. 'His habits, the type of music he likes, nicknames, known friends?'

His mind absorbed every word while he mentally rearranged the photograph. *Beard, moustache, long hair, dyed hair. Combinations.* Sharply, he glanced up. 'Say that again.'

'Some people used to call him Drifter because of his initials.'

Drifter! John kept his eyes bland as he stood up. 'Thank you. I have enough to go on. I'll be in touch.'

'Just a minute.' Ingram Taunt took out his cheque book.

The man had no breeding, after all. 'I'll contact you when he's been located. You'll receive my account in due course.'

John was jubilant as he reached the street, and a rare grin slid across his face. This was going to be the easiest money he'd ever earned. Janey Renfrew came into his mind and he gave a wry smile. A pity, she was a nice kid, and talented.

One of her paintings hung on his wall. Lilies growing along a bank. She had an astute agent. The painting had cost him dearly. He hummed to himself as he headed for the tube station. Already, the painting had appreciated in value. Charles had offered double what it had cost him as soon as he'd laid his eyes on it.

The rap on the door came just after noon. Saffy was taking her nap. Drifter strummed a tune on his guitar. He wondered if he could come up with an excuse to visit Felicity. He hadn't attempted to touch Janey since their argument, she hadn't let him. The atmosphere was strained.

'Hell!' He threw his guitar to one side as the knock was repeated. 'Can't a man be left alone?'

'I'll get it,' Janey said.

A tall, silver-haired gentleman stood at the other side of the door. Green eyes flicked over her, then skewered straight into her. He gave a small, shocked start. 'Where's my grandson?'

'Shit!' Drifter said softly. Coming up behind her he slid his arm around her waist. 'You'd better come in, sir. This is my girlfriend, Janey Renfrew.' He flicked her a pale, sickly glance. 'My grandfather, Ingram Fairfax Taunt.'

She moved away from him, leaving him on his own. This was a decision he'd have to make for himself. 'How do you do.'

'A pleasure to meet you,' the man said, his tone making it very clear it wasn't. 'Young man, your maternal grandfather, Darius Rhodes, is dying. You're needed at home.'

When Saffy gave a cry the man's head jerked up. He gazed questioningly at Drifter, who nodded. 'My daughter, sir.'

Janey went through to the bedroom, leaving Drifter and his grandfather to talk privately. After she made Saffy comfortable, she held her in her arms and stared out of the window. *Drifter will join me soon. He'll tell me he'll stay, and we'll work things out.*

'I'll change,' she whispered. 'I'll learn to please him. Please don't let me lose him. Saffy will be without a father.'

As she watched, the sky piled a mountain of puffy grey clouds one on top of the other. Sunlight speared through them as the rumble of male voices reached her ears.

Words, accusing words. *Duty . . . your country . . . loyalty.*

Words. *If* words – *but* words! Reasonable words like 'family commitment'.

Saffy and I are his family.

The words stacked one on top of the other, like weights on the old-fashioned scale Ada used at the big house. First the balance went one way, then the other. There was a quivering silence when everything hung in the balance, perfectly weighted.

'Disinherited. Disowned!'

The scales fell with a crash, and she hadn't had time to learn to hate him yet. Janey sucked in a deep breath, slid the ring from her finger and laid it on the dressing-table.

Below, a car stood at the kerb, shining and black, like a hearse. Along the street a piece of newspaper blew. It circled slowly on one point at the corner, then was sucked up by an air current. Yesterday's news!

A door closed. Amongst her wounded feelings she found a streak of anger and salvaged it before she broke down. *The weak-bladdered bastard couldn't even face me to say goodbye.*

The two men got into the car and it drove off. Drifter hadn't even looked up. Stunned by the turn of events, she waited by the window in case it returned.

Saffy cried out for her evening meal. Going into the other room Janey fed her some mush, gave her a bottle and placed her in her cot.

Drifter's note was propped against a sauce bottle on the kitchen table.

I love you babe. Don't worry about the rent. It's paid until the end of the year. I'll be back as soon as my grandfather improves. Kiss Saffy for me. Your man, Drifter.

Hope rose in her breast. He'd left everything behind, even his guitar. All he'd taken was a small framed snapshot and the painting of Tower Bridge. There was an oblong of paper lying on the mantelpiece. A cheque for more money than she'd ever seen in her life. Attached to it was a page torn from a notebook.

For the child's upbringing. It will be best for all concerned if this unhealthy relationship is brought to an end. Further contact will not be encouraged.

Unhealthy relationship? What the hell was that supposed to mean? Tempted to tear the cheque up, something stopped the involuntary movement of her fingers. She knew only too well what poverty was like. With this, Saffy would never go hungry or wear shoes bought from a jumble sale.

Ingram Fairfax Taunt hadn't even bothered to look at his great-grandchild, she thought sadly. Her darling Saffy had been judged unworthy of being a Taunt. Not once, but twice!

So be it, Grandfather Taunt, she vowed to herself. I'll take your conscience money. But don't ever try to see her – not ever!

Without Drifter, the occupants of the house crowded in on her.

Connor became a self-proclaimed Guru. The house filled with his hangers-on. John Lennon clones with flowing hair and dark round glasses loitered on the stairs. It was like looking at reflections in mirrors, mirroring reflections.

Girls with bare breasts, filthy feet and rows of silver bells round their ankles stood in groups, their eyes kohl-smudged, soulful and unaware. Someone painted the walls black, the windows purple, the stairs red.

Incense burned incessantly, its cloying sweetness mingling with the odour of stale urine, perspiration, mull, and sexual encounters. Music throbbed. Bells, drums, chants – in ear-suffocating rhythm.

Janey kept herself to herself, painted with a quiet desperation and forgot to eat while she waited for a letter from Drifter. It was a letter that never came. Devlin came instead. They had an argument and he went away.

Griff sent a note saying he was going to Winterbrook for the weekend. Did she want to join him? It would be autumn in Winterbrook. She could taste the leaves in her mouth as they fell from the trees, flame-coloured. She didn't need to see them. She painted them falling from the branches like spears. She painted them, bright flames burning against the sky. She painted them curling into themselves then decaying into lacy ribbed skeletons and crumbling into brown dust.

Devlin called the exhibition *A Season of Glory*. It was a sell-out.

She forgot to answer Griff's note, and started on Mistral paintings, dark abstracts coming from somewhere deep inside her. Saffy and soul-painting kept her fully occupied.

She had another argument with Devlin, but she couldn't remember what about.

Early in December a knock came at the door. From the other side Tim Ryker gazed at her like a friendly dog waiting to be patted. She blinked, and smiled. He looked nice in his uniform.

'I've got two weeks Christmas leave.' A frown creased his forehead. 'You look pale, and thin. My God? What have you been doing to yourself?'

Her face screwed up and tears flooded her eyes. Her bottom lip trembled like a child's. 'I don't know.'

He folded her in a hug, then led her across to the lounge. His eyes took in the child playing on the floor, and he smiled at her. Saffy clambered on his knee, tried to eat his shiny gold buttons and dribbled on his uniform. She captured Tim's heart. His face had the soppy look that Devlin and Griff always wore when they saw her.

Tim's eyes were compassionate as he turned and scrutinized her in her turn.

She felt old and used when he said, 'Drifter's gone, hasn't he?'

She felt lightheaded, as if Tim had brought in too much fresh air for her to gulp at one go. 'Yes, he's gone.' She smiled a faint smile. *There, I've admitted it to myself. Drifter's gone and he's never coming back.*

'You shouldn't stay here by yourself, love. There are some unsavoury types hanging around downstairs.'

An understatement. 'Where will I go?'

'Have you got a friend you can stay with for the time being?'

She thought about it for a few moments. 'My agent. Devlin will help.'

Devlin called Griff, and together they began to move her things into his home.

'What about Drifter's gear?' Devlin said.

'Leave it. It's only clothes. I'll take the guitar in case he sends for it.'

She was taking one last look at the place when Connor strutted in with his entourage. 'Groovy pad. How come you got to keep all this for yourself?'

Her curled lip signified the disdain she felt for him. 'Probably because Drifter paid the rent.'

'Fuckin' right, man,' the cur said.

Felicity hung off Connor's arm like a pale wraith. Her eyes looked like death, scabs tracked her slender arms. Janey couldn't hate her.

Her head cleared of pity when Connor picked up Drifter's guitar. He gazed enviously at it and his voice became beggar-like. 'I wouldn't mind having one like this.'

'If you push drugs long enough you might be able to afford one. Put it down, and get out!'

'Ah, the ice queen speaketh.' Felicity giggled, and Connor's followers snickered. Connor's smile was a nasty little smirk as he struck a chord and imitated Drifter's voice. '*I love you, babe. You turn me on, real nice.*'

She snatched the instrument from his hands and glared at him.

'How did you like your trip, *babe*?' he taunted. 'It's a pity you chickened out. Me and the guys were going to have a party and melt you a little.' He glanced around him, sniggering. 'How about it, gentlemen? It's not too late.'

'Gentlemen? You wouldn't have the brains to know the meaning of the word.' She whacked him in the chest with the instrument. He fell over, staring up at her from surprised eyes.

'You're a no-talent, freeloader,' she spat out, and was about to hit him again when Devlin snatched the guitar from her hands and did it for her. The guitar cracked, and he threw it aside.

'Take Saffy down to the car,' he ordered, grinning as Connor's dogs formed a circle, 'I'm going to enjoy this.' With the devil in his eyes, his hand made a little scooping motion. 'Come on you little yellow chickens – who's going to be next?'

The circle melted away when Griff and Tim slid through the door and ranged either side of him.

Felicity fell to her knees. Her fingers scrabbled desperately in each of Connor's pockets, and she scuttled away with a small cellophane packet clutched to her chest.

Later, when they were sitting in the large cozy kitchen at Devlin's house, Tim took Saffy on his knee. After a moment or two, he gazed at her with a quizzical smile. 'I hate to ask, but has she been christened yet? I'd consider it an honour if you allowed me to be her godfather.'

Griff's dark eyes stared at him, all challenge. 'Unfortunately for you, I've already claimed that distinction.'

'Wait a minute,' Devlin chipped in. 'Saffy and I discussed the issue between us a long time ago. After all, I did look after her for a few days. She's decided on me.'

'Surely that's up to her mother,' Tim argued.

They were all grinning as they turned her way.

It was one of those moments that fixed in her mind like a photograph. *How I love these three men*, she was thinking, as tears pricked the back of her eyes.

Devlin, the keeper of her career was brave, sometimes bad-tempered, but sharp-minded and neat. His astute grey eyes never gave his thoughts away, never allowed her in. Yet, he was always there when she needed him.

Tim, with his friendly face and open nature. There was nothing devious about him. Tim was trustworthy. How could one want for a better friend?

Then there was Griff, dark and enigmatic, who knew the secrets of her heart and soul. He was looking at her now, his eyes telling her he knew what she was thinking.

And what was she thinking? That her daughter had no father, not even a stranger's name on her birth certificate. These three men were offering her support, each of them worthy in his own way – *all* of them more fit to be a father than Drifter. She couldn't choose between them.

And the corners of Griff's mouth were already twitching into a smile when she said, 'I'll be proud to know Saffy has three such fine godfathers.'

Package clutched to his chest and eyes to the ground, Jack Bellamy shuffled out through the prison door.

He experienced panic when it slammed shut behind him and he took a few deep breaths to control it. The air, lacking the staleness and lingering carbolic smell he'd lived with over the past few years, ripped into his lungs. It made him cough. The scar on his face turned livid with the effort.

He turned up the collar of his thin summer jacket. It hung off him now, like an old beige sack. The cold made his joints ache and his nose run. He fished in the pockets for a handkerchief, but they were empty. They'd let him out a month early. Resentment flared in him. He'd had it all worked out on his calender, each day painted a different colour so it spelled out one word: FREEDOM. It had given meaning to his life. Jack didn't know where to go or what to do. He stayed where he was, shuffling in one spot to keep warm and staring at the ground.

Presently, a hand touched his arm. 'The car's over here, Jack.'

He didn't look up. 'They told you, then?'

'They rang us this morning,' Mary said. 'We came as soon as we could.'

Jack glanced up once as the car drove through the New Forest, but the light was so bright it hurt his eyes. The glimpse of green was so glorious he was afraid to look at it in case it disappeared.

'Doug and I heard from Janey this morning,' Mary chatted. 'She and the baby have moved into a flat above her agent's place. Shall I write and tell her you've come home?'

Slowly, Jack unwrapped his package and gazed at the squirrels. A smile touched his lips. 'Has she mentioned me since you told her?'

'No. But she didn't take it badly, did she Douglas?'

Douglas didn't answer.

'Don't interfere again, Mary. If Janey wants to contact me she'll know where to find me.'

'You're *never* going back to Canford Cottage? Don't be stupid, Jack. Why don't you sell the place and come and live with us.'

His eyes came up to his sister's then, and they were wounded beyond belief. 'I was happy there.'

'But people will remember.'

'And you want me to hide myself away, is that it?' He held her gaze until she looked away. '*I* know I'm innocent, Mary. That's all that matters.'

But that wasn't what really mattered to him. One day his daughter might remember he was innocent too, and she might come looking for him.

CHAPTER ELEVEN

It had to be a mistake!

As Eddie rapidly calculated the figures, his guts began to ache. Nothing left! All his years of careful investing gone down the drain in one fell swoop. *Damn William Reith! Damn and blast him to hell?*

Pulling a packet of cigarettes towards him he extracted one and, lighting it, stared through the smoke at the statement on his desk.

He should have listened to Martin instead of that over-fed stockbroker. 'Australian mining is highly risky at the moment,' his son-in-law had said.

But Eddie had been swayed by the more experienced William Reith, especially when he'd promised to make up his previous losses with one big killing. 'Six months and you'll be rolling in cash. Nickel is booming. Everyone I know is buying up big.'

He straightened his shoulders as pain cramped his back. Scowling, he threw the butt in the ashtray, then stuck a fresh cigarette in his mouth. He frowned as he lit it. He could always sell the house and buy a smaller one.

Drawing a pad towards him, he did some rapid calculations. Pamela could go out and earn a wage. Susan was old enough to clean the kitchen after dinner and they needed an evening cleaner in the showroom. He'd have a word with the boss.

He rose when he heard a sharp slap, followed by a cry followed by Pamela's voice. 'What's going on? Why did you slap her?'

Pauline's shrill, indignant voice assaulted his ears. 'Tell Susan to keep her grubby fingers out of my things. I won't have it.'

'It's only a doll,' Pamela said. 'You're too old to play with it, anyway.'

'That's not the point. It's *my* property, not hers. Look at it, she's dirtied the dress. Keep her out of my room. My father bought me this doll and it's about time she learned that taking other people's property is stealing.'

'I was only looking at it!' Susie shrieked. 'You're mean, Pauline. Why don't you and Martin go and live somewhere else?'

'You need to learn some manners. If you don't behave yourself, I'll tell father.'

'He's mean as well. That's why Janey ran away. Tim told me.'

'Janey was thrown out because she couldn't behave herself. Now she has a baby, but no husband. She brought shame on the family.'

'It's better than *your* baby. Yours will be mean and ugly, like you.'

Blood rushed through Eddie's veins, bringing a flood of perspiration to his face. 'What the hell's going on?' he shouted as he opened the door. 'Can't a man get any peace in his own home?'

Pauline indicated the doll. 'Susie's been in my room.'

Why did he have to sort everything out? 'Have you, Susan?'

Susie gazed defiantly at him. 'It's only an old doll.'

'But it's not *your* doll is it? Stealing is a sin, and it must be punished.'

'No, Eddie,' Pamela said when Susie pressed against her. 'She was only looking. She won't do it again.'

He took off his belt. 'She has to learn, and afterwards you can explain to me what she was doing talking to Tim Ryker.'

'She can *have* the doll.' Turning pale, Pauline thrust it into Susie's arms. 'It's dirty now, anyway.'

'No she can't.' Eddie advanced on his youngest child. 'Give it back to Pauline at once, Susan.'

Susie's lip curled as she gazed at it. 'What's all the fuss about? I was only looking at the silly thing.'

'*Give it to Pauline this instant!*' he yelled.

'I don't want it,' Pauline shrieked just as loudly. She clutched pathetically at her stomach. 'All I want to do is rest before my baby's born. Is that *too* much to ask?'

Lifting the doll over her head, Susie threw it as hard as she could against the wall. It bounced back, its head splitting in two. If she was going to be belted she might as well do something to deserve it. She goaded her father with an insolent smile.

Pamela quaked. Eddie would kill her.

Furious, he raised the belt. The belt glanced off Pamela's shoulder as she thrust in front of Susie. It fell to the floor.

He stared at his hand, bewildered. *How did that happen? I can't remember letting it go*. Then the floor canted sideways, and he fell to his knees. Toppling sideways, he found himself nose-to-nose with the doll. It looked grotesque with the two halves of its face split apart.

Then *his* head split in half, too.

Pamela went with him to the hospital.

'A stroke,' the doctor told her.

'Will he recover?' Deep in her heart, she hoped not.

'I'll order some tests. Once he's stable, we'll send him home. You can look after him there. His paralysis should improve in time, but how much is difficult to say.' He patted her kindly on the shoulder. 'It's not much use hanging around here and worrying, my dear. Go home and get some rest.'

Noticing a light on in Eddie's study when she returned to the house, she pushed the door open.

Pauline and Martin gazed guiltily up at her.

'What's going on?' she said. 'It's not right, going through Eddie's private papers.'

Pauline's eyes glittered as she gazed up at her. 'We needed to find his will. You might as well know, Pamela. He's left everything to me.'

'But what about Janey and Susie?'

'Janey's hardly going to get anything, is she?' Pauline scorned. 'And as for Susie?' The expression in her eyes became spiteful. 'If you want something for the brat, you'll have to contest the will in court.'

'And that will be expensive, Mrs Renfrew,' Martin said.

All these years I've worked my guts out for this family, been abused by Eddie and picked up after Pauline. I should have joined Janey when she asked me. What a waste of my life! Something snapped inside her. She began to laugh at the thought of what she was about to do. Eddie *couldn't* take Susie from her now.

Martin gave her an upper-hand stare. 'I assure you, Pamela, you won't find it very funny when you're out on the street.'

She'd never felt so amused in all her life. 'The pair of you are pathetic. You haven't even asked how he is!'

Eyes slanted towards her, half-wary. 'What do you mean? He's dying, isn't he?'

'No. He's going to survive, as an invalid.' She strolled to where Susie waited for her by the stairs and gave her a hug. 'Fetch the brown suitcase from the cupboard and pack your things. We're leaving.'

'Just a minute, Pamela.' Martin joined her, his face a study of sickly charm. 'Perhaps Pauline and I have been a bit hasty. We had no intention of evicting you from your home.'

'I'll give you the benefit of the doubt,' she said agreeably. 'But I'm going anyway. Eddie's bound to die sometime. You'll just have to wait before you cash in on it. He'll enjoy having his favourite daughter looking after him. From now on, you'll have to work for your money, Pauline. The boarders like their breakfast at eight.'

'But my baby's due any day.'

'So it is.' Pamela smiled pityingly. 'I feel sorry for it having parents like you two.'

Pauline was having hysterics as she went upstairs. 'It's Pamela's duty to stay,' she was sobbing. 'She's his wife.'

'Do shut up, old girl.' Martin absently patted her shoulder. 'If Eddie can sign his name, I can get power of attorney over his business affairs.'

From its hiding place inside a shoe, Pamela took a wad of notes. It was money Janey had sent her over the years. She'd never dared spend it, in case Eddie or Pauline had noticed.

'Where are we going?' Susie asked as they walked off down the drive.

They had three choices. They could join Janey in London, stay the night with Mary and Douglas Yates, or go to Winterbrook. Tim, who'd brought her a letter from Janey the last time he'd been home, had mentioned there was a position vacant for a housekeeper at the big house.

She didn't want Susie to be unhappy with her choice, and she didn't want Mary and Douglas to influence her in any way. Janey would welcome them, she knew, but was it fair to trade on her good nature?

All the same, it would be nice to see Janey and tell her what was going on.

Pamela's arm came around her daughter. 'Let's spend the night in a hotel. We can decide where we're going, together.'

Devlin gazed at the woman and girl standing on his doorstep, then giving in to an irrepressible impulse, grabbed up Pamela's battered suitcase and made like Jeeves.

'Follow me, madam. I'll see if Miss Renfrew is receiving visitors this morning.'

'You needn't take the case upstairs. We're not staying for long.'

Devlin's sigh of relief was overheard by the girl. She gave him a long, deliberate stare.

He poked his tongue out at her. 'You must be Susie.'

'Must I?'

Stroppy little baggage! He suddenly grinned. 'Janey didn't tell me you had a wasp stuck up your snout.'

Her eyes widened in astonishment and he winked at her. For a moment she was uncertain, then she gave a strangled giggle. '*You're* not a butler.'

'I'm Devlin Cox.' He turned to the woman. 'You must be Janey's stepmother. Why don't you just surprise her. Follow the stairs as far up as they go.'

Pamela gave him a nervous smile. She hadn't imagined Janey would be living amongst such elegance. She felt out of place in her down-at-heel shoes and scruffy coat.

When Janey set eyes on her she looked as though she couldn't believe what she was seeing. A lump came to Pamela's throat as she gazed from one to the other.

'Susie,' she whispered, then her eyes lit up and she smiled. '*Susie! Pamela! Oh my God! Look at you, Susie, how you've grown, and you're so pretty!*'

Susie eyes widened. Janey was so beautiful it made her heart ache. Her hair was spun gold and she shone with some sort of radiance, like an angel. How could such a person have brought shame on the family?

Bounding across the room Janey pulled them through the door. Tears poured down her face, and she hugged and kissed them both at the same time and cried out. 'I've missed you so much!' and 'How long can you stay?' without a breath in between.

When Pamela muttered something about it being only a short visit, there was a fierce cry of protest. 'I refuse to let you dash off. I haven't seen Susie since she was a little girl. I've missed her so much.'

Susie began to cry, which annoyed and embarrassed her because she was nearly grown up, and hadn't cried for a long time. She felt all mixed up inside, and angry, because Janey had gone away and left her. But then, no one had ever made her feel so welcome before, nor told her she was pretty. So she wrapped her arms around Janey's waist and cried, and remembered when she was small – remembered love.

Drawn by the noise, Saffy waddled through from the other room and stood staring at them. Her thumb came out of her mouth, and she gave a cry of protest at the sight of two strangers touching her mother.

Three pairs of eyes turned to gaze at her, three mouths stretched in a smile. It was all rather odd and frightening. Sitting down with a thump, she screwed up her eyes and began to howl.

'Saffy, my darling. It's all right.'

Scooped up in her mother's arms, Saffy listened to her soft, soothing voice, breathed the scent of her skin in her nostrils and felt it warm against her face. Her world became safe, her crying stopped, and she smiled at the strangers.

Later, when Janey went down to the kitchen to make tea, she approached Devlin.

'I suppose so,' he grumbled when she asked him if her visitors could stay for a few days, even though he'd expected it and didn't mind. 'But don't take too much time off from your work. The American exhibition will bring international recognition for the Mistral signature.'

'All this *Age Of Aquarius* stuff is driving me nuts. Dev. It's not what I want to paint.'

'It's commercial. Make the most of it. Not many artists are doing as well as you are.'

'That's because they haven't got a slave-driver for a manager. I'm tired. My arms and shoulders ache and I'm running out of ideas. Besides, I *need* a holiday.'

'After the exhibition, I promise.' Devlin sighed. 'Look, take a week off to spend time with your family. Afterwards, I'll hire a part-time nanny for Saffy. That will give you time to catch up on your painting. OK?'

Devlin avoided her accusing eyes. He knew he was pushing her too hard, but cult art had a limited life. As Mistral, Janey had fluked her way into it. The rewards had proved to be greater than he'd imagined.

Had she but known it, she'd earned enough money to buy herself a house and live independently for a year or so. He didn't intend to give her that independence, not yet. He wanted more for her – he wanted more for himself. He wanted her!

But her heart was still with Drifter. He could see it in her face when she looked at the seagreen eyes of her child. She had a way of standing then, her head slanted to one side, her mouth a soft smile, her eyes full of daydreams.

Her lips brushed his cheek, as if she was kissing a favourite uncle. 'Thanks, Dev.'

He caught her face between his hands and kissed her mouth, fighting the urge to throw her down amongst the sliced carrots and celery on the bench, and make love to her until his rage was spent. He kept the kiss gentle and grinned at the faintly perplexed expression in her eyes when he finished. She didn't have a clue about men.

The corner of his eye glimpsed Susie coming down the stairs. An odd child that, her face closed as if zipped together with despair when she'd come through the front door. He'd have assessed her as the type of child who'd get into trouble just to lash out at the world. Yet barely half an hour later, there was an adoring shine in her eyes for Janey, and Devlin knew he'd been wrong. All she needed was to be listened to, and given a sense of self-worth.

Devlin Cox. Psychologist, he self-mocked. *Mum said a university degree always comes in handy so let's see what I can do with this odd-bod.*

He waved his hand over the vegetables like a magician. 'Fancy giving me a hand in the kitchen?'

Susie bestowed a cool glance on him. 'I might. Can I make a cake?'

'You like cooking cakes?'

'Didn't I just say so?' She leaned on the bench, saying offhandedly, 'I'm going to be a chef when I grow up and have my own restaurant. Do you like cooking?'

'Yes, when I've got the time.'

An understatement, Janey thought, flicking him a grin. He had a *passion* for cooking.

'Perhaps I'll give you a job in my restaurant.' Susie's gaze darted around the kitchen, at the rack of copper pans, the utensils, and the cooker with the range-hood to take away the smells. 'Not bad,' she said, then inspected the vegetables. 'What are you making?'

'Minestrone soup.'

'You should use shell pasta, not chopped spaghetti. It looks better.' Susie picked up the paring knife. 'The vegetables should be cut smaller, too.'

'I thought you wanted to bake a cake.'

'We'll have to get this mess off the bench first, won't we?' She handed him the knife and selected a recipe book from the shelf under the bench. 'You get on with it whilst I look up a recipe. OK?'

'Just what I needed. An overseer for the kitchen,' he grumbled. 'Thanks, Janey.'

Susie giggled.

As she picked up the tray and left them to it, Janey grinned. Devlin constantly surprised her.

Justin Pitt was born exactly one year after Saffy.

He was small, not very attractive, and quiet – as if the fact that his creation was an intrusion rather than a cause for celebration had affected his development.

There were gifts. A substantial trust account from the Pitt brothers, who promptly enrolled Justin at the prestigious school Martin had attended in Milton Abbas. Teddy bears of various sizes and colours arrived, boxes of chocolates, gift baskets and enough flowers and cards to fill the private room to overflowing.

Miss Frobisher put notices in the paper on behalf of the young Mrs Pitt, and ran herself ragged seeing to her every need.

Pauline gave the chocolates and gift baskets to the nurses when she was ready to leave the hospital, dispensing them with graceful largesse. As an afterthought, she kept one for Miss Frobisher, who shed tears of gratitude when she handed it to her.

Silly old cow, Pauline thought.

Martin used his power of attorney to raise a small mortgage on the Renfrew's house. He put some money aside to pay Eddie Renfrew's nurse, then bought a second-hand Morgan, a car he'd always coveted. It needed a bit of work doing on it, but he could tinker with it himself.

Pauline demanded a nanny for Justin. She'd produced the heir, but had no intention of looking after him. Martin refused. If she was kept fully occupied with the baby she wouldn't make so many demands on him.

'I intend to regain my figure, go on the pill and enjoy myself!' she told him, her eyes narrowing. 'If you think I'm staying at home looking after a kid and an invalid, you can think twice.' When Justin woke them up at night she shouted at him to shut up, and told Martin he'd have to feed and change the child himself.

After a week, Martin was so tired he gave in and hired a nanny. He was forced to renegotiate the loan on the house to pay for it, but told himself it didn't matter. The house would eventually be theirs, anyway.

Pauline smiled with satisfaction as she accepted the invitation to Sarah Wyman's New Year's Eve party in London. They needed to move in the right circles if Martin was to get ahead in 1969, and Sarah Wyman was just the person to help him – and her!

Winterbrook was just as Pamela remembered it, except for a sprinkling of tastefully designed bungalows in the grounds of the old Ryker house.

'They blend in nicely with the old house,' she said, as Phil drew the car to a halt so she could inspect them.

'Aye, they're nice enough. It's mostly city folk who own the village now. They come down on weekends and holidays. Not many of us locals are left. Sam's gone – a bad chest took him off at the beginning of autumn.'

'I'm sorry,' Pamela murmured.

Phil glanced at the child sitting quietly in the back seat. 'The village school has closed. Mister James died two years since, and Miss Robbins has moved on.'

'Susie will be going to secondary school. There's a daily bus service now, I believe.'

'That there is.' Phil's dark eyes caught Susie's indifferent stare and his face creased into a smile. Here was a child who needed to be made to feel a bit special. 'Seems like yesterday you were born, young Susie,' he said, his arm embracing the sky. ' 'Tis said that a child born in a thunderstorm will carry the turmoil in her soul through childhood.'

Susie leaned forward, her arm resting on the back of the seat. 'Are you the gypsy who delivered me?'

Phil grinned when Pamela tried to shush her. This one was blunt – straight out with it! She'd believe only what her eyes told her to.

Not like her sister. Janey's soul was connected to the threads of the universe in many different ways. All feeling, all perception, all trust was Janey, however much she tried to deny it to herself. It was about time she returned to where she belonged.

'That's right, Susie girl. Janey and I brought you into this world. A pretty sight you were too, though squalling fit to bust. You swallowed the storm, all right. Swallowed it down in one gulp. Now, I reckon you'll be spitting it out bit by bit till you're grown up enough to handle it.'

'I *am* grown up enough to handle it.' She sat back in her seat and stared out of the window as the car jerked forward again.

Pamela gazed at Coombe Cottage as they passed. Smoke curled from the chimney, staining the pale lemon sky with grey. The flower bed had been dug over, and turned into a flourishing vegetable patch. Tamed now, wisteria arched twisted bones over either side of the windows. Odd to think spring would cascade fragrant blue blossoms all over the windows.

It looked neat with the dormant flower beds set into the lawn.

She experienced no sense of nostalgia at seeing Coombe Cottage. She'd never had any happiness living there, except perhaps the birth of Susie.

'Someone called John Smith bought it. He's a quiet sort of chap. Doesn't go out of his way to make friends, but pleasant enough to talk to if you run in to him.'

'He's done a lot to the garden.'

'Oh, aye,' Phil snorted. 'He'll have his job cut out in spring. Nature has a way of ignoring such neatness.'

'Which room did Janey sleep in?'

Surprised, Pamela gazed at Susie. 'The one on the right, up under the eaves. Why do you ask?'

'She talked about it in her sleep. She said there was a shadow in her room, that it was hurting her. She was crying out so I had to wake her up. She looked terrified.'

'I expect it was a nightmare.'

'That's what *she* said, but I had the feeling. . . .' Susie bit her lip and shrugged. 'I thought something awful might have happened to her there, that's all.'

Pamela exchanged a glance with Phil, both remembering the night Janey was attacked.

'I've heard Jack Bellamy's coming back to the village,' Phil said a few moments later as the gates of the big house came into view.

Pamela nodded. They'd had a little chat about Jack Bellamy when she'd been in London. Janey was convinced he hadn't attacked her now, but she wouldn't let on who had. 'Let sleeping dogs lie,' was all she would say.

Susie was overawed by the welcome they received at the big house. The cook, whose name was Ada, was as round as a tennis ball and quite old. But she was sprightly, and fussed and clucked when she asked her how the sponge cake she'd set on the table had turned out so light.

'It's in the beating, my dear. Next time I make one I'll show you.'

'Susie's very interested in cooking,' Pamela remarked.

'Good. I was telling Mister Wyman the other day, I could do with an extra hand in the kitchen on Saturday. Perhaps he'll take you on if I asks him nicely. I daresay you wouldn't mind earning a bit of pocket-money for yerself?'

Susie tried not to flinch as her cheek was pinched between a thumb and finger. 'Eh, who would have thought it. The last time I saw you, you was a bonny little baby. I hope you can settle down in the country after the bright lights of Bournemouth.'

Susie would have liked to live near Janey, but her mother had been offered a job in the village and they needed to support themselves. But Janey had promised to visit her next month, and Devlin had said she was welcome to visit any time.

Her main fear was that they'd go back to live in Bournemouth with their father. She'd run away if they did.

That night she slept in a small room, high in the house. Out of habit, she jammed a chair under the doorknob in case someone came in while she was asleep and touched her – like her father had of late.

Putting the finishing brushstroke to a painting, Janey stretched, then sighed with relief. She was one big ache. Every muscle, every finger felt old to her. For the past month she'd done nothing but paint. Now it was done, and Mistral was no more – whatever Devlin said.

A long walk was what she needed. She closed her eyes for a moment, recalling the dark woods of Winterbrook and the track over the hill to the beach. There, the salty wind would sting her cheeks and blow the London grime from her lungs.

She heard the postman and raced down the stairs to scoop the letters from the mat. The house had an empty feel to it as she made her way through to the kitchen.

Devlin was at the gallery, Saffy walking with her nanny in the park. She pulled a face. Her daughter had never been so clean and tidy. Still, the girl Devlin had hired was nice-natured, and didn't mind that it was just a temporary job. She'd explained that she'd just finished training, and at least she'd have a reference.

Splashing orange juice into a glass, Janey fanned the letters out over the shining blue counter top. Two for Devlin, three for herself. One from Tim and one from Mary Yates. Her face paled as she stared at the postmark. 'USA,' she whispered, and feverishly tore it open.

It was from the art gallery in America saying how much they were looking forward to her exhibition. She gave a short, sharp, angry laugh as she screwed it up and threw it across the room. *Why am I trying to kid myself? Drifter is never coming back.*

She felt shut in and restless. She'd ask Devlin for some money, and go away to the country. He'd promised her she could have a holiday. *Why should I have to ask Devlin? It's my money, isn't it? He's taken over my finances, and doesn't even tell me how much I have.*

She went through to his office, then hesitated. It wasn't right to go through his desk, even if her bank book *was* in it. She rang him at the gallery, determined to ask.

'Devlin?'

'Is something the matter?'

His warm friendly voice brought a rush of guilt. How could she even contemplate not trusting him. Devlin was the best friend she'd ever had. He'd given her a home, guided her career.

'Janey, are you all right?'

'Of course. I've completed the painting for the exhibition, that's all. I wanted to tell you.'

'Great. We'll have a bottle of champagne to celebrate when I get home. See you later, angel.'

'Devlin?' she said quietly into the receiver.

'What is it?'

'I don't know. Nothing, I guess. I'm just being silly. I feel . . . sad.' She hung up. She hated this feeling of limbo she got when she finished something. Somebody had once told her it was a form of grieving, that she should start a new project.

Jack Bellamy had said it. Instantly, anger rose in her. Why had he deceived her? He should have told her he was her father right from the beginning. She imagined him penned up for all those years in prison and pressed her fingers against the pain that knotted her temple. *I wasn't to blame – I wasn't!*

But she couldn't *stop* thinking about it. Presently her body became heavy and the floor drew her down to its shining surface and held her prisoner. Through the lights came a shadow, creeping closer and closer. She couldn't move a muscle.

It was Eddie Renfrew. As he smiled at her she tried to scream, but it burned in her throat and her skin fused together. She began to cough and cough and she couldn't stop. '*No, don't, daddy. You're hurting me! I'm choking!*'

'It's OK, Janey. It's me, Devlin? Open your eyes, angel. You're safe.'

She was lying on her bed. He must have carried her up because the last thing she remembered was being in the kitchen. She clung to him for a long time, then when her heart settled down, managed a smile. 'Thank God you came home.'

'I thought you sounded odd.' Anxiety clouded his eyes and she knew she wasn't being fair to him.

'Did you want to know about it?' she asked.

As his eyes engaged hers, he said gently. 'Only if you want to tell me. I'm not stupid, Janey. I've got a good idea already.'

She tried not to cry or sound self-pitying as she told him what she remembered. 'The awful thing is, I don't know what to do about it. My fa . . . Eddie Renfrew has had a stroke.'

Devlin drew her close, his fingers walked caressingly through her scalp. 'It's going to bug you for the rest of your life if you do nothing. Perhaps we can sort something out when I come back from America.'

'Yes.' His fingers felt great against her scalp. Closing her eyes, she sighed. 'That feels wonderful.' His lips touched hers, and his mouth was a provocative exploration. She should have stopped him, but didn't have the will. He made her feel loved and loving, and she needed to give him something in return.

So she didn't protest when he began to make love to her. Once, she detected a little spark of response inside her. But it surprised her too much, and because she thought about it for too long, she sighed with regret when it faded.

He gazed at her then, his eyes dark. He cursed, and rose from the bed, his body taut and defensive, like a beautiful golden puma being cheated of its prey.

'Why didn't you stop me sooner?' He was harsh, accusing, and she desperately wished she could give of herself what he desired.

'Because I love you.'

He knew exactly what she meant. He gazed down at her for a few seconds, a pulse twitching in his jaw. She could have cried at the frustration in his eyes.

'Keep your charity, Janey. If I can't have all of you, I don't want anything.'

When he moved off, all prickly in his affronted male pride, she wondered if anything would ever be the same between them.

CHAPTER TWELVE

Devlin was in America for Janey's twenty-first birthday. When he rang to wish her a happy birthday, he said, 'There's a lot of interest in your work. We'll have to capitalize on it.'

'No, Devlin. I'm finished being Mistral, I feel stale.'

'For God's sake,' he argued, his voice, sharp and impatient. 'This fad could end at any time.'

'No!'

'After what I've done for you?' He sounded hurt for a second, then suddenly changed tactics. 'How's Saffy's cold?'

'Fine,' she said quietly. 'Please stop trying to manipulate me, Devlin. I *refuse* to be Mistral any more.'

'Drifter came to the exhibition.'

She hadn't expected to be hit below the belt so casually. The colour fled from her face and she gulped in some air. 'How was he?'

'He's been drafted.'

Oh no! Please God, not Vietnam! He was so against the war. Hugging the receiver to her ear she gazed at Saffy with tears in her eyes. 'Did he ask after Saffy?'

'He asked.' He'd also asked why she hadn't answered his letter, but Devlin wasn't going to tell her that. 'I told him Saffy was thriving, that both of you were fine.'

'That's all he said?'

'What did you expect? It was over between you the day he left. Surely you realized that?' He could have told her that Drifter had metamorphosed into a clean-cut all American boy – and that he'd looked as miserable as hell when he'd discovered Janey had moved in with him.

'Of course I realized. I'm not stupid, Devlin.' She felt as cold and as sluggish as a river of ice. 'I'm going to Winterbrook for a few days at the end of the week. Perhaps it will give me inspiration.'

Did she need inspiration? People didn't buy the Mistral paintings because they inspired. They bought them because they were fashionable and might realize a profit down the track. She sighed. 'Perhaps I'll paint more Mistrals when I get back. I *can't* promise, though.'

She didn't have to. She knew she would, and so did Devlin. She'd paint under the Mistral signature until every drop of paint Drifter had bought her was used up. Then she'd stop, and put him out of her mind for good.

Taking Saffy up in her arms she covered her in kisses. 'Your dada is going off to war.'

'Dada . . . dada . . . dada. . . .' Saffy giggled and squirmed in her arms.

Saffy's first word. Janey's grin was tinged with sadness when she whispered. 'See what you missed out on, Drifter.'

Later, Griff called in. She hadn't seen him for months. Her heart did a torturous roll when he gave her a ghost of a smile. He looked exhausted.

He sank into the depths of Devlin's leather armchair with an ecstatic sigh. 'Happy birthday. I've got the rest of the day and a whole night off, so I thought I'd take you and Saffy out for lunch.'

As if it were something infinitely precious. She wanted to cry – for his tiredness and his thoughtfulness. Dearest Griff.

It was bitterly cold outside, a bleak, depressing day that fused body and spirit into greyness. Griff looked so comfortable in Devlin's chair that she invited him to stay for lunch instead. Saffy climbed on his lap, murmured, 'Dada,' and curled like a puppy against his chest. By the time Janey had prepared lunch they were both asleep.

There was something irresistible about Griff with a baby curled against him. She sketched them while they slept. With his gaunt, exhausted face relaxed, and his arm curled protectively round Saffy's plump little body, Griff was a heart-warming sight.

Saffy's thumb was in her mouth. Her other hand rested in the hollow at the base of Griff's throat. Every now and then her eyelids quivered, as if she was dreaming. When she woke, Janey lifted her from Griff's lap so she wouldn't disturb him.

Griff slept all through the afternoon. Janey guarded him like a mother with her child, watching the rise and fall of his chest with each breath. He's very attractive, she thought with a sudden start of surprise. A combination of olive-hued skin, high cheekbones, dark eyes and hair gave him a slightly Latin look. His dark raffish curls were a legacy from his gypsy ancestors. She wondered if he had a girlfriend.

How odd and how selfish of me. I've always taken Griff for granted. I never stopped to wonder if he had a private life.

The thought of a girlfriend nagged uneasily at her. It wasn't the sort of thing she could ask Griff. He was the most private person she knew.

But she did ask, later, when they ate supper in the shiny blue kitchen – blurting it out like a curious schoolgirl, because the question had lodged in her mind, and wouldn't be discarded.

His eyes lit up with amusement and his laugh was gently self-mocking. 'I haven't got the time or energy for romance. Only work and sleep.' He held her eyes for a few, lonesome heartbeats. 'One day things will be different.'

'I'm going to the village at the weekend. Can you come?'

The answer was a regretful shake of the head. 'I'm working. Go and stay with dad. He'll enjoy having you.'

Phil's little cottage on the edge of the wood was a perfect retreat for her few precious days. She had an open invitation to stay at the big house, but thought it might embarrass Pamela if she did.

Saffy took to Phil without reservation, climbing straight on to his lap and giving him a hug.

'Friendly little tyke,' he commented. 'Griff tells me he's her godfather.'

'One of them.' Janey gave a soft chuckle. 'Saffy called him dad the other day.'

'Well, she would, wouldn't she, with her not having one of her own around.' His eyes came up to hers, steady and unblinking. 'Jack Bellamy's back in the village.'

'I take it you know he's my father,' she said straight away.

'Folks talk. Most of the village knew your parentage was in doubt when you moved here.'

'Except me,' she said a trifle bitterly.

'There's none so innocent as a child.' Phil placed a comforting hand over hers. 'I guessed it the first time I saw you together. I doubt if anyone else saw a resemblance through the scar on his face. People tend not to see below the surface.'

'I must drop in on Brenda tomorrow,' she said with determined brightness, then chattered on inconsequently about nothing in particular until it was time for bed.

Over the next two days she busily visited her old haunts, and renewed old acquaintances. Annie Sutton, her childhood friend, had married a New Zealand sheep farmer, and the Sutton farm had been sold. She wished Griff was with her. On the surface, nothing seemed to have changed, yet everything had changed – like flat water between tides. Griff would have helped her understand it.

Her visit to Brenda and Charles Wyman wasn't as embarrassing for Pamela as Janey feared. Pamela smiled proudly at her when she bought in the tea tray, and Brenda smiled.

'Is this the cake Susie made specially for Janey's visit? It looks delicious. Why don't you fetch another cup and join us?'

Pamela made some excuse about having to count the linen.

'Remember when you were a child and stayed with us for a while?' Charles said, his face wreathed in smiles.

'And Lord William invited me to tea and took me to the barn to visit his old hunter. He was such a nice old man. We used to have battles with his soldiers and he'd let me win.' She laughed, and bringing out the lead soldier from her pocket stood it on the table. 'This belongs with the set if you've still got it. I couldn't bear to part with it and it became a sort of talisman. Some of the paint's missing, I'm afraid.'

Charles picked it up and turned it over in his fingers. 'The soldiers are yours. Lord William bequeathed them to you along with the money. I thought it better if I kept them until you grew up. They're quite valuable.'

'Will you look after them a bit longer? One day I'll buy a house of my own.' She glanced at her daughter who was seated contentedly in Brenda's lap being fed on cake. 'I'd really like Saffy to grow up in the country.'

Charles leaned forward. 'The Ryker's old place will be going on the market soon. Most of the land was sold off for the bungalows. Even so, there's a decent-sized garden left, and the house itself had quite a lot of character before it was redecorated.'

Brenda made a face. 'It's pink and blue cosy, with tea roses on the walls and frilly cross-over curtains. The present owner has no taste.'

'Now, now, my dear.'

'If I recall, Charles, that last observation came from you.'

Grinning, he threw up his hands in surrender. 'Have you ever been inside it? If you'd like to have a quick look round I have the key.'

After tea, they trooped up to the solid stone house. Janey thought if the fireplace was opened up in the lounge, the paint stripped from the beams and the walls painted a soft cream, it would be so welcoming. The house was a nice size and the converted attic was perfect for a studio. She dragged her mind back to reality and grinned. 'I couldn't begin to afford a place like this.'

'Couldn't you?' Charles's blue eyes were twinkling. '*You* young lady, are in for a bit of a surprise.'

And she was. There was a substantial amount of money invested for her. She decided to leave it in Charles Wyman's hands for the time being. Besides, the house wasn't on the market yet. When it was he was much better equipped to handle the purchase for her.

There was a hunger growing in her, a hankering to build a nest for herself and her child. Devlin was right. Mistral must be capitalized on. The signature would furnish her with the means to achieve it.

Despite her earlier misgivings, she did find inspiration in Winterbrook. Goblin faces in the bog, bats with human eyes in the purple dusk. There were creatures in the dark, mossy tree roots, their faces puckered like lost and abandoned children.

If Griff was with her now she knew she wouldn't have allowed herself to be swayed by money. She'd close her eyes and feel the earth turn, and her hand would know the power of that which lay beneath her consciousness.

'Did Griff say anything about what happened to me in London?' she asked Phil one evening.

And Phil, who knew everything without being told, said, 'Griff wouldn't discuss anything confidential between you.' He placed the kettle on the hob and gave her a comfortable smile. 'Issues don't just go away because you avoid them, Janey love. Jack Bellamy has come out of one prison, and gone into another.'

'What do you mean?' she whispered, feeling the knot of pain gather in her temple.

'He's been in that cottage for six weeks and the shutters are still on the windows. He's living in the dark.'

'He didn't do it, you know. He didn't lay one finger on me.' Her mouth formed into a painful grimace. 'I feel so guilty. I don't know what to do. I just don't know what to do.'

'If you know he didn't do it, you must know who did?'

Her eyes slid from his. 'I told you all I can. I don't know what to do.'

'Yes you do.' There was no bending in Phil as he handed her the cup of tea. 'You know *exactly* what must be done.'

Her hand sought the wooden Griffin hanging round her neck. Instead, it closed around the heart Mary and Douglas Yates had given her.

Tomorrow, I'll visit my father, she decided. *After I've been to the big house to say goodbye to everyone, and just before I go back to London. I'll tell him I know he's innocent. I owe him that, at least.*

The next day Janey put Saffy in her pushchair and walked over to Canford Cottage. She stared at the place. It was depressing with its shuttered eyes. A rusted gutter flaked paint, mould grew on the window sills. The gate sagged open on its hinges. A thin wisp of smoke curled from the chimney.

It was the house of a recluse, set amongst a decaying garden. It needed sunshine to warm it, love and laughter to bring it to life again.

He was inside – her father, frightened to face the daylight. Saffy's grandfather. *His life is in ruins and it's all my fault! How can I face him?*

Her hand trembled as she softly knocked at the door. She waited for the sound of footsteps, her heart pounding. Nothing. She pressed her face against the door to hear only the echo of her heart pulsing in her ear.

She knocked again, without result. He wasn't in. Relief defeated her disappointment. Taking a note pad and pen from her bag she wrote him a polite little note saying she'd called, then stuffing it through the letter box, turned, and hurried away.

Inside, Jack jerked awake. He thought he'd heard a noise. He listened for a moment, but heard only the wind sighing a dirge around the house. Rising from his chair, he threw another log on the fire, stirring it into flames with his foot. He gave a grim smile as he stared at it.

He couldn't get used to being his own master, couldn't remember what life had been like before prison. As for the future? He didn't have the will left to plan it. He'd been robbed of it in that awful place. He couldn't seem to function without being told what to do, where to go.

He'd thought freedom would be easy, but it wasn't. He felt exposed in the daylight, and resorted to doing things at night.

Mary brought him shopping once a week. Poor Mary. She didn't know how to handle him. He didn't know how to handle himself! He'd gone from one prison to another. This one was of his own making, and he couldn't find the key to let himself out.

On his return from America, Devlin found Janey hard at work.

She was painting with a renewed vigour, so he asked the agency to send the young nanny back to them and set about making sure she was kept fed and comfortable.

There was a change in her, a remoteness he couldn't put his finger on. He figured that she felt awkward after what had occurred between them.

He still burned with frustrated embarrassment when he thought about it, but that didn't alter the fact that he wanted her with every breath he took. Damn it! Why had he let it bother him? He should have just taken her, pretended she was a prostitute. But how could he have when he loved her?

She seemed tireless, the work she produced brilliant in its concept. She started the next one before the paint dried on the canvas, sometimes painting two at a time if they were related in some way.

In the corner of her studio was a separate easel, and on it a canvas with a painting taking shape. It interested him. Each day it grew, by one careful brush stroke after another. He'd never seen her work like this, so patiently, so mathematical. After she caught him examining it, a cloth was thrown over it. She gave him a slow, steady look. 'Leave it. It isn't for sale.'

April came. The rain showers sparkled, and the parks glistened with daffodils. The grimy diesel smell of London began to change. People exchanged smiles, joggers came out of the brickwork, ducks wagged their tails in the park and trees blossomed.

Janey didn't notice. She painted non-stop, her concentration absolute.

At the beginning of June there were enough canvasses for the exhibition Devlin had planned. Nothing cheap about this one. He'd invited everybody who was anybody.

She argued with him when he asked her to be at the opening.

'What for? I have work to do. Besides, I have nothing to wear.'

'You need to be seen and it won't hurt you to do a bit of networking.' He bought her a dress of black silk, with a drifting, tied-dyed purple scarf to wind around her neck and trail down her back. He called in a top hairdresser to style her hair.

She looked stunning, and behaved perfectly. She answered questions about her work, accepting the accolades with self-assurance.

Janey enjoyed assuming the role of sophisticate for the evening. There was a lot of pretentious talk going on, each art lover attempting to out-do the other in the art of swallowing the dictionary.

Red dots gradually appeared on her work as Devlin, the astute salesman, conducted his business. He oozed charm and grace. A naturally elegant and charming man, he was in his element working the crowd. A smile here, a flirting word there, a practised laugh.

She grinned widely when she caught his eye, and winked over her glass at him. Then she spotted a black-bearded man in a cloak wearing a pair of round old-fashioned glasses. He was holding a long black cigarette holder, and was smiling and nodding to himself. Her insides churned with laughter. The ghost of Toulouse-Lautrec was nodding his approval. What better endorsement could she have?

She nearly lost her composure open when Pauline came in. She was with an older woman of exquisite beauty. A momentary hush fell over the crowd, then voices began to babble again. She sidled over to Devlin. 'Who's that?'

'Sarah Wyman. She's a bitch, but she's loaded. Rumour has it she's about to marry a viscount.'

Sarah Wyman! Curiously, Janey stared at her. Pauline had certainly worked her way up in the world.

'I don't know who the other woman is,' Devlin said.

'I do. She's my sister.' She glanced frantically around her. 'Is there anywhere I can hide? She doesn't know I'm Mistral.'

A pained expression flitted over Devlin's face. 'Isn't it about time she learned how talented her sister is?'

Recognition dawned in Pauline's eyes when she glanced across the room, then her face was averted.

A snub from her own sister! Janey's face began to burn. Toulouse-Lautrec came to stand next to them. 'Excellent, just excellent. You have talent.'

'Not as much as you,' Janey murmured absently. 'None of the Mistral paintings will ever rival *At the Moulin Rouge*.'

'Quite so,' he said drily. 'Am I to take that to mean you've read my humble reviews?'

Devlin dug her gently in the ribs. There was amusement in his voice. 'Wake up, Janey. Perhaps I should introduce you. Mistral, meet Caleb Price.'

'*The* art critic!' She was laughing as she turned towards him. 'It's lovely to meet you, and yes, I have read your reviews. Devlin's determined to educate me about the art world, and *made me* read them. I wouldn't describe them as humble, though. You were vitriolic about Lee Van Flemming's work.'

Caleb's grin displayed a row of small, shark-like teeth. 'I'll regard that as a compliment. Anyone who paints as badly as him is *masquerading* as an artist. *You*, on the other hand, show great promise. Who did you study under?'

'My father.' Devlin give a swift intake of breath and she smiled at him. 'He's the artist, John Gregory.' A hand closed around her wrist signalled Devlin's annoyance. She slid her hand into his, gently squeezing it.

She wondered why her father hadn't contacted her. Perhaps he couldn't bring himself to forgive her. This public acknowledgment was one small step to compensate him for all those years in prison.

'A competent artist in his field,' Caleb was saying. 'I haven't seen anything fresh of his on the market lately.'

'He hasn't been well. He lives quietly in the country now.'

I'll go to him soon – my father. Try again. I'll ask his forgivenes, and somehow – somehow I'll find a way to make his life whole again.

She excused herself and drifted to Pauline's side.

They kissed the air each side of the other's cheek. 'How's Justin? You must bring him to see me one day.'

'What are *you* doing here?' Pauline hissed.

Beginning to enjoy herself, she raised an astonished eyebrow. 'Why on earth shouldn't I be here?'

Devlin appeared from nowhere to kiss her on the cheek.

'Could you come over here, darling. The press wants a photograph of you with Caleb Price.'

When the photo session was over, there was a sudden shriek from the door. '*Daaahling!*' Dion and Stephen bustled forward, all silk shirts and Afro hairstyles. Each hugged her in turn.

'Love your hair!' Dion shrieked. 'Guess who we ran into? Such a surprise.'

'*I* wanted to tell her that?'

'Don't be such a baby.' Dion gave an exasperated grimace. 'Oh, go on then, Stephen. I can't bear it when you sulk.'

'Sandy Carter.' Stephen's sulk became a smile. 'She's got a small part in *The Mousetrap*.'

She threw up her hands. 'Not the mouse?'

'Very funny,' they both said together.

'You must bring Sandy with you tonight,' Devlin said, laughing. He took her by the elbow and steered her away. 'See if she's got a couple of girlfriends to even things up.'

Janey grabbed a glass of champagne from a tray. 'What's going on tonight.'

'It was going to be a small surprise party for you. Tim's in town, and Griff has managed to get the night off.'

They almost collided with Sarah Wyman. Pauline was one step behind.

Devlin practised his sincere smile. 'Have you met Mistral, Sarah?'

'I doubt it.' A pair of eyes checked her out, like wasps at an apple core. Without turning, she said. 'Go and fetch me a glass of champagne, Pauline. There's a dear.'

Giving the simpering smile she'd perfected as a child, Pauline hurried off to do as she was bid.

'I understand you're Pauline's sister.'

Pauline had obviously decided that association by fame was perfectly acceptable. 'We share a mother.'

Sarah's eyes narrowed. 'I wondered about the lack of similarity.'

In case she chose to think differently, Janey made it absolutely clear. 'Pauline and I are *nothing* alike.'

Giving a bored smile, Sarah nodded. 'I might buy one of your paintings. Which one would you recommend?'

'*Thorns*.'

'Go and buy me *Thorns*,' she said, when Pauline came back with her champagne.

Sarah Wyman was flaunting her power over Pauline, deliberately humiliating her. Although there was no love lost between herself and her sister, Janey didn't like it. She didn't intend to be patronized, either. She took Pauline's hand. 'Would you attend to Mrs Wyman personally, please, Devlin. I'd like to talk to my sister. And check on the price of *Thorns*. I thought the ticket was a little indistinct?'

Expression bland, Devlin nodded.

She steered Pauline through to Devlin's office. 'Why do you allow her to treat you like that?'

Pauline shrugged. 'Martin's set up an office in London. She's helping us meet the right people.' She stared at a painting on the wall. 'I had no idea you were Mistral.'

'You never bothered to ask.' Her head slanted to one side. 'Is Justin in London with you and your husband? I'd like to meet them both.'

'Justin's in Bournemouth. He has a nanny.'

'Have you got a photograph?'

Pauline took a photograph of a pale-looking infant from her purse. 'Keep it.'

There was a helplessness about Justin that stirred the pot of pity in Janey's heart. 'He looks so sweet.'

'Actually, he's a brat,' Pauline said.

And you're a cold-hearted bitch. 'Has your father improved, at all?'

'His hand moves a bit and he can mumble a few words.' Her face took on a martyred look. 'I still can't believe Pamela went off and left him as soon as he took ill. It's costing us a fortune in private nursing fees.'

'You could look after him yourself.'

'With my weak stomach?'

'Then why don't you look after Justin yourself. It would save paying a nanny.'

Pauline shuddered. 'The last time I picked him up he vomited on me. Besides, he cries all the time and I can't stand it.' She stood up, saying casually, 'I really must get back to Sarah. She wants me to help her dress for a dinner party.'

'Has she lost the use of her arms, or is she practising to be an aristocrat?'

'You just don't understand.'

'Yes I do.' She bit back the urge to tell Pauline to just be herself, when she realized she *was* being herself. They had very little in common. 'If you ever need me you just have to ask.'

'I can't imagine why I should.' Her sister's eyes speculated on her for a moment, then she managed a smile notable for its insincerity. 'Thanks, Janey. I'll remember that.'

An hour later the gallery closed. Devlin was jubilant. 'A sell out! And a photo to go in the paper with Caleb Price's review.'

'Priceless,' she murmured. Easing her feet out of her shoes she subsided on to a chair and rubbed her toes against the back of her ankles. 'How much am I worth, Devlin?'

A frown replaced his smile. 'I haven't calculated what today's little lot will bring in.'

'Totally, I mean.'

'Why do you ask?'

'Why have I *needed* to ask? Shouldn't I be getting statements or something?'

'You're right.' He took her hands and pulled her upright, kissing her lightly on the nose. 'I'll have a detailed statement drawn up for you as soon as I've got some spare time. Let's go.'

'Yes, let's. I want to climb out of this shroud before the party.'

Devlin had prepared finger foods for the party, and plenty of them. Griff arrived on the doorstep at the same time as Tim. They both dashed upstairs to see Saffy before she was put to bed.

'I thought you came to see me,' she grumbled when they came down. Immediately, Tim swept her into his arms and kissed her.

Sandy poked her in the ribs. 'Introduce me to the sailor.'

'Introduce yourself' Janey surrendered herself to Griff's hug. 'You look better than the last time I saw you,' she whispered in his ear.

'I'll try and stay awake this time.' He gently bit her earlobe, surprising her.

It was a lovely party. Devlin was a perfect host, her guests well-behaved. Everyone got tipsy enough to lose a few inhibitions. One by one, they all fell asleep where they dropped.

Devlin's glance roved over them all. Tim was on the couch, his arms around Sandy and Blaise, who snuggled against his chest. 'Typical bloody sailor,' he muttered.

Dion and Stephen were stretched out on the floor. He took a smouldering joint from between Stephen's fingers and stubbed it out in the ashtray before he burst into flames.

Griff was in an armchair. Janey leaned precariously against his knees, her hair a fall of silver against his leg. He gazed thoughtfully at Griff for a moment. There seemed to be a special bond between them, almost like brother and sister.

'Bed for you, princess.' He picked her up and carried her upstairs. She didn't stir when he pulled the covers over her. He pressed a kiss against her forehead. 'Don't imagine I'm going to let you go without a fight. I'm going to make myself so indispensable, you won't be able to live without me.'

She turned over on her side, drew her knees up and whispered sleepily, 'Goodnight, Drifter.'

When Mary finished reading the article she cut it from the paper and turned to her husband. 'I'm going to show this to Jack.'

'He told you not to interfere.'

'This isn't interfering. Did you read it? Janey said she was his daughter. She told the whole world.'

Douglas sighed as he took her hands in his. 'This is a personal matter between them. You can't push your way into people's lives like this. I forbid you to mention Janey to him. In fact, I wish you wouldn't go down there at all.'

'If I didn't, he wouldn't eat.'

'Then let him starve. Jack's a grown man. If you stopped babying him, he'd have to fend for himself.'

'I never thought you'd turn against him, Douglas.'

'Oh, for God's sake!' Douglas threw the paper aside and rose to his feet. 'Not one day has gone by over the past few years when I haven't been force-fed your brother's troubles. I'm old. I want to enjoy the time I've got left.' He slammed the door as he left.

Tears came into Mary's eyes as she watched him walk across the garden. He was right. She should leave Jack to fend for himself. It wasn't as if he didn't have transport. His car was in perfect working order, Douglas had seen to that.

Later, she took a cup of tea and some biscuits out to the shed. 'You're right. I'm sorry.'

Douglas took her hand and held it against his cheek. 'It will work out for the best, love. Just you wait and see.'

When Mary didn't come with his shopping, Jack thought she might be sick. He left it a couple of days, living off baked beans, stale bread and fruit from the garden.

When she didn't arrive the following week he began to worry, and wished he'd had the telephone service connected. He supposed it was about time he did something about it.

A couple of days later, his larder was empty and he was hungry. Heart leaping in panic, he made his way to the front door, where Douglas had left the car keys on the hook. He didn't even know if he could still remember how to drive.

His fingers trembled so much that he dropped the keys. They slid across the tiles and under the hall-stand.

Kneeling, he scrabbled around in the dust. A folded scrap of paper came out with the keys.

Janey. The signature startled him. He unfolded the note, smoothing it out on his knee. *Dear Mr Bellamy*. The name been scored through, and *Father* substituted. Jack's eyes squeezed shut for a second or two. *I'm sorry I missed you. If you'd care to write or telephone me, I'd be happy to hear from you. P.S. You have a granddaughter called Saffy*.

The note was date-marked six months previously. All that time wasted. He burst into tears. He'd been stupid hiding indoors and wallowing in self-pity. From now on he must learn to cope with life, be the sort of father she could be proud of. After a while, his tears stopped and he began to smile.

Rising to his feet he threw open the door to the cottage. The air smelled clean and fresh as it poured into his lungs. He'd forgotten how cleansing light was. Eyes narrowed against its glare, he took his first stumbling steps outside in months – out of the darkness and into the daylight.

CHAPTER THIRTEEN

'Charles told me you have some puppies needing a home.'

'Aye, I have that.' Phil stood to one side to allow John Smith into the cottage. 'The poor little buggers were dumped on the main road.'

Gazing at the sleeping pups, John raised an eyebrow. 'What are they?'

'Can't rightly tell,' Phil said comfortably. 'Like most of us, they didn't come with a pedigree.'

Grey eyes battled with black ones for a few seconds. Neither won.

'I meant what gender, Mr Tyler?'

'Titles don't sit easy with me. The name's Phil.' Phil grinned as he held out his hand, leaving John with the uncomfortable feeling he'd seen right through him.

'John.' A small, abashed smile inched across his face. 'I've never owned a dog.'

'They're bitches.'

'I've never owned a bitch, either.'

Phil chuckled 'The kettle's on the boil, I'll make us some tea. The black-eared one is Gypsy. She belongs to Susie up at the big house, though she's boarding with me for the time being.'

'So, I can have my choice of the other two?'

'One will choose you when they wake. The other is for Jack Bellamy. His dog died last year. He'll be needing another.'

'He's the recluse up at Canford Cottage?'

'You don't miss much, do you?' Phil set a mug of thick brown liquid down in front of him. 'There's some who value privacy more than others.'

'And some who have more to hide?'

'Aye.' John was subject to a long uncomfortable stare. 'Perhaps they figure their business belongs to themselves. To my way of thinking, that man got more than he deserved.'

Intrigued, John stared back at him. He knew about the case. Charles had discussed it with him when he'd inquired about buying Canford Cottage. He'd said Jack Bellamy might have been used as a scapegoat. Odd that two such different men should be of like mind.

'It was you who found the girl, wasn't it?'

Phil's body became as still as stone. 'Aye, me and my son. I said my piece at the trial, and see no reason to repeat it to an outsider.'

'An outsider could present an unbiased viewpoint because he lacks emotional involvement,' John said just as bluntly. 'You should consider that before you make snap judgments.'

'Could be I should. I'll think on it.'

Prickly customer, John thought, and as close as an oyster. Uncomfortable, he was relieved when the puppies decided to wake up. One immediately tried to clamber up his leg, peeing excitedly on his shoe in the process. When he lifted her to his lap, she stood against his chest, aiming high-pitched yelps at his ear.

'Stop nagging,' he said, grinning as she leaped up and down, trying to lick his chin.

Phil chuckled. 'She's the liveliest one of the three. She'll need a lot of exercise, but you look as if you could do with some yourself.'

The yelps changed into short yaps as the puppy attacked the buttons on his cardigan. He turned her over on her back and tickled her belly. 'I'll call you Nellie, after Melba, the opera singer.'

'She's the same shape, I reckon.' Phil said, and the tension eased when they laughed. 'I'll be helping Jack Bellamy set his cottage to rights in the morning. Drop over in a day or so and meet him?'

So he hadn't been found wanting, after all. John smiled as he met Phil's enigmatic glance square on, both knowing he would.

There was a mystery here. A horrendous crime had been committed in this sleepy little village. In John's experience, mistakes weren't usually made when bringing a criminal to justice. But the act of rape, especially when involving a child, was highly emotive. People were uncomfortable with it. It would have been dealt with as quickly as possible, then hushed up.

It struck him as odd that the perpetrator of the crime would come back to live in the place where it had been committed, though – very odd!

He stopped at the village store to pick up some cans of dog food and a loaf of bread. When he got home, he installed Nellie in a cardboard box in the kitchen, then went through to the lounge and dialled a number in London.

Within five minutes he had the information he sought.

'Jane Renfrew again,' he whispered, shaken to the core as he gazed at the painting of the lilies. It was almost as if fate had thrown them together. But for what purpose: to investigate the crime? Jack Bellamy had been convicted on circumstantial evidence. The trail was cold. All the same, he didn't like unsolved mysteries.

The next morning, he took the early train to London.

Jack had barely begun to prise the boards from the windows when Phil Tyler arrived.

'You look like a man in need of companionship, and I've got a pup who needs a good home. Her name's Daisy.'

Jack stared at him for a second, not knowing quite what to do until the plank of wood in his hands was exchanged for a fat, brown puppy. 'Where do you want the wood stacked?'

Jack's brain scrambled in panic when faced with this decision. He thought for a while. 'The woodshed, I guess.' Then faster, more decisively as the puppy licked his hand. 'Yes, the woodshed. I'll just settle Daisy in the kitchen.'

They worked in silence for most of the morning, then by common consent downed their tools.

'They do a good lunch up at the Thatcher's Arms,' Phil said.

A knot of worry inched across Jack's forehead. 'Is Joe still the landlord?'

Phil's thumb jerked towards the churchyard. 'Joe's over yonder. He and his missus passed on several years ago. A young couple have taken over. They keep a good table.'

Panic attacked and Jack searched for an excuse. 'I haven't been to the bank lately.'

'No problem,' Phil said gently. 'I reckon young Janey would be upset if I couldn't manage to buy her dad lunch.'

Jack thought he might burst with the sudden uplift of pride be experienced. 'Did she tell you I was her father?'

'Aye, she told me the last time she came to visit. She's doing quite well for herself from what I gather.' Phil took the newspaper cutting from his pocket. 'See, here's her photograph with some weird-looking feller.'

'What does it say?'

'Don't rightly know. I'm not much good at reading and such. I thought you might tell me.' Snatching the cutting from Phil's fingers Jack began to read, his words tripping over each other in their eagerness to get out. 'She's using the name Mistral . . . sell out . . . another exhibition in America.' He glanced up at Phil, his eyes shining. 'She said she's my daughter.'

'Aye, well why shouldn't she? 'Tis nothing for her to be ashamed of.'

'But that means? Tell me about her,' he said, eagerly. 'How is she, what's she been doing?'

Phil shrugged into his jacket. 'A man can't talk on an empty stomach, and half a pint of bitter would slide down real well on such a warm day, I reckon.' He ambled off towards the road, leaving Jack to follow.

Within two days, Canford Cottage was clean inside and out, and they'd started on the garden.

There was a certain enjoyment in physical work, Jack thought, enjoying the motion of the scythe slipping through the long grass. He tired easily though, and his muscles protested every time he took a rest. For the last two nights he'd slept like a dog, waking in the morning with every joint aching – and Daisy eager to greet him.

'Take it nice and easy,' Phil had said. 'It's not a race.'

But it seemed like a race to Jack. He was ashamed of the state he'd fallen into.

He wanted his house in order before he contacted Janey and invited her to visit.

He winced as he stopped for a breather. Lowering himself to the ground under the shade of a tree, he drew the chamois gardening gloves from his hands and flipped the top from a bottle of brown ale. Carefully, he flexed his palms. 'My hands haven't been this blistered since I was apprenticed to my father's boatyard.'

'They'll soon harden up.' Phil handed him a pastie, courtesy of young Susie. She often visited, using his kitchen to practise the recipes Ada taught her. She was a right nice little cook. Sometimes Pamela came with her, and they'd sit and jaw over a cup of tea. He didn't usually feel comfortable around women, but Pamela was different. Phil grinned. The only thing wrong with her was the ring on her finger. It was no good hankering after something that couldn't be.

'Tell me about the process of building boats. I suppose it's a bit like making cars.'

'Nothing like it.' Leaning back against the tree, Jack grinned with pleasure. 'A boat . . . a real boat, is alive.'

'*Oh, go on!*' he teased.

'It's true. Have you ever been on the ocean?'

'Can't say I've ever needed anything but the earth beneath my feet.'

'One day I'll take you out. When you feel a boat respond to your touch, when you experience the deck quivering beneath your feet and the wind in your hair, when you feel the ocean singing in your veins, then you'll *know* she's got a heart and a soul, just like a woman.'

As clearly as if she'd spoken on the wind, Phil heard Janey on the man's breath. He blinked back tears when Jack's eyes clouded over. 'I had a good boat once, with a brave heart. She was named *Margaret Jane*. Somebody set fire to her. She burnt to the waterline, and it damned near broke my heart.'

'Did you ever think of building another?'

'She'd have been too expensive, and I didn't really have time, then.'

'You have now?'

His brow furrowed in thought. 'And the money from the sale of the yard.' Leaping to his feet Jack stepped out into the sunshine. Sliding his companion a sideways look, he grinned. 'I have the original plans my father drew up. Would you like to help me build her?' He threw his arms wide as a cloud moved over the sun. 'We could call her *Saffy Jane*.'

'That we could, but I doubt I'd be much use to you. I prefer to plant seeds and watch them grow.'

Jack cast a long shadow shaped like a cross when the sun returned in all its brightness. Hairs prickled at the nape of Phil's neck and he was filled with a sudden sense of urgency. 'How long will the boat take to build?'

'*She*.' Jack's grin was as wide and hungry as the ocean. 'A boat is a she. Twelve months if all goes well.'

They turned as the gate squeaked a protest.

'Good day, Phil.' John stepped forward, introduced himself and said to Jack, 'I hope you don't mind me dropping in.'

'Not at all. We were just going inside to look at some plans. I'm trying to talk Phil into helping me build a boat.'

'I grew up on a barge, if that's any help, and I've got plenty of spare time on my hands.'

Phil gazed from one to the other and thought: *you're exactly the sort of help he needs.*

Janey received her father's letter at the end of July. Immediately, she was all smiles, all bounce, reading bits out to Devlin as he prepared a side salad to serve with the Chicken kiev.

'He's building a boat in his back garden. Griff's father is helping him, and John Smith.' Her eyes were shining blue as they came up to his, but they were focused somewhere in the past. 'John Smith? He keeps cropping up in my life. How very odd.'

'Very,' Devlin muttered, grinning as he wondered who the hell John Smith was.

'I'm going to see my father at the weekend.'

'I'll drive you.'

She was distant, evasive. 'There's really no need. I can take a train.'

'I'd like to meet him,' Devlin persisted, still annoyed that she'd kept her relationship with John Gregory a secret.

'Not this time.'

'What's got into you, Janey?' He gave her the benefit of his frown. Not that it did any good. Of late, she'd displayed an unexpectedly independent streak.

She worked like one possessed, rising early and only stopping for meals. She spent an hour or so playing with Saffy before her bedtime. Often she forgot the time, and sometimes, the day.

She glared back at him. 'Do I have to spell it out for you? I didn't think you were totally lacking in sensitivity, Devlin.'

Christ! He'd forgotten the circumstances of this meeting. How could he have? His pride deflated like a punctured balloon. 'Of course! How stupid of me.' Placing the salads into the refrigerator he slid his arms around her.

'Don't,' she said, pushing him away.

He was losing her. Inch by inch he was losing her, and he didn't know what to do about it.

He stared at her in angry bafflement. 'Why did you do that?'

'Do what?' She looked totally mystified.

'Push me away when I touched you.'

She slid from her chair and stood up. Her body was a mass of pent-up energy. 'I feel edgy. I have to get back to work.'

How infuriating she was. 'Haven't you done enough for one day? You're going to have a breakdown if you're not careful. You need to relax. I'll take you out dancing or something.'

Her jaw tightened. 'I can't dance very well. Besides, if you want Mistral paintings I have to work.'

He took her by the shoulders and gently shook her. 'Something's wrong, Janey. What is it?'

'Nothing's wrong. I just want to work. I want to get everything over and done with.' She shrugged away from his touch for the second time. 'Damn it, Devlin, stop pushing me.'

He was devastated when she placed her hands against her face and began to sob.

'Janey, angel, what is it?'

'Leave me alone,' she shouted and ran from the room.

He let her cry for a while. Later, when he thought the time was right, he took up a tray with a pot of tea and some dainty asparagus and chicken sandwiches.

She was working on the abstract, but she quickly threw the cloth over it and joined him. Her face was set and pale, her eyes red from crying.

'I'm sorry,' she said straight away. 'There's nothing wrong. I was listening to a news broadcast about Vietnam before I came down.'

Devlin said nothing, but his jaw tightened.

'How is it they managed to put two men on the moon last month, but can't stop the war in Vietnam?'

'Drifter isn't in Vietnam, if that's what's eating at you.'

Her mouth and eyes formed three surprised ovals, reminding him of a Modigliani portrait.

'Grand-pappy pulled strings and got wonder boy a nice little desk job in Washington.'

'Why didn't you tell me?'

How can you look so accusing? I'll put a stop to this, right now I'll crush Drifter and make you spit him out. Be damned if I'll spare you, this time.

'Wait there. I want to show you something.' Taking the stairs two at a time he removed a file from the cabinet in the office. When he returned, he slammed it on the table in front of her.

'I wasn't going to show you this, but it's time you faced facts. I don't imagine you'll thank me for it.'

One finger cagily touched it, as if it might suddenly spit venom at her. The smear of paint she left was as blue and wounded as her eyes. He felt like all kinds of a heel, but it was too late to change his mind. He left her staring at it, and strode away – out through the front door into the evening sunshine. He had no idea of where he was going, and didn't really care. All he needed was a pub. He intended to get drunk. Janey could get her own damn dinner if she wanted to eat! He was through babying her.

It didn't take Janey long to open the file. It contained a dozen or so published articles, titled *An American in London*. They were biting accounts of the life of the people who'd lived in the Finsbury Park house. She read each one carefully.

Connor, Felicity, Stephen and Dion – everyone was there, including Devlin and herself. Drifter had examined every weakness, and with the cruelty and delicacy of a cat with a nest of mice to play with, had shredded the skin from them all.

Why hadn't she noticed he was studying them like insects impaled in a skin? *Because I was blinded by stupid, adolescent first love.* It had been a long, lingering sickness, one she hadn't quite recovered from yet. But this dose of medicine was designed to have the effect of a laxative.

The writing was slick and sardonic. It was an exposé of the cruelest sort, as if Drifter had imagined himself some superior being standing judgement over them all.

There was a talented female artist who'd lost the meaning of subtlety when dealing with people. Because her emotions came in tubes of primary colours, when she mixed them she only got shades of grey.

There was enough truth in the statement to shatter her. Crushed, she flung herself into a chair. Drifter had been nothing but a voyeur. Why had he done this to her, to any of them! There were three other papers in the file. One was a newspaper cutting announcing Darius Taunt had been posted to Washington. She examined the photograph, imprinting it on her mind. This was a different man to the one she'd known. Clean-shaven and smart in his uniform, he was smiling into the camera. How sincere he looked, she thought bitterly, and how perfectly charming. *She despised him!*

Then there was Drifter with Ingram Taunt, his paternal grandfather. They were attending the funeral of Darius Rhodes. They looked very much alike as they gazed at each other. The third cutting was a biographical article about the Taunt family, dated fifteen years previously. Drifter's parents had drowned when he was young. A boating accident in France. There was a picture of his mother, tall and slim, her hair flowing about her shoulders in long fair ripples. *Lost in the mistral wind*, it said, making her death seem somehow romantic.

The mistral wind! She suddenly felt sick. Taking the article she strode to her bedroom and stared at herself in the mirror. Her hate was transferred to Devlin. He'd known. He'd always known!

'Devlin!' she yelled down the stairs. 'Why didn't you tell me I looked like his mother?'

Saffy's nanny gave her a slightly apprehensive glance when she stormed into the kitchen to confront him.

'Mr Cox has gone out,' she said. 'I saw him turn the corner as I came across the park. Is everything all right?'

Janey's bad mood melted away when Saffy smiled and held out her arms. 'Mum, mum, mum!'

'Everything's fine. I'll take over if you like. You can go home early.'

'Well, if you're sure. Thank you, that's very kind of you.'

Left alone with Saffy, Janey finished spooning a bowl of mush into her mouth, then gave her half a banana to eat. Afterwards, she took Drifter's child upstairs, playing with her until it was time for bed.

'D'you know something?' she said, exchanging kisses with her daughter. 'Your father wasn't all bad. At least he gave me you.'

Just after she went to bed she heard Devlin arrive home. She was surprised when he knocked on her door. Hurriedly, she threw on her robe.

He peered owlishly at her. 'I s'pose you hate my guts.'

'Not really.' She'd never seen Devlin drunk. She grinned as he swayed unsteadily on his feet. 'Go to bed, Devlin. I'll lock up.'

He wagged a finger at her. 'This can't go on. Being in love with you is hell. I haven't laid a finger on another woman since I met you, let alone anything else. I'm as frustrated as hell. Kiss me goodnight, Janey.'

He ignored her peck on the cheek. Sliding his hand to the back of her head he turned her mouth around to his. Passion was lost in the whisky fumes on his breath. She found it hard not to recoil when he backed her into the room and against the bed.

He was precious to her, and she took him so very much for granted. She wished she could love him the way he wanted – wished she could offer herself to him without reservation. What was the matter with her? Her emotions were shades of grey, Drifter had said. *Shades of grey?*

'You don't have to worry,' he whispered. 'I've had too much to drink to get a hard-on.' He released her with a lop-sided grin. ' 'Sides which, I wouldn't hurt you for all the tea in China. Marry me, Janey.'

Shades of grey, like a winter sea stretching to a grey horizon. Beyond that, more shades of grey. He deserved more woman than that.

'Ask me in the morning, Dev. When you're sober.'

He gazed at her for a moment, his eyes all silvery and sad. 'I don't think I want to hear your answer when I'm sober. Goodnight, angel.' He turned and ambled away.

They were awkward with each other at breakfast.

Devlin's face was haggard as he swallowed a couple of codeine tablets with some coffee. He winced when Saffy banged her spoon on the table. 'Can you do that quietly, my darling?' he said piteously. 'Uncle Devlin is dying.' A pair of red-rimed eyes touched her for a second, then slid away. 'Did I say or do anything I should apologize for last night?'

Her hand covered his for a moment. 'Nothing. Why don't you go back to bed for a while?'

'I think I might.' He turned at the door, his teeth worrying at his bottom lip. 'You're absolutely sure?'

'Positive.'

He looked so relieved she wanted to giggle. She waited for a decent interval, giving him time to get out of earshot.

Janey had taken the early train. Paying the taxi off, she gazed at Canford Cottage, marvelling at the change in the place. She had not told her father she was coming.

Someone had tamed the garden wilderness, and the windows gleamed with morning sunlight.

She inhaled the subtle mixed fragrances of wild herbs, summer flowers, and newly-mown grass. Joy filled her to the brim. Before too long she'd come back to live, and she'd never go away again.

'Doggy,' Saffy whispered, pulling at her hand. And there was a dog, a fat brown puppy sniffing in the long grass at the base of an apple tree.

Releasing her daughter's hand, Janey watched the child run towards the pup, waving her arms and laughing.

Jack emerged from the house just as Saffy and dog met in the middle of his lawn. His eyes widened as the pair collided, then Saffy was flat on her back, giggling, and the pup was standing on her, its tail whipping back and forth, licking her face.

'Get off, Daisy.' Taking the pup by the scruff of the neck he dragged it aside and stood Saffy up. He squatted on his haunches in front of her and said wonderingly 'Now, young lady, where might you have come from?'

'Dadda,' Saffy said, one finger reaching out to touch his scar.

'No, I'm not your dad.' He glanced towards the gate and a grin dawned on his face when their eyes met. 'But I've got a wonderful feeling I could be your granddad.'

Janey was tall and graceful in flared jeans and a smocked, cheesecloth top. The sun was behind her. Her hair absorbed the rays and shone with a silver brightness that made his eyes ache.

Jack wanted to laugh, and he wanted to cry. He wanted to leap into the air and swing from the branches of the tree, hollering like Tarzan. The first two were undignified, the second, although just as undignified, was also impossible for a man with his aching bones. He couldn't stop grinning, as if his lips had been starched into position.

She came towards him on brown-sandalled feet, her bag swinging from her shoulder. She wasn't much like her mother. Perhaps a touch about the mouth. There was a scattering of freckles across her nose, like grains of golden sand.

Up close, he saw the resemblance to himself. Not that he'd ever doubted Janey was his daughter. He was seeing her through fresh eyes, a grown-up woman with a child of her own. The last time he'd seen her she'd been a child. *The last time he'd seen her?* He didn't want to recall what she'd suffered. Instead, he allowed pride to swell up inside him until he thought he might burst.

'You've come, then?' Banal words, designed to hide the emotion churning inside him.

Her eyes closed for the few seconds it took her to blurt out, 'I'm so sorry you went to prison. It wasn't your fault, I know that now. Can you forgive me?'

He couldn't prevent the tears coming to his eyes. Dear God! What had it cost her to say that? Had she been blaming herself? She'd been a frightened child at the time. He didn't hold her responsible for anything she'd said.

Reaching out, he took her hands in his. 'It's over, Janey love. Forget it and let's concentrate on getting to know one another.' His eyes slid towards Saffy who was charging around the garden after the puppy. 'Perhaps I can be a successful grandfather.'

'Do you think?' Her eyes were uncertain, almost shy. 'Do you think it would be all right if I hugged you? I mean, you wouldn't mind or anything?'

Their arms came round each other, both of them careful at first, stiff, each ready to withdraw from the other's embrace. Slowly she relaxed, her head against his shoulder. Her tears dampened his shirt as he cuddled her against him.

'Hush, Janey,' he comforted. 'Everything's over now.'

Nothing is over, Janey was thinking, *and nothing will be until I can prove your innocence. But I don't know where to start, and I don't know who I can confide in.*

Jack did nothing to change his plans for the weekend. Some of the material for his boat was being delivered. Phil and John came to help him unload them.

Phil greeted Janey with a nod and a smile. 'Griff's taking a week off at the end of September. Why don't you come down for a holiday then?'

'I'll try, but I have work to finish.' It was possible her paintings would be finished by September, that Mistral would be no more. The present series were the best she'd done, full of darkness and power. Each brush-stroke and slash of the palette knife had eradicated a little bit more of Drifter from her heart.

Soon she'd be free of him, her last painting already planned in her mind. A woman in a boat, her hair streaming in the mistral wind as she was ferried across the River Styx. She would keep it for the right time. A moment she was sure would come.

John gave nothing away of his thoughts when Jack referred to her as his daughter. It only confirmed what he already suspected. Then she was laughing at him, teasing him because he hadn't contacted her like he'd said he would, making him splutter apologies and give excuses.

He was flattered by her attention, but bounced back to tell her he'd bought one of her paintings. She was interested in which one, more interested still when he said Charles had offered double what he'd paid for it.

'My agent will be pleased. He'd tell you not to accept the first offer to buy.'

'I have no intention of selling it. I bought it because I love it.'

'Those lilies grow on the banks of the stream in the woods. When spring comes I'll show you the place in the painting.' Her eyes became far away. 'When I was small I used to think the place was my secret, but I daresay you've been there already.'

No . . . no, I haven't. I'd very much like to see it.'

'Then you shall, in the spring.' She moved off then, to stop Saffy eating a snail, admonishing her gently before sliding a kiss through the child's sparse, silky curls.

Saffy's father was Darius Taunt. John felt a twinge of remorse. He'd been responsible for the child losing her father, even though he hadn't known of her existence at the time.

Later, he went into his study and stared at a graph on the wall. He removed a question mark from Janey's name, then picking up a ruler, drew a thin red thread from her to Jack Bellamy. There were already two other lines, connecting her to Pauline Pitt and the late Margaret Renfrew. The jigsaw was slowly taking shape.

At the centre of the graph, like a spider in a web, was Edward Renfrew's name.

CHAPTER FOURTEEN

Concentrating hard, Eddie gathered a ball of spit in his mouth.

'Come along, Mr Renfrew, I'm sure we can do it if we try.'

Filled with loathing, he stared at the smiling face of the nurse. She treated him like a child. He couldn't breathe, eat, or take a crap without her. He hated her, he hated his useless shell of a body and he hated Pauline for never being at home when he wanted her.

'Rest for a moment, left foot forward like a good little soldier, that's right. My, we are being a good boy today.'

Does she have to use that singsong voice? Upstairs, Justin started to cry. He never stopped whining. Tears slid from under Eddie's eyelids. Where was Pauline? She was hardly ever home. It wasn't fair, leaving him here all alone. She wasn't much letter than Pamela.

Anger burned bright in him. He'd never imagined Pamela would find the guts to leave him. When he was better he'd go after her. He'd soon teach the ungrateful bitch what was what!

'Right foot. Try not to drag it, Mr Renfrew . . . wonderful . . . *whoops-a-daisy!*' His face lodged between the pillows of her breasts when she caught him. He caught a whiff of body odour and pink carbolic soap.

'Naughty, naughty!' she said archly, pushing him upright. 'You men are all alike.'

He rolled the ball of spit on his tongue and let it fly. It had no momentum and rolled down his chin. He let out a frustrated cry as she carried him back to his chair and applied a tissue to his chin.

'There, there, Mr Renfrew, don't let's get upset. You did very well today, doctor will be pleased. I'll sit you on the lavatory for a while. You can do your duty whilst I have a little break. We don't want any accidents, do we?'

Eddie did. He hoped she'd fall down the stairs and break her neck. She didn't allow him any privacy by shutting the door! He was seated on the pedestal, his trousers round his ankles when a movement caught his eye.

There was a girl standing in the passage outside. Her back towards him, she was looking out of the window and gazing out to sea. She was wearing some sort of school uniform. She reminded him of Margaret, his first wife. He paled.

'*Pauline?*' When the figure slowly turned towards him and smiled, he tasted her ashes in his mouth. He blinked and she was gone, leaving him shaken.

It's my illness. I imagined Margaret standing there, accusing me with her eyes.

He saw her again the next day. This time she spoke to him. '*Repent your sin.*'

'Never.' His voice came out quite clearly. 'The sins of the parents are visited on the child. You all had to be punished.'

The nurse smiled broadly as her head came between him and Margaret.

'Well done. Hardly any slurring. Now, tell nursie who you were talking to? Has my naughty little man got an imaginary friend?'

Eddie wanted to cry. He hardly ever got visitors. She had no right to interrupt his conversation. Margaret needed to be shown the error of her ways, then God would repent and take her into his fold.

He stared at her, his eyes full of hate. With all the venom he could muster, he whispered, 'Piss off!'

She recoiled for a second, her smile forced, her eyes mean brown marbles. 'My, my, we are in a bad mood today. Perhaps a sedative might improve our disposition.'

The sedative made him feel like shit, and she knew it. He watched her pour a colourless liquid into a glass, hating her.

He pursed his lips, and this time, his ball of spit reached its mark.

'You dirty sod.'

He clamped his mouth shut when she held the glass against it. Her finger and thumb took a grip on his nose, shutting off the air. After a few seconds his mouth fell open and the liquid trickled sweetly across his tongue and down his throat.

'There,' she said, wiping the spit from her face. 'That should keep you quiet for a while.' Her buttocks jerked self-righteously up and down as she marched from the room.

Someone gave a soft giggle. He could see Margaret from the corner of his eye. His crotch became tight as he smiled at her.

Sarah handed Pauline a diamond necklace. 'Do this up, there's a dear.'

Pauline gasped as the stones caught the light. She'd never seen anything quite so beautiful. 'Did Lord Conley give you this?'

'No. It was a gift from an admirer.' Sarah's eyes were faintly malicious as she gazed at the girl's avid face in the mirror. 'Try it on if you like.'

It looked good against the young woman's firm skin. Renfrew's daughter had turned out to be quite pretty. Money would furnish her with style. 'It's a pity you married Martin. You must hate being short of cash all the time.'

A sulky pout came to Pauline's mouth and she flushed. 'My father invested unwisely, and so did Martin. He's hoping to recoup his losses. Noel Chatterton is advising him. Besides . . . I love Martin.'

It sounded as if Pauline was trying to convince herself. Sarah wondered what she'd do when she discovered that Martin and Noel had become lovers? A gleam of amusement came into her eyes. It might be fun to turn this silly little daughter of Renfrew's into a high class whore.

Edward had been so prissy about her, she mused, and although she'd paid him back satisfactorily for his disloyalty, it still rankled. How would he feel if he received photographs of his precious daughter *inflagrante delicto* through the post?

'Why don't you come to the opera with us tonight, dear. I'm sure Martin won't mind me borrowing you for one evening.'

'He's having Noel Chatterton over to play cards,' she said breathlessly. 'I was going to see *The Graduate*, but I'd rather go out with you. You know such interesting people.' Her face fell. 'I haven't got anything suitable to wear to the opera, though.'

'The wardrobe's full of clothes and we're the same size.' Strolling to the wardrobe, Sarah selected a lilac evening gown she'd been photographed in several times. 'Wear this. You may have it if you like.'

'It's lovely,' Pauline gushed. 'Thank you so much.'

Sarah watched her undress. Her figure was petite and perfect. 'I must take you in hand. Strip everything off, then go and shower off that cheap perfume. And we can't have you ruining the line of the dress with granny-type underwear.' Her eyes began to gleam as Pauline self-consciously stepped out of her panties. 'We ought to do something about that bush of yours. It's so prolific. Heloise, see to Mrs Pitt's grooming.'

'*Oui, Madame*.'

So Pauline was waxed, powdered and pampered. Her hair was dressed in a smooth chignon by Sarah's new French maid. She loved the feel of the expensive clothes against her skin, and adored the amethyst necklace Sarah lent her.

'You know, you're quite exquisite when you're dressed properly. You really should have a male escort. Shall I ring a friend of mine and ask him to join us. He's a charming companion, and very generous. It was he who gave me the diamond necklace.'

Pauline's eyes widened.

Yes Pauline, I did have to earn it, but it was a delightful experience as you're yet to find out.

Two hours later, and acting on Sarah's instructions, Lord Conley's Daimler drew to a halt outside the Pitts' rented apartment in Chelsea.

'Tell Martin we might be going on to a party afterwards,' Sarah drawled. 'We don't want him to worry about you being late.'

There was no one in the lounge. Martin's laugh came to her from the bedroom.

'Martin?' she said, pushing open the door. She gasped when two shocked faces turned towards her.

'Oh, dear, we've been sprung,' Noel said lightly. 'I do hope you're not going to be tedious about this, Pauline old thing.'

Martin was dressed in a black negligee. Taken aback, she muttered. 'I'm sorry, I didn't realize.' She wasn't as shocked as she should have been, nor as upset as she ought to have been. In fact, she felt like laughing, because Martin looked like a schoolboy who'd just been caught masturbating by the headmaster. She mustn't let it throw her. That would be too *passé*.

She thought of the man waiting downstairs in the car with Sarah. He was wealthy, and quite handsome if one didn't mind older men of middle-eastern origins. His manners were charming too. 'I popped in to say I won't be home tonight.'

'Next time it would be better if you phoned,' Martin said, looking relieved.

'If you'd told me you were entertaining, I would have done.' Slightly stunned, she rejoined her hostess.

'Is everything all right, dear?' Sarah cooed. 'You look pale.'

Pauline eyed the diamonds glittering at Sarah's throat, then at the man standing on the pavement, waiting to help her into the car. A diamond set in gold winked discreetly on his little finger as he gently stroked the inside of her wrist.

'Everything's perfect,' she said.

The purchase of the Ryker house was negotiated privately by Charles Wyman early in September. Not wanting another confrontation with Devlin, Janey kept the purchase to herself.

She rang Hackney hospital and asked Griff if he'd witness her signature on the papers.

'I'm just about to go into theatre,' he said. 'I should be through by lunchtime. I'll meet you in the hospital cafeteria. I won't be able to stay long.' He gave her instructions on how to get there.

She was there at twelve, feeling out of place amongst the chattering nurses, orderlies and office staff. Twenty minutes later, Griff came hurrying in, white-coated and with a stethoscope slung casually around his neck. He didn't seem to notice the glances he drew from women as he joined the queue and piled his tray up with sandwiches, fruit and a pot of tea.

He nodded to a couple of people as his glance roved over the room, then his glance connected with hers. Breath held, she waited for his serious Griffin face to be transformed by the smile she loved so much, experiencing a rush of pleasure when it did. He added an extra cup and a couple of doughnuts to the tray. It seemed as though a thousand pairs of eyes turned to look at her when he headed her way.

'You found it, then?' Leaning over the table he kissed her on the cheek, then asked to see the papers. Swiftly, he witnessed her signature, then folded the documents back into the envelope. 'So, you're investing in real estate?'

'It's not an investment. It's going to be my home.'

His eyes were dark and searching against hers. 'Does Devlin know?'

Guilt niggled at her when she shook her head.

Griff's hand covered hers. 'Shouldn't you tell him?'

'He'd only try and talk me out of it, then we'd have a big argument. I'll tell him when it's all settled.'

His hand slid away to peel the wrap from his sandwiches. 'I never thought you had it in you to treat him like that.'

She gazed at him in puzzlement. Did he think? *He did think!*

A grin spread across her face. 'How long have you thought Dev and I were an item?' she teased. 'Really, Griff, you, of all people.'

His hands stilled their movement as he met her eyes square-on. 'Aren't you?'

'Has he ever indicated otherwise?'

'No, but I assumed, as you were living there?'

'You assumed wrong. Dev and I are friends. There never has been, nor ever will be, anything between us.'

Griff's lips twitched into a wry grin. 'That won't stop him hoping.'

'I know.' Their eyes met in complete understanding. 'I'm messing up his life, Griff. I don't want to hurt him any more than I have to.'

'When will you move back to Winterbrook?'

'As soon as I've finished the series of paintings I'm working on. Before Christmas, I hope. I can stay with my father until I furnish the place.'

A smile touched Griff's lips. 'I'm glad you've come to terms with your father. Have you had any more ill effects from the LSD?'

'One or two minor episodes. I can handle them.'

'If you ever need me, you know where I am.'

She would have asked Griff's advice about her father then, but he was paged over a loudspeaker. His smile was rueful as he rose to his feet. 'No rest for the wicked, I'm afraid.' He kissed her again, very gently and lingeringly on the mouth. 'I'm sorry I can't stay longer. Enjoy my lunch for me.'

Watching him walk away with long unhurried strides, Janey felt so proud of him she could have burst. She wished Phil could see his son in this environment. He looked so sure of himself, so confident. Griff had always known the path his life would take, and had never once deviated from it.

She followed shortly afterwards, made self-conscious by the speculative glances aimed in her direction. Had Griff kissed her to discourage female attention? He couldn't work in such a big hospital and be unaware of it.

She lingered on the way home, walking through Hyde Park and enjoying the balmy weather. People were everywhere, clad in summery clothes. But the leaves were turning, and the heat had left the sun. Soon, the mists would creep from the river to blot out the light, the trees would be bare, and the earth would lie dormant once again.

There was music playing. A group of bare-footed hippies lolled on the grass. *Flower-power entwined in an untidy heap.* The smell of pot drifted to her nostrils as she walked past. It reminded her of Drifter. 'Make love, not war,' one of them chanted. Easy to say when he'd never be involved in Vietnam.

Dear Mrs Jones, it is with great pride that we write to tell you your son has been drafted to serve his country.

She was glad Drifter hadn't gone to Vietnam, hadn't been forced to kill somebody's mother, somebody's father, somebody's precious child. A child like Saffy, only sloe-eyed and dark haired.

Dear Mrs Jones, we regret to inform you. . . .

Peace-through-love, Janey shivered. The hippy philosophy didn't stand a chance against the will of governments. Democracy was just a myth.

When she was home, she wrote to Tim telling him she'd bought his childhood home. She hoped he'd never have to become involved in a war. She tossed up whether to ring Mary and Douglas, but decided against it. Mary would only invite her down, and she couldn't spare the time.

Still haunted by her melancholy mood she started work, and was soon absorbed.

September merged into October. Leaves turned from yellow to orange, then brown, littering the gutters until they were sucked into the hungry jaws of the roadsweepers. Grass became pocked with boggy black patches. She ran out of autumn colours.

November brought fireworks and wet, clinging mist. It intruded into the nostrils and throat. Foghorns honked like dying swans, chimneys smoked, people's faces turned pale, cold-pinched and miserable. She ran out of winter colours, and rejoiced.

The woman in the ferry boat gazed enigmatically out at her from the canvas. Her hair was pale tendrils that snaked around a man-child on the shore, naked and vulnerable. She felt emptied out, as if someone had turned on a tap and allowed her essence to flow from her body. Sinking into a chair she stared at the painting until there was no light left. Mistral's hair glowed, even in the dusk. It was the best Mistral painting she'd ever done. She threw a cloth over it.

After a while, she went downstairs.

'I've finished, Devlin.'

'Finished?' he said stupidly. 'How can you be finished. There's a waiting list for Mistral paintings after the American exhibition.'

'Mistral's dead. I've run out of paint.' Her smile was triumphant, her voice adamant.

Devlin laughed. 'What do you need? I'll get you some.'

'I don't need any. I've given up painting.'

His eyes were as uncertain as the smile that came and went across his mouth, but his eyes had taken on a murderous gleam. 'Either you're joking, or you're sickening for something.'

'Neither.' She stretched her aching muscles. 'You're the businessman. Mistral must have made us both a fortune by now. You never did give me the detailed statement you promised.'

'I forgot.' He came to stand in front of her, taking her hands in his. She was making a stand. OK, she was entitled to. 'Is this what this farce is all about, Janey. You're mad at me, yes?'

She felt her heart begin to break. 'I'm not mad at you, Dev, I'm tired in body and spirit. I've bought myself a house in the country and I'm going to raise my child there.'

Nothing he could say would make her change her mind. He was furious, and made an ass of himself by ranting. She dissolved into tears, making him feel guilty – but she wouldn't be swayed.

He pleaded with her. He promised her the earth, the stars and the moon – all the planets of the universe rolled into one. Still, she cried, long shuddering sobs that cracked him up.

He steeled himself against them. She'd never painted so well, now she was going to chuck it all away. Well, damn her! He wouldn't let her waste her talent. He'd changed her mind twice. He'd do it again.

'Be reasonable. If you don't work, you won't have enough income to pay the damned mortgage,' he told her.

Her sobs became a watery, mutinous voice. She was fighting him with every weapon she had. 'I haven't got a mortgage. I bought it with a legacy.'

He was affronted. 'You bought a house without telling me!'

'Don't do this to me, Devlin?' she said softly. 'Don't make me hurt you.'

'Hurt me! What the hell does that mean?' He resorted to blackmail. 'I made you, Janey. I gave you my friendship, my home to live in. I looked after you and Saffy. Damn it! You owe me something.'

She hit him squarely below the belt. 'I only owe you for your commission, and room and board.'

'How can you throw that at me?' he shouted, wounded beyond measure. 'You're my guest. I love looking after you. I haven't taken a penny from you in commission. I'd do anything for you – *anything!*'

'Then let me go.' She turned and walked away from him.

'Where are you going?' He followed after her up the stairs, desperate, knowing he'd lost. 'We haven't finished this conversation.'

Her voice was choked with tears when she spoke. 'I have something for you.'

It was the abstract she'd taken so long to paint. It was executed perfectly in shades of blue, grey and silver. Mirrored shards converged like a web to capture a bubble. There was a naked figure curled inside, a woman with long, silver hair winding around her body and binding her wrists and ankles. Her eyes were closed tight, and the whole was reflected in the shards of glass, coming from different angles.

It shattered him. He stared at it, unbelieving. It was brilliant – it made him despise himself.

'You've got to let me go before we destroy each other. I'm suffocating.'

He should have listened to her before. He shouldn't have forced her to prove herself the stronger. He felt like a middle-aged man as he walked towards the door, his heart as fragmented as the mirror shards in the painting. 'I'll move into a hotel until you sort yourself out.'

'Please don't go.' She threw her arms around his body, keeping her too him, begging him to stay. 'I don't want us to be enemies, Devlin.'

'Damn you, Janey.' Extricating himself from her grip he glared at her. 'Can't you leave a man any pride?'

'Don't go. I need to know you forgive me.'

There were tears in her eyes. Paint streaked one cheek, a slash of purple. She smelled of turpentine and linseed oil. Her hair was a straggly mess where she'd drawn it into an elastic band. Bits stuck out all over the place.

It was agony, loving her, but he knew he'd stay with her until the bitter end – to the day she walked out of his life.

He'd forgive her for doing this to him, but he wondered – would he ever forgive himself for what he'd done to her?

CHAPTER FIFTEEN

Although they were gradually establishing a relationship, living in the same house with her father wasn't all that easy.

There was a natural tension between them, too many things left unsaid, as if they'd erected a dam, that once breached, would sweep them away on a tidal wave of recriminations.

Behind the wall of that dam, the pressure was building up. Seeking ways to lessen it, Janey asked him about her mother one evening.

Jack gazed sharply at her. He didn't want to be reminded of Margaret or the manner of her death. Sat crossed-legged in an old-fashioned armchair, she was darning a hole in one of Saffy's mittens. Her braided hair hung over her shoulder, her mouth was pursed in concentration as she wove the needle in and out.

'Why do you want to know?'

She looked up then, her eyes registering surprise at the roughly uttered query. 'I can't remember her, you see.'

'Does it matter after all this time?'

A tiny flicker of hurt replaced the surprise. Her teeth bit through a length of blue wool. She replaced the needle in a small sewing box, shut the lid, then set the mitten on top of its twin.

'I suppose not. They say what you've never had you never miss. I'm curious, that's all. I've never even seen a photograph of her.'

Why did she have the ability to make him feel so guilty? 'I'm sorry. I should have realized.' Fetching a dog-eared album from the cupboard he placed it in her lap. As she flipped past sepia photographs he heard himself saying inconsequential things like: 'Your grandparents. Mary when she was little. Me when I first joined the air force.'

Janey slipped him a smile. 'We're alike, aren't we?'

Her observation pleased him. He'd thought he was beyond ego, thought he'd been purged of it in prison. Embarrassed by its re-emergence, he ruffled her hair before stabbing a finger at the album. 'That's Margaret.'

Her breath swooped in surprise. It could have been Pauline gazing out from the photograph, only a softer, less poised Pauline. Her mother was sitting on a park bench, a baby on her lap. There was a self-conscious smile on her face.

'Is that me on her lap?'

Jack had lived with the photograph all the years he'd been inside. That, and the painting of the squirrels. He'd lived in the past, had resented Mary telling him of Janey's success. He knew now that he hadn't wanted her to grow up without him.

'Yes, that's you.'

It's hard to imagine this woman is my mother, that she fed me from her breast, loved me and looked after me, Janey thought. *I bear no resemblance to her, and she looks too much like Pauline for comfort.*

She stared at it for a long time, as if by doing so she could establish some thread of rapport. But it was only a photograph, and all she experienced was a faint sense of regret. It was Pamela who'd been her mother, Pamela who she loved. She closed the book with a sigh of regret.

'There's a couple more.'

'Not now.' Her eyes engaged his. 'Tell me about her.'

Jack's eyes clouded over and he turned away. 'It's not a good idea to rake over the past.'

'I'm not asking you to. I'm asking you to tell me about my mother.' Anger clawed at her insides. 'All my life I've been told that she was wicked, that she brought shame on the family. Her actions reflected on my life in ways you'll never know, ways I'm just beginning to come to terms with. I'm your daughter – *your child and hers.* I need, and have the *right* to know her. Tell me, did you love her?'

Her anger took him by surprise. She'd been a baby when Margaret had died. He'd never stopped to consider her death might have had a ripple effect. But of course, it would have. He shouldn't deny Janey knowledge of her mother. 'Of course I loved her. How could you imagine otherwise?'

'Quite easily.' She gave a short, bitter laugh. 'Men say one thing and mean another, Saffy is proof of that. Even so, I didn't contemplate doing what my mother did.'

Now it was his turn for anger. 'You know nothing of the circumstances. Perhaps if you'd been as desperate as Margaret, perhaps if you'd been married to a man who abused—'

'I was abused by the same man,' she reminded him.

He gazed into the wounded eyes of a child he'd so carelessly fathered. 'Your mother wasn't wicked. She was confused and at the end of her tether. If she'd only told me she was pregnant.' He put his head in his bands. 'She phoned me the night she died. She said she loved me, that she was going to leave him and marry me.'

'It's all right.' Her hand stole up to claim his. 'I'm not asking you to justify what you both felt, nor am I blaming you.'

'I would have died for her then.' He shrugged. 'Now she has no substance for me. I don't know what to tell you.'

'You've told me all I need to know. Shall I make us a cup of tea before bed?' The tension relaxed and they became easy with each other again.

*

It was wonderful to watch her father's boat taking shape in the garden. He was skilful with his hands, each part lovingly set into place, plank by plank, fitting perfectly together.

'She's going to be beautiful,' she said one chilly day as she took him out a mug of tea to warm him. 'When she's finished we'll sail out into the sunset and find a warm island to winter on.'

He grinned as he curled his hands around the mug's warmth. 'She's not built to sail, you'll have to make do with power. The original engine was salvaged, and is still in the boatyard.' He was boyish in his enthusiasm. 'It's being overhauled. If all goes well, *Saffy Jane* will be seaworthy early in June.'

He needed the boat, she realized. He needed the companionship of the two men who were helping him build her. It amazed her how well the three of them, so different, got on together. John constantly surprised her. He was astute, the possessor of a chameleon-like quality which enabled him to fit into village life as though he'd been born to it. His knowledge was infinite, his mind a sponge that retained everything he learned. Her respect for him constantly grew.

It was John who told her of country house sales, who advised her on what was a bargain and what was not, who helped her gather together the bits and pieces to furnish her home. Among their finds was an oak dresser covered in chipped cream paint, which he was in the process of stripping back and restoring for her. For next to nothing she'd picked up a trestle table and six ladder-back chairs. An upholsterer in Dorchester was recovering the comfortable old-fashioned lounge suite she'd bought at the same auction. Charles had raided his attic, donating a hallstand and matching oak settle.

As soon as she'd finished stripping and painting the necessary bedrooms, she intended to buy new bedroom furniture and move in.

They'd have company. Tim had written to say he was being posted to the navy base at Portland in the new year. *If you're prepared to offer me bed and board I'll held you redecorate*, he wrote. *I'm a dab hand at slapping on paint and it will be better than living in navy quarters.*

She accepted his offer, posting the letter when she was in Bournemouth shopping for Christmas gifts. It was hard to juggle with a toddler and overloaded bags amongst the crowds. By lunchtime, Saffy was tired and wanted to be carried. Bundling herself and parcels into a taxi, she headed for Mary's house in Westbourne.

I should learn to drive and buy myself a small car, she thought, as half her parcels slid to the floor on Mary's doorstep.

'You look worn out, dear.' Mary relieved her of the burden of Saffy, and Douglas took the bags. 'Come through to the lounge where it's warm. Have you had lunch?'

'A cup of tea and a sandwich would be welcome. I don't know if Saffy will eat anything. She's half asleep.'

Saffy managed a smile when Mary removed her coat and hat, but her eyelids were drooping. She fell asleep on the couch, a rag doll Griff had given to her clutched against her chest.

'How are you and Jack getting along?' Mary asked as she busied herself with lunch.

'*Mary!*' Douglas warned.

She laughed. 'Dad and I are getting along just fine. Are you coming to spend Christmas with us? He specifically asked me to invite you, and told me not to take no for an answer. Please say yes right away, because I haven't got the energy to argue.'

'In that case, we'd love to.'

'We've invited John Smith as well. He's helping Dad build his boat. He's very easy to get along with and I think you'll like him.'

After lunch, she pulled some of her purchases from the bags and tried to fit them in better. She'd bought her nephew a brightly coloured push-pull toy for Christmas, and set about wrapping it. 'You won't mind if I pop out while Saffy's asleep. I rather thought I'd leave Justin's present at his grandfather's office. It will save me carting it home.'

'I'll drive you there if you like,' Douglas offered, lumbering to his feet.

When she directed him to Andrew and Robert Pitt's office, he expressed surprise.

'I hadn't realized. We've met several times at various conferences. You won't mind if I come in to renew my acquaintance with them.'

'I'd be pleased. I haven't met them at all, so you can introduce me. I haven't even met my nephew.'

To her surprise, she met Justin in the office, being unsuccessfully placated by a harassed-looking middle-aged lady who introduced herself as Miss Frobisher. The inner door was slightly ajar and a woman was talking in a loud, determined voice.

'I'm afraid not. Nothing would induce me to stay on in that household. I wrote and told Mrs Pitt I'd been offered another position. It's not my fault if she forgot to hire someone else.'

'I must apologize,' Miss Frobisher said, trying to be heard above Justin's din, and looking distractedly from one to the other. 'I'm afraid it's a bad time to call. Do you have an appointment? Perhaps you could see Mr Andrew. Oh dear, I forgot? He's absent from the office at the moment with a cold.'

'I'm Justin's auntie. Let me take him from you,' Janey offered, feeling sorry for the woman when the telephone rang. 'Now then,' she soothed when he was handed over. 'What are you making all this fuss about? Tell Auntie Janey all about it.'

The chaos of the office gradually calmed. Justin stopped screaming and gazed at her hair as she talked quietly to him. He was a pale, thin little thing and her heart went out to him. She smiled as he took a handful of her hair in his fist, and kissed his soft cheek. 'You can do that if you don't pull too hard.'

He was soaking – no wonder he was upset. Within a few seconds she'd located a plastic bag containing nappies, and Justin was made as comfortable as possible, considering his behind was almost raw from nappy rash.

'What will I do with him?' a distinguished looking man pleaded as he followed the woman marching from his office. 'Justin's parents are in Paris. I've got no idea how to look after a baby.'

'*Parents?*' the woman snorted. 'They don't know the meaning of the word. The last time they saw their son was four months ago, and then only for half an hour.'

The office door was too dignified to slam, but it managed a muted thud under pressure.

'Oh dear,' Miss Frobisher said again, sounding distressed.

Smiling at Robert Pitt, Janey held out her hand. 'Don't worry, I'll look after him. I'm his aunt, Janey Renfrew, and this is my uncle, Douglas Yates, whom I believe you know.'

The man looked so relieved she began to laugh. 'I guess this is one of those occasions of being in the right place at the right time.'

'Or the other way round,' he said drily. 'Either way, I'm very pleased to meet you.'

It was Robert Pitt who went to collect Justin's belongings. He drove them all back to Winterbrook, with Justin's cot strapped to the roof rack of his car. He became suddenly anxious that he might be doing the wrong thing by giving his grandson into the care of a complete stranger.

She showed him round her house before they went to her father's. 'We'll be moving in after Christmas. I hope you and you brother will visit Justin often. You'll be quite welcome to come to my father's house for Christmas Day, too.'

'I don't know quite how to thank you,' he said. 'I'll arrange another nanny for Justin as soon as possible.'

Her heart sank at the thought of Justin being brought up without love. 'Please don't. I'm quite willing to care for Justin, and long-term if necessary. In fact, I'd like to. The country air will do him good, and he and Saffy will be company for one another. His other aunt lives in the village, so he'll be with family. I'm sure Pauline won't object to me looking after him.'

Robert Pitt's lips tightened a fraction at the mention of her sister. 'I'm inclined to agree with you.' He said nothing more, he was too gentlemanly, but it was obvious he was disenchanted with his daughter-in-law. 'Thank you once again. I'll be in touch.' He refused Jack's offer to stay for a cup of tea, and inclined his head before he drove away.

Her father was unconcerned by the sudden arrival of Justin in their midst. His cot was erected with a minimum of fuss in a corner of Saffy's room.

The cottage became an obstacle course of baby clothes drying round the fire, toys and pushchairs. Jack bought a playpen to keep Justin out from underfoot.

Knowing a car was now imperative, Janey fit in a few hasty driving lessons with Pamela, and asked everyone to keep an eye out for a suitable car.

Saffy was fascinated by the new arrival. It soon became apparent that Justin felt the same way about her. Where Saffy went, Justin followed, crawling after her as fast as he could go.

'He's a solemn-looking little chap,' Jack said one day. 'I don't think I've seen him smile once.'

'He's not complaining quite so much, though. I wish he were mine.' The grave, unwanted, and unloved infant had found his own personal niche in her heart.

Christmas Eve came. The small pine tree Phil brought them was decorated with tinsel, coloured balls and frosting. Jack set an angel on top as she placed the parcels underneath.

'You can open yours now, if you like.'

She watched anxiously as he tore the wrapping from the parcel.

'A compass! How did you know?' His eyes held the suspicion of tears despite the smile on his face.

'I hope it's all right. It was the one I saw circled in your catalogue.' Suddenly anxious, she began to gabble. 'I asked John if that was the one you wanted. Well, anyway, the shop said they'd change it if it was the wrong one for the boat. I've kept the receipt just in case. I don't know much about these things, so if it's not—'

'It's perfect.' Placing it carefully on the dresser, he took her face between his hands and softly quoted, ' "And all I ask is a tall ship and a star to steer her by." This will be my star, Janey. I'll have your name inscribed on it, and it will guide and inspire me, as it always has.' He gently kissed her forehead and let her go, his gruff voice telling her he'd been embarrassed by his show of affection. 'Don't think I'm going to give you your present now. As far as I'm concerned, you're one of the children.'

A bitter-sweet sadness welled up in her. He loved her, he'd always loved her. That love had kept him going in prison, year after year.

Her hand touched his wrist. 'Was it very bad in there?'

He seemed to hunch into himself. 'Being imprisoned robs a man of his pride and spirit. It strips him to basics, forcing him to face his own worthlessness. All he's got left to fight for is his own survival. If he loses the fight then he becomes dehumanized.'

How unemotional he sounded. No bitterness, no self-pity, just a factual statement. Even so, she was moved by this unexpected confidence. 'You survived.'

A faint smile hovered on his lips as his eyes engaged hers. He straightened up. 'I had something worth surviving for.'

'I wish I'd known you were my father when I was young.' She heard in her voice the wistful longing for something she'd missed, a father's love.

'Perhaps it was for the best. You might have grown up hating me, or spent your life yearning for something you couldn't really have.'

'Did *you* do that?'

He nodded. 'I was wrong to believe I owned you body and soul. Nobody has a claim to another person's emotions.'

This lapse into the personal wasn't entirely comfortable, but it was a hurdle they must overcome if they were ever to be completely at ease with each other.

'I don't know what I feel for you, except I like you a lot,' she said honestly. 'When Mary first told me you were my father it was a shock. I couldn't imagine how my *own* father, a man I'd grown to respect and love as a teacher and friend, could leave me for dead. Of course, I didn't know it wasn't an accident, then.'

He gave a small anguished groan.

'Later, when I realized you were innocent, I felt guilty, and somehow to blame. I was ashamed of myself and angry at you. It took me a long time to come to terms with the fact that neither of us was responsible for what happened.'

'Perhaps now is a good time to forgive ourselves.'

So they hugged each other for the second time as father and daughter, and a small flicker of longing began to grow in her heart. Perhaps one day she could bring herself to love him as unreservedly as he loved her. When all the obstacles were overcome she might be able to come to him and say: *It was never good enough for me to tell you I know you're innocent – now I can prove it. Now I can allow myself to love you.*

When she could do that, perhaps it would be the right time for what he'd asked of her. But right now – on the eve of Christmas, when the whole world was filled with forgiveness and love – she couldn't find the charity in her heart to completely forgive herself.

They went to the early-morning service on Christmas Day. The fields and hedgerows were sugared with frost. The peal of church bells was so sharp and clear it was a wonder the enthusiasm of the village campanologists didn't cause them to crack, Janey thought.

Glossy, dark holly wreaths with blood-red berries decorated the church, candles glowed on the altar and in the sconces, and the nativity scene was a serene reminder of what Christmas was all about. Feet stamped against the cold in the porch, faces and noses glowed red, arms wrapped around bodies for warmth.

'Cold enough for snow, I reckon.'

'Not before the New Year's rung in. You mark my words.'

'Is that your Pauline's young-'un?' asked Ada, rounder than ever and waddling a bit.

'Yes.'

'He looks as if he needs feeding up to me. Plenty of cream will put some roses in his cheeks.'

Phil, self-conscious in his best suit, doffed his hat to smile at Pamela. Susie bounded up the path with the energy of a puppy. She was wearing a matching Fair Isle hat and scarf Ada had made for her, and her brown curls bounced energetically against her face. Everyone was enveloped in kisses and hugs.

There were sidelong glances at her father's scarred face, mostly from the people who used the village as a weekend retreat. Briefly, she wondered how he stood it, then realized he had no choice.

The weekenders tried desperately to fit in, arriving in estate cars with the required number of golden retrievers in the back. The men wore polo-necked jumpers and flat checked caps. The women wrapped their heads in Queen Elizabeth headscarves.

When the bell stopped tolling, villagers and weekenders became one, scrambling for places in the pews.

The vicar was a short, genial man with a highly-polished head and a beaming smile. His sermon, a simple narrative about the meaning of Christmas, was well received. John arrived in the middle of it, sliding apologetically into a seat at the back.

There was a sense of togetherness amongst the congregation as they sang the carols and took communion. Saffy was delighted with the singing and slipped from the pew to dance in the aisle. Afterwards, she clapped enthusiastically, which earned her several smiles.

She was swiftly scooped into Jack's lap when he sensed she'd enjoyed the attention so much she was about to do a repeat performance. He stuck a jelly baby in her mouth before she could protest.

Justin, snuggled in Janey's arms, sucked his thumb and stared around him with round wonder-filled eyes. 'Your first Christmas of many, Justy,' she whispered in his ear. 'How do you like it?'

His eyes swivelled up to hers, then his thumb left his mouth and the corners of his mouth twitched upwards. He gave a soft gurgle of laughter and her eyes widened in surprise. *Who said miracles didn't happen?* She covered his face with kisses and he chuckled again, longer and louder.

'Me 'swell.' Saffy's face was sticky sweet, her eyes merry and shining like emeralds. She giggled as she received her kiss, then the three of them were all kissing each other and laughing, until Jack elbowed her gently in the ribs.

The congregation's heads were bent in prayer. She and her father gazed with amusement at each other for a moment, sharing the gift of happiness the children had just given them. Then she slid her hand into his so they were joined. They bowed their heads too.

They lingered for only a short while, exchanging greetings with friends and acquaintances before taking the children back to the warmth of the cottage for the excitement of opening their gifts. Afterwards, Janey put them down for a nap. They'd been up early, and still had the excitement of the rest of the day to get through.

Mary came down early from Bournemouth to help Janey prepare dinner.

'How's Douglas going to get here?' Janey asked her.

'It's a surprise,' she said mysteriously, and Jack choked back a laugh.

Later, after John had arrived and Douglas hadn't, and she'd begun to wonder if he was going to turn up in a Santa costume to amuse the children, there came a toot on a horn.

Taking her by the arm, her father led her outside. 'Happy Christmas, Janey love.'

Green and red bows decorated the door handles of a shiny green Ford Anglia.

'Oh?' She couldn't stop smiling at everyone. 'It's the most wonderful gift I've ever been given.' *Except for Saffy, Justin and my father.*

'Then you'd better get some practice in so you can get your licence.' He took a couple of L-plates from behind his back 'Once around the village so I can see how you're getting on.'

She threw her arms around his neck and kissed him. 'You shouldn't have,' she scolded. 'It's too expensive.'

'Enough of that,' he said gruffly. 'Just get behind the wheel and let's go.'

She lurched off to the cheers of those left behind, then laughing, drove her father round the village, waving proudly at anyone who was abroad. When they got back to the cottage, Robert Pitt's car was parked outside the cottage.

Drawing the Anglia to a halt, she gazed with sudden alarm at her father. 'You don't think he's going to take Justin back, do you? I couldn't bear it.'

He gave her a hug. 'You invited him down, remember?'

'So I did. I hope we've got enough dinner.'

'If the turkey was any bigger it wouldn't fit in the oven.'

There was more than enough, and soon everyone declared they couldn't eat another scrap. It seemed that now Justin had learned how to smile, he decided to smile all day, charming everyone in the process.

Taking her aside, Robert Pitt told her that Pauline and Martin had agreed to her fostering Justin. 'If you're still of the same mind I'm happy with the arrangement. I've discussed this at some length with Douglas and have agreed not to insult you by offering a wage, but I think you'll find the amount provided will recompense you for his material needs.'

'You needn't have bothered, but thank you anyway.' She surprised him by kissing him on the cheek. 'Justy's settled down very well with us, and I'd hate to lose him now.'

'No fear of that. I have to say this, Janey. My son has proved a great disappointment to me in his choice of both partner and lifestyle. I'm coming to the conclusion they're unsuitable parents for Justin.'

She stared at him, wide-eyed. This man was quite formidable.

'I'm going to ask my son and his wife to place the legal guardianship of Justin in my hands, although I wouldn't discourage them from seeing him, of course. Should anything happen to me, I'd stipulate guardianship be handed over to you. Would you be happy with that arrangement?'

Of course I would, Pauline has shown by every action and deed that she doesn't love or want her son. Janey *did* love him. Justin was a darling, and the thought of losing him was as painful as the thought of losing Saffy.

She nodded, but warned. 'If – and *only if* – your suggestion is acceptable to both Pauline and Martin.'

'Thank you, my dear. I feel much happier about the situation now.'

They went through to the other room. Douglas was sleeping off his dinner in an armchair, Mary was deep in conversation with John. Saffy had climbed into the playpen with Justin, and they were playing quietly with their new toys.

Her father took Robert Pitt outside to see his boat.

She began clearing the dirty dishes from the table and carrying them through to the kitchen. 'Leave the washing up until I come back,' Mary said, rising to her feet. 'John and I have decided to take the dogs and walk off our dinners.'

Janey decided to do it anyway, her eyes dreamy as she gazed out through the kitchen window at the two grandfathers. They were talking animatedly, her father waving his arms over the boat, taking imaginary measurements.

I should ring Devlin and Griff and wish them a Happy Chrisimas, she suddenly thought. She left it until everyone had gone and the children were in bed for the night.

There were the sounds of revelry in the background when Devlin answered. The sound of his voice made her realize how much she missed him. 'Hello, angel. Have you called to tell me you're coming back?'

'Don't give me a hard time, Dev. I've called to wish you a Happy Christmas.'

'Thank you, but you needn't have. I got your card.' He suddenly chuckled. 'Are you sure you don't want to come back?'

'*Devlin!*'

'All right, I'll behave myself. Have you started painting yet?'

She ignored his question, explaining about Justin instead, then telling him about the house and that Tim was moving in to help her redecorate it.

He whistled. 'It's just as well you're not coming back. I don't want to end up with a house full of other people's kids.' There was a short pause, then he said cautiously. 'You don't intend to give up painting completely, do you? You've got too much talent to waste it.'

'I don't know. Perhaps once I get settled in the new house I'll start again.'

'I won't push you, I promise, but you won't forget I'm your agent?'

He was so transparent she began to laugh. 'How could I, Dev, you wouldn't let me? Besides, if it wasn't for you—'

'If you're about to say you're grateful to me, don't bother,' he warned. 'I'm not into sentimentality.'

'I'll let you get back to your guests, then.'

'It's Sandy. She's brought a crowd of actors over and they're eating me out of house and home. Do you want to say hello to her?'

'Just tell her I said Happy Christmas. Keep well, Dev. Once I get sorted out, I'll be having a house-warming party. You're top of my guest list.'

'Forget it! I have no intention of tramping around in cow dung and squeezing myself into a rustic cottage with blackbirds twittering in the roof and no running water.'

'House martins.'

'Same difference.' He chuckled, then smacked her a kiss down the line. 'I miss having you around,' he said, and hung up.

She couldn't get hold of Griff, but a message was relayed back to her by the nurse. 'Doctor Tyler's in emergency. He said he'll contact you as soon as he's able.'

'I hope you have a Happy Christmas,' she said. 'I tend to forget there are people like you who have to spend Christmas at work.'

'Thank you, that's very kind of you. The job has its compensations.' A smile came into her voice. 'A child's life has been saved tonight.'

Janey waited until midnight before she went to bed, then lay awake marvelling about the dedication of people like Griff and the nursing sister she'd spoken to. In an increasingly commercial world, how better to demonstrate the spirit of Christmas than to save a child's life? It made her feel humble.

At Coombe Cottage the light in John's study burned into the early hours.

It had been easy to get Mary Yates talking on their walk over the hill to the beach, though it was she who broached the subject. 'I'm surprised Jack's decided to build a boat at his age.'

'He can't be more than sixty, surely.'

'Fifty-eight.'

'That's not too old, besides . . .' he chose his next words carefully '. . . it's always been his dream, I believe. The ocean represents freedom to him. I understand the boat's a replica of the one your father built.'

A smile twisted her lips. 'Both Jack and my father were crazy about that boat. She was called *The Maggie* originally. My father took her across to Dunkirk. It killed him. Jack renamed her *Margaret Jane* after Janey was born. I've never seen him so upset as the night the boat was burned, except perhaps when Janey was attacked.' She shrugged, and took a deep steadying breath. 'He still thinks Eddie Renfrew had a hand in destroying the boat, though nothing could be proved.'

John's eyes narrowed. 'Eddie Renfrew?'

'Janey's stepfather.' Distaste laced her voice. 'They used to live in the cottage you bought. He's a bad bit of work. No wonder his wife left him. She works up at the big house now, a nice woman, and good to our Janey. I don't know how she put up with him all those years.'

'I've met her.'

Mary bit her lip and flicked him a sideways glance. 'I think Pamela must know more than she's telling.'

'In what way?'

'About what Eddie got up to. After all, she was married to him. It wouldn't surprise me if he committed the crime that put Jack in prison, or all those crimes against young girls at the time.' She suddenly put her hand to her mouth. 'You won't tell anyone I mentioned this? Douglas said I've got to keep my nose out.'

'I know how to be discreet.' He took a punt, because Mary had grievances she needed to unload, and he had an insatiable curiosity that needed fuelling. 'I'll let you into a confidence, Mary. I used to be a detective before I retired, so crime is a hobby of mine.'

He could almost hear her mind ticking over. In a hopeful voice and without looking at him, she said. 'Would you be interested in helping me clear Jack's name? I couldn't pay you.'

'I might, if the evidence is there.'

Her face fell. 'I haven't got any evidence except the word of Janey. She knows he's innocent, she said so. And I think she knows who attacked her. But I daren't ask her. Jack has made it very clear she's off limits in that respect.'

'That's understandable. If Renfrew *was* the culprit, there are many other people whose lives could be affected. Janey's sensitive. She'd have had enough to cope with just being the victim. Jack loves her. He knows if she destroyed the happiness and well-being of the people she loved, it would live in her conscience for ever. I'm sure you wouldn't want that.'

Mary flushed. 'I wouldn't do anything to hurt her. I love her too.'

'Tell me about the other crimes you mentioned?'

'Three young girls were lured into a man's car, then drugged and interfered with. They all said the car was blue. Eddie Renfrew had a blue car at the time. The police weren't even interested when I pointed this out to them.'

Her indignation made him want to grin, but he suppressed it as he allowed her get it all out of her system.

He'd sifted through what she'd said, finding bits and pieces amongst the conjecture that could prove useful or relevant as threads to follow. Now, he stood in front of his chart and stared at it. He didn't like loose ends.

Picking up a pen he put a question mark against the name of Pamela Renfrew. An uncomplicated woman, but she could hold the key to everything.

Persistently, the unsolved rapes ran through his mind. Mary Yates was right. It was an area worth investigating. Through fear or shame, those sort of crimes often were unreported, or were dropped before charges were laid. It wasn't easy for a young woman to face her attacker in court and prove his guilt. More often than not, her own reputation was irreparably damaged in the process. It might prove useful to compare the three reported cases in the New Year, and see what he could make out of it.

He yawned as he went downstairs. Making himself a cup of chocolate, he turfed Nellie out of her basket by the fire, sending the reluctant dog into the cold night to relieve herself. Hands wrapped around the mug of chocolate, he sat in front of the fire and stared into the flames. One thing was certain: Janey had to be protected. He usually managed to avoid emotional involvement with his cases, but the sudden murderous rage he felt rocked him.

He could only imagine what she'd gone through as a child, and if he could bring her attacker to justice he would – whoever he turned out to be!

CHAPTER SIXTEEN

Janey had just finished painting a circus on the walls of the children's bedroom. A red and white striped tent was painted around the window, which represented the entrance. She intended to hang matching curtains at either side. Elephants trumpeted, seals balanced balls on their noses, lions roared. There were jugglers and clowns, trapeze artists and dappled ponies with plumes on their heads. It looked good against the sunny yellow background of the walls.

'You've forgotten the ringmaster.'

Heart thumping, she spun around. 'Griff! What are you doing here?'

'Visiting you. I was taking Gypsy for a walk and saw the light on. I brought her into the hall. I hope you don't mind.'

She glanced at her watch. 'I didn't realize it was so late. I wanted to get this finished before the bedroom furniture is delivered tomorrow. We're moving in at the weekend, the day after the children's birthday.'

One dark eyebrow rose. 'Children? Did I miss something, or were there two of Saffy to begin with?'

She laughed. 'Didn't your father tell you? Pauline's son is living with me now. Justin's so sweet. You'll adore him.' Her eyes searched his dear, familiar face. 'It's good to see you, Griff.'

His smile came, his eyes had a teasing light. 'What are you waiting for? Come and give me a hug, then.'

She stopped breathing for a second, then she was in his arms and squeezing him tight. There was an aura of night air clinging to him.

Griff kissed the top of her head, then held her at arm's length, making his own inspection. Clear blue eyes, her mouth peachy soft and kissable – and best of all, the tension she'd displayed the last time he'd seen her, was gone. A smudge of green paint decorated one satiny cheek. She looked good enough to eat, he thought, making a superhuman effort to prevent himself from running his finger down her cheek. 'You look great.'

A shy laugh dismissed his observation. 'Your eyes need testing. I'm wearing a pair of my father's overalls cut off at the ankles, my hair's a mess and I'm covered in paint. *You*, on the other hand, look wonderful, and more rested than I've seen you in a long time.'

'That's because I'm no longer burning the candle at both ends.' A self-conscious grin spread across his face. 'I'm now a fully qualified surgeon, and a member of the Royal College.'

'Oh, Griff, I'm so proud of you.'

'Stop sounding like a mother. How have you been?'

'Who's talking like a doctor?' she retorted, knowing exactly what he was referring to. 'I'm fine. How long are you here for?'

It seemed as if they couldn't stop grinning at each other.

'A couple of days. In February I've got a whole month off.'

'Good, you'll be here for my birthday and house-warming party. I intend to invite all my friends, both old and new.'

'Stephen and Dion might come as a bit of a shock to the locals,' he murmured, giving a chuckle as he slipped his arm around her waist. 'Show me around the house, then I'll walk you home. It's getting late.'

'I have a car. It was a Christmas present from my father.' Eager to show off her driving skills, she offered to drive him home.

'I didn't realize you had a driving licence.'

She gave a small, ashamed grin. 'I haven't quite got my licence yet. I only drive myself here at night, when nobody can see me. Will you wait while I bank up the Aga? I want to keep the chill off the house so it's warm for the children when we move in.'

'I'll do it.'

He kissed her goodnight when she dropped him off, a small friendly kiss she couldn't read anything into. 'Want a hand with the furniture tomorrow?'

'You're a brick. It's arriving about eleven. If you come earlier and help me hang the curtains, I'll cook you breakfast.'

He gave an easy laugh. 'How can I resist.'

It was almost pitch black when she drove away, her headlights a small friendly tunnel showing her the way. There were no stars, no moon and the cold was bitter. The warmth of her breath steamed up the window. She rubbed it away with her palm before it turned to ice. A light in Coombe Cottage burned in the distance.

She would be glad to get home. The high hedges either side of the lane seemed to curve in over her. A panicky terror suddenly took a grip on her. She'd avoided coming this way since she'd been back. She began to perspire as the cow-shed came into view. Sweat trickled between her breasts in a clammy stream, and soaked through the underarms of her overalls. The erratic thumping of her heart was startlingly loud in her ears.

This is where it happened! This is where I was beaten and raped by the man I thought was my father. Her mouth and throat dried up and she began to feel sick. Her foot pushed the accelerator to the floor.

Then she was past it, her mouth salty with adrenalin, blood pumping against her ears and tears streaming down her face as she raced by her former home with its unhappy memories. Only then did she slow down. She was trembling all over when she finally drew the car to a halt. A few minutes later she was safely inside Canford Cottage and retching violently into the pedestal.

Her father was waiting for her when she emerged. His concern made her want to cry. He'd spent years in prison paying for someone else's crime. He should hate her, not stand there looking at her with love in his eyes.

'I passed the spot where . . . it happened.' She took a deep breath. 'I felt sick, that's all.'

He made her a hot drink, and adding a dash of brandy, sat her by the fire. 'Would you like to talk about it?'

Talk about it. How could she? Eddie Renfrew was too ill to even consider bringing to justice. She didn't want to be responsible for causing his death. Then there was Pamela and Susie to take into account. Pauline, who loved her father. How would they feel if she told them? Even if they believed her she might lose Justin. What good would talking about it do, except make everyone else's life miserable? It wouldn't give her father back his lost years.

I'll beat this fear, she thought. *I'll go back there one day in the daylight, walk right into the cow-shed, face my ghosts and say boo!*

She pulled herself together, summoning up a smile for her father's benefit. 'There's nothing to talk about. I was just being foolish.' Her hand covered his. 'I'm all right now. Go back to bed, dad. I'm sorry I woke you.'

'You're sure?'

Why didn't he just go, she thought wearily. Couldn't he see she wanted to be alone? 'I'll be going to bed myself in a minute. I've got a busy day ahead tomorrow. Griff's coming over to help, and Susie's promised to keep an eye on the children for me.'

'That's good.' His voice contained a tiny nuance of hurt. 'Goodnight, then. I'll see you in the morning.'

She followed shortly afterwards, crawling into her bed like a rabbit seeking the safety of its burrow. Her sleep was restless, as if she'd fallen into a deep, dark hole filled with unseen terrors. When she fought her way out of it, it was into a cold, pewter-coloured ghost of dawn.

Pauline and Martin were having an argument. Eddie could hear them from his seat in front of the window.

He squeezed the rubber ball in his hand. *Squeeze and release – squeeze and release.* His strength was returning. He could walk unaided now, taking little shuffling steps. He could talk too, with only a slight slurring in his voice.

Martin's voice was cold and precise. 'We'll have to sell the house.'

'What about my father? It's his home too. We can't just sell it from under him.'

Eddie nodded to himself in the sudden silence. Pauline knew where her duty lay.

Then Martin drawled. 'Of course, if you looked after him we wouldn't have to pay for a nurse. That way, we could afford the mortgage, old girl.'

His mouth twisted into a smile. Pauline and Margaret together again. He'd like that.

'Like hell!' Pauline's voice had a decisive snap to it. 'I can't stomach that sort of thing. What about the church nursing home? Perhaps they'd take him. We could sell the house then. I'll talk to the priest.'

The ball dropped from Eddie's hand and rolled across the floor. Shock pounded at his temple like a jack-hammer. How could she consider such a thing?

'Poor Eddie,' Margaret said in his ear. 'Pauline turned out to be a selfish bitch, didn't she?'

'She doesn't mean it. She wouldn't turn me out of my home.'

'She sent her baby away, didn't she?'

'Only because he screamed all the time. She did it for me. She loves me.' A self-pitying tear slid down his face. 'She's the only one who ever did.'

'You're a fool, Eddie. The baby's with Janey. Remember Janey, Jack Bellamy's daughter? Remember what you did to her? That was wrong.'

'She had to pay for her sin – so did Jack Bellamy.'

'We were the sinners, Eddie. I paid the price, now you must too. You have to confess.'

'I've confessed to the priest. There's nothing on my conscience.'

'God wants you to do it the right way. He wants you to clear Jack Bellamy's name. He told me so himself.'

Eddie was surprised she'd try to trick him into pardoning her lover. 'God must tell me that himself. Bellamy has to pay for what he did.'

'He *has paid*, Eddie.' She came and stood beside him, looking as sweet and innocent in her gym slip and long socks as she had the day he'd made her his. 'Jack led me astray, I know that now. We could go away afterwards, just you and I. You'd like that, wouldn't you?'

'Yes,' he said eagerly. He loved Margaret, he'd always loved her. She hadn't died, she'd just gone away for a while. Now she was back and they'd be together always. 'Tell God to come and see me, Margaret. I'll do whatever he commands.'

'You can't bargain directly with God. You know the rules.'

'An angel, then. Ask him to send an angel to guide me.'

The door was pushed open. It was Pauline, with her painted Jezebel face and her bright, false smile. Something about her reminded him of Sarah Wyman. He glared at her.

'I thought I heard voices.' Pauline's nose wrinkled as she gazed at her father. He smelled dreadful. 'I can't stay very long, I'm afraid. I have to go back to London. Did you have a nice Christmas? The nurse said you've been behaving yourself lately. That's good. We can't afford to lose her, can we?'

A swift, pulsing rage filled him. She needed pulling into line. He began to stutter, anything to bring her nearer.

'What is it?' She came closer and bent her face to his. 'Speak a bit more clearly?'

'*Traitor!*' he hissed, spitting in her face.

She screeched like a parrot as she recoiled. 'You vile pig!' Frantically, she scrubbed at the spittle with a handkerchief. 'This is the last time I visit you. As far as I'm concerned, you can go and rot in a nursing home.'

'*Honour your father and mother!*' he thundered. 'Get down on your knees, Pauline. Repent your sins or God's wrath will fall upon your head. He has no patience with disobedient women.'

'Shut your mouth,' she hissed. 'I had enough of that rubbish when I was growing up.' One venomous glare and she was gone, banging the door behind her.

From the corner of the room, Margaret gave a soft giggle. 'My, she's like you, Eddie. If you hadn't been so blind, you would have seen this coming.'

'More toast?'

Griff leaned back in his chair and grinned. 'No thanks, I've eaten enough to last me for a month. Another mug of tea would go down well, though. The stuff they serve at the hospital is like dishwater.'

Susie hastened to refill his mug. 'You're nothing like my doctor. He's an antique. He smells of mothballs and looks as though he's swallowed a lizard.'

'Like this?' Griff pursed his mouth and bulged his eyes.

'Almost.' Susie made the same face, only worse. Looking down her nose at them she said in a strangled voice, 'What can I do foah yew, young lady?'

Griff exchanged a glance with Janey and they burst into laughter.

'It's not funny.' Susie rolled her eyes to the ceiling. 'I ask you, how can a girl confide anything personal to a wrinkly in tweed plus-fours? As soon as I'm old enough, I'm going to sign on with somebody modern, like Doctor Kildare on the tele.' She sighed. 'He's so handsome.' Her eyes darted to Justin, whose rear end was disappearing out of the door after Saffy. 'Wait for me, you little pest. I don't want you falling down the stairs into the coal cellar.'

Griff's eyes were full of amusement as he watched her go. 'I've never met anyone quite like Susie before. Did you know she's asked me to deliver a fruit cake to Devlin?'

'And will you?'

'I don't see why not. I'll have an hour or so to spare before I start work, and it would be nice to see him again.'

'Susie and Dev got on like a house on fire. They're quite alike in some ways. She was delighted when he sent her a cookery book for Christmas. I think she has a crush on him.'

'She's the right age.' A teasing light came into his eyes. 'Didn't you have a crush on me, once?'

'At an early age,' she said ruefully. 'You became my hero after you saved the life of that mouse.'

Puzzled, he stared at her. 'Mouse?'

'Surely you've not forgotten. You told me off for keeping it in a glass jar.'

Eyes clearing, he laughed. 'That mouse was a definite case of rigor mortis. Not even a miracle would have brought it back to life.'

'It was alive when you gave me it back.'

'A simple enough procedure. I swapped it for a live one.'

'You tricked me? I'm disappointed.'

'Your hero has clay feet, after all,' he mocked.

'Couldn't you have just told me it was dead?'

'I could have.' He finished his tea and stood up, his gaze dark on hers. He reached out and gently touched her cheek. 'To be quite honest, I couldn't bear to see you cry. Where are the curtains you want hanging?'

'In the bedrooms I've painted. I'll go fetch the hooks. The other two bedrooms can wait.'

'I take it this is the guest room?' Griff said a little later. He attached the last hook to a pair of straw-coloured curtains, and gave them a test run. 'It's got a nice view over the village.'

'It's Tim's room.'

From his perch on top of the ladder, Griff turned and stared at her.

'Didn't I tell you? He's been posted to Portland for three months and has offered to help me redecorate in return for bed and board.'

'Is that wise?'

'What do you mean?'

'Don't act the idiot, Janey. You know exactly what I'm saying.'

Her face suddenly flamed. 'Oh, come off it. First it was Devlin, now Tim. Don't you know me better than that?'

The sigh he gave signalled his exasperation. 'For pity's sake get off your high horse. This is a small village, remember?'

'I don't give a tinker's cuss what anyone thinks.'

'You haven't just got yourself to consider. There's Saffy and Justin.'

Their eyes locked in silent battle, hers indignant blue, his dark and implacable. The man she'd always thought she could count on for support had suddenly become an adversary.

He cares, a voice in her head said. *Griff's risking our friendship because he cares. And I do give a tinker's cuss. What if Robert Pitt jumps to the same conclusion and takes Justin away? Being a single mother is already a strike against me in some people's eyes.*

She capitulated a fraction. 'OK, so I hadn't considered people might gossip. Is that a crime?'

Griff hurled her a dark look. They were silent as they stalked into the next room. His back was so stiff she could almost see hackles ridging along his spine. She bared her teeth in a snarl as he climbed the stepladder. 'OK, damn it! I admit you're right. But I can't cancel the arrangement now. It's too late.'

Savagely, Griff hooked the curtains into the rings. 'Why is it?'

'Why?' she spluttered. 'Because I don't want to go back on my word, besides which. . . .' Her brain scrambled around for a plausible reason but only produced a lame answer. 'I need Tim's help.'

'Plenty of people would help. I have a whole month off in February. Why didn't you ask me?'

He was so infuriating! 'How could I have asked you? I only found out myself last night. Why didn't you tell me sooner, come to that?' Briefly, the thought crossed her mind that his attitude might be more than just caring. Was he a tiny bit jealous because she'd accepted Tim's offer of help before asking him?

'I didn't realize you were such a stuffed shirt. It must be the gypsy in you.'

Her prod brought an unexpected reaction. He tested the curtains with such force, the runner dislodged from one end and bent under the weight of the curtains. As if they were attached to a set of miniature roller skates, the whole lot slid down the runner into a heap on the floor.

So much for injured pride. Sense of humour fuelled by the event, she snorted with laughter. '*Never* take my appendix out, Doctor. You're too clumsy.'

He turned, his eyes laced with reluctant amusement. 'If you dare say another word I'll stitch your tongue to the end of your nose. Then we'll see who's clumsy.'

She stuck it out in the most provoking manner she could manage. When he made a flying leap from the ladder she was ready for it. Dashing out on to the landing she galloped down stairs two at a time with him after her. He caught her at the bottom in a rugby tackle. They rolled across the carpet in a tangle of arms and legs until he managed to pin her down, her hands above her head. Laughing and breathless they gazed at each other.

'Apologize for calling me a stuffed shirt,' he demanded.

'I refuse. You were totally out of line.'

His smile became rueful. 'I was, and I'm sorry. Let's kiss and make up.'

Something hit her in the solar plexus, turning it to liquid. 'Griff, I—'

'Be quiet.' His mouth touched against hers so gently she could have curled up and died from the pleasure of it.

'*Janey, are you there?*'

'Damn!' he murmured, then rising swiftly to his feet, pulled her upright.

They moved apart when Pamela came into the hall. 'Hello, dear. You look a bit flushed, I hope you're not catching a cold. Hello Griff. Nice to see you back home. I've just been talking to your father.'

'If he's been bragging about me again, I don't want to know.'

'He's very proud of you, and no wonder.' Pamela's smile was turned her way. 'Ada has sent over a steak and kidney pie for lunch. I just have to warm it through. I'm sure there will be enough to go round if I do some vegetables to go with it.'

She giggled when Griff winked at her.

Pamela gazed from one to the other, suddenly awkward. 'I hope I didn't come at a bad moment.'

'It was a perfect moment,' Griff said, almost keeping his face straight. 'Wouldn't you agree, Janey?'

'Perfect,' she said faintly, then burst into laughter.

'Mum!' When Susie came running through from the back room Pamela sighed with relief. She had the feeling she'd just made a fool of herself. 'Come and see the house. It's fantastic. The kitchen's groovy. I wish it was ours.'

The solution to the problem Tim had unwittingly caused suddenly presented itself. Janey grabbed at it, wondering why she hadn't thought of it before. 'Actually, I wanted to talk to you both about that. There are two spare bedrooms. If you'd like to move in we could be a family again.'

If Susie had been born with a tail she would have wagged it. 'Can we, Mum? I hate being all by myself in that tiny little room at the big house. There's never anyone to talk to, and Saffy and Justin are here. I'll be able to bring the dog as well.'

Pamela smiled when Saffy and Justin appeared. 'That would be very nice if Janey doesn't mind, but only until I can afford alternative accommodation. We mustn't impose.'

Susie dismissed the notion with a snort. 'Can I have the bedroom with pink roses? It's ever so pretty, and right next door to the nursery.' Eyes shining, she picked up Justin and smacked a kiss on his forehead. 'Wait till you see the nursery. It's got a circus on the wall. Bring Saffy, Mum. I was just going to show it to them.'

The cheeky look Janey shot at Griff was met by a grin. 'Shot down in flames. I guess I'd better go and get that curtain rail sorted out before the furniture arrives.'

'Griff?' she said as he ambled away.

He turned, his eyes liquid darkness in the shadowed contours of his face.

'Thanks, for everything.'

A wry smile touched his mouth. 'My pleasure, I think?'

The children's birthday party was a family affair, because neither of them were old enough to know what birthdays were.

Susie made an iced sponge cake covered in brightly-coloured sweets. The godfathers had remembered to send presents, with Griff and Devlin providing an extra one for Justin.

John Pitt had phoned the day before, saying he had a cold and couldn't make it. He'd visit as soon as he was better, and what did she consider a suitable present for the two children?

'They've got plenty of toys,' she said. 'What they do need is some sort of harness for the car. I'm taking my driving test next week, and although the Anglia has no back doors, I'd feel much happier if the children were restrained in some way.'

'I'll make enquiries,' he said hoarsely. 'Whilst I have you on the phone, I'm happy to inform you that Justin's parents have agreed to my suggestion regarding his guardianship. If you're of the same mind, I'll bring some papers down for you to sign. Your signature will need to be independently witnessed by someone of good standing and character.'

'I'll ask Charles Wyman. He's been named in the honours list, and is about to be knighted.' Hearing his hacking cough, she implored, 'Please go to bed and rest, Mr Pitt. You should look after yourself with that cold. A glass of hot lemon with a teaspoon of honey and a tot of whisky in it will help ease the cough.'

'Thank you. That sounds like a sensible, and delicious remedy. I'll try it. And please, could you bring yourself to call me Robert from now on in?'

It wasn't until the day after the party that Janey realized Pauline and Martin hadn't sent their son a birthday card.

Pauline appeared in the social pages now and again. *Sarah Wyman, Noel Chatterton, Pauline and Martin Pitt at the hospital charity ball.* Twice, she was with an older man. *Pauline Pitt at the opera with financier, Ibn Faisal Gamal. Mrs Pitt and Ibn Faisal Gamal at Covent Garden. Mrs Pitt was wearing. . . .*

Diamonds at her throat, around her neck, on her fingers, a designer gown, fur coat. Pauline looked absolutely stunning.

Within a week, Janey had unpacked the boxes that had been stored in the house. It struck her as odd that she'd done all those paintings and didn't have any to put on her walls.

Except Mistral! Going into the room she'd chosen as a studio she unwrapped it, and placing it on the easel stood back and studied it. It was a good painting. The woman looked steadily back at her through luminous challenging eyes, her hair blowing in the wind.

'Who's that?' Pamela said, coming up behind her. 'Did you paint it?'

'Yes. It's Saffy's paternal grandmother.'

'Oh!' There was a moment's silence, then Pamela said hesitantly, 'She looks a bit like you.'

'Yes, I know.' She threw the cloth back over it. 'She's dead.' *Only she hadn't been dead in Drifter's memory! It's odd how I hardly ever think of him now, the man who'd once meant so much to me.* She wondered if she'd ever see him again.

New Year came and went. She passed her driving test with flying colours, coming home triumphant. It snowed the day after, enchanting the children who clambered up on an armchair and gazed at it out of the window. She and Susie built them a snowman, but it turned to slush overnight.

Justin found his feet, lurching from chair to chair with an intense, determined look on his face. He'd gaze silently at her afterwards, seeking approval for his achievement. She praised him often, with kisses, and cuddles and tender words. He wasn't confident like Saffy, and she'd begun to realize he was a child who needed lots of encouragement.

Robert Pitt visited, bringing with him some child restraints, which he fitted to the back seat of her car. She hesitantly asked if she could consult him about her finances. 'My agent has just sent me another cheque. I haven't had time to deposit the last one yet.'

'Has any tax been paid on this?' he asked.

She gave a helpless shrug. 'I really don't know. Devlin Cox has been handling my finances.'

'I'd better ring him and find out. Is he trustworthy?'

'Absolutely,' she snapped, feeling suddenly affronted on Dev's behalf.

'One can't be too careful,' he said drily. 'Have you enough for your day-to-day expenses without this?'

'For the next two years, at least. Longer if I'm careful.'

'Mortgage payments?'

'I bought the house outright.'

Robert looked impressed. 'Then we should be able to make this money work for you.'

She hesitated again. 'There's also Saffy's account. She laid the passbook on the table. I'm not quite sure if I did the right thing with it. It's quite a lot of money.'

His eyes widened when he saw the amount. 'Money like this should be accounted for, and properly handled. Where did it come from?'

'Her father's family. I was tempted to tear the cheque up.'

He gave a slight smile. 'And you're not going to tell me their name?'

'Taunt?' she said stiffly. 'Saffy's grandfather is Ingram Fairfax Taunt.'

'I've heard of him. Publishing, I believe.'

It was funny how Robert managed to cut the tycoon down to size with one terse sentence. She gave him a small, wry, smile. 'I guess you could say this was a pay-off.'

His eyes were bland as they gazed at her. 'Why *didn't* you tear it up?'

'Because I was brought up in poverty, and Ingram Taunt wouldn't even have missed it. I didn't want Saffy to be raised the same way. I didn't take this for myself. It's for her future. Besides, her father loved her, despite what happened.'

'He hasn't tried to contact you?'

She shook her head. 'To be honest, I think our relationship was over a long time before the end came. We just didn't see it.' This was the second time in days she'd reopened this old wound, and although there wasn't as much scar tissue as she'd imagined there would be, it still hurt. *It's only my pride that's hurt*, she rationalized. 'Both of us had a lot of growing up to do, I guess. If her father wants to see her in the future, I won't object. He wasn't a bad man, and I'd like her to know who he is.'

'My dear, girl.' His hand closed over hers for a second. 'I'd say you've managed to grow up most admirably.'

Robert had a depth of feeling, despite his stern, old-fashioned exterior. She was relieved when he offered to manage her financial affairs.

A few days later she watched from an upstairs window as Tim tore up the road. He was driving a noisy motorbike and sidecar with blue smoke trailing out the exhaust. It backfired as he drew to a halt.

She was downstairs in a flash, throwing open the door before he had time to knock. Smiling broadly, he dropped a couple of suitcases on to the hall floor, then kicking the door shut behind him, grabbed her up in his arms and whirled her around. 'Sorry about the noise. Something dropped off when I went over a pothole. Guess who I picked up on the way in?'

'Griff?'

'How did you know?'

'Just a guess. I knew he was taking a holiday this month.'

'I dropped him off at his father's place. *Good God!*' He set her on her feet. 'Look at the state of this place. Pink roses everywhere!'

'Not everywhere. There are also blue and yellow ones. However, I've painted your room a pale yellow. You know where to find it.'

Saffy wandered out from the lounge to see what all the fuss was about.

Tim held out his arms. 'Look how pretty you've become. Come and give your favourite godfather a kiss.' Saffy was shy for a few seconds, then she launched herself into his arms with a smile on her face. 'That's what I like, a girl who's easy.' Tim's glance suddenly went to the doorway. 'Hello, who are you, young fellow?'

Justin stuck his thumb in his mouth and stared at Tim, uncertain.

Scooping him into her arms, Janey kissed him. 'This is Justin. He's Pauline's son and lives with us.'

Tim stared unbelievingly at her for a few seconds, then his mouth relaxed into an ironic grin, and he shook his head. 'That figures.'

Justin pointed at the shiny buttons on Tim's coat, chuckled with laughter, then buried his face in her neck.

'If you imagine you're eating my buttons you can think again, young man. Saffy chewed the last lot. My superior officer told me I was a disgrace to the British Navy.'

How uncomplicated he is, Janey thought, as she watched him lower Saffy to the floor and open his suitcase. Justin wriggled to be put down and went to join her, watching solemnly as Tim brought out a brightly coloured box.

'I guess you'd better have this, Saffy.' He touched the catch and a jack-in-the-box sprang out. Saffy squealed with delight. Astonished, Justin took a step backwards and fell over.

'And this is for you, Justin. A genuine plastic toy radio made in Hong Kong.' Tim wound the knob in the middle and animals went round a dial as it played a tinkling tune. A smile spread across Justin's face and he began to rock backwards and forwards with it held in his arms.

'Wasn't it clever of me to bring two presents? I must be a mind reader.'

Dear Tim. He'd matured into an easy-going man with a great sense of humour, she thought. Pauline would never know what she'd missed out on. She hoped he'd find a woman more worthy of him, one he could share his future with.

'Let me make you some tea before Susie gets home from school.'

'Susie?'

'My sister, surely you remember her?'

'Oh *that* Susie.'

'She and my stepmother live here, too.'

His eyes met hers for a second, then he gave an easy, self-effacing laugh. 'I can take a hint. Nice move, Janey. No wonder Griff looked so damned smug?'

Smug? Why would Griff look smug? Then she remembered his kiss and an unexpected blush warmed her cheeks.

Tim laughed as he ruffled her hair. 'I might just give him a run for his money.'

'Don't be silly,' she said as he grabbed up his luggage and headed up the stairs. 'There's nothing but friendship between Griff and myself. Absolutely nothing.'

CHAPTER SEVENTEEN

Tim's energy seemed inexhaustible. Within days he'd stripped the wallpaper from the downstairs rooms, painted the hallway a soft green and was now inspecting the ivory satin wallpaper she'd chosen for the lounge.

'This will look a bit bare,' he commented, standing back and gazing critically at it. 'Have you got any pictures to hang?'

'No.'

'You're supposed to be an artist. Paint some.'

There was a strange reluctance in her to paint. The domestic routine of the house and children occupied her time fully, leaving no room for the creative urges which had once ruled her life. 'I haven't got time.'

'Sure you have, after the children are in bed.'

'You don't understand, Tim. I can't just paint a picture. I don't feel inspired.'

He threw her a wolfish grin. 'Let me inspire you.' Closing one eye, he measured a patch of wall with his fingers and thumbs. 'Four foot by three. A window with lace curtains, and a sunny garden outside. Wallflowers, daisies, sunflowers, foxgloves and hollyhocks, a stone garden bench with an old-fashioned girl sitting on it.'

'Forget the windows and lace curtains, it would make it too fussy.' Her eyes narrowed in concentration. It might be fun to paint something for her own house, something that wasn't commercially inspired. 'No, not sunflowers,' she muttered. 'Their brilliance would overshadow the child. Light diffused through an arch of climbing roses, perhaps, illuminating the girl's face. She could be gazing at a kitten in her lap, teasing it with a ribbon.'

'Tabby?'

'Tortoiseshell, to tone in with the colours of the wallflowers.'

'Are you sure? I've never seen a tortoiseshell wallflower.'

'Don't be ridiculous, Tim. I'll just blend the colours.' Tim's chuckle brought a grin to her face. 'You rat? Just for that you can get your own lunch. I'm going into town to stock up on paints as soon as the kids wake up from their nap.'

'Go now, if you like. I can manage them for a couple of hours.'

She needed no further encouragement. Within minutes she was on her way, mentally listing the materials she'd need. She bought the materials in bulk, then ruefully gazed at the bill. *Why do I need all this? I'm only painting one miserable picture*. Only it wouldn't be miserable. Her subject would be modelled on Saffy, her green eyes alight with mischief, her smile impish.

Griff arrived on the doorstep just as she was unloading her purchases. 'You take this. I'll bring in your parcels.' He pulled a kitten from under his jacket and placed it in her arms. 'Dad said you might like to give this orphan a home. It's from the barn. A fox killed his mother and the rest of the litter.'

The kitten was a tabby, long furred and velvety soft. *An omen. I'll paint a tabby in the picture*. 'He's beautiful. Thanks Griff.'

Tim was lying on the floor, the kids clambering all over him. Laughing, he rose to his feet with one captured under each arm.

Griff eyed the one piece of wallpaper pasted to the wall. 'It looks as though you need help with that. It's crooked.'

'The wall's crooked.'

'You should have hung a weighted piece of string from the picture rail as a guide.'

There was a moment of tension when the two men eyeballed each other, causing her to hold her breath for a second. Then it slipped past as Tim's good-natured grin reasserted itself. 'I've never hung wallpaper before. I'm better with a paintbrush and roller.' When he put the two children down, Saffy immediately transferred her affections to Griff, who swung her up in his arms.

'You've done an expert job on the hall,' Griff conceded. 'I'll give you a hand with the papering, if you like.'

Men! Janey thought, making a dive for Justin who was heading for the bucket of paste as fast as his legs could carry him. The sight of the kitten stopped the squawk of protest he was about to give.

'This is Fluffy. Isn't he sweet?'

'*Fluffy?*' Griff's eyebrows nearly disappeared into his hairline and a grin spread across his face. 'Dad will die laughing.'

'She'll have him on the vet's operating table before the month is up,' Tim chipped in.

'Tarzan, then. Will that suit your macho image better?' Giving them a dirty look she took Saffy from Griff's arms and stalked away. 'I'll get you both rugged up and we'll walk to the village shop to buy kitty some food.'

She left the men to sort themselves out. As she manoeuvred the pushchair out through the front door, she could still hear Griff and Tim laughing.

'Idiots!' she snorted.

Pamela had just rounded the bend on her bicycle when she hit a patch of ice and skidded across the road into the fence surrounding Coombe Cottage. Climbing to her feet, she gazed ruefully at the twisted frame and buckled wheel.

'*Pamela!* I heard the bang. Are you all right?'

'A couple of scrapes, that's all.'

John placed his hand under her elbow. 'You're trembling. You'd better come inside and I'll make you a cup of tea.'

'I'm all right, really,' she protested as she allowed herself to be led inside. 'I should have taken more care.'

It was odd being inside Coombe Cottage again, though she wouldn't have known the place. One wall had been lined with shelves containing a stack of books, records, and an expensive-looking record player. Three comfortable chairs were arranged around an oblong coffee table, their dark blue covers toned with the blue-checked curtains. The walls had been painted white, the floor carpeted in pale grey.

On one wall was a painting of lilies growing along the bank of a stream. She swelled with pride when she recognized it as Janey's work. She wished all her paintings were like this. Although the one she'd seen at the house was good, she didn't quite understand it, or like it half as much.

'Janey's very talented' John said, watching her eyes stray to it for a second time as he examined her hands. 'I'll fetch a bowl of warm water and the first aid box. You can fix yourself up whilst I make you some tea.'

'It's kind of you.'

As he went to pick up the sheets of paper he'd been studying, her glance fell on them. A puzzled frown creased her brow. Not a normal reaction, he would have thought. Curiosity, yes, but puzzlement? Acting on a hunch, he moved them to one side, then left her to it whilst he went into the kitchen.

When he came back with the bowl of water, she had one of the papers in her hand, and was studying it. She flushed, and placed it back on the table. 'I'm sorry. I hope you don't think I was being nosy. It's just, I thought I recognized the girl's face on this one.'

'They're all crime victims.'

'Yes, I know. These are newspaper cuttings from several years ago.' She applied herself to the task of bathing her wounds, her face a study of concentration.

She knows something, or thinks she does.

'Why have you got them?'

'Criminology is my hobby. I used to be a policeman, then I became a private detective. Much more money in it and I enjoyed being my own boss.'

'I see.' Her eyes came up to his. They were clear brown and honest, but troubled. 'They didn't catch the man who attacked those girls, did they?'

It was more of a statement than a question.

'No,' he said gently. 'A pity. There would have been other victims too, unreported at the time. It's not an easy thing for a woman to admit to, especially girls as young as these.'

She worried at her lip. 'What if somebody knew something, but hadn't said anything?'

'The police can be very understanding under certain circumstances.'

'What circumstances?'

'In the case of a husband and wife, for instance. She wouldn't have to give evidence against her husband in court.' He stood up and smiled at her. 'The kettle must be boiling. I'll go and make the tea.' By the time he came back she'd finished dressing her wounds, and didn't resume their former conversation, talking instead about the garden.

'You should plant a lilac in the corner of the garden, right against the fence. It would look pretty, and the blossoms have a lovely perfume. Dig a big hole so it's got plenty of room for the roots to spread out.' She seemed ill at ease, drinking her tea quickly and obviously eager to get away.

'I'll drive you home.' He waved aside her objections. 'Janey would never forgive me if I allowed you to walk.'

She was silent in the car, her face set and pale. He hoped he'd given her something to think about. Mary Yates's suspicions had been correct. Eddie Renfrew *was* involved in the rapes. Pamela either knew it, or suspected.

'You won't forget the lilac,' she said when she got out of the car. 'I'll ask Phil to drop you one off. He's always taking cuttings of things.'

Later, when Janey came in and fussed over her, Pamela couldn't look her in the face. She should have guessed Eddie had attacked Janey. He was vile! How could he have committed such a crime and allowed Jack Bellamy to take the blame?

Janey must know that he'd attacked her, but she couldn't ask her outright, she just couldn't! She cried that night, her sobs muffled by the pillow. She wished she'd never heard of Edward Renfrew.

A hand touched her shoulder. 'Mum, what's wrong? Why are you crying?'

'It's nothing. Go back to bed, Susie.'

'It's him isn't it? My father? You're going back to him!' There was an undertone of fear in the accusation. 'I won't go, I won't! I love it here with Janey. I'd rather die!'

'Hush, baby, you'll wake everyone up.' Pamela drew back the covers and allowed Susie to slip in beside her. 'I'll never go back to him. Whatever gave you that idea?'

Susie shuddered as she snuggled against her mother's shoulder. 'I'm so glad. I couldn't bear living with him again. He came to my room when I was asleep once, and *touched me*.'

Blood suddenly pounded against Pamela's eardrums. 'Oh my, God! Susie?'

'You know how he used to rant on about religion? He kept telling me I was a sinner, that I had to suffer. It was horrible. I put a chair under the door handle so he couldn't get in after that. A normal father wouldn't do that. He's insane, isn't he?'

Pamela had never considered that possibility, now she began to wonder. 'Why didn't you tell me before?'

'I was scared.' Susie's tense body began to relax. 'He said you wouldn't love me any more if you knew. But you do, don't you? It wasn't my fault.'

'Of course I love you.' Holding Susie in her arms while she drifted into sleep

Pamela thought of Janey and what she must have suffered at Eddie's hands. Hate for him glowed white-hot inside her. Wide awake now, she carefully eased herself from the bed and made her way downstairs. The kitchen was warm, and the sight of the kitten curled against Gypsy in the basket made her smile a little.

Tarzan emerged whilst she warmed herself some milk, rubbing around her ankles and mewing. She drew it into her lap. It was so sweet and helpless, motherless and seeking love, like Janey had once been. She'd failed Janey and Susie, the two people she loved most in the world.

Her decision was made as soon as the thought left her mind. It was time Eddie was brought to justice!

Between them, Griff and Tim completed the redecorating in two weeks, just in time for the house-warming. There had been some good-natured rivalry between them over the past few days. It culminated with Griff saying to Tim over lunch 'Now it's finished you'll be moving into navy quarters, no doubt.'

Tim's eyes gleamed. 'I don't know what gave you that impression. I know a good billet when I see one. Besides which, I adore my landlady.' He slid his arm around Janey's waist and pulled her to his side. 'You're not going to be heartless enough to chuck me out, are you?'

She disentangled herself with a light laugh. 'Not if you behave yourself.'

Tim was subjected to a hard look from Griff. 'I'll come over and fix up the garden whilst Tim's at work. Dad said he's got some shrubs that can be planted along the fence line.'

'You'll spoil your pretty surgeon's hands doing manual labour,' Tim mocked.

A smile inched across Griff's mouth. 'Let me worry about that. Just go and play with your battleships.'

'Submarines. Portland is a submarine base.'

'Shut up, you two. I'm trying to work out what shopping I'll need to get for the house-warming.'

'Plenty of booze,' Tim suggested. 'I'll chip in for it.'

'I'll help you shop, if you like,' Griff offered. 'We could go in the morning, early.'

Her face lit up in a smile. It was hard work shopping with two small children in tow. 'Thanks. Griff. I'd really appreciate it. You can look after the kids while I buy myself a new outfit.'

Tim snorted with laughter. 'Typical woman. Give her an inch and she'll take a yard.'

Griff arrived at half past eight on the dot. Soon they joined the rush hour traffic into Poole, arriving just as the shops opened for business.

Janey bought herself a pair of black velvet pants and a waistcoat. To go under it a pearl-buttoned white silk shirt, its cuffs edged with a tracery of delicate lace. It was wildly expensive, but she hadn't been able to resist it.

With Griff in charge, Saffy and Justin suddenly became model children. They stopped for lunch before loading the contents of the heavily-laden trolleys into the back of the car, then headed back home. The children fell asleep, and she deposited them on the couch whilst Griff brought in the shopping.

'Will you stay for a cup of tea?'

'Some other time. I have to go back into town. I'll see you tomorrow night.'

Looping his grey scarf about his neck she gazed at him. 'Thanks for all your help, Griff.'

He brushed his mouth across her forehead. 'I enjoyed it.' Then he was gone, his long legs taking him rapidly down the driveway. He turned at the bottom, blew her a kiss and disappeared from view.

Half an hour later the telephone rang and a woman inquired, 'Is Tim there?'

'He'll be in about half past five. If you leave your name and number I'll ask him to call you.'

'It's Wendy. It's just, well, I haven't seen Tim in ages.'

'I'm having a house-warming party tomorrow. Bring your boyfriend. Tim told me you're practically engaged.'

'Not any more, we've split.'

'Oh, I'm sorry.'

'Don't be. He was hand-picked by my mother.'

'All the more reason to come to the party, then. I'll send Tim to pick you up, if you like. It will get him out of my hair for a while.'

'I've got my own car. I'll surprise him. Would I be able to stay the night? I don't fancy driving home late, especially if I've had a drink or two.'

'Sure. You can have Tim's room. He can fight the others for possession of the couch.'

There was a thud from the lounge, followed by an outraged cry. 'I must go. Justin's just fallen off the chair. I'll see you tomorrow.'

The party proved to be a huge success. Despite his remarks to the contrary, Devlin arrived, bringing with him Sandy, Blaise, Stephen and Dion. Laughing, they spilled out the back of the van, limping and clutching various parts of their bodies, and making disparaging remarks about his driving skills.

'If you ungrateful bastards don't belt up, you can walk home. It's not my fault the road's full of potholes.'

'*Daaahling!*' Dion trilled, catching sight of her. 'You look ravishingly medieval.'

Enveloped in a mass hug, Janey managed to scramble out of it just as Wendy arrived on the doorstep. Dressed in a short, cream jersey shift, her hair was a fall of burnished copper curving gently into her jaw line. She'd become a beautiful woman.

They smiled at each other, then Wendy stepped forward and hugged her. 'I wouldn't have recognized you. You look great.'

'You look absolutely stunning.'

'She's a dream.' Devlin stepped forward, as smooth as butter, his eyes alight with curiosity. 'I'm Devlin Cox, Janey's agent. I'm fairly well off, unattached, and you're the woman of my dreams.'

So much for undying love, Janey thought, grinning.

Wendy eyed him up and down, saying coolly, 'I'm Wendy Ryker.'

Devlin groaned. 'If you tell me you're Tim's wife, I'll strangle him with my bare hands and turn you into a widow.'

'I'm his sister.' Wendy batted her eyelashes. 'Can I buy you a drink?'

Janey laughed as the pair of them walked off without giving her a backward glance. Confidence was all it took, and Wendy seemed to have plenty of it. She envied her.

She turned to open the door again, giving a big smile at the sight of Griff. 'You've arrived.'

'So I have' His glance wandered to the Griffin medallion, which she'd hung on a black velvet ribbon. 'You still have it, then?'

'I've never taken it off. It's always been my talisman.'

Her words seem to annoy him. 'It's a piece of wood with a carving on it. I can't believe I was egotistical enough to ask dad to give it to you.'

'My hero, Griff,' she mocked. 'Remember?'

His hand reached out to close around the medallion. For a moment she thought he was going to jerk it from her neck, but he merely applied pressure, and pulling her relentlessly towards him, kissed her.

There was nothing friendly about this kiss. It was a slightly savage reminder he wasn't to be taken lightly. She didn't know whether to be sorry or angry when he released her. She only knew she'd enjoyed it, which surprised her. Astonished, she stared at him, watching the amusement dawn in his dark eyes, the smile slowly inching across his face. 'That's to remind you I'm just a man.'

Some man! If you hadn't been dear, dependable, Griff, who I've known all my life, I might go after you. She mentally shook herself. It was stupid allowing her thoughts to run in that direction. A relationship, *any* relationship, was out of the question for her now. Her life was full with her house and children. Now she'd begun to paint again, she didn't have room for a man in her life, even if she'd had the inclination.

'Why are you so frigid?' Drifter had asked, and she hadn't been able to tell him. *Spoiled goods! Griff deserved better than that.*

Everybody arrived at once. Her father with Mary and Douglas, all of them giving her a hug at once. John Smith with a huge box of chocolates. The Wymans, both of them looking content, and not a day older than when she'd been a child. Ada, a self-conscious smile on her lips, her cheeks pink and puffed, and looking for all the world like a female toby jug. Then there was Phil in his best suit, a potted hyacinth clutched in his work-worn hands for her kitchen window sill. Justin's grandfather gave her a clock with a swinging pendulum, which she hung immediately on a hook in the hall.

The salt of the earth, all of them, accepting the peculiarities of her London friends with good grace and good manners, apart from a few raised eyebrows at the antics of Stephen and Dion. As the evening wore on and they all relaxed together, even they lost their novelty.

By midnight, everyone began to drift away. Pamela tidied up the kitchen as best she could, then went to bed, taking a reluctant, and protesting Susie with her.

'Goodnight, Suse.' Devlin called out after her. 'We'll cook Sunday lunch together tomorrow, and dazzle everyone with our expertise.'

They reminisced about old times, drank wine and played jazz. Wendy fitted into the crowd as though she'd always known them. She embarrassed Tim by relating his boyhood misdeeds, flirted with Devlin, teased Stephen and Dion and encouraged Sandy and Blaise to tell tales about the theatre, which had them in fits of laughter.

Stephen and Dion mentioned their dream of opening a hairdressing salon in the West End as soon as they raised the capital, a constant topic with them.

'I wouldn't mind selling my salon in Bournemouth and going shares,' Wendy said. 'I could do with a change of scenery.'

'Mum and dad would kick up a fuss,' Tim said.

Wendy's laugh had an edge to it. 'Let them. I'm a big girl now.'

'I wouldn't mind throwing in a few quid,' Devlin said casually.

Leaning against Griff's knee, Janey felt a bit left out as they all began to discuss the viability of the business venture. London seemed unreal to her now, part of her past. There was a sense of something ending for her tonight, as if the tide had turned and was taking them all in different directions.

As if he sensed her thoughts, Griff's finger stroked down the back of her neck. Griff would never be an integral part of the crowd. The others liked and respected him, but they'd never known the essence of him. He was a disturbing man, enigmatic even to her, who knew him best.

'I'll make us some coffee, shall I?' She rose, unseen and unheard by anyone but Griff. Leaving the room, she stood in the quiet hallway.

The voices faded to a buzz. The house was solid, real to her, breathing secrets into the night. The clock ticked, its tone solemn and reliable. It was a good clock, made to last a lifetime. She loved her home, loved the secure feeling it gave her. Its walls hugged her close, she and her children, protecting them. She'd been fortunate in her life, in her friends. On balance, the good outweighed the bad. She had much to be thankful for.

'Thank you,' she murmured, remembering with fondness the old man who'd provided the roof over her head. 'I'll call it William's House in your memory.'

'He would have appreciated that.'

She hadn't heard Griff follow her out. She turned, her eyes seeking his face in the dark. 'I was listening to the house.' If anyone but Griff had caught her talking to herself she might have been embarrassed. He understood, he always understood.

'I'll make you a nameplate for the gate.' He slid an arm around her waist and led her towards the kitchen. 'Come on, I'll help you make the coffee before I go.'

Before her guests left for London the next day, Devlin asked to see what she was working on.

He gazed at her current project with pleasure in his eyes. 'Not bad at all. We could have a Renfrew exhibition in the summer.'

'This is for me, Dev.'

His eyes brooded on hers. 'I know I said I wouldn't push you, but you need to consolidate on what you've already done.'

'I will, I promise.' The urge to paint had returned as soon as she'd put the first brush stroke on the canvas. She smiled. She'd been foolish to imagine she could give it up. 'What about the following spring?'

'Now you're talking!' He pulled the cover from the Mistral painting, staring at it in silent contemplation. 'I could get a good price for this.'

'It's not for sale.'

'You're brilliant at painting tombstones. Why are you keeping it?'

How perceptive he was. 'I'm not. I'm looking after it.'

He turned, a despairing look in his eyes. 'You still think Drifter's coming back, don't you?'

'No. It's over.' She threw the cloth back over the painting. 'Like you said, it's a tombstone.'

'He told me he wrote to you.'

Just like that! Squashing the hurt she experienced, she stared at him. 'Where's the letter?'

If Devlin was capable of guilt he managed to hide it under an aggressive shrug. 'How the hell should I know? That little shit Connor probably read it and threw it away. I should have beaten his tiny brain into pulp when I had the chance.'

There was no anger in her, just a faint curiosity to what the letter had contained. 'You should have told me before, Dev.'

'I know, but I thought I had a chance with you then.' He gave an ironic smile and gently kissed her on the cheek. 'Tell your father I enjoyed talking to him. He's very proud of you, and so am I. Be happy, Janey.'

There was a curious silence in her after he strode away, as if something vibrant and alive had abruptly ended.

The following week a bitter wind blew in from the north, bringing with it shafts of sleet that froze the earth solid. The furrows in the fields resembled tiny waves white-capped with frost. Icicles quivered on the bare tree branches, a fantasy of silver flora flung from the frigid sky.

Pamela was chased inside Coombe Cottage by a gust of wind that sent papers flying from the table and smoke billowing into the room from the chimney.

'I really must build a decent porch on this house,' John grumbled, helping her off with her coat. 'You look frozen. Why don't we go into the kitchen before we turn into smoked kippers. It's warmer in there. I'll make us some tea, then you can tell me what you wanted to see me about.'

She didn't wait until the tea was made. 'Just before we vacated this cottage I found a suitcase in the roof containing photographs. They were of an indecent nature. I buried it in the corner of the garden.'

'Where the lilac should be planted?'

'Yes. Stupid of me, wasn't it? I was hoping you'd find them by accident.'

'When you say indecent, do you mean the type of pictures found in magazines aimed at men?'

Pamela blushed. 'I've never read that type of magazine.'

'Quite so.' John placed a cup of tea in front of her, and giving her time to recover from her embarrassment, turned and opened the pantry door. 'Would you like a digestive biscuit to go with that?'

'Thanks.'

Sliding some on to a plate, he set them on the table and took the chair opposite her. 'Tell me about it. You needn't be embarrassed.'

'They were photographs of girls. I recognized one of them from those newspaper cuttings.'

'You think your husband was implicated?'

'Well he must have been, mustn't he?' She took a deep breath. 'I have no proof, but I know he was. He was a cruel man, that's why I left him. Now Susie has told me he went to her bedroom and tried to . . . touch her.'

Pamela was a mother defending her young. She looked as if she were about to cry. Touched, he waited until she'd taken control of herself then placed his hand over hers. 'This must be distressing for you.'

'It wasn't just Susie,' she said flatly. 'I think he must have abused Janey too. I know he ill-treated her, but I never thought he'd do anything like that to her.' She buried her face in her hands and began to sob. 'She's never said anything to me about it. I should have left him when he first started beating me, I suppose, but I was scared. Besides, I thought if he took his temper out on me, he might leave Janey alone.'

'You're the only mother she's ever known. Janey's very fond of you.' He fetched a handkerchief and handed it to her. 'Have you thought of discussing this with her?'

'How could I?'

'Has it never occurred to you that she might be trying to protect you and Susie by keeping quiet?'

There was a sudden, terrible stillness about her. 'No . . . no, it hadn't. It would be so like her. She might have needed another woman to talk to. I've been so selfish. Perhaps I should start by telling her about Susie's experience.'

John smiled to himself, knowing Janey would see right through her approach. But that didn't matter if the end justified the means. If Janey signed a statement naming Edward Renfrew as her attacker, and the buried photographs were still usable, it wouldn't necessarily bring the man to justice, but it would give him a lever to clear Jack's name. 'I'd say you were the most unselfish person I've ever met. How is your husband, by the way?'

She managed a watery smile. 'Your questions are never as casual as they appear. Why do you ask?'

'When people are faced with their own mortality they often take stock of their lives. I know of several instances where people have cleared their slates because they thought they were going to meet their maker.'

She gave a disbelieving snort of laughter. 'The only person he'd confess to would be the priest.'

'Then it might be worth paying him a visit.'

'It won't do any good. He can't divulge that sort of confidence.'

Gently, he suggested. 'It's possible he might be able to persuade Eddie to confess to the authorities. It's worth a try.'

She stood up, a determined look on her face. 'Will you let me talk to Janey first? She might want to let things lie.'

'Of course, but if those photographs have survived, they're evidence. I'm legally bound to hand them over to the police. They'll probably want to interview you.'

Her face paled, but she gave a resolute nod.

'I'll drive you home,' he said, feeling sad for this perfectly nice, perfectly ordinary woman, who'd only sought to do what she'd thought best for her family.

'I'd rather you didn't.' She fixed a woollen scarf around her head and pulled on her gloves. 'Walking will give me time to think about things a bit.'

After she'd gone, John fetched a spade from the shed. As it hit the frozen earth a shock ran up his arm. He made several attempts before running out of breath, then leaned on his spade and swore in frustration.

From behind him came a chuckle. 'You'll be needing a pick-axe before you'll make an impression on that, I reckon. But even then you won't get far. The earth's set like concrete. Best wait until it thaws.'

For a man who'd always prided himself on his patience, John's own sense of urgency surprised him. 'How long will that take?'

Phil looked up at the sky with a knowing eye. 'Wind should change soon. A couple of weeks should see you right for planting that lilac Mrs Renfrew was asking me about. I'll drop it off when it's time.'

'To everything there is a season,' John quoted with a frustrated sigh.

'And a time for every purpose under the heaven.' Phil finished, grinning at John's surprised expression. 'The vicar taught it to me. He's right nice at reading. I could never quite get the hang of it mesself. The bible has a lot in common with nature, I reckon. In the next verse it says something about, "a time to plant, and a time to pluck up that which is planted".' Touching his cap, Phil continued on up the lane with John staring after him.

Whistling to himself, Phil grinned now and again, and wondered at the ignorance of city-bred folk.

CHAPTER EIGHTEEN

The train pulled out of the station, taking Griff with it. His face at the window grew smaller, his eyes glowing dark in the pale oval. She lifted her hand in a final wave. He blew her a kiss. Then he was gone and she felt alone.

'Daddy's, gone,' Saffy wailed. Immediately, Justin's bottom lip began to tremble in sympathy. She took them both in a hug, then fished around in her pocket. 'Look, Griff's left you some Smarties.' She stuffed a couple in each mouth, then hurried them out to where she'd left her car.

'I've applied for a position at the hospital in Poole,' Griff had told her, leaving it until just before he got on the train, as if the information was somehow inconsequential. 'If all goes well I'll be back for good in May.'

'I'll keep my fingers crossed.'

'Will you, Janey?' He'd sounded slightly remote, as if his mind had shifted into another sphere.

She'd hugged him then, bringing him back to her in spirit. 'I'll miss you, Griff. So will the kids.'

The slow curve of his smile had warmed her heart. He hadn't kissed her, just touched her lips with his finger. 'And I'll miss you.'

Tears pricked her eyes as she strapped the children into their restraints. It's March tomorrow, she told herself firmly. With a bit of luck he'll be home for good soon.

She was half-way home when a thought came out of nowhere and punched her squarely in the midriff. *Could you be in love with Griff?*

'I've always loved him,' she argued out loud.

Of course you have, but this feels different.

It would be wise to deny the notion before it took a hold on her. To fall in love with Griff would be a disaster for them both. A horn tooted behind her, alerting her that the lights had turned green. She must stop thinking about Griff. She managed it for the half hour it took her to get home, singing nursery rhymes at the top of her voice to keep the children amused.

As she turned into the gateway she saw it – a wooden plaque screwed into the gate post: *William's House*. Pulling to a halt she gazed at the beautiful copperplate lettering and the border of dog roses carved around it, and began to love him all over again.

*

Pamela had prevaricated, never quite finding the courage to approach Janey. Watching the girl bring the car to a halt, she knew she could no longer afford to wait.

John had phoned whilst Janey was out. He'd dug up the suitcase. Although most of the photographs had deteriorated, he thought there might be enough of them left for identification purposes. 'Did you talk to Janey?' he'd asked.

He didn't pressure her when she'd confessed she hadn't.

'Well, it's not an easy thing to do. We might be able to get by without involving her. I've talked to the priest. He's agreed to come with me to see your husband tomorrow, but I have to warn you – he said Eddie's mental condition is deteriorating. He's been living in the church hospice since the house was sold, and he doesn't get any visitors.'

Pauline was showing her true colours with a vengeance, Pamela thought.

'He's being assessed soon by a psychiatrist. If he's found to be of unsound mind he'll be moved into an institution. I doubt if a confession would be admissible under those circumstances. It's highly unethical, but I'll hold back on the photographs for a couple of days. The best we can hope for now is to clear Jack's name, I think.'

A statement from her stepdaughter had suddenly become imperative.

Pamela's heart was thumping when she approached her. 'Can we talk when you've got a minute?'

Janey's smile was replaced by alarm. 'What's wrong, there hasn't been an accident or anything?'

'Nothing like that.' She managed a smile as she turned towards the kitchen. 'I'll make us some tea.'

Janey divested the children of their outdoor wear and placed them in the charge of a sober-faced Susie, who giving her a quick hug, whispered fiercely, 'Whatever happens, I love you.'

Hurrying through to the kitchen, Janey gazed at Pamela, whose hands trembled as she poured tea into two big blue-hooped mugs. 'I can see from your face that something serious has cropped up. Don't keep me in suspense.'

Pamela's eyes slid to her hands. 'I don't quite know how to start.'

Janey got the feeling she wasn't going to like what Pamela had to say. 'Straight out, please. Have I done something to upset you?'

'Nothing as easy as that.' Pamela sucked in a lung-full of air. 'I need to know. Was it Eddie who attacked and raped you when you were a child?'

The colour drained from her face. Feeling as if somebody had punched her in the stomach, she eased herself into a chair and whispered. 'Oh, God, I didn't expect this!'

'I'm sorry.' Pamela rushed to put her arms around her. 'I'm so sorry.'

Janey's hand groped up to cover hers. 'How did you find out?'

'Susie told me he touched her. I started putting two and two together.'

Horrified, Janey gazed up at her 'Poor, darling Susie.'

How typical of Janey to think of someone else. Pamela hugged her tight, loving her generous spirit. 'Susie got off lightly. It's you I'm worried about. There's worse.' She put some distance between them, but not too much, taking the seat beside her, taking her cold hand between hers. The words tumbled out of her. The rapes, the photographs, John Smith's involvement. When she said, 'John knows someone in the Home Office who might be able to help, but he thinks you should make a statement,' colour edged into Janey's face.

'I'd love to clear my father's name, but what about Susie? How will she feel.'

'I've already told her. I thought she'd take it better coming from me.'

'Was she upset?'

'More angry than upset.' Pamela managed a wry smile. 'You know Susie. She's resilient. She wants me to divorce him.'

Janey smiled at that. 'You've certainly got grounds.'

'Yes, I suppose I have.'

A knock came on the door. It was Susie, ever practical. 'Have you finished talking yet? Gypsy has knocked over the potted palm and I need the dustpan and brush. Stupid dog! She needs to be taken for a run before it gets dark.'

'I'll take her if you can manage the kids a bit longer.' She exchanged a glance with Pamela as she rose to her feet. 'I thought I might go over to Coombe Cottage.'

'Great.' Susie beamed a smile. 'Would you deliver a slice of fruit cake for me?'

'A slice of fruit cake . . . to John Smith?'

'It's a sample. Devlin gave me the idea. He said the fruit cake I sent him was the best he'd ever tasted. So I thought if I sent out samples, I might get some orders. Ada's offered to teach me how to ice and decorate. Once I've learned that, I'll be able to take orders for wedding and Christmas cakes.'

Janey stared at her for a moment, at the too bright eyes, the trace of tears on her face. She took Susie's face between her hands and gently kissed her forehead. 'I'm so sorry this has happened, Susie. I wouldn't have hurt you for the world. We don't have to do this, you know. We can just forget about it.'

'Yes we do.' Susie took her in a fierce hug. 'I'll never forgive him for what he did to you, never! I hope they put him in prison and throw away the key.' She broke away, dashing the tears from her eyes and saying gruffly, 'Don't forget my cake. I've decided to become a millionaire by the time I'm thirty, so I've got to start now.'

One encouraging remark from Devlin and they had an entrepreneur in the family. Janey was grinning to herself as she set out with the dog pulling at the leash. Her other hand contained a portion of cake, prettily wrapped in a paper napkin, The phone number and price was listed on the label, as was the legend: *Susie's country fruit cake*.

It was still cold, though the February sting had gone. Now the wind carried with it the smell of pine resin, as if it had blown through every nook and cranny of the woods, picking up fragrance on the way. There was a hint of salt too, fine spray thrown high by the winter seas, to be captured by the wind and borne over the land. She breathed it in, letting it fill her body. Nothing in London had smelled quite as wonderful as this.

John saw her coming from the upstairs window. As she neared the cottage she slowed to a halt and stared at it. Reluctance was written on every inch of her body. The way she stood, half-turned, reminded him of a deer poised for flight from danger. He didn't go down, didn't move. She had to make up her own mind.

She stood still a long time, the dog sitting patiently at her feet staring up at her. Then her head slowly turned, and she gazed up the lane towards the old cow-shed. Indecisiveness was plainly written on her face, and his heart went out to her. That's where she'd been attacked, and God only knew what must be going through her mind. After a while, she gazed down at something in her hand – she gave a disbelieving shake of her head.

She was grinning as she opened the gate and made her way to his door.

Something was in Eddie's head. He could feel it moving, shifting about as if it had taken up residence. Sometimes it used his eyes as windows, pushing at them, blurring his vision as it tried to break out. It made his head ache. He thought it might be a demon.

He sat in the chair by the window. He didn't know what he was doing in this place. The men here were old. In the dormitory at night, when they took out their teeth, their shrivelled up mouths dribbled and flapped with each rasping snore.

Margaret had visited him last week. It had been a long time since he'd seen her. She hadn't brought the angel with her.

'Be patient, Eddie,' she'd said, laughing when he'd started to cry. 'I'll bring him soon.'

'But what shall I tell him?'

'Everything, if you want to go to heaven.'

The priest came in and drew up a chair next to him. 'There's someone here to see you, Eddie. If you don't want to talk to him, you needn't.'

'My name's John.'

Excitement raced through Eddie's body. *One of the disciples?* He was a bit of a disappointment. No wings or halo. Still, he wouldn't want to advertise his presence on earth. Eddie crossed himself and glanced around for Margaret. She smiled approvingly at him from the chair in the corner.

'I want to ask you about some crimes that were committed some time ago,' John said gently, and showed him some newspaper cuttings. 'Do you remember these girls?'

Eddie nodded. 'They needed to be punished.'

'Can you tell me how you punished them?'

The demon in his temple jabbed him with a fiery fork. 'I can't remember.'

'Yes, you can, Eddie,' Margaret said. 'Try and shock him, like you did the priest. You'll enjoy that.'

Eddie grinned. 'The little scrubbers had it coming. They shouldn't have flaunted themselves before a married man. They led me into temptation, like Eve did to Adam. I punished them.'

John exchanged a glance with the priest as Eddie spat out the foul details of that punishment. Finally, he slowed to a halt.

'Have you got a cigarette?' Eddie said.

The disciple pulled a packet from his pocket. When the two of them had lit up, he asked him about Janey.

Eddie's eyes narrowed. Since when had disciples smoked? He needed proof that this was the messenger. 'Ask Margaret. She's over in the corner.'

John turned his head and smiled. 'Hello Margaret. You'll be happy to know Jack Bellamy's out of prison and reunited with Janey. They're very happy.'

Margaret smiled coquettishly at the disciple.

'You little slut,' Eddie snarled. 'This was all your fault. I should have killed her,' he snarled. 'She didn't utter a squeak that first time in the cottage. The second time was different. She was older then, more aware.' He began to laugh so hard that tears poured out of his eyes and ran down his cheeks. 'She begged me to stop. Bellamy can have her now. She's rubbish.'

'Calm down, Eddie,' the priest soothed. 'It's time for your rest. You needn't say anything more.'

Eddie's face crumbled. 'I want to tell John about my diaries.'

The disciple leaned forward, a compassionate smile on his face. 'What diaries, Eddie?'

'It's a secret.' Eddie crooked his finger to urge him closer.

'Careful. He spits when he's angry,' the priest warned.

'I hid them under a loose floorboard in my study. There are photographs of Pauline as well.' His face became suddenly vulnerable. 'Destroy them. God has already punished Pauline for her sins by giving her to the devil's mate. Sarah Wyman has led her into temptation. *Promise you'll destroy them!*'

John managed to hide his surprise at the mention of Sarah's name. 'I promise.' He turned to the priest. 'Is Pauline his eldest daughter?'

'That's right. Mrs Pitt lives in London.'

The demon prodded Eddie with his fork. *The diaries will shock the disciple.* Eddie didn't want to laugh, but the demon made him. He laughed and laughed until his chest began to ache, then he began to cough. Above the noise he could hear Margaret giggling in the corner. 'Bitch!' he shrieked. 'You said I'd feel better if I confessed.'

Pity flared in John's eyes. He experienced an unexpected surge of guilt at having tricked such a sad, disturbed man. The priest pressed an emergency button, drawing him aside as a black-gowned sister bustled into the room to sedate him.

'He's becoming agitated and we can't risk him getting violent. The doctor is visiting him in the morning. I'm very much afraid he'll be committed. I'm sorry I couldn't help you further.'

He'd been helpful . . . *most helpful indeed*, John thought as he left the hospice. He contacted Pamela at work, told her about the diaries and asked for the address of the Bournemouth house.

'Eddie used to keep a spare key on a ledge over the door,' she offered, after telling him where the study was located.

'Shame on you, Pamela,' he teased. 'Are you suggesting I enter illegally?' He could almost see the blush rising to her face as he replaced the receiver. *All the same, if all else failed, it was a thought!*

As it happened, he didn't have to. The house was in the process of being demolished, a sign stating that a hotel was to be erected on the site. He could hear workmen talking, and the chink of tea cups from the back of the house. Grabbing up a clipboard and donning a handily-placed hard hat, John picked his way over the debris towards the study.

Just in time! Half the floorboards were up, the others loose. He discovered the package exactly where Eddie had told him it would be. He shoved it hastily inside his coat when a voice said from behind him.

'Who the hell might you be? This is private property.'

'John Smith, Ministry of Safe Work Practices.' Gazing down at the clipboard, he turned, frowning. 'You should have danger warning signs on display.'

'I don't know nothing about any signs. You'll have to see the boss. He'll be back in a tick.'

'I haven't got time to hang around. Tell him if they're not in evidence by the day after tomorrow he'll be fined. Good afternoon to you.' The man stood respectfully to one side when John walked calmly past him towards the door.

That night, as John burned the photographs of Pauline Pitt, he realized the sending of them had been little more than a malicious act by someone. If blackmail had been the intention there would be no negatives. He dropped the negatives on top of the photographs, watching them melt on to the glowing coals.

The diaries were on the table. Six of them, bound in black. There was a reluctance in him to read them – but read them he must. It was gone midnight before he finished, and any compassion he'd felt for Eddie Renfrew had been completely and utterly eradicated.

In the early hours of the morning, Eddie was woken from sleep by the demon pounding on his temple.

Frightened by the intensity of the pain he thrashed his head from side to side and groaned. The demon was relentless, pushing behind his eyes, burning them with his fork and clawing to get out. *Bastards!*

'Margaret,' he screamed, his eyes bulging under the pressure. 'Help me? Fetch the priest.'

'Go to hell,' she mocked. 'There's no extreme unction for you.'

He heard her giggle as the demon burst through. It was the last thing he heard.

Janey and Susie refused to attend Eddie's funeral. Pamela went. She needed to convince herself she was finally free of him.

Amongst the sprinkling of mourners were Pauline, and Martin, looking bored and sulky as he slouched in his seat. Exquisite in an expensive black suit, a discreet diamond brooch attached to one lapel, Pauline's face was composed into a mask of sorrow as the priest dispatched Eddie.

Hypocrite, she thought, watching the girl apply a delicate lace-edged handkerchief to the corner of each dry eye. Sarah Wyman sat next to her, a faint smile on her lips. She caught Pamela's eye. Recognition dawned and she inclined her head in a slightly regal manner. Pamela remembered Ada telling her Sarah Wyman had married again, and was now a viscountess.

'Trash is trash, whatever the title,' Ada said self-righteously. 'Anyone who treats a lovely man like Sir Charles the way she did, is trash.'

As the widow, Pamela might have well been invisible. The nod was the only recognition she received, except for Pauline briefly confronting her after the service.

'I don't suppose you know if father had any life insurance, do you?'

'Not to my knowledge.' Memory jogged, and remembering the policy she'd taken out on Eddie's life just after Susie was born, Pamela managed to hide a smile. And to think she'd nearly cancelled it after she'd left! It wasn't a grand sum, but it might be enough to buy a modest house.

Neither Pauline nor Martin asked about Justin. They stepped into Sarah's sleek, chauffeur-driven car and sped away, leaving her to walk alone through the dismal rain-swept cemetery to the bus stop outside.

Umbrella bent towards the wind, each step she took seemed to get lighter and lighter. She was free of Eddie at last. *Free!* Giving in to impulse, she held her umbrella aloft and skipped round it like a young girl, laughter bubbling up inside her.

The priest shook his head as he watched her dancing in the rain, until he remembered this rather shabby-looking woman was Eddie Renfrew's widow. A soft, pitying smile lit his face as he murmured, '*Give unto them beauty for ashes, the oil of joy for mourning, the garment of praise for the spirit of heaviness.*'

He chuckled when a gust of wind caught her umbrella and turned it inside out. Still laughing, she turned and gazed at him, then lifting her hand in a wave she dropped the useless article in the nearest rubbish bin and scurried off towards the gate.

April arrived, bringing a special symphony to nature. Bluebells rang a welcome and clumps of daffodils trumpeted out of the earth. Daisies were a thousand open-mouthed choirboys singing in unison to the sky. The lilies gathered in dignified conference on the banks of the stream and unfurled their creamy throats.

As she'd promised, Janey took John to see them. The heady perfume assailed their senses as they walked towards the bog.

John said, 'I've never seen flowers like this in their natural habitat. I hadn't realized how beautiful this place is.'

'When I was a child I used to hide behind a tree and watch the bubbles rise from the boggy patch. I thought goblins lived there and if I stayed long enough I might catch a glimpse of one.'

John chuckled. 'Did you?'

'Only a frog.'

He gazed at her, eyes twinkling. 'It must have been a prince in disguise.'

'Have you ever been married?'

'Yes. I lost my wife and daughter during the war. An air-raid.'

Janey could have bitten out her tongue. 'I'm so sorry. I shouldn't have asked.'

He gave her a surprised look. 'Why not? Pain fades with time and asking questions is the only way you get to know people.'

'You didn't ever think of marrying again, then?'

He shook his head. 'I tried to enlist, but like the proverbial copper I had flat feet. So I joined the police force and threw myself into my work.'

'What did you do before that?'

'Worked on my father's barge up and down the Thames.'

Dreams coloured her eyes. 'I did a painting of Thames barges once. It must have been wonderful working on them.'

John grinned. 'You're taking the utopian standpoint. It was actually hard, dirty work, with very little to show for it at the end of the week.'

'What made you abandon your police career to strike out on your own?'

'The realization I wasn't going to rise above detective sergeant.' He shrugged. 'A few years after the war ended a lot of bright young men poured out of the universities into the force. Joe Plods like me were shelved in the promotion stakes, and politics came into the job.'

'Did you like being a private eye?'

He stopped walking and engaged her eyes. 'I've been doing it long enough to know when someone's leading up to something. What do you really want to ask me, Janey?'

'I don't know.' She worried on her bottom lip for a second. 'It just struck me as an odd coincidence that we lived in the same building in Hammersmith, then met again at Charles and Brenda's wedding.'

'You want to know who I was working for then, is that it?' He smiled when she nodded, relieved she hadn't guessed about his involvement with her former partner. 'I can't answer that. My clients are confidential.'

Colour flooded her face. 'I wasn't prying. I just wondered if it had anything to with me. I mean, you weren't there to spy on *me*, were you? If you were working for my stepfather, it wouldn't break confidentiality now he's dead if you told me, would it?'

'Good God, no! Whatever gave you that idea? I used that bedsit to store files and things. It was cheaper than finding a bigger office to work from. Sometimes, I slept there if I had a lot on. It really was a coincidence.'

Glancing sideways at him, she grinned. 'So, you were telling lies when you told me you were a chauffeur.'

'Not entirely.' Half-smiling, he shrugged. 'Sometimes it's necessary to assume another identity in my game.'

Her eyes took on a mischievous glow. 'Sandy was right. It was cloak and dagger stuff. There's a lot of Peter Pan in you. It's refreshing to meet a man who's never quite grown up.'

'I've never really thought of it that way,' he said, biting back a laugh. 'But you could be right.'

Her laughter faded. 'Have you heard anything more about our case since we gave our statements to the police?'

'The photograph of Eddie was identified by the victims, so those files have now been closed.'

'What about my father?'

'The evidence of his innocence is in the hands of the Home Office. I must warn you, Janey, government departments are notoriously slow. It could take years.'

'I was hoping I could give it to him for a Christmas present. You haven't told him?'

He could almost taste her disappointment. 'I have a great deal of respect for your father. It would be unfair to build up his hopes after what he's been through.'

'You mean the application might be turned down?' Her chin tilted and her expression became fierce. 'If that happens I'll contact the papers and blow the lid off it. I swear, if I don't hear anything by Christmas I'll write to the Home Office and tell them so.'

As they strolled back towards the village, John thought it might prove judicious to contact his colleague in the Home Office and inform him of her intentions. Once brought to light, an injustice such as this could cause heads to roll.

He invited her back to Coombe Cottage for coffee. She declined. 'I promised Susie I'd pick up Pamela's birthday present and hide it before she gets home from work.' To John's surprise, she kissed his cheek. 'Thank you for being such a help,' she said. 'You're a lovely man, and I count myself lucky I can consider you one of my friends.'

Spring fever hit the village like an epidemic. Curtains flapped from washing lines, windows were polished to a gleaming brightness. Rugs hung limply over fences, like defenceless boys who'd forgotten to wash themselves all winter. Women with set, determined faces and robust arms, thrashed the dust from them with cane paddles.

Pamela's birthday came and went, weeds encroached on the flower beds, April became May. The weekenders became more evident.

Some of them joined the fête committee, which caused a bit of friction until the villagers realized their organizational skills were far superior to their own. It was to be a grand affair. There were rumours that Princess Margaret would come down to open it, followed by Laurence Olivier then The Beatles.

Painting steadily in every spare moment, Janey wouldn't have noticed if it hadn't been for the gossip-loving Susie. 'I'm entering a cake in the competition, but don't you *dare* tell Ada. She's entering one too, and she always takes off first prize.'

Janey was approached to donate a painting for the auction. She decided on a scene of the village pond with a pretty thatched cottage to the right of the foreground, and the church beyond. The fact that the cottage was the weekend retreat of a wealthy coach tour operator hadn't escaped her notice.

Tim had been posted to Singapore, and much as she loved him, Janey wasn't sorry to see him go. As a house guest, he'd been rather like a large, over-friendly – and untidy – puppy.

He had given her a passionate kiss goodbye at the station. She thought it might have been more for the benefit of the fellow officer who was travelling with him, than any declaration of undying love. Judging from the amount of phone calls from females he'd received, and the late hours he'd kept, Tim was definitely not a one-woman man!

'Tell Susie to send me a fruit cake,' he yelled from the window as the train pulled out, a request Janey decided she'd be wise to ignore.

She was expecting Robert Pitt that last weekend in May. He'd accepted her offer of Tim's old room for the night, and she was looking forward to his company.

When the doorbell rang on Friday evening she was in the middle of bathing the children, readying them for bed. He was a day early.

'I'll get it,' Susie yelled out.

'Ask him if he'd like a cup of tea. I'll be down as soon as the kids are in their nightclothes.'

Both Justin and Saffy were being their uncooperative bedtime selves. Justin was wriggling and giggling, and Saffy egging him on. Finally, she managed to dry them, then took them into the bedroom and dumped them both on Saffy's bed.

'Behave yourselves, you two. Saffy, see if you can be a clever girl and put your nightie on by yourself.' Trying to stuff the flailing legs of the giggling Justin into his pyjama bottoms was proving an impossibility.

'Need any help?'

Griff? It was Griff! Her eyes absorbed him in one glance. 'Why didn't you tell me you were coming? Saffy, you're putting your head in the sleeve!' Justin escaped her clutches and bounced up and down on the bed. 'Stop it, you'll fall off!'

Trying to fight her way into her nightie, Saffy's head was a wailing lump in the middle. Her arms flapped like a pink flowered ghost. *'I can't see anyfink, mummy.'*

Griff's grin was a mile wide. One hand grabbed Saffy's nightie and jerked it down over her head, the other cut Justin's legs from under him in mid-flight. 'Pyjamas, young feller,' he said as Justin flopped on his back.

Ten minutes later the bedtime story had been read, eyelids drooped shut, and peace reigned.

Janey feathered a kiss on each soft cheek. 'They look like angels now. How did you manage it?'

'They need a father.' His eyes were dark on hers, enigmatic, giving nothing away – but his glance strangely disturbing to the orderly rhythms of her heart.

Yes, she thought, turning away. *I do love you, Griff, but you deserve someone better.*

CHAPTER NINETEEN

Although he worked long hours, Griff became a regular visitor. Sometimes Phil came with him. He'd eye her garden, shake his head and pick up a fork. Soon, lilac and rhododendrons were growing along the fences, apple in the lawn and a hawthorn in the hedge for May perfume. A slender ash sapling was set in place at the front. Eventually, the spreading branches would shade the house from the summer sun, and flame into glory in autumn.

His work-rough hands were tender on the young plants, almost loving as he set their roots into the crumbly brown soil. When he knew Pamela was home he brought her flowers. They'd sit together in the garden on the stone retaining wall, self-consciously apart, but exchanging glances now and again.

'I think he's courting her,' Griff remarked one day.

Janey had reached the same conclusion. 'Your father's such a lovely man, and Pamela deserves some happiness after all she's been through.'

His smile was as mellow and rare as old brandy. 'Don't you deserve the same?'

There was heartache ahead if she wasn't careful, for both of them. She must guard herself against what she saw in his eyes, or *thought* she saw. She'd never be able to read Griff, and loving him was too easy.

'I'm happy. I have everything I could ever need. Saffy, Justin, my career and good friends.' Mischief came into her eyes. 'If things work out I might have the best of those friends for a brother.'

A pulse beat in his jaw as his eyes collided with hers. The chair scraped harshly against the floor as he stood up. 'Don't count on it, Janey.'

Startled, she gazed up at him.

His finger traced a gentle path down her cheek, making her want to curl her face into his palm. The intensity of the moment shook her.

'I'll always be your friend, and who knows, one day I might even be your lover. But a brother?' He shook his head. 'I wouldn't even contemplate the thought.'

She closed her eyes. 'It's impossible. I can't be your—'

A finger was pressed firmly over her lips. 'Stop denying what you've always known. I'm sick of talking round it. I love you, Janey. I've always loved you. Let go of the past, and for everyone's sake let go of Drifter. Stop being a tragedy queen and get on with your life before it passes you by.'

Tragedy Queen? Drifter? What the hell did *he* have to do with her and Griff? Flaming with anger she rushed out to the gate, shouting up the road after him. 'You're wrong. I haven't thought about Drifter in months.'

He kept going without turning round.

Picking up a small pebble she hurled it at him, scoring a bull's-eye in the middle of his back. 'Don't you *dare* ignore me, Griff Tyler. I *refuse* to be ignored by *you*!'

He was laughing when he turned to face her. 'I'll pick you up at eight and we'll go out dancing.'

'Go to hell! You know I can't dance.'

'I'll wear my safety boots.' He blew her a mocking kiss, then ducked as her second missile flew past his ear.

'Bloody men!' she snorted, turning her back on him and stomping into the house. 'If you think I'm going dancing, you can think again.'

She was ready at eight at the dot. And she discovered, when they joined the crowd stomping and swaying on the dance floor in what seemed to be some weird tribal ritual, that she could dance, after all.

When Griff kissed her goodnight, his lips a teasing, tender exploration of hers, everything she'd starved herself of became suddenly apparent. There was a silent scream of panic inside her, as if something was dying, bit by painful bit. All her self-doubt flooded back.

Sensing her withdrawal, Griff touched her mouth with his fingertip. 'It's all right, Janey. I can wait.'

Will it always be like this for me? she was thinking a few moments later, as she stood inside the darkened hall. *Will I never be able to love Griff as he should be loved?*

It seemed as though the whole village had turned out to watch *Saffy Jane* depart.

The retired couple who'd bought a cottage nearly opposite, once the district nurse's abode, made a pretence of watering the garden. They looked like a couple of chickens, their necks craning this way and that.

The villagers were more open in their curiosity. Stood in small groups, the women placed hands on hips and the men puffed on cigarettes or waved pipes in the air as they talked.

'I ain't seen the like of that before in the village, has 'e, George?'

'You gone blind or summat, Bert? That there boat has been growing in the backyard for nigh on a year.'

Bert cackling. 'Fancy that, and here's me thinking it was a bloody giant mushroom all this time.'

As the crane swung the boat over the wall into the cradle on the back of a truck, Jack ran a satisfied eye over her hull. Once the engine was fitted he'd just need to put the finishing touches to the fittings. It had taken longer than he'd estimated to build her. *I used a young man's calculations, but I no longer have a young man's energy*, he thought, grimacing as the wasted years came into his mind.

'The garden looks empty without her.'

He laughed as he slid his arm around Janey's shoulder. 'She's not a garden gnome, she's a working boat and needs to be in the water.'

'It was nice of the boatyard to allow you to finish her off there.'

'And much easier. I'll be able to launch her from the slipway. I'm thinking of taking her on a pilgrimage to Dunkirk in May or June of next year. John said he wouldn't mind making the trip with me.'

'You get on well with him, don't you?'

Her father looked surprised. 'I suppose I do. He's the sort of man who grows on you. He plays a damned good game of chess.'

A cheer went up as the truck moved off. 'A pint of bitter says 'e don't get round the bend without touching that there oak tree.'

'You're on, George Higgins.'

'Daft old so-and-so,' Mrs Higgins muttered as the truck missed it by a mile. 'He wouldn't see a train coming unless it ran over 'im.' Excitement over, they drifted away, the men towards the pub, the women towards the cottages.

Jack exchanged a smile with his daughter. 'Are you staying for lunch? I might be able to rustle up a sandwich.'

'I promised my house a good clean. Come up for dinner on Sunday.' Leaving a sunny smile behind she was gone, tooting her horn as she rounded the bend.

Hiding his disappointment, he made his way indoors and slumped into an armchair. He was so tired these days. Perhaps it was time he got a check-up.

After the boat's finished, he promised himself. I haven't got time, now.

A sleek black Daimler was parked in the drive when Janey got home. With a strange sense of foreboding, she left her car outside the gate, gathered the children together and hurried towards it.

The driver respectfully touched his grey peaked cap when she peered in the window. 'Mrs Pitt has gone inside, ma'am.'

His face was beaded with perspiration and Janey was willing to bet he'd driven all the way from London. It was too bad of Pauline to leave him hanging around outside.

'Thank you.' *Pauline could wait!* 'You look hot. If you'd like to follow me inside I'll find you something to drink.'

'That's very kind of you, ma'am.'

She left the chauffeur in the kitchen with a generous slice of Susie's sponge cake and a mug of tea, gave the children a glass of milk and hurried through to the lounge. Justin was drooping with tiredness, but she couldn't put him to bed if Pauline had come all this way to see him.

Pauline was in the process of reading a bank statement Janey had left on the coffee table.

'That's private.'

Unabashed, Pauline allowed it to flutter from her hand. Janey's wraparound skirt and T-shirt received an inspection. Pauline's smile was derisive.

Janey let her annoyance show. 'Why didn't you tell me you were coming?'

'I didn't think I'd need to make an appointment to see my own son. I take it that's him?'

'You should know.'

'Don't try and be smart, Janey. It doesn't suit you.' Smiling a little, Pauline examined her perfectly manicured fingernails. 'Actually, I was thinking of taking him back.'

Heart squeezing like a concertina, Janey picked Justin up and cuddled him tight. 'You can't. Robert Pitt's his guardian.'

Pauline gave a light laugh and gazed at Saffy. 'A good lawyer would soon overturn that. After all, the court might decide that a woman who'd given birth to an illegitimate child was an unsuitable parent for him.'

There was a roaring sound in Janey's ears. *Dear God. Don't let her take him from me.*

'Put the child down, Janey.'

Justin began to grizzle. 'He's tired,' she argued, 'he needs his nap.'

'*Put him down!*'

Reluctantly, Janey lowered Justin to the floor. Her heart went out to him as he clung to her knees. 'It's all right, darling. Don't cry.'

'I don't like her,' Saffy muttered.

'Come to mummy, Justin darling,' Pauline cooed.

Justin buried his head in her knees and began to howl. Saffy patted his head in comfort.

Rising from the couch Pauline dragged him away. Janey's nails dug into her palms when she hissed 'Come here you whining little brat. *I'm* your mother, not her.' Justin's howls became a fully blown tantrum. Kicking and yelling he screamed blue murder at the top of his lungs.

Pauline looked rattled. 'I'll give you a good smack if you don't stop that noise.'

Justin sank his teeth into her arm. When she loosened her hold on him he ran for safety behind her legs.

'Look what he's done,' Pauline screeched, displaying the bite mark. 'He's an animal. I'll give him a good hiding when I get hold of him.'

She picked Justin up. 'No you won't. I'm putting him down for his nap. Saffy, come with me. You can have a nap too.'

She wanted to applaud when Saffy poked her tongue out at Pauline, but knew she couldn't let her get away with it. 'That's naughty, Saffy. Say sorry.'

'Won't!'

'Yes you will. Say it now, please.' It was debatable whether Saffy's muttered response was an apology, but she decided to let it pass.

She paused at the door, her rage hidden by a veneer of calm. How dare she upset a defenceless child like that. 'I won't let him go without a fight! If we are to go to court I need to let his grandfather know. If you'd like to wait, I'll ring him when I get back. I'll tell you now, Pauline. I intend to fight tooth and nail for custody of Justin.'

When she returned, Pauline had a sullen expression on her face.

'Actually, I didn't come here to see Justin. I don't care if I never see him again. He's too much like Martin.'

'What's wrong with Martin?' *Apart from the fact he's as rotten a father as you are a mother.*

'He's a homosexual. He's just moved in with his boyfriend.'

Janey's eyes flew open in shock. 'Does Robert Pitt know?'

'Of course. I informed him of the fact just over an hour ago. He took it badly. Men of his age are amazingly stuffy about such things. They have no concept of the real world.'

What a lousy thing to do.

'I came down to see if you had any spare cash.'

Janey eyed the diamond on her dress. 'Can't you sell that?'

'It was a gift.'

'What happened to the cash from the sale of the house in Bournemouth? And if you're so hard up, why are you driving around in a fancy car with a chauffeur?'

The expression on Pauline's face would have soured cream. 'Martin mortgaged the house to the hilt. As for the car?' She shrugged and unconsciously fingered the diamond brooch. 'It belongs to a friend of mine.'

'I see.' Janey had an urge to laugh, and couldn't resist a jibe. 'Didn't you train to be a secretary? You could always find a job.'

Pauline's eyes narrowed. The smooth beige mask of her make-up couldn't quite disguise the flags of colour rising to her cheeks. 'If you must know, I'm going into a private clinic to have an operation. I don't want any more children, and I suffer so every month.' Her voice became a whisper and she suddenly looked vulnerable. 'It makes me remember *her – our mother!* I can't put up with the bleeding any more. It turns my stomach.'

And that was the only thing genuine about Pauline, her inability to come to terms with the circumstances of their mother's death. What her sister had witnessed had burned itself into her mind, leaving an invisible scar. Children were so impressionable, so needful of love and stability in their lives. Reluctantly, Janey's heart reached out to her. Then what she'd implied suddenly sank in. Horrified, she stared at her. 'You're having a hysterectomy, aren't you?'

'Exactly.' Pauline's recovery was swift, her mouth etched into a smile. 'That's why I need the money. In return, I'll consider letting you have Justin permanently, adopt him even. Martin wouldn't care. He loathes children as much as I do.'

'That's blackmail.'

'Take it or leave it.'

'And if I don't agree to give you the money?'

'I'll start proceedings to remove Justin from your care.'

Sadly, Janey gazed at her. 'Please don't use Justin as a pawn. He doesn't deserve to be punished.'

'Good old, Janey,' she sneered. 'You're always looking for someone to love, and never quite succeeding. How jealous of me you must have been when we were growing up. I often wondered about it, until the truth came out. Jack Bellamy of all people, the man who assaulted you.'

Unwittingly, Pauline had given her a stand to fight from. It was about time she learned the truth. 'It wasn't Jack who beat and raped me. It was *your father*, Pauline.'

The colour drained from Pauline's face. 'You're lying. You're just saying it to upset me.'

'He also raped at least three other young girls,' Janey said relentlessly. 'It was all in the diaries he left behind. His victims identified his photograph. If you don't believe me, go and ask the police.'

'This will ruin my life if it gets out,' Pauline whispered. 'Oh, my God! I'll never live it down.'

No thought for what I went through, no thought for the man who spent all those years behind bars for a crime he didn't commit. Pauline first and last, always Pauline.

'You needn't worry, it won't get out . . . unless it *has* to, of course. I wouldn't want Justin growing up knowing his grandfather was a rapist.' Janey pulled her cheque book towards her and started to write. 'How long will it take you to decide about the adoption?'

'You certainly know how to go for the jugular when your back's against the wall.' A mean look disguised the previous fright in Pauline's eyes. 'Add another nought to that, and make it out to cash, would you?'

Pen poised, Janey engaged her eyes. 'How long?'

'Six months, say?'

Six months? Could Pauline be trusted to keep her word? Janey wavered between wanting desperately to believe, and not believing at all.

Pauline's eyes were riveted on the cheque. 'As soon as possible. I'll consult a lawyer to find out the legalities involved.' The cheque was practically ripped from her hand as soon as Janey added her signature. It was tucked into Pauline's expensive calfskin purse.

Pauline didn't linger. Snapping her fingers at the chauffeur, who was waiting in the hall, she swept regally past and waited for him to open the front door for her.

Bitch! Janey thought. You don't deserve a beautiful child like Justin. After she'd gone, Janey went to the children's room and gazed at the little boy she loved so much. She wondered if Pauline would try to exact a higher price? She'd pay it willingly if Justin's happiness was at stake, but not without a whimper. She pressed a kiss on his cheek, then quietly closing the bedroom door, returned to the lounge and dialled the number of Robert Pitt.

June brought the village fête. As anticipated, it was a grand affair with a small fairground, and a mediocre-sounding pop group to add to the attractions. It was opened by Charles Wyman. Brenda stood by his side, elegant in a blue dress and matching hat.

Afterwards, the men headed en masse for the beer tent and the women hurried towards the white elephant stall to hunt out the best of the bargains.

It was a beautiful day. The sky was marbled with tiny clouds, and there was just enough breeze to temper the warmth of the summer sun. Janey took the children on the merry-go-round, then wandered over to the food tent where the cake judging was taking place.

Susie was staring anxiously at the judge, a plump-looking woman who wrote the cookery pages for one of the women's magazines. She prodded and felt, smelled and tasted. Finally she was down to two. Susie's and Ada's.

Ada had a complacent look on her face. Susie looked so worried that Janey died a thousand deaths on her behalf whilst the woman deliberated. Then she smiled, and stuck a blue ribbon on one of the cakes.

'Susan Renfrew,' the vicar announced, beaming a smile in Susie's direction.

As Susie moved forward to be presented with her award, her face flushed with pride and happiness, Ada huffed to a neighbour, 'It was me who taught that lass to cook. I shouldn't be at all surprised if that wasn't one of my recipes she was using.' Ada took it with good grace after that barb, kissing Susie soundly on the cheek. 'I'm right proud of you my love. Right proud.'

Griff joined her after lunch, his face all smiles. Before she could stop him, he kissed her soundly on the mouth.

Her face was heated when he let her go. 'Stop it, Griff. What will people think?'

'That he's mad about you,' Devlin's voice whispered in her ear, 'and they'd be right.'

She spun round. 'Dev, what are you doing here?'

'Your father told me he had a painting in the auction. I have a client lined up who's been trying to get hold of a John Gregory. I thought I might put in a bid for it.' Picking up Saffy he smacked a kiss on her cheek. 'How's my favourite girl?'

'Daddy,' Saffy said holding her arms imperiously out to Griff.

Devlin's glance went from one to the other. He smiled as he handed Saffy over, and held out a hand. 'You seem to have been upgraded. Nice to see you again, Griff.'

'Likewise.'

'Hi, everyone!' Wendy strolled towards them, a smile on her face. 'I see Tim's motorbike managed to find its way to the white elephant stall.'

Janey laughed. 'He was forced to donate it when it wouldn't sell. It nearly broke his heart.'

Wendy slipped her arm through Devlin's. 'Can we buy a hot dog or something before the auction, darling. I'm starving.'

Devlin gave a self-conscious grin when Janey chuckled. 'I notice you have a painting in the auction,' he remarked.

'Yes. Do you like it?'

'It's cosy. You're not going all chintzy on me, are you?'

'Would I dare? It was you who taught me to be commercial, Dev. The man who owns the cottage is loaded. I thought he might pay a good price for it.'

Devlin secured the John Gregory, then proceeded to push the price to the limit for her painting. He allowed himself to be outbid.

The owner of the cottage gave Devlin a dirty look, then strutted off, his prize clutched against his chest.

Griff couldn't stop grinning. 'There's a few people round here could be done for conspiracy.'

'He got a bargain,' Devlin said. 'I could have sold it for more.'

'Wanna go wee's, Mum.'

Janey hastily exchanged the pushchair for her daughter and headed for the nearest bush. She returned to find Robert Pitt chatting to Griff.

'Ah, my dear. I'm sorry to arrive without notice. Something has come up and we need to talk.' His glance slid apologetically to Griff. 'You won't mind if it's in private?'

Alarm leapt into her chest. 'It's Pauline, isn't it? She wants Justin back. I knew I shouldn't have given her that money. I knew she wouldn't keep her word.'

Griff stared at her. 'You gave Pauline money in return for her child? I understood the bartering of children's lives was illegal these days.'

How cold he sounded. 'That's not how it was.' *I'm lying to myself. That's exactly how it was. Don't look at me like that, Griff, as though I was a stranger. I did it for Justin as well as myself.*

'How much?'

'A thousand,' she said, shamefaced.

Griff managed a twisted smile as he gazed down at the oblivious Justin. 'I guess he's worth it, at that.'

'I think you misunderstand, Doctor Tyler,' Robert cut in smoothly. 'Janey was given very little choice.'

'It's a pity she forgot to tell some of her *friends* about it.'

'Griff.' She placed a hand on his arm. 'You don't understand.'

A pulse worked in his jaw. His eyes were remote as he jerked away from her touch. 'Perhaps you'd like to enlighten me sometime, when you've got the time, of course.'

'I have to ask you this, Janey,' Robert said, watching Griff move stiffly away. 'Is there any reason why you *should* have told Doctor Tyler?'

'I guess so.' An aching chasm appeared in her heart. 'You see . . . I'm in love with Griff, and he loves me.'

'That's wonderful, my dear.'

'It is?' It didn't feel wonderful. She'd hurt Griff's feelings in a way he didn't deserve.

'You see, it solves the very problem standing in the way of adoption. Pauline's lawyer rang me this morning. She and Martin agree it would be best for Justin to be permanently placed in your care by adoption, but he thinks the fact that you're a single woman will go against you. Once you're married, there will be no obstacle.'

No obstacle? How wrong could the man be? This was the biggest obstacle ever. How could she marry Griff now? He'd think she was using him as a means to an end.

Griff didn't come up to the house later. Devlin and Wendy stayed for dinner. Susie monopolized him, proudly showing off her cup and chattering all the way through the meal.

Finally, when Pamela shooed her off to bed, Devlin caught her eye. 'OK, let's see what you've done.'

Wendy drifted off to help Pamela wash up.

Devlin walked along the row of paintings. There was a sun-washed wall with a weathered window and a creamy clematis growing up it. An old man leaned on a garden fork with a dog at his feet, staring at a sunset. A woman prayed, her face illuminated by light streaming through a stained glass window. Then there was the boy on a bicycle, a jar of minnows swinging from the handlebars.

Devlin gazed at them a long time. She knew better than to disturb him, but she did when he flicked the cloth from the second easel.

'That's not for sale.'

'The one on this easel never is.' Slanting his head to one side, he mused. 'It's funny how blind a man can be. Does he *know* how you feel about him?'

She joined him, gazing at the painting of the sleeping Griff and Saffy through newly opened eyes. Saffy's fist was curled into the hollow of Griff's throat, his arm circled her protectively. He was achingly beautiful to her. Hollow-cheeked, his lashes were a dark sweep, his mouth relaxed. She usually smiled every time she looked at it. Now she couldn't. She should have seen then how much she loved him.

A lump gathered in her throat, choking her words. 'He knows, I think, but I haven't told him. Now, I never can.'

'Tell Uncle Dev all about it, Janey. You've been like a cat caught in a thunderstorm all evening. I've never seen you look so miserable.'

Words tumbled out of her without sequence. Somehow she got everything out, *everything*, as if a damn had burst inside her. Although he winced on occasion, he didn't interrupt her. 'Now, I just don't know what to do, Dev.'

'Let's sort this out a bit. You're going to have to learn to live with the abuse, because you can't undo it. As for your father, it sounds to me as if the legalities are being taken care of. Let it rest, and stop worrying about it. If you start pushing government departments around they nail their well-fed backsides to their seats.'

She nodded.

'Now, the fact that you feel you can't have a relationship with a man is poppycock. You managed it with Drifter.'

She gave him a half-shamed look. 'He said I was frigid.'

Devlin grinned. 'You should read that as *his* inadequacy to turn you on. Men often shift blame on to their partners. It makes them feel better in a one-sided relationship. Besides, you never gave yourself the chance to try anyone else, did you?'

Colour crept to her cheeks.

'As for Griff, if I were you I'd give him that picture and see what happens. If he's half the man I think he is, he'll soon put two and two together.'

'You make everything sound so simple.'

'What's simpler than two people who have the hots for each other. Most men carry their brains between their legs, and I very much doubt if Griff's balls are made of wood.'

He grinned when she started to laugh. 'That's better. Right, now I've sorted you out I'd better find Wendy before she starts giving me hell. Now, there's a woman who gives as good as she gets. She's coming to the States with me next month. I might propose to her if she plays her cards right.'

'Oh Dev, that's wonderful. Congratulations.'

'Don't be premature. She might say no.'

'She'll be mad if she does.'

His smile became an ironic self-mocking slice. 'Will she, Janey?'

Her foot nudged against the easel. Time to change the subject. 'Do you know Drifter's address?'

His eyes came sharply to hers. 'I might.'

She waved her arm at the parcel in the corner. 'I thought you might like to take Mistral with you.'

'My pleasure.' His arms came round her in a brief hug.

'Thanks, Dev. You've made me feel heaps better. You've missed your vocation, you should have been a psychologist.'

'I was one before I became an art dealer.' He began to chuckle when she stared unbelievingly at him. 'I guess it came in handy, after all.'

'Why did you give it up?'

'I got crapped off by people who blamed their problems on everyone else. Life's too short to waste time being miserable.' His eyes swept over her paintings again. 'Keep on painting. You're a bloody knockout.'

Wendy arrived to take possession of him. 'Are you going to be much longer, Dev? It's nearly midnight and I've got work in the morning.' She did a double-take. 'Hey, did you do all these? You're not bad.'

'*Not bad!*' His face assumed a pained expression. 'Janey's sensational!'

After they'd gone she went back to her studio to gaze at the painting of Griff and Saffy.

She was smiling when she went to bed.

CHAPTER TWENTY

Janey chose a time when Griff was at work.

'He looks just like his Ma,' Phil said, gazing at the painting with a smile. 'She was a bonny, lass, right bonny. She'd be proud of him now, I reckon.'

'It's you who raised him. She'd be proud of you, too.'

The compliment drew an abashed grin from Phil. 'There ain't nothing to raising a young-un. It's like growing a plant. Give it the right food and plenty of attention, make sure its roots are firmly established, then prune it back hard if gets out of hand.'

The thought of Griff getting out of hand made her chuckle. 'How often did you have to prune Griff back?'

'Oh, he had his moments.' Berry-bright eyes slid her way. 'He can be right stubborn when he sets his heart on something he wants, but in a quiet sort of way so a body never notices until it's too late.'

Her cheeks bloomed in a confusion of pink.

'Damn me, if you ain't as pretty as a border full of peonies,' he said. 'If I had a bit more spring in my step I'd be after you mesself.' He was still laughing when she left.

She sat at home and waited for Griff to call. One day, two, a week went by. Finally, she could stand it no longer. She *had* to talk to him, had to explain. She picked up the receiver and dialled his number.

'He's gone out,' Phil told her, speaking loudly because the telephone was still an unfamiliar novelty to him. 'He went to the hill to watch the bats.'

He's waiting for me.

She whistled for Gypsy, and throwing a cardigan over her shoulders called out to Pamela, 'The kids are asleep so I'm taking the dog for a walk. I might drop in on Dad, so don't wait up.'

The undersides of the clouds were bordered with magenta, fading into shades of purple and pink. She watched it shift and change as she walked, the red tones assuming a gentler blush, the purple darkening into grey. Soon the sky would be clothed in darkness and the creation of time would be displayed in all its mystery and splendour.

She quickened her step. *Griff's waiting for me.* She could feel the pull of him, as though they were attached by an invisible thread. *My journey has brought me in a circle back to him.*

'The tide comes in and goes out,' she murmured. Her own tide was running high, racing through her body like waves rolling in to shore. She couldn't doubt its force as it carried her towards the shore that was Griff.

Deep in thought, the cow-shed remained unnoticed until something rustled in the undergrowth. Her feet suddenly became lead blocks, anchoring her to the ground. She hadn't intended to come this way.

The tumbled stones looked like a skull in the dusk, the windows, dark, hollow eyes watching her. Eddie Renfrew had stood unseen behind those eyes, waiting like a venomous snake. His poison had found its mark. She could feel it inside her still, drying her mouth and throat, squeezing her lungs until her heart lunged with panic.

'You're going to have to learn to live with it.' Dev's truth, easier to speak than face.

Now is the time to say boo to my ghosts! Brave thoughts, only it wasn't daylight, it was dusk with its unseen terror. She shuddered. Had Eddie's revenge been sweet? Had he gloated over her father all those years?

Eddie Renfrew's dead. She took a deep breath. Yes, he was dead – but whilst this was hanging over her she was half-dead too. She gazed at the cow-shed.

From the top of the hill Griff watched Janey make her way up the lane. He had known she would come eventually. He gave a wry grin. So much for ego. If he hadn't let pride get in the way of phoning her he would have seen her sooner. A smile illuminated his face as he squinted into the rapidly descending darkness. The painting was her way of telling him she loved him – had always loved him.

A puzzled frown replaced the smile. Why had she stopped? She seemed to be staring at the cow-shed? *God, no!* Heart in his mouth, he uncoiled to his feet and began to run.

Hand against her heart, Janey spun round to face him as he burst through the doorway, her face contorted with fear in the yellow glare of a torch. Instantly, the torch was turned against him, the beam becoming a weapon to blind him. A tiny, relieved sigh reached his ears.

'Oh, it's you, Griff! You scared me.'

The daddy of an understatement! If he never saw that look on her face again it would be soon enough. 'Turn that damned thing off!' White dots danced in front of his eyes when she aimed it at the floor. 'What the hell are you doing in here?'

'Saying boo to ghosts.'

'Don't be so bloody flippant. You should have had somebody with you. What if—?'

'Why are you so angry, Griff? I *did* have somebody with me.' Her hand closed around the wooden medallion. 'You're with me every minute of every day, as you always have been.'

'I care for you, that's why, and if you think some stupid juvenile carving will protect you from harm you need your head examined.'

Her snort of laughter pulled him up short. 'I've been analysed adequately by Devlin. He said I can't change what happened, so I've got to learn to live with it. I haven't been able to pass this place without getting a panic attack, so laying this particular ghost to rest was a priority. I had to face it alone.'

'And the next priority?'

'It might be harder.' Her teeth chewed on her bottom lip for a second. 'You might decide I'm not worth loving.'

'Damn it.' He was unable to keep the gruffness from his voice. 'Are you saying you love me, Janey?'

He felt the smile in her as she threaded her hand in his. 'Not in this place. The memories are too sordid. Let's go to the hill and watch the bats. I need to explain something to you.'

They talked as they walked. About her quest to clear her father's name, about the adoption of Justin and the reason she'd given Pauline the money. 'I know you might think her awful for doing such a thing, but she was badly affected by what she saw as a child. She can't help how she is, Griff. She doesn't want or love Justin. I know I was wrong to pay her, but I was so frightened I'd lose him. He needs to be loved so much.' When they reached the top of the hill she turned to face him. 'When Robert Pitt told me the lawyer said I'd stand a better chance if I were married, I just *couldn't* tell you.'

He pulled her down on the grass beside him. 'Tell me what, Janey?'

'How much I cared for you. You might have thought I was trying to catch myself a husband for Justin's sake.'

'Uh-huh!' He began to smile. 'Putting all that aside, how much *do* you care for me?'

She wondered if the dusk concealed her blush. Did he have to make her say it? A red neon sign with *I love Griff Tyler* written all over it would be less obvious. 'You know how much.'

'Say it, Janey.' She could hear the laughter in his voice. 'It's only three words.'

'I love you, dammit!' Her whole body seemed to become one big grin and she laughed aloud. 'I love you.'

The bats came flying out of the hill with a suddenness that made them jump. The air was thick with an untidy swirl of black, squeaking shapes before they swooped off into the darkness in search of food. Gypsy chased excitedly after them.

She laid her head against Griff's shoulder when his arms came round her. 'I'll adopt both the kids, and we'll have a couple more when the time's right.'

'Griff, I don't know. I don't think I'm much good at . . . relationships.'

His lips traced a path across her cheek, coming to rest against her ear. His breath was a soft shivering whisper. 'I guess there's only one way to find out?'

If she failed him she wouldn't be able to bear it. 'Griff, I'm so unsure about this.'

'Close your eyes.'

Her eyelids drifted shut as his mouth touched hers, loving her, filling her to the brim with longing.

Stop thinking, listen to your body. It's singing a different song. We're one mind, one heart . . . always have been.

Lips against lips, fire in the touch of his fingers, flesh cool in the evening air, skin, flowing silk against silk, his mouth warm and honey-moist against hers. How did he learn to be so tender, so exquisitely loving?

Stop thinking, experience.

Her body alive, a sculpture shaping to his caress, breasts smooth, moon-kissed pale, hips curving to his touch, thighs satin soft. Her hair, strands of liquid silver spread upon the grass, upon his face, binding him to her with threads of love.

Night-dark eyes absorbed the sky of hers. Her mouth accepted, sought, took, gave. His voice whispered, urged.

Listen to your body now. There was a wild, turbulent song in her, as if the earth, the sea and the sky had come together as one. She pulsed with it, with a bitter-sweet poignancy, as if she were drowning in a sea of sensuality.

Hear your body sing.

Griff, muscles fluid, skin rough, salty to the tongue. Lion-strong in his possession, feral sharp. Dove gentle.

This is how it should be, abandoned and wild, bodies and minds exchanging an exquisite loving, passion at one with the rhythm of nature.

The world began to turn upon its axis, faster and faster. Her fingers curled into the grass, anchoring her body to the earth when the rest of her spun off into an eden of infinity.

She and Griff, one voice, one heart, one body – one love.

The moist night air kissed her buttocks as she lay against his chest. His heart was an erratic beat under her ear, his breathing tumultuous, as if he'd just run a race. Gradually, they tuned into a gentle unison.

Above them the sky was an arc of stars, the moon an incandescent crescent. Beneath, the earth was solid again, turning them towards dawn.

Her finger traced the moon curve of his smile, the pulsing skin that protected his heart. *Her Griff, her heart.* 'Say something nice to me, Griff.'

His chuckle was a trickle of warm honey against her ear. 'The Greeks didn't discover Aphrodite. I just did. I adore you.'

'How on earth did you manage to graduate from anatomy class, Griff Tyler? Allow me to demonstrate the difference between myself and *Venus de Milo*. See, I have arms and fingers.'

'So I notice, and if you don't stop doing that . . .' he rolled her over on her back and pinned her arms to the ground above her head, 'I'll be forced to do this.'

And how wonderfully he'd done it, she thought a little later when she let herself into the house. She'd never felt so fulfilled, so loved, so in tune with everything around her.

Pamela glanced up and smiled when she crept into the kitchen to make herself a drink.

Immediately, Janey became aware of her dishevelled state. Her hair was tangled with grass, her blouse was creased and hanging outside her skirt. Her feet were bare because she'd lost a shoe in the darkness.

'I thought you'd be in bed.'

'Gypsy came back by herself so I was a bit worried. I rang your father and he said you weren't there. Then I rang Phil, and he told me you were with Griff on the hill. I hope you don't mind me waiting up. I wanted to be sure you were safe. Gypsy brought home one of your shoes.'

She'd forgotten about Gypsy. She blushed as she tucked in her blouse. How alive she felt, how supremely happy. *I must share it with her . . . my mother.*

'Griff and I are in love.'

Pamela's arms came round her in a big hug. 'I'm so happy for you, darling, but I can't say I'm surprised. Griff's such a nice man.'

'Just like his father.' Her smile widened when Pamela avoided her eyes. 'I've got a feeling you might end up being my mother-in-law as well as my mother.'

Pamela gave a funny, embarrassed sort of grin. 'Who knows, you might just be right.

'Sarah Wyman is dead. Listen to this.'

The body of Lady Sarah was discovered amid the mangled wreckage of her car. It's believed she farewelled friends at a nightclub in the early hours of the morning and was on her way to join her husband in Kent. The viscount is being consoled by close family friend Pauline Pitt.

There was a picture of a tragic-looking Pauline being assisted into a car by a middle-aged man. A wry smile twisted Pamela's lips. It was hard to equate this smart-looking stranger with the sullen and malicious child she'd once known.

'No one round here will miss her, I'll be bound.' Ada's fist punched into a bowl of dough and buried itself to the wrist. 'That Sarah was a bad-un all right. The way she treated a fine gentleman like Sir Charles. It just wasn't right.'

'My father used to work for Sarah Renfrew once.'

Ada flicked Susie a glance. 'Little pitchers have big ears.'

'I'm not a little pitcher,' Susie said indignantly.

'As far as I'm concerned, you are. Now you just polish that silver properly, miss. Just because I said you could work today instead of tomorrow morning doesn't mean you can take it easy.'

Turning the dough out on to a floured board, Ada grumbled as she began to knead. 'I don't know what's so all-fired important that you have tomorrow off, anyway. Is there something going on I should know about? The pair of you have been as jumpy as fleas on a mangy dog lately.'

Pamela exchanged a grin with her daughter when Ada hardly paused for breath.

'Like I was saying before I was interrupted. No one's going to miss Sarah Wyman. I remember the time. . . .'

The tragedy was discussed over a pint in the Thatcher's Arms by the men, and tossed back and forth over fences by the village women. Sarah was forgotten when a juicier bit of gossip replaced it. Pamela and Phil Tyler had become man and wife.

'Just upped and did it without telling anyone,' Mrs Higgins huffed. 'Last Saturday, mind you. Off to the registry office, and her not even widowed a year yet.'

'Marry in haste, repent at leisure,' George answered in the tone of one wise after the event, then pulling on his boots. 'I'm off. I've got work to do on my motor bike.'

'You can weed the vegetable patch first, George Higgins. I don't know why you bought that noisy, smelly thing, anyway. They seen you coming if you ask me. No wonder Tim Ryker donated it to the white elephant stall.'

Pamela didn't let the gossip worry her.

Ada had been put out at first, but had soon come round with: 'I suppose it couldn't be helped, him being part-gypsy and all. A secretive lot, them gypsies. It's in their nature.'

She was still living with Janey. She and Phil had pooled their money and were negotiating to buy one of the bungalows nearby. It wasn't grand, but more convenient than the estate cottage Phil had always lived in. If all went as planned, they'd be living in their own home by the beginning of September.

Janey hadn't seen much of her father over the preceding few weeks. Every spare moment had been spent with Griff or her children.

At her insistence he'd dropped in for dinner that week, but he hadn't eaten much. He'd fallen asleep in a chair at the table. Struck by how pale and exhausted he appeared, she asked him if he felt all right when he woke.

He brushed aside her concerns with an irritated comment that he was perfectly healthy, and would she stop fussing.

Tears sprang to her eyes. 'I'm sorry. I didn't mean to.'

He rose to his feet and hugged her close. 'It's me who should be sorry. I didn't mean it, love. I've been working too hard of late and I'm a bit tired. Once the boat's finished I'll be able to ease off. I'm putting her into the water this week. Why don't you come and look her over on Sunday. We could drive in together, then go over to Mary's for lunch.

Sunday dawned bright, a faint drifting haze adding a touch of humidity to a perfect August day.

Everything had a fullness to it, the roses looked like plump maidens in gaudy crinolines. Overloaded with fruit, tree branches bowed towards the ground.

Prickly green shells guarded the chestnuts. Soon, they'd split and throw the shining nuts to the ground.

Janey knew she would take the children to gather blackberries soon, and rise at the crack of dawn to pluck mushrooms from the dew. She was looking forward to autumn with an ever-increasing impatience. Summer had made her full, like a bumble bee who'd supped too much nectar but was ever-greedy for more. She was bursting with love, with her own ripeness.

Her father was waiting for her at the gate. He's growing thin, he has dark circles under his eyes, she immediately thought. I'll ask Griff to take a look at him and tell me what he thinks. She hugged him long and hard. *I love this man – my father. I want him to know it deep inside where it counts. I want him to be as happy as I am.*

They used her car. The conversation between them was desultory as they drove to the harbour at Poole, as if he found it an effort to speak. There were lines of strain about his eyes, a tense stretch to his mouth. She must ask John if there was any progress with the Home Office.

He brightened as the boat came into view. *Saffy Jane* was solidly beautiful, her umbilical cord a stretch of white hawser tying her to the land. She tugged gently at it, eager for her birth. Her hull was navy blue, her name painted in gold lettering, her cabin white.

'We could go around the harbour for a quick trip, if you like. Just make sure you keep an eye on the children. She's not finished off inside, and I don't want them to hurt themselves.'

Cables hung from the bulkhead, the woodwork was still raw and the seats lacked upholstery. But her brass-work gleamed bright, and her deck gently quivered as they headed around Brownsea Island. The two children stared in round-eyed wonder at the sight of gulls weaving about them and the water slipping by.

After a while her father brought her back to harbour, his experienced hands placing her in exactly the right position so he could slip on to the quay and secure her to the bollard. A smile played around his lips as he helped them ashore, relaxing his mouth a little. 'What do you think of her?'

'She's wonderful. You must be so proud of yourself.'

'I can't really claim the credit. It was my father who designed her.'

'But you who built her.' She was laughing as she teased. 'I *insist* on being proud of you, whether you like it or not.'

He gave a self-effacing smile. 'I guess I do like it at that. I'm just not used to it.'

'Well, get used to it. I love you.' *There, it had slipped out quite naturally without her even thinking about it.* She grinned when his eyes caught hers and she saw a misting of tears. 'I do love you, Dad, more than you'll ever know. So I want you to promise me that you'll look after yourself.'

'Stop pushing me around, woman,' he said gruffly. 'We'll be late for lunch if we don't get going.' Touched beyond measure, he told himself that his tiredness was probably something simple. He'd been living on nothing but sandwiches lately, and had a thirst on him he couldn't believe. But it could wait. He'd try a pick-me-up from the chemist first.

'I'll get a check-up soon, if only to put your mind at rest. Remind me tomorrow.'

His casual answer didn't fool her one little bit. 'I'll do better than that. I'll make an appointment with your doctor and drive you in.' She placed a finger over his mouth when he began to protest. 'Don't bother arguing, because I won't listen.'

Jack didn't let his annoyance show as he gently kissed her on the forehead. She was his daughter, she loved him. That was all that mattered to him. He'd do nothing to jeopardize their precious growing relationship.

Nevertheless, the day placed a great strain on him. Mary made too much fuss, commenting often on how pale he looked. With both her and Janey's eyes on him he managed to force down most of his lunch despite his lack of appetite. He felt bloated afterwards, and longed for the solitude of the cottage so he could sink into his favourite armchair and sleep it off.

When he stood up from the table he felt dizzy, and had to clutch the back of the chair before anyone noticed. He made an effort to appear alert on the way home, jerking himself awake each time he felt himself drifting off. The trip seemed interminable.

When he finally closed the door of Canford Cottage behind him he was trembling with fatigue. All he needed was solitude and sleep, he thought, heading for the comfort of his armchair.

It had arrived! Suddenly and unexpectedly, there it was on her mat, an official envelope. Janey couldn't believe it as she turned it over in her hands.

OHMS. PRIVATE AND CONFIDENTIAL. *John Bellamy, Esquire. c/o William's House. Winterbrook. Dorset.*

She rang John.

'What does it say?'

'I haven't opened it. It's addressed to him and marked confidential.'

John laughed. 'Then what are you phoning me for? Go and give it to him.'

'What if it's bad news? I couldn't bear it.'

There was a short silence from the other end, then a cautious, 'How can it be bad news? It seemed cut and dried to me.'

'But what if it is? He hasn't been well lately. In fact, I'm picking him up in an hour to take him for a check-up. I know it's an imposition, but would you mind—'

'Ringing my contact and asking him the contents of the letter?' Her sigh of relief made him chuckle. 'It's a little unorthodox and I can't promise he'll give me an answer, but yes, why not?'

Fifteen minutes later he returned her call. 'My contact refused to divulge the contents of the letter, but he indicated he'd prefer to receive it as soon as possible were it addressed to him.'

Eyes shining, Janey waved the letter jubilantly under Pamela's nose. 'It's arrived!' She kissed Saffy and Justin, twirling them exuberantly round before setting them on their feet again. 'Be good for Nana. I'll be back as soon as possible.'

Her heart warbled a duet with the birds as she jumped into the Anglia. Butterflies took up residence in her stomach. *No, they were more like helicopters.* Her mouth seemed to be reaching for her ears.

If I don't calm down I'll swallow my head. In her eagerness, she selected the wrong gear, leaping out through the gate in an inelegant series of hops before she stalled. She took a deep breath and counting to ten, restarted the engine and pulled smoothly away. In sixty seconds her father would be the happiest man alive!

But her father didn't answer her knock and the door was locked. Daisy whined forlornly at her from the other side. Dropping to her knees she gazed through the flap of the letter box, calling outl 'Dad! Are you in?' *Of course he's in. His car's parked in the drive. He must have overslept.*

No amount of shouting of knocking brought a response. Uneasily she walked around the cottage, gazing through the windows. The kettle spouted steam so he couldn't have overslept. All the windows were shut, the only movement inside was Daisy, shadowing her from room to room. The dog's tail was wagged furiously as she gazed hopefully back at her.

'Go and fetch your master,' Janey ordered, gazing thoughtfully at the upper storey. His bedroom window was ajar. She cupped her hands around her mouth. 'Dad, I know you're in there. Answer me?'

She thought she heard someone mumble. Five seconds later, Daisy's head poked over the window sill and she began to bark.

Something was wrong. Heart pounding, she gazed desperately around her. Her glance lit on an old wooden ladder lying in the grass by the shed. Struggling under its weight, she dragged it across to the house and placed it against the wall. It was slippery with moss, and didn't quite reach. But if she was careful and tested each rung first, she'd be able to see inside.

The ascent was precarious. The ladder was rotten in parts and crumbled away under her feet. But as long as she held her breath it seemed to hold together, so she held her breath. Finally the top was reached. Pulling the window open and rising to the balls on her feet she leaned forward on to the inside sill.

Her father was lying in the doorway to the hall, still in his pyjamas. If she got a grip on the window sill she could probably get inside. Throwing caution to the winds she took a grip on it, exerted pressure on the ladder, swung one leg up, then exhaled with relief.

There was a sharp crack as the rung disintegrated beneath her. She lurched sideways, her hands taking her weight, her foot caught under the ledge on the other side. It felt as though her muscles were being stretched beyond endurance as she hung there for a moment. Then a superhuman effort saw her up and over, dropping to her knees on the other side.

She crawled on all fours to her father. 'Dad!'

He mumbled something incoherent.

At least he's alive. Thank you, God. He was perspiring heavily, and was deathly pale. Shudders racked his body now and again but nothing she did or said would rouse him. He was unconscious.

Griff! I'll call Griff! Calm down and think clearly. Griff will be at the hospital. Call for an ambulance. Get him to hospital, fast!

She dialled emergency and explained the symptoms to a calmly reassuring voice at the other end of the line – then remembering the dog and kettle, dealt swiftly with those before going back upstairs. As instructed, she turned her father on his side and kept watch over him.

I love him so much, she was thinking as she sponged the sweat from his dear, scarred face. Please let him be all right.

She followed the ambulance to the hospital, tears streaming down her face, then sat in the emergency waiting-room for what seemed like an age. The place was crowded with people coming and going. Doctors, nurses, patients, all wheeling about in a purposeful frenzy. She half stood up when she saw her father being wheeled away on a trolley, then sat down again.

The nurse had told her in no uncertain terms to wait, that she'd be informed in due time.

A half-hour passed, an hour, two, three. Was he dead? *No, his face would have been covered. Pamela will be wondering what's happened to me.* There was a telephone in the hallway, so she called her.

'Can you ring Mary and tell her what's happened?'

Two men in white coats emerged from a room at the end of the corridor. They were moving away from her, talking. The walk was as familiar as the dark curly head. '*Griff!*' She dropped the receiver back in its rest. 'Griff, wait!'

He turned, his puzzled frown becoming a smile when his eyes met hers. She practically ran up the corridor, then she was in his arms and gabbling it all out against his shoulder. A sharp odour of disinfectant lingered about him. 'I've been here for hours. Can you find out how he is? Everyone is rushing about in there and I'm frightened to ask in case it's bad news.'

'I suggest you take your young lady to the staff room with you, Doctor Tyler,' the older man said with an indulgent smile. 'Tell me the patient's name. I'll make enquiries and join you there.'

Griff's reassuring presence and a large mug of tea did much to calm her nerves, and when the man returned she managed a smile.

'*Hypoglycaemia.*'

She glanced uncertainly at Griff.

'Low blood sugar.'

'Is it serious?'

'It could have been if you hadn't found him in time.' The older man exchanged a glance with Griff. 'There's a possibility of *diabetes mellitus*. He'll be hospitalized for a day or so to undergo tests.'

'Is he conscious, can I see him?'

'Doctor Tyler can take you up to the ward in fifteen minutes.' He nodded to Griff and glanced at his watch. 'I'll see you in theatre in one hour.'

'Thank you,' Janey said as he walked away. 'You've been most kind.'

'I'd better explain.'

She winced when Griff took both her hands in his. 'You don't have to explain. I know what diabetes is. Just tell me he'll live.'

'Of course he'll live.' Griff turned her palms over and stared at the lacerations and splinters. 'How did you manage this?'

'I climbed up the ladder to dad's bedroom and the top rung broke.' She managed a grin. 'I was left hanging from the window sill like a damned monkey with one leg over the edge.'

'That must have been quite a sight.' He fetched a bowl of warm water and a first aid box. 'Put your hands in there.'

'Will it sting?'

His eyes met hers, dark and serious. 'It will hurt like hell, but I have the perfect anaesthetic in mind.'

He was right, it did sting. The kiss he gave her numbed the pain nicely. She yelped a couple of times when he picked out the splinters, bringing the same response. Finally he peppered her palms with antiseptic powder. 'There, that should do nicely.'

She kissed him. 'I love you.'

His eyes were as soft as his voice. 'It would be advisable not to continue with this line of treatment. I have afternoon theatre to get through. I'll leave you with your father and drop in on him later.'

She remembered the letter as the lift bore them swiftly upwards. With a flourish she withdrew it from her pocket. 'This came from the Home Office. Will it be all right to give it to him now?'

'If that's what I think it is I'd say it was the best tonic he could have.'

Griff left her with the sister.

'Five minutes, no more, Miss Bellamy. He's very tired.'

Miss Bellamy? It was the first time anyone had called her that. She didn't bother correcting her.

Griff was right. Gazing with disbelief at its contents, her father smiled through his exhaustion. 'How did this come about?'

'Mary, Pamela, myself and John Smith. We've been working on it for some time.'

'I told Mary to leave it alone. I didn't want you to have to go through it all again.' Tears came to his eyes and he shook his head. 'This is a most wonderful surprise. I can't believe it.'

'Then why are you crying?' She was crying with him, the tears trickling down her cheeks. 'Hurry up and get better, you've given me enough trouble for one morning.' She hugged him tight as the sister bore down on them, her love for him so fierce she never wanted to let him go. 'I love you so much. You're the best father anyone could wish for.'

Griff smiled as he watched them from the doorway. For once, his father's sixth sense had failed him. Jack Bellamy would survive this.

CHAPTER TWENTY-ONE

The September sun rose though the morning mist, scattering the shadows in the village. The thatch of each tiny cottage glowed mustard bright, the windows winked orange gleams and the church tower began to blush.

It promised to be a lovely day, as soft as love and as tender as dreams. The trees were ablaze with glory. Tangy tangerine, yellow fiesta, hot-blooded red and lush burgundy. It was a gypsy Autumn.

The air tasted like wine on Janey's tongue, the earth drifted with fragrance, the dew pressed cool lips against her skin. She embraced the sun with her arms and laughed with sheer exhilaration. It was nonsense, of course.

Bathe in the breath of a September dawn, and if the cock crows thrice, nature will endow your marriage with a wealth of love, long life and everlasting happiness.

Gypsy folklore.

The whole of the village seemed to take one quivering, drawn-out, waking yawn. A hundred chickens began to cackle, geese honked, milk churns clanked, an engine started.

A cock crowed thrice!

She was smiling as she made her way home. The earth was a precious jewel. Spiders' webs were pearls of dew. Little ruby berries had replaced the flowers in the hedges, diamonds of mist sparkled where the sun touched.

I've bathed in the breath of a September dawn. The cock's crowed thrice. I'll be happy with Griff forever. What else could I desire?

There was to be a wedding in the village and everyone had been invited to the reception in the garden of the big house.

Suits had been sent to the cleaners, hats trimmed with lace, dresses inspected for traces of last year's Christmas pudding. Shoes were shone, corsets unearthed, nylons inspected for ladders, permanent waves applied. A ton of confetti was secreted in various pockets.

Gifts had been wrapped, an opportunity presented to get rid of Aunt Emily's vase, or the leather desk set with glass ink pots that had been lacking a desk to recline on for the past thirty years.

'He's a doctor, he's bound to have a desk, ain't he? It polished up real nice, just like new.'

'Lady Brenda's arranging the flowers herself. Roses picked from her own garden. The church looks a real treat.'

'Ada reckons the cake is going to be four tiers high.'

A derisive snort. 'That Ada allus was a show-off. Serves her right that young-un takin' the prize off her this year. It might teach her to be a bit more humble in future.'

Lacy white stockings sliding up her legs.

Something old. The lead soldier. Lord William, buried deep in her pocket. A drift of white silk whispering against her skin.

Something new. A tiny gold Griffin hanging on a chain at her throat. A gift of love. Satin over silk. Hair elegant and smooth, courtesy of Dion and Stephen, who'd clucked and fussed over her and hadn't quarrelled once. Tendrils curled at the nape of her neck, pearls were threaded like dew drops on the spider webs. Edwardian style, like her gown.

Something borrowed. A lace-edged handkerchief from Pamela at her wrist. Satin button-up boots that pinched her toes.

Something blue. A garter circling her thigh. Saffy was adorable in pink with a posy of flowers, so proud of her white patent shoes she kept tapping her feet and staring down at them with a smile. Susie, her long dress a deeper shade of pink, was self-conscious in her touch of make-up.

The veil was a white mist about her head and secured in a circle of pearls. A cascade of pink rosebuds spilled from her hands down the skirt of her gown.

Is Griff nervous this day? Is he already at the church, standing at Devlin's side? I shall be late of course, but not too late, It's the bride's prerogative.

She looked like a stranger in the mirror. *I bathed in the September dew. My marriage will be happy.*

Then she was alone with her father. He looked so proud she thought her heart might break. His voice was choked with emotion. 'I love you, Janey. Be happy.'

There was a slow clip-clop of horses down the road – Brenda's idea. The Victorian carriage emblazoned with Lord William's family crest had gathered into itself a hundred years of dust. Repaired and refurbished for the occasion, it creaked and groaned, but was burnished bright. Phil handled the reins with a casual aplomb, as if he'd been born to the job.

Church bells rang. A flower-bed of hats, the organ wheezing Handel's wedding march. There was a sudden flutter of nerves when faces turned her way, her father's arm was supportive under her elbow. Familiar faces, faces she loved – strangers' faces, smiling at her, wishing her well.

A collective sigh went through the church, a long drawn out: '*Ahhh!*'

Justin wriggled on Pamela's lap. 'Mum, mum, mum.' The procession stopped whilst she leaned down and kissed him.

Griff waiting. Grave, loving her as she walked towards him, perfectly at ease, tall and elegant in his wedding suit. His dark eyes sought hers, pulled her towards him like a magnet. His hand, her hand, each seeking the other like twin souls.

Devlin took a step back.

The vicar beamed a smile at her and nodded at Griff. The reverend's head shone in the light streaming through the window as he began to speak in a strong resonant voice.

'We are gathered together in the sight of God.'

Her father giving her away – giving her to Griff just when they'd found each other.

Outside, a taxi pulled to a halt. The passenger was a man in his mid-twenties, tall, clean-shaven and handsome.

'Wait, would you, man?' he instructed the driver.

The cabbie watched him walk towards the church and slip inside.

'*. . . let them speak now, or forever hold their peace.*'

Clear green eyes roved over the congregation then came to rest on the bride.

'*Do you, Jane Elizabeth Renfrew. . . ?*'

She was gorgeous, the sight of her stunned him. His mouth twisted into an ironic smile. Doc Tyler of all people. If he had to lose out it couldn't have been to a better man.

'I do.'

'*Do you, Griffin Philip Tyler. . . ?*'

Doc Tyler's eyes seeking Mistral's, his love glowing transparent for all to see as he spoke to her alone.

'I do.'

'*With this ring I thee wed.*'

A small girl in a pink dress caught his eye. His smile became tender. '*Saffy*,' he breathed. She looked like her mother. When she turned, he saw her eyes, as clear and green as his own.

'*. . . I now pronounce you man and wife. You may kiss the bride.*'

Such love in their eyes. She'd never looked at him like that. It was time to make himself scarce. Half-hidden behind a tree Drifter watched them emerge, watched the mill of people laughing and chattering, posing for photographs, the confetti floating in the air. Janey's happiness made him ache. The way Griff kissed her, and the way she responded made him die inside.

Saffy was dancing on the grass, her dress floating out around her like the petals of a flower. She tripped over a tussock and fell flat on her face. It was Doc Tyler who picked her up and cuddled her tight. Doc Tyler who dried her tears and made her laugh again. She called him daddy.

Damn my grandfather! Why was I so weak? I should have defied him. Vietnam! He was dreading it, but too many of his countrymen had died and he'd felt guilty sitting behind a desk.

The crowd was moving away, some following after the horse and carriage on foot, others getting into cars.

Devlin drove off with a classy-looking chick. Devlin, who'd delivered her message, whose eyes had been cruelly amused when he'd watched him unwrap the painting. At least he hadn't got her. Doc Tyler he *could* forgive.

A man gave him a cursory glance as he walked by, a man so ordinary-looking that Drifter forgot what he looked like before he was out of sight.

Darius Taunt! John felt a twinge of guilt until he recalled how Griff and Janey had looked at each other in the church. Then he smiled and put it out of his mind.

The church grounds were empty now. Drifter wandered over to where Saffy had fallen over – to the white object lying on the grass.

A tiny shoe made of shiny material with a pink rosebud on it. He held it to his cheek for a second, smiled, then slipped it in his pocket and sauntered back towards the waiting cab.